"Like a combat-ready Cobra, *Maverick* is 'good to go,' and 'the rotor is in the green.' It's rude, crude, and real."

—Richard Herman, Jr.,
author of *The Warbirds* and *Force of Eagles*

"The telling of the story is as raw as the subject matter, filled with curses, cynicism and black humor; it brings to mind warriors back at their camps, discussing the day's events."

—Tampa Tribune

"From the first page, I was captivated by the writing. This marvelous narrative voice, wry and witty, both entertains and illuminates as it spins out Marvicsin's gripping, deeply moving story. The people are drawn with such skill that they step out of the pages and into our hearts."

—Herbert Crowder,
bestselling author of *Ambush at Osirak*, *Weatherhawk* and *Missile Zone*

"The authenticity and realism of *Maverick* grab and hold the reader. It captures the essence of not only the Vietnam War through the eyes of a Cobra pilot, but the horrors of war itself. Marvicsin and Greenfield's ability to bring the reader inside a tiger cage is uncanny. You don't read this book—you feel it."

—Colonel Dave "Bull" Baker,
USAF, Former POW

MAVERICK

The Personal War of a Vietnam Cobra Pilot

DENNIS J. MARVICSIN
AND
JEROLD A. GREENFIELD

J
JOVE BOOKS, NEW YORK

This Jove Book contains the complete
text of the original hardcover edition.
It has been completely reset in a typeface
designed for easy reading, and was printed
from new film.

MAVERICK

A Jove Book / published by arrangement with
the author

PRINTING HISTORY
G.P. Putnam's Sons edition published October 1990
Jove edition / September 1991

ISBN 0-515-10662-3

Jove Books are published by The Berkley Publishing Group,
200 Madison Avenue, New York, New York 10016.

PRINTED IN THE UNITED STATES OF AMERICA

10 9 8 7 6 5 4 3 2 1

We'd like to express our sincere appreciation to our families for their support; to Sharon Less for bringing us together; to Gloria Greenfield for keeping us together; to Michael Sisson and Catharine Bushnell for many things; to Frank Harvey, author of *Air War: Vietnam,* for his encouragement.

This book is based on true experiences.
Certain liberties have been taken with chronology
and many names have been changed
for the protection of privacy
and reputation.

Otherwise, it all actually happened.

Dick Fortenberry and Ken Smith are real people.
So, by God, was Tyrone Hisey.

This book is dedicated to the memory
of all the names on the Wall.
And to the men and women who served their time in hell.

MAVERICK

ONE

When Maverick came to, he was in a tiger cage, lying on a grille of hard bamboo rods, every inch of his body incandescent agony, hot-metal fire from his skin to the bottom of his bowels. It was a kind of pain that began in some fundamental part of his soul and ate its way to the surface with hideous persistence. Throbbing waves of nausea told him that inaccessible organs had been outraged nearly to the point of fatality.

When Maverick came to, he had no idea how much time had passed, but as soon as he saw the bamboo bars and realized where he was, no amount of pain could keep his scarred right hand from scrabbling toward the upper-left breast pocket of his flight suit, where he always kept the derringer. It contained two little .22 Magnum hollow-point pills that he would swallow eagerly, a brief burst of piercing light ending his captivity almost before it could begin. He was convinced, indeed had always known, that sudden death is far better than the infinite pain, indefinitely prolonged, that Americans could expect from the VC. Despite the appalling insult to his body, he was more than ready to stick that pistol in his mouth, and the sooner the better.

Briefly he grabbed at the idea that this was a dream. He was unconscious because he'd been shot down—again—had made another of his many unscheduled landings. None of this was real. But then his searching hand felt his chest on the right, the left. He had no derringer, he had no flight suit. This *was* real. He *was* in a tiger cage, barely able to move, on fire inside, wearing a floppy set of black pajamas.

There's a difference between the liquid silver light that a full moon spreads before you and the eerie glow of a night sky full of stars. This was the second kind of night. This night, the sky was a fortune in diamonds. The thumbnail sliver of moon stood modestly aside, not daring to compete with the glitter. In the middle of the Asian countryside the glow was riotously intense in the absence of the arrogant glare of electric civilization from below.

Pilots call this a field-grade night—light enough so you can see features on the ground. Maverick could. The countryside unfurled below his Cobra gunship east of the Angel's Wing just south of Tay Ninh. There were two Cobras from the Assassins in the brilliant air that night, black locust shapes against the gray sky, long and sleek, pointed and unspeakably sinister.

In the lead, low and away to the right, just out of bed and still warm, was Maverick. He sat high in the rear seat, looking over the head of the copilot just in front of him. This was supposed to be Woodrow's mission, but Woody had died two days before, so horribly burned, so wasted, and Maverick's stomach was filled with cement because of it. He'd be calm for a while, perhaps several hours, then he'd start crying again, the tears running stupidly through the little off-center furrow in his chin. He had put his name in Woodrow's place in final black on the dull white mission assignment board, a gesture, a farewell, and now it would cost him in ways he could not imagine. He was suspended in the starlight, his machine pulsing around him, on the way to *someplace* because at some ARVN outpost *somebody* thought he heard *something* going on along the border.

In the front seat was Quinlan, a young warrant officer halfway through his first tour. He'd already been in breathtaking situations; he thought he'd seen everything. This night would show him the very last thing he would ever see.

Hanging just above and behind them in the second threatening machine, Connell and Warren flew wing.

Ahead, not more than three kilometers, they can see the ARVN compound because tracer fire arcs up from it across the night, little red neon streams in the sky. Is it a battle, or is it just some assholes shooting because they like the noise, or a little harassment here, a little there? No problem. An easy night.

"Tiger radio, this is Assassin Three Six. Can you report your situation, over?"

Maverick gets back the voice of one of the American advisers in the ARVN camp, a voice that, even on the radio in the middle of Southeast Asia, never left Brooklyn and never would.

"Ahh . . . Roger, Assassin Tree Six, dis is Tiga Six. It don't seem to be dat big a thing here, we been gettin' a little snipa fiah, a couple mortuhs . . . but it's been goin' on awl night long. And it's comin' from all different directions. Could be a big unit building up over dere in Numba Ten country. Ovuh."

"Roger that," Maverick responds. Where *did* that motherfucker learn to speak English? "What do you want us to do?"

"Be nice if you could pop a couple rockets about three hundred meters to duh west along da canal and quiet the fuckers down. We'll light the arrow."

"You got it, Tiger Six. You hire, we fire."

The two dark Cobras bank left in a broad sweeping turn, sinking down for the first rocket run directly over the compound. The arrow lights up, brilliant yellow dots on the ground. It swivels around, points accusingly at the enemy. The ships take turns making runs, just like the drill, first Maverick and Quinlan nosing down to release their rockets, ripples of high explosive or white phosphorus, then breaking up to the right, pulling a few G's as Connell dives in under his tail, spitting rockets, sputtering minigun fire at thousands of rounds a minute, belching grenades. Nice and easy, like a practice run, no return fire, just the muzzle flashes from small arms and the red tracers from the M-60's at the camp.

But then there are big guns, *big* guns that assert themselves all at once from the left, unmistakable flashes of fire, probably from a 12.75. Bigger than an M-60, smaller than a cannon, it is the Asian version of the fifty-caliber machine gun. It surprises.

"What's this shit?" Connell's voice yells from the other Cobra, shrill in Maverick's headset. "Where the hell did *he* come from?"

"No problem," says Maverick. "Let's take a run at him. Come in behind me and we'll wax his ass."

"Roger that." Maverick pulls the cyclic toward his stomach to slow the ship down as Connell gets into position. They circle once, nose down, and dive into the fire.

The 12.75 opens up again, long fingers of sparking green light that reach for the Cobras, clutch, and miss. Maverick runs right through it, releasing his rockets, Quinlan's stubby hands busily squeezing triggers, pushing buttons, pouring minigun fire and grenades out through his turret. They swoop, they break, Connell and Warren roll in underneath, firing, firing, breaking to the right, following the lead ship around in a long lazy circle. They come in for the second time, the ground rushes up at them, another 12.75 reveals itself from the right.

"Jesus Christ in a wheelchair," Quinlan says from the front seat. "*Two* of them! That's some weird shit."

"Roger that," Maverick says. "But we gotta have another crack at the bastard." And so they do.

Maverick leads in again, and halfway through the run all he can see is flashbulbs going off around him outside the bubble cockpit, like the world press is out there, he's famous and everybody wants his picture. This is not heavy machine-gun fire, this is a more recent development, courtesy of their Chinese neighbors to the north. This spectacular light show comes from a motherfucking radar-guided thirty-seven-millimeter antiaircraft *cannon* that releases deadly bursts of fire in a computer-controlled area, throwing huge heavy bullets that explode into angry shards of hot screaming piercing tearing metal.

Maverick knows what it is because he's seen it before, but in the distance, shooting at some *other* poor bastard. This one is different. This time the poor bastard is him, and he's getting pounded like a hack fighter who's stumbled into the ring with the champ.

A noise, then a volcano of smoke. Eruptions and billows in the cockpit, instruments go berserk—*red lights!*—and perish in the night, the unspeakably lovely life-supporting eternal whine of the turbine engine sounds a long glissando down the scale as the machine first tries to go AWOL, then decides to desert. It decelerates completely, absolutely, utterly, finally.

The controls get stiff. Maverick strains as hydraulic fluid bleeds out into the pearl night sky from wounded tubes and pipes. The violated Cobra begins to lurch inevitably toward the ground as Quinlan screams the litany of distress into the radio. Maverick begins the all-too-familiar autorotation sequence, trying to make the ship settle more or less gently to the ground, collective down to make the blade pitch neutral, maintain the rotor RPM, aircraft straight, hold a sixty-knot attitude—or as close as you can come while the thing is shot to pieces around you and the controls won't respond—nose down as they fall and fall, uprushing air making the rotor blades pinwheel enough to provide some lift, then closer to the ground, closer, and Maverick turns on his landing lights and (thank God!) likes what he sees, a long, straight beautiful rice paddy. No trees, no hills, just enchanting rapturous level terrain. If he can't put it down on the American base at Tay Ninh right now, this luxurious sweep of clear planet Earth will do nearly as well. At least it's not trees and mountains. He flips the lights off. The Cobra continues to settle.

At a hundred feet—he thinks—he puts the light on again, just to be sure this God-given landing spot is not an optical illusion, a cruel hoax, or the wishful thinking of an American boy in deep, deep trouble. No, it's still there, thank you, God, pull—*pull!*—the cyclic back to slow the forward airspeed (it barely responds), level out the chopper, then, just before impact, jerk that collective up as hard as you can to take a big bite out of the air and cushion the impact. But Maverick never was much good at killing that forward airspeed in emergency landing situations, and besides, the controls work a shitload better when they have at least a dribble of fluid left in the lines, and Maverick can think a bit more clearly when he isn't sitting in all this fucking fire and smoke, so they hit the ground at sixty knots, which is only about fifty-six knots faster than the owner's manual says. This causes the wounded machine, slave as it is to the laws of gravity, momentum, friction, conservation of energy, and possibly even Coriolis force, to stumble forward on its skids, aquaplaning across the shallow brown water. The rippling glare of the landing lights surprises them with a view of a three-foot paddy dike dead in front of them, running precisely across their path like the edge of a knife.

It is the last thing they see. Rotors windmilling, skidding, slewing from side to side, the Cobra hurls itself into the paddy dike, reaches again for the air, flips over forward, collapses, then topples off to the side, rolls once, twice, comes to rest right-side-up, is still.

TWO

Lynn was so pretty *the first time he saw her, by* God . . . *Brownie, get that shit away from me, I don't* need *another rum and Coke, goddamn, I'm fucked up enough already . . . God, you were a prince in that bar tonight knockin' back those shooters, but did I keep up with you or what? But we put it over on you, you prick, you don't even remember falling down in the driveway, but then,* then *you opened the front door and* surprise! *the Snake Ranch is ass-packed with people and it's your birthday and you can puke if you want to.* Jesus, *don't everybody look* cute *in their little Navy uniforms, and if I don't sense an intensification of the emotional level sometime soon, I'm gonna go outside and barf or take a walk . . . Girls? Well, shit, didn't what's-his-ass over there say he'd invited what's-her-ass and some of her girlfriends from Memphis State? (Maverick, we* got *you a date.* Maverick! *Her name's Lynn. Hey, can he understand me?) Shit, she better, she better, listen, she better* look *like something, 'cause if she don't, well, I'm gonna go outside and call Ralph on the big white phone where's my* drink? *over* here *and she can talk about college to somebody else.*

(Maverick, you are such *an asshole.) What? What? (How the fuck can you meet your date in* this *condition?) Well, shit, between the shooters me and Brownie did in the bar and the two or six rums and Coke I had since I carried him in the front door and you all jumped out and yelled . . . Look, she comes in, you point her out to me, if she looks okay I'll talk to her and if she doesn't I'll just go outside and drive the big white bus. (You're a charmer, Denny, you really are.) Jesus, I hope this all stays down. Mingle mingle mingle.*

What's that old saying, you never get a second chance to make a first impression? Hello, um . . . Lynn, I'll say, that's what I'll say. Hello the first thing. Okay. Then I'll say wanna mess around . . . no, I'll get her a drink first, a double, then ease *into the subject, be more* oblique, *like do you think you might like to have sexual intercourse with me, say, right now. . . . I love that, God, I love that.*

(Maverick . . . Maverick? *Excuse me, son, but you are truly a sotted slut, and by the way, your date is here.)* Here? *(Yeah, for about three and a half hours.) Where here? (On the couch, the blond one on the left.) Her?* Her? *Shit, I been looking at her all night, she isn't bad! She* isn't bad! *In* fact, *she looks goooood . . . how good? . . . so good that I'm almost sorry I had that last rum (did I put Coke in it?) Coke? God, I sure would like a nice tall cold Coke right now, with lots of ice . . . there's too many fuckin'* people *at this party and I'd go over and talk to (what was her name?) Lynn, if it weren't so* hot, *if I weren't so* fucking thirsty!

The air was hot and it was heavy and damp and close. He burned from fever. Rivulets of sweat trickled down his scalp, off his forehead, into his eyes. He rolled his head from side to side (careful!) *and discovered that the cage was on stilts, a few feet off the ground, inside a straw hooch with walls that came nearly to the bottom, but not quite. Finally his curiosity, powered by a strong sense of dread, made him bite down hard and pull himself up to his elbows. The jolt of nausea almost made him fall back again, but he had to know where he was.*

The walls of the hooch ended about two feet from the ground, so outside he could see naked brown feet walking back and forth in the red dust. He was alone. No other cages, no other POW's (Jesus! Where was Quinlan?), *nothing. He listened to the sounds from outside the shelter, straining for the familiar timbre of an American voice, anything. He didn't hear it. Nothing but a constant high-pitched rapid-fire gabble of Vietnamese. He settled back down on the mat, groaning the breath out of himself.*

He lay there all day, thirsty to the point of obscenity, burning, sweating, images racing behind his eyes, all that shit in flight school, Dick and Ty and everybody else. He was a long way from Fort Wolters, Texas, and he felt it.

Nobody came in to look at him, nobody brought him food. The little brown feet walked past incessantly and the people ignored him utterly, as though he were a forgotten man, and no longer part of life.

He passed out.

• • •

First, there's Fort Wolters, Texas. It's in Mineral Wells, and if you know where *that* is, you're either a Mineral Wellsian, or an Army helicopter pilot, or you used to go there to "take the waters." Maverick arrived in September 1964, and nobody on the whole planet had ever been half as excited as he was then. It had taken him forever to get there, to finally fulfill a dream that had possessed him ever since he could remember. Looking out the window from the bus, he was so excited he almost slid off his seat.

But even as he arrived, he had the feeling that something was just waiting to bite him on the ass. It wasn't any one thing, actually, just a pattern of events, a series of small happenings that started to take form almost from the start. He knew he was probably going to fight a war, but he didn't know—none of them did—just what kind of war it would be.

When Maverick was five years old he crept out of the bedroom window of his grandmother's house in the middle of a cold blinding rainstorm and walked three miles to the local airport because he wanted to hitch a ride on an airplane. Somebody there recognized him and called his uncle to come fetch him home. Such was his lust for flight.

He joined the Navy in 1958, right out of high school, because they offered a program called NAVCAD, which meant that they'd let him fly without a college degree. No other branch of the service would. All he had to do was survive a series of insanely difficult exams and place somewhere in the top one percent. The Navy doesn't let just any miscellaneous individual fly its aircraft. While he was waiting for the semiannual testing, the Annapolis qualifying exams rolled around, and having nothing better to do, he took them. About thirty days later the NAVCAD exams came up and he suffered them eagerly.

He passed them both. Got accepted to NAVCAD, prep school for Annapolis, whichever he wanted. But instead of NAVCAD, instead of Annapolis, he got married and became instantly ineligible for anything. Love is wonderful.

Anyway. He left the Navy in 1962 and joined the Army about eighteen months later because they had this warrant-officer training program for helicopter pilots. By this time the Army, too, was willing to overlook the empty spot on the wall where the sacred diploma should have been.

There was another reason the Army attracted him. A Scripps-Howard reporter named Jim Lucas had changed Maverick's life with newspaper articles about some Southeast Asian country that nobody ever heard of and some Communist insurgency and how helicopters, being remarkably versatile aircraft, were playing an increasingly important role in fighting a whole new kind of war and how the country's soldiers were learning to fight from the Americans and how American involvement was gradually getting deeper and with all that shit going on Maverick was dead certain that the Army would need pilots so badly they'd let him fly even if he were a married three-headed purple atheist.

Some people went into helicopters thinking that the chance of war was remote but if they ever *did* get sent into one their country would have a damn good reason for putting them there. Maverick *knew* he was going to war because of what Jim Lucas had written, and didn't give much of a rat's keister what the reasons were. He *really* wanted to fly and was none too finicky about the specific conditions under which he did so. Besides, he wanted to be a career officer, and in the military, considering what they do for a living, going through combat is considered *de rigueur* and you don't get much peer-group respect if you've never been shot at.

Maverick decided that this was exactly what he needed. He didn't want to get hit, exactly, but he had to get as close as he could, comfortably. He would, in fact, get *too* close. He would discover just how much of a prophet Jim Lucas really was, and would not be comfortable.

Send me anywhere, Maverick thought, send me to French Equatorial Africa, as long as you teach me to fly.

When he got to Mineral Wells in late September 1964, he had nothing on his mind but getting into one of those seductive rotary-wing dream machines and making like Igor Sikorsky.

He was young, slack-jawed, agape and glassy-eyed, drooling, practically, at an entire Army base dedicated to the aspiring helicopter pilot. A place that existed for the sole purpose of teaching people like him, or smarter, how to drive a helicopter. Across the tedious horizon he saw rows and rows of the magnificent creatures (for that is how he thought of them) shimmering in the heat. Around him, there were hundreds of people who just climbed into those glorious machines and took right off with a casual practiced ease that made his gut ache. And in the air were more choppers, at least five or six, than he'd ever seen aloft at one time. Maverick was awestruck right from day one, and stayed that way the whole time. If he survived this, they'd let him fly!

But he almost lost all capacity for amazement the day they brought the class together for the first time.

It was in one of those peculiar boring military-looking light green bare-walled rooms with the Texas sun cascading into the windows, glinting off the shiny beige floor. A hundred and twenty guys stood around, some still filing in, checking each other out (kind of like in the locker room, but with a different kind of nakedness), wondering who was going to make it and who was going to wash. Most of the men he saw in the room probably had some time in service, but there was a bunch of guys who looked awfully young. Maverick was twenty-four.

He was thinking that he'd pick this helicopter-pilot shit up right away, but how were they ever gonna teach it to these *kids,* when across the room Tyrone Hisey walked through the door.

Ty Hisey and Maverick grew up together. They were kids together. They had lived within blocks of each other. They went to high school in Mansfield, Ohio, together, and did all those Bob Seger teenage growing-up night-move things together. And even though Ty was a year older, such a wide gulf in high school, that was never a factor in their friendship. When Maverick was a senior, Ty went off and joined the Marines. So with Maverick a year behind him in school and the Navy right afterward and Ty being Always Faithful someplace, they had lost track of each other for over seven years.

Of all the United States Army Primary Helicopter Flight Training Centers in the world, he had to walk into this one.

Ty was about five-ten, half a head taller than Maverick, 150 pounds, and physically dense to the point of impenetrability. He was spare and he was solid, like a Marine.

He didn't have much of a nose. What there was of it had a curious shape, almost concave, like someone had used the heel of a hand to mash it back level with his face. It was perfectly flat across the bridge and did a little ski-lift thing at the end. On either side of it were eyes of a color that is seen only in the sky, and only just before the tornado strikes.

Ty never said much, but when he did, every word was golden. To turn Will Rogers around a bit, he never met a man who didn't like him.

Perhaps it was because he loved to laugh. During the bull

sessions he'd sit in the corner, quiet, listening. Then the laugh would burst out, hard. Too hard, sometimes, till the tears came.

Turned out he too was a frustrated pilot, and couldn't get what he wanted out of the Marines, so he applied, like the rest of the thirsters after glory, for the WOC program. Eight years from high school, light-years from central Ohio, but not as far away as they were to get, deep in the heart of Texas they were together again for the first time.

The first sight of Ty in that room was all Maverick thought about the day they sent his body home to his mother.

Of course, they roomed together all through flight school, along with one other candidate they picked up along the way. His name was Dick Fortenberry and he was a skydiver. He was not, however, just any skydiver. No, this skydiver had just won the championship of the whole fucking world in some aviation capital like Dubrovnik, so he was automatically a Quality Individual, earning a bye on any macho test you'd care to administer. He'd been on the Army parachute team, the Golden Knights, and had more national and international titles than he had walls to hang them on, his young fresh-faced picture on the cover of *Sports Illustrated,* everything but the Nobel Prize. But everybody liked him anyhow, and besides, he played killer guitar, as Maverick found out in the barracks one day when Fortenberry snatched one out of his hands because he'd reached the limit of his capacity to suffer.

In some ways, Dick looked kind of like a ten-year-old. He had one of those open faces with laugh lines and chuckle crinkles around his gunpowder-gray eyes. People invariably liked him at once. They listened when he spoke, partly because he made sense, something every new warrant-officer candidate believed was in woefully short supply at Fort Wolters, and partly because he had a great voice, a motivating voice, a Voice that began somewhere down around his knees, modulated delicately in the cranial cavities, and emerged with a glorious meshing of overtones and harmonics. When he played the guitar and sang, nobody walked.

Dick Fortenberry was another one blessed with an uncanny kind of physical strength. What with being a skydiver and a member of the Golden Knights and a runner, if he ever got shot in Vietnam, he'd walk around for a month before he fell over.

• • •

Warrant-officer candidates in flight school occupied a position exactly like plebes at a military academy. That is to say, lower than the proverbial whale shit on the bottom of the ocean. They were constantly being humbled, subject to the sadistic caprice of upperclassmen, TAC officers, and instructor pilots. But their abased social position had at least the benefit of promoting physical fitness, since every candidate was given ample opportunity to do push-ups. The TAC officers would make them drop for twenty or thirty. Or fifty. After a time, Maverick would have claimed the title of Texas Regional Push-up Champ, if the honor hadn't been stolen by—you guessed it—Tyrone Hisey, and all because he'd been a Marine.

The TAC officers in charge of training . . . well, you know all about them. They scream up your nose, they make you scream back. "I can't hear you, Candidate! *I can't hear you, Candidate!*" They don't even call you Mister, because that's the title used to address a warrant officer, and you, as a candidate, are certainly not a warrant officer, are anything *but* a warrant officer, are not worthy of aspiring to the title, are not even worthy of recognition as a human being, in fact you as a candidate are wallowing at the aquatic mammalian fecal stage, groveling to rise above. Yes, TAC officers make you run everywhere, they make you sit on the edge of your chair in the mess hall, and for months you have burning hot spots of pain in your heels, in the back of your head, and in that little bone that sticks out just above your ass, from slamming yourself against the wall to pull a brace. This builds the "character" so indispensable to the Military Aviator. They are immortalized in dozens of movies, they wear little flat hats. They're larger than life, classic characters of the American military myth.

There is one thing to tell, though. No, two.

Thing number one: those hard-core all-Army born-in-the-USA TAC officers leaned on Tyrone Hisey something fierce because of his four years in the Corps and they dropped him for twenty with numbing regularity out of sheer caprice, whim, and fancy.

"The sun's out today, *Marine,* drop and give me twenty."

"Sir! Candidate Hisey! Yes, *sir!*"

And down he went, arms pumping, ass bobbing. One day he gave them twenty just like he was supposed to and then pumped out one more and grunted, "And one for the Corps."

The TAC officers were stunned, stupefied at this maniacal heresy, so after they recovered their voices they handed him another twenty. Ty did them, and again threw in "one more for the Corps."

They couldn't believe it. The more they dropped him, the more extras he'd dedicate to the Few Good Men. Self-perpetuating punishment. It went on for days.

There were, well, *reasons* the TAC officers couldn't allow this rebellion to continue. The TAC officer exists in our particular space-time continuum solely to deliver intolerable bullshit by the metric ton to unfortunate candidates at every opportunity, every day, till said candidates wash out, walk off, crack up, knuckle under, or rise above. But here they had a Special Case on their hands. There are only two things more fearful than a TAC officer: a TAC officer who's had it up to here with a smart-ass candidate, and God when he's pissed off at the Jews.

Thus, the turning point.

"Candidate," the TAC officer yelled, glaring down into Ty's face. If his nose got any closer to Ty's, they could kiss like Eskimos.

"Sir. Candidate Hisey. Yes, sir!"

"Candidate, if I drop you for twenty, are you going to give me one more for the Corps?"

"Sir. Candidate Hisey. No, sir!" Even though the rest of the candidates stood at attention so hard their eyes were getting bloodshot, a collective sharp intake of breath could still be heard. Fortenberry whispered to Maverick out of the side of his mouth, "Shit, I think they broke him."

"All right, Candidate. Let's see twenty. *Exactly.*"

"Sir. Candidate Hisey. Yes, sir."

Ty dropped, his nose not an inch and a quarter from the TAC officer's shoes, gave him twenty textbook-quality push-ups, twisted his neck up and sideways to look him in the eye, pumped twice, and said, ". . . and two for the Corps."

The rest of the candidates didn't need a revelation from on high to understand that they had to get behind the poor bastard, and at once. Such a flagrant display of free will by a candidate surely demanded a rallying of forces, mutual support, brotherly cohesion in the Grand American Tradition, exactly the kind of group *gestalt* that flight school is designed to foster. If they didn't back Ty now, he'd either wind up in the stockade charged with felonious insubordination or have to do so many push-ups that his arms would fall off and he'd never be able to fly.

So at that very moment the entire formation, every single soldier, dropped like he'd been gassed, did twenty, and, counting out loud, counting in unison, threw in two more for the Corps. When it was over and they shuffled to their feet, all that could be heard was the wind flowing across the prostrate Texas landscape. The TAC officers were apoplectic. They dropped Hisey again, and everybody dropped with him. Whenever he gave them one more for the Corps, they *all* threw in one more for the Corps. Everybody did it, every time. After ten or twenty episodes the TAC officers were so embarrassed that they wouldn't drop him anymore.

Thing number two: the only candidate they picked on more than Ty was Dick Fortenberry. They had a hard time dealing with Ty, because he was competition, but they stayed in Dick's shit all the time because he was the skydiving champion of the entire Third Planet from the Sun. Ty was guts, but Dick was glamour.

"So, this is a world-champion skydiver? What do you know about helicopters, *Candidate?* Gimme twenty and tell me all about it."

"Come here, *Airborne.* How much time you got in helicopters? Drop right here and build me some time on the ground."

"Do you know how to *fly* airplanes, Candidate, or do you just know how to fall out of 'em? Why don't you skydive to the ground and give me twenty."

"Sir! Candidate Fortenberry! Yes, *sir!*"

This was especially hard on Dick because of the cruel contrast. He'd won the world title not three weeks before reporting to Fort Wolters, standing on the dais in Dubrovnik basking in the adulation of his peers, flushed from the primal exhilaration of free-fall, gold amulets dangling from his neck, surrounded by willing international pussy. Then, practically overnight, he is here, forced to become a cowering submissive before some asshole with a little rank and no flight time, his nose bobbing up and down inches from the Texas tarmac.

After Maverick's first tour, he found himself back at Fort Wolters. As a TAC officer. And was *he* ever an asshole. What the TAC officers had given him, he passed right on down the line at every opportunity. He just *loved* to see those boys do push-ups. But Maverick was a combat veteran with almost a square yard of ribbons on his chest, so he could be the biggest asshole in the world and get away with it. And at five feet, seven and a half inches he spent most of his time screaming up some guy's nose, right into the little hairs.

The first months of flight school were just like basic training all over again, only worse. But it all became worth it when the Days of Amazement began and Maverick was finally assigned to an instructor pilot to begin actual hands-on leave-the-ground flying lessons. Except for an orientation ride when he arrived at Fort Wolters, he'd never even been in a helicopter.

Helicopters are like love. You never forget your first one. His was a Hiller H-23, an orange bubblenose thing that was so small it looked like they built it from a kit. And you never forget your first flight instructor. In this case, a young man named Ken Smith.

Draw a picture of the perfect Texan and you draw Ken Smith. He was tall, lanky, kind of dark, swarthy almost, with "wet-look" hair just a bit longer than maybe the military would like. Thin face, even a bit cadaverous, and the rest of him looked like if he drank a Coke he'd slip through the straw and fall in. He was so thin that the smallest flight suit they could give him, considering his height, was at least two sizes larger than he deserved. He was an anorexic elephant, skin sagging to the ground in great looping folds.

Since he was a helicopter pilot and a natural hot dog, he rode a snortin' Norton motorcycle, wore black Wellington boots and black sunglasses. Not those teardrop-shaped aviator glasses that everybody wore on his way to hot-dog warrant officerdom, but Buddy-Holly-East-by-God-Central-Texas Wayfarers that made him look like if your sister brought him home to dinner your father would kill him without hesitation.

Out of his mouth flowed a classic south Texas butter-'n'-honey drawl so thick that his mother used to spread it on toast. It never raised in pitch and never got excited, which was yet another source of amazement to Maverick. Over the course of time, Maverick did plenty of things to Smith in that helicopter that would not only raise the pitch of your voice but also make your balls crawl right back up where they came from. Ken's genitalia, however, remained in place.

He carried one of those collapsible pointers that look like a pen, and used it to keep the interest of his student pilots when their attention span began to shorten. When they fucked up, *whack!* he gave them one upside the helmet, just to keep their young minds right. It was like hitting a house pet with a rolled-up newspaper—a lot of noise, not a lot of damage. Brutality in a minor key.

Like all instructor pilots, Ken was a civilian under contract to the military, bringing to the party about thirty-four hundred hours' flight time in crop dusters, of all things. Now, crop-duster pilots have a peculiar personality profile, composed of equal parts unquestionable aviation ability, irritating self-assurance, and total bull-goose lunacy. Six feet off the ground in a tiny little single-seat plane with a great big honker engine hanging out the front, and it doesn't mean a damn, trees whizzing by on every side, *close.* You just clear those power lines at the end of the field, or maybe go under them, pull a few G's, stand the sucker on its wingtip, turn back, and do it again. Maverick thought the very idea was deranged, but in Vietnam he'd do things with his helicopters that would make crop dusting seem genteel.

Thing was, Ken Smith had never flown a helicopter in his life till the day he walked into the flight commander's office, put a thousand dollars down on the desk, and said, "I want to be a helicopter pilot and I want you to teach me."

So they did. He picked it up in no time, which was more than we can say for Maverick. Then they gifted him with Maverick as his very first student.

When he met Maverick for the first time, this is what he said: "You're *not* gonna learn how to fly this thing mechanically, you're *not* gonna fly it technically, and I don't give a damn if you know diddly about flight theory. You're gonna fly it by the seat of your pants. You'll become part of the machine, and the machine will become part of you. Everything you need to know, you'll feel right through your ass."

Maverick found out later that most instructors were obsessive to the point of anal retention about watching the instruments and what they tell you about your engine and what they show about the position of the helicopter in the air, but Ken, well, he just didn't give much of a shit about that stuff. He taught Maverick to keep his head up and his eyes off the little round black-and-white dials.

When Ken strapped him into that Hiller for the first time, he thought the guy was Jesus in a flight suit. Maverick didn't know it, but the skinny little joker was barely twenty-four years old and had all of about eighty hours in helicopters.

A few miles from the flight line, the flat Texas landscape breaks up by Army decree into "stage fields," areas the size of about three football fields, where student pilots can freely push expensive government machinery beyond its design parameters and frighten their instructors to the point of infarction. Each student was assigned to one specific area so he could screw up without running into anybody.

The morning of lesson one, Maverick was shaking with equal parts of anticipation and fear. There were huge cold pools of dark sweat under the arms of his dark gray flight suit. He clutched his brand-new helmet and gazed in awe. Smith flew the tiny chopper out to the middle of the field, put it in a hover, gave Maverick the controls, and told him to keep it like that. Then he folded his arms and sat back.

Keep it in a hover? Maverick couldn't keep it in Yankee Stadium. His sweaty hand strangled the controls. They swayed left and right like they were at the end of a long string. They drifted up and lurched down. They bounced. They rolled and pitched and yawed along every one of the aircraft's many axes. The helicopter had seen a vision of the Virgin of Guadalupe and was seized with the inspired fervor of trembling religious ecstasy.

Smith reached out, rested his hand ever so gently on the controls, and miraculously healed the machine.

He gave the controls back to Maverick and helicopter epilepsy promptly began all over again. Up, down, back, forward, wobble wobble wobble shake. They experienced motion in as many as six dimensions, they went around time and again—hold *still,* you bitch—and Maverick was more and more humiliated. Or mortified. He couldn't decide which.

Back on that first day of class, he'd *known* he'd be able to fly one of those things. The thought of his first lesson had kept him going through all the horrors and testing and hazing and happy horseshit of the month before. But now he was fucking up by the numbers, and it was becoming dead obvious that he didn't have the merest scrap of the kinesthetic aptitude that this task required. He thought: What if the guy who invented this goddamn thing couldn't fly it either?

Helicopters fly nothing like fixed-wing aircraft. At least regular old airplanes *want* to fly. If you get them rolling forward fast enough, flying is about all they can do. But helicopters don't want to do shit. The very fact that they can fly at all is like the case of the bumblebee, an affront to the laws of aerodynamics. Halfway through the course, Maverick was so frustrated he had to cry for an hour and a half all over some goddamn pay phone in Mineral Wells at three in the morning while Lynn talked him out of saying fuck it and coming home.

"Okay, Maverick," Ken finally yelled over the clatter. "I'm going to tell you the secret of keeping her steady."

He pointed to a little bulbous chrome toggle switch on the side of the cyclic, the lewdly symbolic hand grip that comes up from the floor between the pilot's legs and controls the roll and pitch of the aircraft.

"See this switch here on the side?"

"Yeah."

"We call this switch the 'hover button.' I didn't want to tell you about it before, but I'm gonna tell you about it now. It's like an automatic stabilization system. Flip it on and the aircraft will hover. With the switch off, it's a bitch to keep it steady."

"You must be kidding," Maverick said. "I've read a lot about helicopters and never heard of a 'hover button.' "

"Just watch. I'll turn the switch on, and you take over."

Instant miracle. Maverick sat shaking in his seat, gripping the cyclic like a month-old banana, and the chopper held so steady they could both have stood up and walked around. It was one of Life's Proudest Moments. I'm flying, thought Maverick. I'm flying!

"Okay," Smith said, "now I'll turn it off." He thumbed the switch down. But the machine still sat there nice and steady, pointed toward the scrubby gray tree on the horizon just like they wanted . . . for all of three seconds. Then the Blessed Virgin reappeared and the chopper's frenzied worship began anew.

"Hold on," Ken yelled. "I'll flip it on and settle her down." Which he did. Instantly they were floating, rajahs on a magic carpet three feet off the ground. Maverick's grin slowly returned. "Hey," he said to Smith, "I'm just a little pissed you didn't tell me about the hover button sooner."

Smith took over, set the machine on the ground, and throttled down to idle.

"Maverick, you dick," he drawled as the dust swirled up

around the chopper, "there's no such thing as a goddamn hover button. This thing here on the cyclic is the fucking landing-light switch. Flying a helicopter is nothing but mind over matter. All psychological. You got to have the feeling in the seat of your pants, and now you do."

Here's what it feels like to fly a helicopter. No, here's what it *doesn't* feel like. It doesn't feel like patting your head and rubbing your stomach at the same time. Too easy. It's more like patting your head, rubbing your stomach, juggling four eggs, doing the samba with your right foot, the Watusi with your left, and whistling "The Minute Waltz" in fifty-eight seconds.

You have the cyclic in your right hand, the stick which curves up from the cockpit floor and controls the angle of the rotor system, thus propelling you forward or back, right or left, sometimes whether you want to go or not. Your left hand, not to be outdone, is busy with the collective, which has two functions. It looks like a hand brake coming up from the floor to the left of your seat and has a twist-grip on the end that works like a motorcycle throttle. Pulling up on the collective changes the pitch of the rotor blades and provides lift. Twisting the throttle, of course, feeds gas to the engine and makes the blades turn faster. The two actions are intimately related.

If this still sounds a bit too commonplace, we offer for your consideration a couple of nasty little foot pedals that control the antitorque rotor on the tail. Since the blades above your head are rotating, they develop a load of force called torque. This makes your fuselage want to follow the rotors around in the opposite direction. Nature is wonderful. So the antitorque rotor, smaller, mounted at ninety degrees to the overhead rotor, counteracts that tendency.

Of course, all these controls have to be in balance. Pulling up on the collective for lift means the blades are taking a bigger bite out of the air which requires more power so you have to twist the throttle which develops more torque so you have to push harder on the pedal. You get the idea . . . but it took Maverick almost forever.

So Ken taught Maverick to fly like a crop duster, since that was the only way he knew. While all the other obedient little candidates were up at altitude flying the pattern and doing their drills, Maverick was where no pilot wants to be—down, down between the trees, ground hurtling past just below, screaming along three to ten feet up from the deck, terrified.

A few months later Maverick was belted into a Huey in Vietnam, blessing Ken Smith in his heart for teaching him to fly with his ass right on the deck. It kept him alive.

The morning of October 21, 1964, started out normally enough. Maverick and Ken went out early for their daily two hours of terror while the wind was calm, and about halfway through the lesson, Ken told him to set it down on the taxiway.

"Maverick," he said, looking at him through his trademark weird-ass greaseball sunglasses, "you may be the most dangerous son of a bitch that ever left the ground in a powered vehicle, and I'm tired of you scaring my ass every day. I just can't take this shit anymore." Then he opened the door and got out.

Maverick was stunned. Was this it? The Big Washout? The end of the dream? Smith stood on the hot pavement, his head tucked into his shoulders like people do when they stand under rotor blades, leaned over into the cockpit, pointed one long bony finger in Maverick's face, and said, "Give me three times around the pattern. Three approaches to a full stop. And for Christ's sake, don't kill yourself, 'cause the school's busy and we need all the choppers for training. Besides, it'll make me look like an asshole. Understand?"

Solo? Now? Maverick was too afraid to be scared. Or vice versa.

"No, I *don't* understand. I got only eight hours! Nobody solos before ten . . . or twelve. I'm not ready. What are you trying to do to me?"

"You're readier'n you think, cowboy. Besides, I'm a brand-new instructor and I want the glory of turning out the first student to solo with practically no time at all. You're him. You are now the pilot in command, Candidate. Take her up. Now or never."

Now or never. Maverick sat there, rotor blades idly slapping the air over his head, watching Ken walk away with his head pulled into his shoulders, unbending a bit when he got out from under. Maverick looked over at the other seat, now ominously empty, no familiar, reassuring presence to take over if things got out of control. This was his first time alone in a helicopter and he never felt more in the shit.

Courage. A shaking left hand reached down, fingers curled

deliberately around the throttle, a small contraction of muscle pulled the collective up, and the machine lifted him miraculously into a hover, then instantly drifted to the right because there was no weight in the other seat like there had been before. Shit again. He should have figured for that.

He floated down the hover lane to the end, and set the tiny helicopter down in the box to wait for takeoff clearance.

Deep breath. Another. Checked all the gauges, called the tower, heard the magic words, "You are cleared for immediate takeoff." Official permission to be a pilot. Up to a hover again, clearing turn to the right, clearing turn to the left (so far, so good), a 360 clearing turn just for jollies, push the cyclic forward, build a little speed, and shudder into the air. All. By. Him. Self.

Around once, twice, three times, perfect approaches each time. He could hear the controller on the radio informing other flights that there was a solo student in the pattern, so as he approached the runway for the third time, from a hundred feet above the ground he could see the whole class standing on the long narrow apron, hands shielding eyes from the sun.

There were only two things different about flying solo. One was the conspicuously vacant left seat. The other was the stupid grin. Maverick smiled with all his might and giggled through all three landings. When he touched down, his face hurt.

He reached forward and shut down the engine, feeling like . . . like you feel when you've just flown all by yourself for the first time after spending most of your life wanting to. Proud, humble, satisfied, giddy, hysterical. One of Life's Memorable Moments. When Maverick climbed out and shrugged off his helmet, Ken was waiting on the apron, looking pissed off.

"And here I thought you could be a pilot." Was that the merest hint of a smile? "I never seen such a shitty performance in my life! You? A chopper jock? I must have—"

And that's as far as he got because the whole class rushed forward, screaming like the Mongol hordes, hauled Maverick into the air, and, with a flurry of arms, legs, and elbows, carried him across the brown dirt road and discharged him into the thick rancid water of a pond in the middle of the pasture. It smelled terrible. He loved it.

Because of Ken, Maverick made his first solo after only eight hours of flight time, which at the time was a record at Fort

Wolters. Some candidates soloed before him, but none with less flight time. Then the Powers discovered that they didn't like the idea of anybody being considered even minimally proficient with a chopper after only eight hours, so they boosted the hour requirement to twelve, thus assuring Maverick's modest place in the history of Army aviation.

Maverick was bitten on the ass once more before leaving Fort Wolters, because he lacked about an hour and a half of solo time to finish piling up the necessary eighty-five that would get him on to advanced training at Fort Rucker, Alabama. It was winter. Cold, raining, icy—perfect flying weather for a high-time student pilot certain that he knew everything.

In the rain, he slogs out to his little Hiller, cranks up, and begins to practice takeoff and landing procedures. He enters the pattern for his first approach. It is there, just as he makes a sweeping left turn onto final, just as he sees the runway stretching before him like a welcome mat, it is there that he discovers he can't roll the throttle off. It's stuck in the open position. The engine remains at full speed, roaring heartily.

Maverick reaches down, twists that goddamn hand grip, and yanks it and bangs on it till his knuckles bleed, but all those cylinders above his head keep up their racket, rotor and engine tach needles comfortably matched up in the green, turning out big power at 3200 rpm. All set up on final approach, right altitude, right forward airspeed, lined up with the runway—and no throttle control at all. Way too fast for a landing descent. Since he can't land in that condition, he calls for a go-around and, in a shrill voice shot through with little yellow bolts of terror, begins explaining his problem to the tower.

Probably it's frozen or maybe he's just fucking up again, but oh, Lord, you can't land a helicopter at full throttle without just twisting the blades right off the thing and when that happens you glide like an anvil . . . and what is he going to *do?*

Is this maybe the scaredest he's ever been in his short life? Those blades are going *whacka-whacka-whacka* over his head just as fast as they can and he can't get them to slow down and his poor fucking left hand hurts *so* bad from banging on that goddamn frozen throttle and he strangles the microphone to scream at the tower again. That's when he discovers that Ken Smith taught him a lot, but not how to keep his voice pitch down in extreme situations. Mickey Mouse yells Mayday.

"Three-four-one-niner, are you declaring an emergency?"

Is he declaring an emergency? His helicopter won't stop flying no matter what he does, he has no control whatsoever, and his only alternative is to fly it into the ground under full power or wait till the fuel is gone and let it fly into the ground all by itself—yes, he is declaring an emergency. He goes around the pattern a second time while fire trucks pour onto the field and little ambulances skitter out, their headlights poking bright fingers onto the runway. Why do they think they need more than one? Do the drivers fight over the pieces?

A major part of learning how to fly is learning what to do when the machine decides to stop flying. But somehow they neglected to teach him what to do when the machine doesn't want to stop flying.

At this juncture it seems to Maverick that his only choice is autorotation. It's one of the things pilots love best about helicopters. When the engine quits, the uprushing air will keep the rotors turning like a pinwheel as you fall, giving enough lift to cushion the eventual and inevitable impact. It's a natural law and you have to be a genius to screw it up. Everybody in the class had proceeded through flight training with little incident, learning how to handle autorotations and emergency procedures till the movements were programmed into the muscles like walking or breathing, and even though a few of those Hillers had been bent pretty badly, nobody had crashed and nobody had died. Maverick could be the first and only.

But autorotation will require him to turn the engine off on purpose, which is a goddamn stupid thing to do. Every person who has ever been at the controls of a powered aircraft will tell you that flying is best when the engine just keeps on running smoothly until the very end of the flight. You never want the noise to stop. You *never* want to turn the engine off.

So he turns the engine off.

He's all set up on final approach (for the third time), with an engine that he has just killed on purpose, thoughts of the Ultimate Bite on the Ass running through his head, trying to remember everything that Ken Smith taught him about emergency procedures. Let's see . . . first you drop the collective. That disengages the transmission from the rotors and lets them spin freely. Done. Now, drop the nose and get the airspeed to sixty knots—son of a *bitch,* it's cold and rainy and he's going to die tonight—get the helicopter straight, line it up with the runway, jacking those foot pedals back and forth, hold it, hold it, sixty knots, don't let the airspeed drop, put her straight down the lane, the ground, the hard cold frozen ground, is coming up at seven hundred feet a minute, through seventy-five feet, time to pull the nose up and take off some airspeed and slow the rate of descent and if he has to think of one more thing his mind will shut down and go to the Bahamas without him, fifty, forty, thirty, waiting for ten feet so he can level this sucker, then pop that collective *all* the way up into his drenched armpit as hard as he can to increase the pitch of the rotor blades and take a big bite out of the air *now!* and settle that foul machine down onto the lane like he does this all the time . . . *bang!*

Well. It is tempting to say that he executed a perfect textbook emergency landing in front of all those medics who were just aching for something bloody and surgical to do, but the bald fact is that he didn't slow the aircraft down quite enough. Ken liked to see the machine skid less than three feet once it touched, but Maverick just couldn't bring himself to pull the nose up that hard, and when he got to the bottom he hit with forty knots' worth of joyous forward motion. The bewildered machine careened down the cold icy lane like it was on ball bearings before they both came to a skidding, drifting, shuddering halt. He was down, he was alive, and he wasn't sitting in anything nasty. Pilots like to define a good landing as any landing you can walk away from. On rubbery legs, Maverick walked away.

Bad news: what with the emergency and all, he logged only an hour and ten minutes of flight time . . . short of what he needed to graduate. Good news: they gave him the other twenty minutes, not as a reward for surviving the emergency, but as a reward for not bending the chopper. The school was busy. They needed every one.

It was good practice, though, Maverick was to discover, because in Vietnam helicopters tended to suddenly stop working all the time, especially if you hit them with enough bullets. Maverick would be offered plentiful opportunity for autorotation practice under much less hospitable conditions.

He was learning an important Lesson of War: how to screw up as far in advance as possible.

• • •

Fort Rucker, Alabama, was the base for advanced helicopter training. There all the hot-dog pilots who were so proud to make it through Texas and thought they knew just everything about rotary-wing flight came eyeball to eyeball with the abyss of their ignorance. It is a big step up from a two-place Hiller to a Sikorsky H-19, and not just because the latter sits higher off the ground. Gone were the TAC officers, the hazing, the push-ups. Instead, they flew Hueys, they learned tactics, they learned instrument flight. When they arrived, they were helicopter operators. When they left, they were pilots. More or less.

And warrant officers. At Rucker, they were accorded officers'-club privileges and other minor niceties of rank. All the juvenile shit went out the window. They had to start growing up.

Of the original one hundred and twenty in the class at Fort Wolters, only fifty-two made it all the way through the second stage, and of those, almost all went to Vietnam. Maverick and Fortenberry, in homage to a time-honored military tradition, dissipated themselves monumentally in San Francisco for forty-six hours before leaving. Memories of this period are vague, details lacking. They were checked onto the plane virtually as baggage, and made the flight to Saigon together. They were separated when they arrived, but would find themselves again an unlikely duo once the plot, and the war, started to thicken.

Not all the graduates were sent to Vietnam right away. Some went to Fort Benning, Georgia, to train in the Eleventh Air Assault, which later became the First Air Cavalry. Ty went with them.

All sorted out? Everybody in place? Good. Now that the ground has been so carefully prepared, it is time to discover which of these aspiring heroes, driven by a cruelly insidious John Wayne fantasy, will finish the war walking upon it, and which will finish the war lying beneath it.

THREE

Maverick spent hours staring at the lock. The door to the cage was secured by a huge rusty chain held in place by the largest, most comically overblown padlock he'd ever seen. It was an enormous lock, an impossible lock, heart-shaped with a dark brown rusty surface, the metal flaking off in tiny curling pieces. In the center was a classic keyhole-shaped keyhole, the kind Alice could stare through into Wonderland. It was an old lock, an antique, the kind that might have held a castle gate closed against determined assault by the infidels. It reminded Maverick of the first time he saw his grandfather's pocket watch, how huge it had seemed, round and golden and glittering, dangling, just as the lock did, on the end of a ponderous chain. It was ridiculously disproportionate to its task, and all the more disheartening for its absurd enormity.

After sundown on the second (third? fourth?) *night, four men he could not see came into the hooch, pushed long bamboo rods through the cage, lifting him up like a nabob in a sedan chair. They carried him out of the hooch into the evening air, threw the cage none too gently onto a cart pulled by a water buffalo, and set off into the jungle.*

They may have hauled him all night long, he didn't know. If they put him down and took a break, he couldn't feel it. The hurting never stopped, and he found it best to lie very still on the strict bamboo rods. Early in the morning, his unlikely cortege emerged from the dense green into a syrupy golden light that flowed through the low thatched huts of a different village. How far had they carried him?

By that time Maverick could focus on the men at the ends of the bamboo poles. Four North Vietnamese Army regulars. No black pajamas here, but full uniforms, with khaki shorts, shirts, gunbelts, and those ridiculous narrow-brimmed pith helmets.

Real soldiers, not VC, which may have explained why he was still alive, if only just.

As they carried him, the dusty trail opened out into the main area of the village. People appeared, bent old women, painfully thin boys, gaunt old men. A furious noise swelled from their angry faces, a wave of palpable hatred. Many had long bent sticks or poles, and shoved the ends through the bars to jab at his face. His fear shot a numbing bolt of strength through his system, defying his pain and rolling him over to curl up in the classic damage-control position.

They carried him into a hooch, arranged his cage on stilts, and disappeared. He gazed into the dimness for many minutes, breathing heavily, hurting. He fell asleep staring at the lock.

Here's how war usually works.

First you give everybody guns. Then you draw a line between the two armed forces. Put the good guys—whichever side you're on—over on one side and the bad guys on the other. Then they try to get over here, and you try to go over there.

The whole idea is to push that line as far toward the enemy as you can, and see how much ground you can gain. That gain, or lack thereof, measures how much of the battle you actually won or lost. Sounds a lot like football, which even has something like a body count. What a surprise.

The places where those lines are drawn are called by many names: "DMZ's" (demilitarized zones), "fronts," "no-man's-land." In Vietnam they were called "FEBA's"—Forward Edge of Battle Area. Now, normally, if you're lucky, the FEBA is miles away. If you're not at the lines, you're not in combat.

But what made war in Vietnam really different, as everybody soon found out, is that the FEBA was a three-foot circle around you, and around everyone friendly toward you. You never, ever knew who your enemy actually was. Not a bit like the Steelers on one side and the Cowboys on the other.

In Vietnam there was no turf, there was no line of scrimmage, and you got no points for gaining yardage. You could buy it in your bed almost as easily as you could buy it on the battleground. Sounds obvious enough now, but in 1965 nobody knew it, and even five or six years later they still hadn't gotten it through their heads. And what a surprise it was for them to discover that the people they were fighting weren't even all men. Or adults. Like the girl in Dong ba Tinh.

• • •

The flight from Travis Air Force Base in San Francisco to Tan Son Nhut in South Vietnam takes twenty-one hours, with stopovers. By the time they landed at Guam, Maverick's head had cleared to the point where he could lift it off Dick's shoulder, where it had rested for the better part of six hours, and ask himself some serious questions. Where were the inhumanly crowded troop transports Maverick used to see in the newsreels? Where was the hardship? Good thing John Wayne wasn't around to see him marching off to war with a plastic tray of Airline Dinner on his lap and a Bloody Mary in his hand. Common sense told him that this couldn't last. Could we have a little destruction here, please? And another bag of those peanuts?

After the refueling stop in Guam, after all the partying on the plane was over, surely he would walk directly into a bit of combat, suffering, and deprivation? Well, he did, but none of it happened like he expected. When does it ever?

Many hours later, in the air over Southeast Asia, the pilot, who had obviously flown the route before, announced, "Gentlemen, welcome to never-never land. On the right side of the aircraft, you will see the beautiful coastline of the Republic of Vietnam. We are about to begin our final descent"—appropriate choice of words, it turned out, for many of them—"into Tan Son Nhut airport. You may notice the approach is a little steeper than usual, but I'm sure you can figure out why. The crew and I would love to stay and have a drink with you, but we have pressing engagements elsewhere." Smart-ass.

War at last! Maverick looked out the window expecting to see those bombs going off, smoke columns rising, tracer fire, Hollywood pyrotechnics. But he saw none of that. When they got off the plane they could have been in Miami or Atlanta. Through hot damp air screaming with the noise of dozens of aircraft, a hundred and sixty of Uncle Sam's Finest shuffled into a plush terminal waiting area and, except for the uniforms, damned if they didn't look for all the world like college kids at O'Hare going home for Christmas.

But gradually, small observations disclosed the danger of their situation. This was not college. And when they started to discover where the FEBA was, they were certainly not in Kansas anymore. Everybody's first little jolt: the buses that took them to the in-processing center had heavy wire-mesh screening on the windows, because the citizenry, at least some of them, might ride up alongside the buses on bikes or motor scooters, slam-dunk a grenade through the window, and blow your ass away.

Welcome to our ally, the Democratic Republic of South Vietnam. Welcome to the Forward Edge of Battle Area.

But still no war.

In 1965 Maverick found himself assigned to the A Company of the 502nd Aviation Battalion in a place called Vinh Long, about fifty miles southwest of Saigon in the Mekong Delta. The war was going to hand him some big shocks, and Vinh Long was the very first. In a way, it was a shock in reverse. He came prepared for exposure to the Horrors of War and they'd sent him to the Palm Beach Polo and Country Club instead. He expected the rockets' red glare and saw nothing but blue sky. The place was absolutely astonishing.

Yes, they landed in a compound on a pierced-steel-planking runway, and yes, there were all these olive-drab aircraft around and ungainly square bunkers made of vast numbers of sandbags, and there were tin roofs and lookout towers, but even the fifty-caliber machine guns on the top didn't look all *that* ominous. There was a perimeter, and barbed-wire fences, and you knew that there were mine fields outside, but when you got out on the street and walked around the place, Christ, it felt like Clark Kent's hometown. Or yours.

There were little low square hooches set out in perfect rows. Tan, with walls halfway up, screening and a metal roof. They were so neat, so precise, that Barbie and Ken could have made a lovely life inside. There were paved sidewalks, lawns that were manicured so hard it hurt, a chapel and a theater, an officers' club and an enlisted men's club with patios and barbecue pits and a great big bar and real live electricity. There was probably more hot water on that one base than in all the rest of the country.

It was obvious that it had never even occurred to the Americans to adapt to the culture of the people whose hearts and minds they were attempting to win. They had brought their own culture with them, thank you, right down to the movies, magazines, and iceberg lettuce. It didn't look a thing like war.

They had houseboys who took their clothes to the convent for the nuns to wash. They were starched, pressed, creased, spit-shined, and fed. They had one of those inevitable signposts in the middle of the base, a white wooden pole with cutout arrows imprinted in big square black letters: "Jacksonville 11,578" . . . "Chicago, 10,754." They had the sun in the morning and the moon at night.

Of course, it was 1965, just before the big escalation, when Dean Rusk and McGeorge Bundy and those well-meaning but totally mistaken gentlemen were beginning to be heard in the White House and before Lyndon Johnson decided that the enemy could be bullied into submission like everybody else he had ever dealt with. The Americans were still in an "advisory capacity." But even so, was it supposed to be so comfortable? If this is war, thought Maverick, it isn't bad. Not bad at all.

The accommodations were more than satisfactory, but conditions soon got lots better and lots worse. When U.S. combat troops were finally brought in later that year, the people who preceded them were suddenly up to their asses in the profligate abundance of the American consumer industrial miracle. Handling the logistics as only Yankees can, they flooded the country with an embarrassing cascade of liquor, cigarettes, cameras, perfume, toilet paper, talcum powder, stockings, panties, rubbers. They didn't want the American fighting man to go to war without his necessities. Maverick was no different . . . you start to miss toilet paper real fast. The shit poured into Vietnam after 1965, and created the most incredible black market you ever saw.

After all the orientation flights and in-country checkout rides, one would get up in the morning, have breakfast, fly a few missions till noon, eat some lunch, take a siesta, fly a little more, and consider the war over for the day. When the sun went down, it was Witching Hour, so they'd have dinner and start drinking as soon as possible thereafter. Nobody bothered them. They were safe on the base, they thought, and the only people out there who didn't like them were the VC, they thought, but nobody took the VC seriously, and besides, this was Vinh Long, not exactly in a front-line combat area. The VC and the Americans both were involved in a part-time war. Sure, a mortar round would sail into the compound once in a while, or "One-Shot Charlie" would crawl out of his hole and squeeze off a few with his antiquated captured French rifle, but anybody on the base who shot back at him would get his ass kicked because the Americans were afraid that if anybody killed Charlie he'd be replaced by some putz who could actually shoot. Every base had a One-Shot Charlie living outside, and none of them ever hit anything. The enemy was a joke.

But the little incidents of hostility were just diversions. For weeks, Maverick remained stunned by how *nice* it all was. The war was being fought at a leisurely pace. It was great.

The first thing that happened to helicopter pilots when they arrived in Vietnam was assignment to a platoon that flew "slicks," the Hueys used for troop and cargo transport, or "Ash and Trash" missions. They were called "slicks" because, except for an M-60 machine gun in each cargo door, they were unarmed. That should have told Maverick something, but he was a newby then, and inexcusably stupid, and too happy just to be flying. He was assigned to a platoon that called itself, in the tradition of taking pride in viciously malicious names, the Outlaws.

Obviously, a first assignment as a slick copilot allowed the newbys to build time, learn how the aviation company operated, find out what it was like to fly under extreme conditions. You got your in-country checkout, your orientation and standardization rides, then you officially had the confidence of the American taxpayers and were ready to be trusted as a copilot of one of their UH-1D helicopters.

The minute Maverick got to Vinh Long, he wandered, agape, to the commanding officer and handed over his orders.

The commander pointed his round face and brown mustache at the paperwork and looked at it the way you'd look at a document from the Albanian Foreign Office. He stared at the name, raised his ruddy face, and said, "How do you pronounce this, son?"

"Mar-vic-sin, sir."

"Mmm. That's kind of tough. You got a nickname or anything?"

"Well, sir, sometimes they call me 'Maverick.' "

That stopped him for a second. Then he sort of half-smiled under his thin brown mustache and said, "Maverick, huh? Well, *Maverick,* it's pretty clear to me where you're gonna wind up."

"Sir?"

The commander never told Maverick what he meant, and Maverick, having just arrived, didn't know that there was a gunship platoon called the Mavericks based out of Vinh Long. He was a newby. Stupid. The CO called it, though. With his nickname and his attitude, it was inevitable that he would find his way out of the Outlaws and into gunships. But it took a while. He needed that exposure first, the experience that would show him just how soft the human body really is.

That night, his very first in Vinh Long, was hot, sticky, and oppressive. Some anonymous EM directed him over to the slick hooch to meet the rest of the pilots and the platoon commander. The PC's name, they told him, was Captain John Weber, which gave Maverick a little tingle, a small disturbing tug of unpleasant familiarity just below the short light brown hairs at the back of his neck. When Maverick arrived, the platoon had just come back from a mission. He walked into the middle of the debriefing.

Up to the front door. Nobody there. Go around to the patio behind the hooch. As he rounded the corner and got his first sight of his new outfit seated on low benches under yellow light, the captain was in the middle of a sentence:

". . . time of war, and you fuckers better remember that. As far as the platoon commander is concerned, the Law of the Forty-five is in full effect. The next time one of you assholes pulls the shit that you pulled today, so help me Christ, I'll blow your fucking head off."

It all came back in a rush. John Weber. Of *course!* Weber was the WOC company commander at Fort Wolters, an inflexible, inhuman, by-the-book automaton who had "asshole" written all over him. Everybody hated him in Texas, and he'd apparently brought all his charm with him to Vietnam.

Maverick got the whole story later. The platoon had inserted some troops into a landing zone, and while they were on the ground they got surprised by fifty-caliber machine-gun fire. They'd landed in the middle of an ambush, a common occurrence, he was to discover, and instead of making a disciplined departure behind the flight leader, two of the pilots had panicked, pulled their aircraft straight up, done a one-eighty, and flown back *over the top* of the formation. Not a good idea. When you do that, you pin your buddies down on the ground. They can't lift off because you're above them. If you get shot down, you crash on top of one or two or three other aircraft. It's not considered acceptable behavior, and Maverick had walked into the briefing as Weber was making that very point in the most vehement possible terms, punctuating each phrase with the dark round hole at the end of his service pistol. As an attention-getting device, it more than served.

Maverick thought: Am I walking into some kind of funny farm here? I've been in some military service or other for five years, and this is the first time I've ever heard an officer threaten his men with death. First day in-country, first day in the war, and the only gun pointed at me in anger is in the hands of my platoon commander.

('Scuse me, Captain, but while we're protecting the Vietnamese from the Communists, who's gonna protect us from *you?*)

Is *this* the Forward Edge of Battle Area?

About a week later, after all the check rides, Maverick's very first mission out of Vinh Long was to fly his longtime idol, a newspaper reporter named Jim Lucas. Back home Maverick had a scrapbook of his articles that weighed about six pounds, and Lucas was the whole reason he had learned to fly helicopters and gotten himself sent over. So far the Southeast Asian experience had been considerably less than uplifting and woefully short of expectations, and Maverick couldn't decide whether he wanted to ask Lucas for his autograph or shoot him.

Out on the dusty morning flight line, he recognized Lucas at once. Tall, skinny, black brush-cut, long face. Maverick was twenty-four and the reporter was the most "famous" person he'd ever met. He stuck out his hand.

"Mr. Lucas, this . . . this is a pleasure. An honor. You won't believe this, but I've been reading your articles for years. I mean, I have 'em all in a scrapbook back home. You inspired me to become a helicopter pilot."

"That's nice," Lucas said in a dull, dusty voice, and heaved himself through the big square cargo door into the chopper. Maverick yanked open the triangular cockpit door and pulled himself into the left seat, crushed. So much for boyhood idols. He didn't know it at the time, but the months to come would deal his idealism even heavier blows.

The first time Maverick saw a man die, he'd been in-country only a few days.

His third mission out of Vinh Long was a flight to take the crew chief and gunner to an area just south of the Cambodian border near the Parrot's Beak. They called it the Gunnery Range and had designated it a free-fire zone. They could shoot at anything that moved, and the populace had been warned to keep clear.

The area was a wasteland. No rice paddies, no cultivation, no people, not if they wanted to stay alive, just swamp and marsh and tall waving clumps of elephant grass about six feet high that was perfect cover for VC movements. Desolation. Nobody could possibly want to go there. So of course the VC and North Vietnamese delighted in moving troops through the area at night.

Every once in a while the Army sent a helicopter out to look around, and the slick pilots would give the gunners a little target practice.

Like today.

"Hit that clump." *Baddabaddabadda!*

"See those birds?" *Baddabaddabadda!*

The slicks were troop transports, armed only with M-60 machine guns that hung out the cargo doors on each side. Not much, but better than being naked. When they were inserting troops into an LZ, the gunships, Hueys loaded to the tits with practically every device known to man that could throw fragments of hot metal rapidly, would fire rockets, machine guns, grenades, and other miscellaneous ordnance into the tree lines to prep the area and keep the enemy's collective head down. When the slicks were on short final approach, the on-board gunners could open up on the tree lines to help with the cover. Very noisy. And they'd fire like mad on extractions, too, so the choppers could get away without being too badly perforated.

Okay. Back to the Gunnery Range. Maverick eases down on the collective and the Huey sinks toward the desolate earth in a gentle glide.

The gunners start firing into a small stand of trees, just to see what they can hit. Suddenly a small figure, like a little black beetle on hot summer ground, bolts from the underbrush and starts to scuttle across the clearing. He's in loose pajamas and carries something that looks like a weapon. (Shit, in Vietnam, *everything* looked like a weapon). Well, the poor bastard must have heard the chopper coming and hidden in the trees, but when bullets start whizzing by him for no reason whatsoever, he gets a bit hysterical.

He doesn't get very far. Those deadly little puffs on the

ground tap-dance toward him as he runs, and they stitch him through and he whirls and he falls, rolling over once, twice, on the scruffy grass. As the aircraft moves up and away, he lies, becoming smaller and smaller, like a little black X, arms and legs open to the sky.

Just like that.

Maverick is stunned, amazed, astonished. He thinks: What an easy thing this is to do! You just . . . you just pull the trigger, and the tracers, the long hot glowing fingers, walk up to the man with baby steps, the bullets tickle him, he falls down. That's all there is to it.

What a puzzling sensation. Not godlike or powerful or heroic. Not glorious. Not even sickening. Just bewildering, like somebody yelling at you in a foreign language. It doesn't seem fair that making a human being die should be so . . . simple. And Maverick himself hadn't even pulled the trigger. But he would.

The emotion didn't last long. You see a few beheadings, you lose a few friends, you come upon a classmate skinned alive—the VC were big on that and Maverick never figured out why—and the softness goes right out of you. A subtractive kind of magic.

Seeing that instructive death gave Maverick his first revelation, and perhaps his most basic. Killing is easy. Dying is hard.

When Maverick arrived in Vietnam, Americans were acting in an "advisory" capacity. Mostly what the chopper jocks did was ferry ARVN troops, called "Reaction Forces," on various kinds of operations. These were mounted in response to reports of enemy activity, rumors of enemy activity, suspicions of enemy activity, dreams of enemy activity, even, at times, actual enemy activity. Anything. The pilots called the RF's Rat Fucks because they never knew what the hell they'd be flying into. A routine mission could turn into the worst chapter of the book of Revelation in half a second.

A normal mission: long lines of Hueys at the staging area arranged in a perfect straight line, their rotors pointing exactly front to back, painfully symmetrical. Clouds of omnipresent whirling red dust. ARVN troops, ten ARVN's per load, including pots, pans, rice, live chickens, teacups, and sometimes weapons and ammo, wait on the ground in single lines next to each chopper, clamber in, are taken into landing zones, and extracted when the operation is over. More times than not, when they get to the LZ's, the choppers swoop in amid deafening clatter, settle down in a whirl, and the ARVN's just jump right out, hit the dirt, sit down, light a fire, kill a chicken, and eat lunch. None of this screaming out of the aircraft, weapons at the ready, forming up like an organized military operation, and charging into the teeth of the enemy. Nope. A camping trip instead. Only thing missing is the merit badges. The chopper pilots shake their heads.

But they didn't call it the "Nine-to-Five War" just out of puckishness. When the boys were finished with a hard day at the war and all the ARVN's were back home, there was always a hot meal, a hot shower, the officers' club, liquor . . . and "One-Shot Charlie" squeezing off an occasional round just to remind them that they were too far from home.

It didn't take long for Maverick to go from the lap of luxury to the heart of darkness. After about a month in Vinh Long, the whole unit was moved to a place in the northern highlands called Dong ba Tinh.

Dong ba Tinh was nothing but a dirt landing strip across the road from a perfectly square Special Forces camp that contained a few American Green Beret advisers and a battalion-size Vietnamese strike force. The camp had been gouged out of the ground in a so-called "pacified area" about two hundred miles to the north. The Viets lived there with their inevitable chickens, wives, children, everybody.

The camp was perched on a hill overlooking Cam Ranh Bay. It was the prettiest place Maverick ever saw. Before the American buildup, before they started towing entire concrete piers all the way across the goddamn Pacific to build a major harbor, Cam Ranh Bay would have brought saliva to the lips and fibrillation to the heart of the most jaded condo developer. The hills were an unspoiled emerald-green crushed velvet rolling down to the white beaches along the bay. It was quiet and hot and tropical. The birds and trees said gentle things to each other all day long.

The condos were never built, but the place *was* Americanized, in a perverted sort of way.

A bit different from Vinh Long, was Dong ba Tinh. Yes, indeed. No mess hall, no showers, no officers' club, no nothing.

Just dirt and a couple of hooches across the road for the American and ARVN officers, maybe. Concertina wire, Claymore mines. No place for anybody to live. Amid much grumbling, none of it good-natured, they camped out on the dirt strip and slept on air mattresses on the ground, covered by a shelter half. That's kind of like a lean-to that you wear. Once inside, you be sure to drape the mosquito netting over it, because in Vietnam the mosquitoes were known to carry off livestock and, on occasion, small children.

When it wasn't being dry and dusty it was being tropically rainy instead. Air mattresses would turn into pool floats and Maverick would often wake up about thirty yards down from where he went to sleep.

Even though it was his first experience in the field, Dong ba Tinh was peaceful, there wasn't really any enemy activity, and Maverick's troop slept safely on the ground across the road from the hooches. He didn't get really scared until the American troops arrived. They were young, so young, and so green you could use them for camouflage and so scared you could hear their assholes snap shut. All they knew was what they'd heard, and what they'd heard wasn't good. All at once they were in the middle of a war and the enemy could be anywhere and there was nothing outside the compound but jungle and VC, so they'd shoot at absolutely anything. Sometimes firefights would start up in the darkness, silly bastards shooting at each other. One guy thinks he hears something and pops off a round, so somebody else pops one back at him, and before you know it there's a dandy little war under way and not an enemy in sight. Officers stopped short at confiscating all the ammunition.

Every night, the 101st set up an ambush position about a hundred yards behind the area where the chopper crews slept. First thing in the morning, Maverick would see the patrol come straggling back to camp. One morning, as he was standing at the piss tube—those were rocket casings that were driven into the ground at an angle and you stuck your dick in them . . . when they filled up, you pissed somewhere else—Maverick felt his usual annoyance as the patrol shuffled past him, because the boys liked to salute officers who were pissing so they'd have to change hands to return the gesture, and get their feet wet.

But something was wrong. The grunts were in their fatigues as usual, flop hats on, faces painted up, dark green apparitions with black under the eyes. They were so tense you could almost hear them buzz. Usually they laughed and joked like people do when the night shift is over, but on this particular occasion they looked like the Nightmare on Elm Street. They all had the thousand-yard stare and nobody was saying a word.

"Sergeant," Maverick said. "What's wrong with these guys?"

"You wouldn't believe it, sir." This particular sergeant had a rugged, craggy face that featured all-too-evident lines of tension. Little white creases ran from the corners of his eyes and mouth, where the rolling sweat had washed his camouflage away.

"Try me."

"Well, you know what a full moon we had last night?"

It had been one of those exotic, rare pearl nights . . . perfectly clear, with an opalescent shimmer that the moon can give only when she has pure, innocent air to work with.

"We'd set up our ambush positions like normal," the sergeant continued, "in a horseshoe. And a little after midnight these two huge dark forms appeared right in the middle of the open end."

"Enemy?"

"Tigers. Big-ass fucking tigers."

Maverick was stunned. Tigers? It had never occurred to him that there would be wildlife around there. How many of those good clean American boys had ever seen one outside a zoo? In central Ohio they were virtually nonexistent.

"Tigers?"

"Yessir. Two of the biggest motherfuckers you ever saw, all silvery under the moonlight. They walked right up the middle of the horseshoe, making these little snuffling sounds, kind of purring low in their throats. God, they were fuckin' gorgeous. Then they split and went down each side sniffing out every single firing position. They met in the middle at the open end and just . . . melted into the jungle. We were so scared we couldn't even shoot 'em. Didn't know whether to shit or go blind. Couldn't scream, couldn't run . . . Jesus."

Well, god damn. Before the 101st arrived, they'd hardly had any security at all. Spent thirty days sleeping on the ground, in the open, nobody to speak of standing guard, lying out there every night with all this man-eating Asian fauna prowling around, and nobody had any fucking idea.

It's true what they said about Vietnam. You never knew when you were going to get it, or how, or from whom, or from what, or from where.

FOUR

He woke up. It was probably late morning, since the heat was already extreme, the inside of the hooch stifling. Maverick had never been in a steam room, but he imagined it would feel just as he was feeling then. It was wet and heavy, fetid with the smell of rotting vegetables and old fish sauce. Every breath was an act of conscious volition because of the pain in his chest. The air was a pillow over his face.

He heard a shuffling noise. At one end of the cage, near his feet, two little brown heads containing four little brown eyes peered at him from floor level. He was lying flat on his back and could barely see them.

The forms walked around the cage to stand next to his head. Two little boys about six years old. The darker of the two was missing his right arm below the elbow. His upper arm terminated in a crude stump, crumpled with white scar tissue. Maverick felt sick.

It apparently had never occurred to them that, despite his appearance, Maverick didn't speak their language (aside from his astounding vocabulary of scatological references), since they'd never met anybody who spoke anything else. So they began a chummy conversation with him, like old friends who have just reunited after long separation. They gabbled for a moment, then paused politely, waiting for a response. It was apparent they hadn't gotten the word that he was the Yankee Imperialist Devil Dog Enemy.

Maverick's instinct was to respond less politely, but he stifled it. They were just kids. Briefly he remembered the girl in Dong ba Tinh. She, too, had been just a kid.

"Hey! Bring me some food. And water!"

The boys smiled at him, at each other.

"I'm hungry. Feed me!" He made weak but unmistakable

"hungry" signs, stabbing his finger toward his open mouth. The movement cost him dearly, but he suddenly realized that he was hungrier than he was hurting. He considered it a good sign.

The boys exchanged a few comments, then whirled and ran off. Maverick hoped they'd gotten the idea. In soft waves, new hunger and old pain washed over him.

It was at Dong ba Tinh that he met the girl. She was about eight years old, and if anything could give a Caucasian an appreciation of Asian beauty, it was her. Round face, big smiling eyes, long straight black hair that was always immaculately clean and shiny (Maverick looked at all the red dust and dirt blowing around the compound and considered the girl's hair a superhuman achievement). She must have washed it six times a day. She wore a little cotton blouse and shorts that looked like they came from the bottom of the stack at the charity bazaar, but they were always spotless too. Her good looks stopped at her ankles, because she had the kind of feet that every Vietnamese peasant had. She had never worn shoes in her life, except maybe sandals to go into town, so her feet looked like little armadillos, brown and scaly, with toes that curled over like she could perch in a tree. Everybody loved her. If she ever grew up in one piece, she'd be a heartbreaker.

Among other commonalities of the Vietnam experience, almost all of them horrid, one memory that everybody took away with at least moderate fondness was that of the green bottle with the red-and-white label—the ubiquitous, inevitable Ba Muoi Ba beer, drinkable only by desperate men and only in wartime. Nobody in Maverick's platoon could pronounce the name, so they just called it Bom-de-Bom. It had this unhealthy, barely yellowish cast that reminded him of the joke about the horse with diabetes. The girl would bring it to camp every day, along with Cokes and some alien odd-colored local soft drinks, carried on a joystick, a long pole across her narrow shoulders with a big can on each end. She'd put ice in the cans, cool the drinks down, and lug them all the way up from the village. It was a constant source of incredulity that such a little girl could carry so much weight. At first the guys wanted to help her, but events soon erased the impulse.

Ice was a very precious substance in Vietnam. Except for the likelihood of wet pockets, it could have been used as legal tender. There were two kinds: the kind that would kill you and the kind that wouldn't. One was the village icehouse variety, which was frozen water and never you mind where it came from. It contained additional bonus ingredients, like rats and cockroaches, assorted vermin, and quite possibly fecal matter. Plus those microscopic things that few have the stomach to discuss. One did *not* use this ice for drinking. The second kind was potable ice, occasionally available in the cities.

It was a relief of sorts to see a happy kid every so often, so all the troops at the base, except for the most alienated, used to fuss over her. They called her Lisa and gave her candy bars and C-rations and stuff. She didn't speak much English, and some of the less refined brethren would try to teach her dirty words. She liked it.

Until one day. Some of the Outlaws were standing around drinking whatever she had brought, and one of the crew chiefs, a big ruddy guy, picked her up for a piggyback ride. He ran her around the helicopters one time and she laughed and squealed and said incomprehensible things at a million miles an hour. When he started to set her down, his big hands tight around her waist, the little white blouse she was wearing blew up over her head, and Maverick caught sight of . . . something.

A piece of paper? Cloth? Taped to her brown midriff.

The crew chief saw it too, and set her down.

"Whatcha got? Is it a love letter from your boyfriend? C'mon."

She pushed his hand away and started to back off.

"C'mon, you can tell me. What is it? Bet it's a love letter."

He reached around her again, and her eyes got wide. Fright? Wariness? What had happened to the fun?

"Tell me, pleeeese. Is it a big secret?"

She stared up at the circle they formed around her like the classic cornered animal. By this time, smiles had faded. The crew chief grabbed her by the arm, pulled her to him, bent down, reached under her blouse and ripped the thing off her chest.

It was a piece of paper, folded to about the size of a playing card, but it kept opening and opening like some sort of perverted road map.

Exactly right. But she didn't get it down at the Shell station, and the AAA had never handed out anything like it. It was, in fact, a drawing of every single helicopter parking position in the camp, outlines of where the ammo bunker was, roads, hooches, ditches, everything, drawn to painstaking scale, laid out in meters, showing distances between aircraft, how far to the crossroad leading to the Special Forces camp, where the troops slept, how the shelter halves were arranged, location of the mess facility, privies, and so on and so on and so on. Did she draw this? Did she sell her drinks and goodies and pace those distances off so precisely with her twisted little feet all at the same time?

It was as apparent as it was appalling. She had been coming into camp every day, taking a look at a position, memorizing it, going off into the bushes, and making a little sketch, till she damn near had the layout of everything in the area. She could've gone to work for the National Fucking Geographic Society.

Maverick just stood there in the heat and the damp and the inevitable blowing red dust for a long time after the girl was led away across the road to the Special Forces camp. Nobody needed much time in-country to be stunned by the poverty and the horror and the utter inhumanity of the Vietnamese toward their enemies and toward each other. Many have told the story. And there were a thousand ways you could get demoralized and disgusted and disappointed by the kind of war you had to fight and the kind of people you had to fight it with and the kind of people you had to fight it against and the kind of people you had to kill. Maverick would fly along with an ARVN officer about fifty feet up, looking at the people on the ground, and the officer would say, "No VC." Next group of people. "No VC." Next group of people. "VC." *Baddabaddabadda.* Maverick never knew how the ARVN could tell. He never asked.

But nothing disheartened him more than seeing that little girl disappear into the low brown hooch across the road. The Americans, good clean models of fair play and sportsmanship, had landed in a country and a culture and a war that showed them ideas and concepts they couldn't begin to begin to imagine. Maverick thought he was prepared for the combat part, but he was never prepared for the collision of cultures. It never occurred to him—it couldn't occur to him—that they'd use children in a war.

Can I really call her a VC? he thought. Who told her to do what she did? Was she ordered? Threatened? Did she even know what she was doing? She seemed a bit young for that kind of political commitment. Should I shoot her now or later?

Fuck me to tears, he thought, shaking his head. If they're willing to sacrifice their children to the cause, we haven't got a chance against them.

Maverick lost so much compassion that day, more than the "normal" sights of war could ever have driven out of him. He realized for the first time that he was in a place where the innocence of childhood didn't exist. Kiss your pity good-bye, soldier. Welcome to the Forward Edge of Battle Area. It starts right over there with the smiling little girl who sells you soft drinks.

FIVE

If I could just kinda combine these two images . . . I can see her out of my right *eye and I can see her out of my* left *eye, but the two don't seem to* coincide *somehow, there's no* congruence *here, shit, I can't even make 'em* overlap. *Sit. Talk. She is nice and blond and healthy with that clean middle-American milk-skin wide-hipped bear-many-children Arkansas look and that slow way of talking, or maybe that's just me, mind-warped by viciously addicting alcohol, shit, I was blasted when I got here and now she must think I'm all kinds of an asshole but . . . but I still got enough sense left to know I got no sense left.*

And then the party's over and we go have breakfast—she drives—and then I call and call and call and she won't go out with me. She does *think I'm all kinds of an asshole because I drunkenslobbered all over her at Brownie's party. I didn't have any sense, I didn't have any fuckin' sensitivity, still don't, but then all of a sudden we're dating and then we're in the car on the way to Mansfield to* meet the folks *and then,* the very next day, *seems like, we're at NAS Jax, just me and Lynn and little Michael Paul, one month old, God bless him. . . .*

At Dong ba Tinh the Outlaws flew nothing but resupply missions to ARVN troops and American advisers stationed in little villages and hamlets in the mountains. There wasn't much else in the area . . . just Cam Ranh Bay and mountains and jungle. But no enemy. While a stray round came their way every so often, and while the grunts went on patrol around the camp every day, Maverick still, after almost three months in-country, was waiting—itching—for his first encounter with the Real Thing.

The villages in the mountains around Dong ba Tinh were inhabited by tribes called by the French name Montagnard, though the Vietnamese called them the Moi—the Wild Men—and not without some justification. Even though Vietnam, to Maverick's Ohio eyes, overflowed with strangeness, the Montagnards gave a whole new meaning to the concept. They were beyond strange, almost outlandish, as if they'd stepped out of a flying saucer. Maverick never gave a thought to the fact that the Montagnards felt the same way about him and his towering American buddies.

It wasn't enough of a jolt for the U.S. Armed Forces to dump a whole gaggle of corn-fed or inner-city American boys into a jungle half a world away and let them try to function in the middle of a bewildering ancient civilization. Most times, thought Maverick, we can't even figure out where the Canadians are coming from, and they live right next door. And the Mexicans? Shit, they can't even speak English. But here we are trying to win hearts and minds in the middle of some jungle in a country so far away that it's tomorrow already. Then, just to put a little icing on the whole experience, once in the jungle, the Americans are sent to villages stuffed with tribes of short-statured people who are more different from the Vietnamese, almost, than the Americans themselves are. The initial shock is compounded, the way it would be if a foreigner arrived in New York and, just as he started getting used to the alien culture, was shipped off to the Indians in New Mexico and told, "This is America too, buddy."

Except for their incredibly sophisticated sense of family relationships, the Montagnards were one step away from primitive. A very small step. They lived in thatched huts built up on poles. They hunted with crossbows and blowguns that shot darts made of heat-treated bamboo slivers. Even though many of them had been exposed to the French ten or fifteen years back, most had never seen a white man, and certainly not a black man, until the day the Special Forces brought the American war machine to town.

The Montagnards are to the Vietnamese what the Indians are to the Americans. Aboriginal inhabitants. First ones in the country, first ones fucked over. They dressed in loincloths, wore beads around their necks, and had a heritage of religion, superstition, totemism, whatever, that dated almost from the dawn of time.

A Montagnard settlement is about as far as you can get from Mansfield, Ohio, and still be on this particular planet. Maverick, at five-seven-and-a-half, was unaccustomed to having any sort of height advantage over anybody, but the villagers barely made it up to his shoulders. He'd stand in the middle of them and feel like Dorothy on her way to the Wizard, his inferiority complex blissfully in remission. If the Montagnards played basketball, a five-footer could have signed for three or four mil.

Fortunately, Maverick had it all explained to him by his crew chief, an honest-to-God cowboy with the unlikely name of Szabo, who was born and bred in Tucson, Arizona, and looked it. He was tall and lean and square-shouldered, fair and sandy-haired, with that Roy Rogers cowboy squint you get from looking at the desert all day. He'd been in-country about eight months. Just after they'd landed at the village, he sat with Maverick, legs dangling out the open door of the cargo hold, in the heat and dust, looking out over the thatched huts up on poles, feeling very far from home.

"Why do we care about these little fuckers at all?" Szabo asked rhetorically. Maverick knew that he needed only to wait for the answer. "Glad you asked. Y'see, the Montagnard tribesmen have two basic personality traits that make us love them to pieces."

"They eat garbage and piss beer?" Maverick asked.

"That'd be nice. No, actually they love to kick ass and they absolutely hate the shit out of the Communists. Only problem here is that they hate the Vietnamese almost as much. We been out on cooperative missions, with a bunch a ARVN's and Montagnards, and when there's no more VC to fight, the Montagnards turn around and start in on the Vietnamese. They don't much give a shit who they kill. The tough job is teachin' 'em to kill the fucking VC and leave the ARVN's alone. And there's one more thing."

"Spill it," Maverick urged.

"Once they start killing, they just hate to stop." Szabo spit in the dirt.

The Special Forces trained the Montagnards as reactionary forces and set them up in listening posts along the VC trails from Cambodia and the north. They ran their own ambushes and reported troop movements back to the Americans. The system worked because there were no ARVN's around and when all the VC were dead the Montagnards would stop killing all by themselves.

Just before the Outlaws arrived, the village had been harassed by a tiger, which nobody even realized until some of the youngest and tenderest inhabitants disappeared mysteriously in the middle of the night. The village chief, who had lost one of his small sons in this fashion, found native crossbows insufficient to the task and asked the Americans for help.

Six of them went on the hunt: Maverick in the right seat; a Special Forces sergeant named Casper, who was five-eight and built like a toll booth; a newby ccpilot; Szabo; a door gunner; and the village honcho. The sergeant took along an M-79 grenade launcher, an innocent-looking device that would remind you of a sawed-off blunderbuss. It flings quarter-pound 40mm projectiles that explode with obscene and terrifying results.

Sweeping back and forth just above the treetops, swaying in the air, blowing the brush aside, it didn't take them long to flush out the tiger. The sergeant and Maverick spotted him at the same time, running and bolting through the underbrush, a flash of orange in one direction, then another, scared out of his wits by the sound of the helicopter directly above and the fierce downrush of wind. He was big, about the size of a banker's desk from his nose to his tail. And he was absolutely stunning. Orange and black and yellow and white and all those colors tigers are—raw animal power in the wild, no bars, no little concrete waterfall, no Mommy and Daddy and Buddy and Sis standing around pointing and throwing peanuts on Sunday afternoon.

"Jesus, would you look at that," yelled the Special Forces sergeant over the intercom. "He's incredible."

"Sure don't want to kill something like that," Szabo said from the back. The animal was majestic even as his territory was being violated by humans and their machines and their weapons. Above him, fluttering in the sky, Maverick knew the tiger had much more right to be there than any of them did.

But when the village chief caught his first glimpse of the tiger through the jungle canopy, he started losing his mind in buckets—only Montagnards and Munchkins can jump up and down in a Huey—and screaming and cursing him for making a Friskies buffet out of his family, and yelling the Montagnard equivalent of "I want you, tiger. I want *you!*" He could have jumped from the chopper and killed that cat with his teeth and toenails.

The Montagnards were essential to the war effort, and what's one tiger when Democracy is at stake in all of Southeast Asia? They knew what they had to do.

The noise and the wind panicked the beast absolutely, causing him to run in three directions at once. Like orange lightning he jerked one way, then another, then back, taking no more than three or four steps each time. Finally he took cover under a group of trees and looked back up at the evil machine, at the round faces staring through the open doors, exhausted, trembling, his long pink tongue hanging out of the corner of his mouth under his black nose, dripping, breathless, defiant.

The sergeant cracked open the launcher with one smooth motion, dropped one of those fat little pointed green rounds inside, took aim, and fired. Grenade launchers make a kind of *thoink* sound, a funny little Saturday-morning-cartoon noise that doesn't seem the least bit fatal. But on the ground, in glittering suddenness, thousands of shards of stainless steel flew in all directions. It was gore, it was not the least bit sporting—the British in India wouldn't have approved . . . no sahibs in this group, just a bunch of scared motherfuckers with plenty of high explosive—but by the time they were finished tossing the products of the American weapons industry at the tiger, he had lost not only his appetite for Montagnards but also most of what he needed to digest them with. Thank God it was quick, Maverick thought. If we'd wounded him and lost him in the jungle, I'd be real hard to live with for a long, long time.

Killing that tiger was the hardest thing he'd had to do in Vietnam. So far.

Financial statement: counting the use of the helicopter, fuel, manpower, transportation, equipment, ammunition, and sales tax, it probably cost the taxpayers about twenty-three thousand dollars to kill that poor beast. Cheap. It cost over a million to kill one VC.

Well, the Montagnard chief considered Szabo and the sergeant and Maverick the greatest thing since ancestor worship and gave them each a tiger's claw as a token of his appreciation. They were white, curved, pointed, evil-looking toenails almost two inches long. The gift also served to make them members of the tribe. Blood brothers. Maverick had his claw mounted in an eighteen-karat-gold setting and wore it around his neck for years, another of his many talismans against the misfortunes of war. A kind of totemism, perhaps, but in Vietnam people cut off all sorts of parts from once-living creatures, many of them more intimate, and took pride in them as trophies or good-luck charms. Some of these amputated pieces could be redeemed for cash.

As if killing tigers weren't heartbreaking enough, the country was also full of elephants, which the enterprising VC would employ as deuce-and-a-half trucks. They could carry enormous loads, travel long distances, eat whatever was around, go anywhere. Early in the war, before the Ho Chi Minh Trail became a freeway with supply depots, gas stations, rest stops, everything but a scenic overlook and a Howard Johnson's selling picture postcards, elephants were critical to the VC and NVA in hauling supplies down from the north.

What does all this mean to your average Army warrant-officer helicopter pilot? Simply that anytime you see an elephant you blow the poor bastard away. Just depriving the enemy of an important means of transportation, that's all. Think of it as a living truck. If you have even a dram of conscience, it breaks your heart.

Everybody who goes to war knows he'll see things he'd never get to see under any other circumstances. Otherwise, why do it? And even though he had that old John Wayne war-as-glory syndrome, Maverick still understood that war involved dead people and guts and refugees and atrocities. He didn't know, nor could he ever have guessed, about exploding elephants. After that, the circus was never the same for him again.

Enough of this. After thirty days in Dong ba Tinh, after the tigers and the elephants and the little girl who would haunt Maverick forever, the Outlaws received orders to move farther north. A place due west of Qui Nhon, toward Pleiku. A place called An Khe.

SIX

Maverick felt like he hadn't moved in months. His injured immobility made the time go on forever, but his mind was feverishly busy. He had unfocused sensations, mere wisps of semicoherent sadness, that, with passage of time, would thicken and clot into despair. Lying on the thin straw mat that covered the bottom bars of the tiger cage, he made one foolish attempt to heave himself up, but collapsed under a torrent of bright pain. It occurred to him that his neck or back might be broken, so he remained very still, trying to get in touch with his body one part at a time. Small movements with one foot, then the other, then a finger, wrist, elbow. All pieces present or accounted for, no broken bones. But the pain, *God* damn *the pain, it was so widespread, so unremitting, so* everywhere *that the normal signals from his nerves were tentative, confused, uncertain. And his mind had backed off from the pain so that, even as he ached and sizzled, he wasn't absolutely sure it was happening to him at all.*

All he could do was stare up and around at the long tan knobby bamboo bars that made up the cage. After a while they started to look like bones, long bones. The corners of the cage, where the rods were tied together with dark thin fuzzy strands of hemp, were the joints. He was inside a skeleton, some sort of ghoulish square creature that had died in the sea, dragged to the bottom by the weight of the massive lock and chain.

Between Qui Nhon and An Khe, there is a lovely expanse of fertile land that nestles within two ranges of vivid green hills. It is called Happy Valley. You fly there over the An Khe pass, which, because of the high hills on either side, was a notorious VC ambush point. When the ceilings were low, choppers would have to fly through the pass instead of over it, and the VC would shoot down at them.

Again the Outlaws arrived at a new destination, and again were greeted by a complete absence of civilization. A small pierced-steel-planking runway and a Special Forces camp sitting in the jungle on the east side of the Song Ba River. Another one of those dream landscapes with a plateau of terror in the middle.

The 101st immediately hired a few thousand natives from the vicinity, gave them machetes, and put them to work clearing away the jungle on the west side of the Song Ba. They did such a good job manicuring the broad flat area that the clearing became known throughout the country as the Golf Course.

None of the troops knew exactly why they were there or why they were building the camp, but the answer came quickly. The First Air Cavalry Division, Ty's unit, would arrive in Vietnam shortly, and this was to be their base camp. The First was to be the first cavalry division in history with total air mobility. Platoons of slicks would ferry the grunts into battle, escorted by platoons of gunships. Everybody thought they would be The Answer, because obviously, getting around in the jungle using tanks and trucks just wasn't cutting it. No, the First Air Cav, with its hordes of helicopters, and its ability to insert troops anywhere at any time, would certainly Solve the Problem. But meanwhile, things were beginning to get a little ghastly.

The slick platoons spent a lot of time transporting the 101st and their ARVN counterparts on missions into the surrounding countryside. The grunts would fight for a piece of land, take it, pull out, then go back a week or so later and fight for it again.

A few weeks after they arrived in An Khe, Maverick was assigned to fly a resupply mission to some troops working around a small village to the north. Six choppers flew in, loaded with food, ammunition, and toilet paper, Maverick third in the formation. As soon as they hit the ground, dozens of olive-drab figures burst from the underbrush, scuttling toward the choppers to unload. But suddenly a jeep raced out of the jungle into the clearing. On the front of each fender was a human head mounted on a short slender pole. The operation had had some success against the VC and the boys were riding these heads around the village just to show the citizenry that the good guys had come out on top and were comfortably in control. Maverick just stared. What a great way to Win Friends and Influence People. Show them heads on a stick.

The sight reminded him of his first trip to the Grand Canyon.

You stand on the South Rim looking at a sight so impossibly big and so impossibly deep that your eyes and brain just toss their little cookies. There's no human scale to give you a sense of proportion. Your senses become lost in the immensity of the vision. Well, that's exactly how he felt. No sense of human proportion at all. His eyes had never seen a severed head before, and his brain was trying to create some kind of new image classification, opening a file in his mind called "Horrors of War." He knew, in his head, anyway, that war was a horror show, but suddenly he was being exposed to sights that could make *The Bride of Frankenstein* look like *Cinderella.* Is the veneer of civilization really this thin? Thinner, perhaps?

The jeep did a few turns around the clearing, kicking up great clouds of red dust, then trundled back down the path toward the village. Stunned, Maverick watched till it disappeared, shook his head, and walked along the flight line to the platoon leader, a sandy-haired Cracker named Clemens, who had eyebrows and eyelashes so blond they were barely there at all. It gave him an odd faceless look. Clemens was sitting on the ground in front of his Huey, legs crossed, smoking the very end of a Lucky Strike.

"Did you see that?" Maverick asked.

"Sure. But don't worry 'bout it none. Them wasn't any of our boys. It's just something the ARVN like to do. Makes 'em feel proud." Then he took the last hit off his Lucky, burned his fingers, put it out, tore it apart.

Once they had settled in at An Khe, they lived a little better. The Golf Course was well under way, they were living in pretty decent six-man tents arranged in precise rows, and the food wasn't bad.

Maverick was eating his C-rations in front of his tent. A beautiful open day, warm and sunny. Quiet. The day's lunch was turkey loaf. He had grown to enjoy turkey loaf, since he had little choice, with fruit cocktail or pears and pound cake. He loved to soak the pound cake in the fruit cocktail. Franks and beans were terrible. Lima beans were hell if you slept in a sleeping bag. Each box of C-rations was a new little adventure, with all kinds of packets and cans and surprises inside. There were mini-packs of Luckies or Philip Morris, packs of sick-looking crackers that tasted like communion wafers. If they tasted like communion wafers to him, what did the Jewish guys think they tasted like? he wondered. It was a GI smorgasbord of infinite variety and astonishment, almost like those cheese trays you mail-order at Christmas.

Most highly prized were the tiny white rolls of toilet paper, held together with little beige paper bands. Nobody ever traded those, because in Vietnam, defecation was often involuntary, uncontrolled, and spontaneous.

This particular day was a waiting part of the war, so the sound of an incoming Huey made Maverick look up. He tried to make out the markings of the clattering machine as it settled into its cloud of red dust on the ramp. The triangular door on the right side opened and a handlebar mustache disembarked, attached to a short wiry guy wearing green from head to toe. This was the trademark of the First Air Cav. They took everybody's clothes, put them all in a big vat, and dyed everything green. Underwear, socks, T-shirts, jock straps. Didn't matter a rat's ass what it was; if it went on your precious body, it was green.

Maverick damn near fell over. The green man was Ty Hisey.

"You son of a bitch," yelled Maverick, which is what soldiers yell at each other after long separation. He dropped his lunch and ran, stumbling, toward the chopper. "What are you doing here?"

Ty grabbed him and he grabbed Ty and they waltzed each other around in the dirt for a minute, like any two countrymen who meet far from home.

"Well"—Ty grinned through his steel-gray eyes—"we got here a few days ago on the aircraft carrier and they were putting the choppers together to ferry them into Qui Nhon. They sent me out to resupply a convoy about twenty miles east of here, but shit, I musta got lost because this doesn't look anything like where I'm supposed to be."

"You got lost because you're a shitty pilot."

"Nah, I ran into somebody in Qui Nhon who told me you were here, so I just let the wind blow me off-course. Besides, this country isn't known for its radio navigation facilities, so I got an excuse."

If Ty stayed too long, his absence would trigger a major air-sea search-and-rescue operation, and if they found him sitting on Maverick's veranda they would make him do a shitload of push-ups. But the two of them did manage to bullshit each other unmercifully for a little while about what had happened during the last few months. Ty told Maverick about living in luxury aboard an aircraft carrier, and Maverick told Ty about living in shit in Dong ba Tinh. And flying Ash and Trash.

Finally Maverick took one last look at Ty's round face with its curious flat bridgeless nose. Ty looked back at him, a good friend far from home, laughed, cranked his machine, pulled up on the collective, and pushed the cyclic forward the least little bit. The dust and the wind lifted him. He disappeared into the sky.

Maverick found himself wishing he had looked at Ty longer. He was to get only one more chance.

SEVEN

He must have dozed off, because the noise startled him. An old woman, gray of hair and skin, bent into the hooch on bare feet and pushed a gray metal bowl of rice through the largest space between the bars. The bowl was unmistakably from an American mess kit. Maverick briefly wondered where she'd gotten it. She sneered at him, showing stumps of teeth stained red from betel nuts. In her eyes Maverick did not read wishes for his speedy recovery, nor did he perceive any charitable desire to feed and nourish him. Rather he saw too clearly the fervency of her loathing, a look of such murderous detestation that he actually recoiled from it. She looked at him the way you look at the man who has cold-bloodedly slaughtered your entire family, right down to the second cousins, pigs, chickens, and goldfish. It was probably the closest she'd ever been to an American, but she had met him before. She said nothing.

Maverick picked up the bowl and looked down into the sodden white heap. It was full of suspicious brown specks. He glanced at the woman one more time, and one more time felt her tangible hatred. Dared he eat anything she gave him? Had she poisoned it? Spit in it? But there was no red color from the betel nuts in the bowl, and besides, his hunger had the best of him even though the scanty portion probably contained microbes that would cause a core meltdown in his bowels. He was very much past caring. He was hurt, he was hungry, and this, after a fashion, was food. He shoveled it into his mouth with two fingers and felt a little better.

The next day he saw blood in his urine.

A few days after Ty left, Maverick pulled another boring assignment, but at least this one let him run into Dick Fortenberry. He ferried a sick Huey up to Qui Nhon for some high-level maintenance, and when he got there, Fortenberry was waiting for him on the ramp, standing next to a sparkling Huey gunship. Maverick could feel himself sag. Dick, the bastard, was flying gunships and loving it. Maverick was driving a bus and hating it.

Fortenberry absolutely glowed as his mellow voice talked Maverick through the armament and weapons systems. This Huey had one sole purpose on this earth—to lift fearsome armament into the sky, and then to discharge it. The chopper had weapons up the ass. Guns and rockets sticking out of every opening, pods that launched 2.75 rockets on each side, hydraulically operated 7.62 machine guns mounted as flex kits, swiveling and firing at the command of the copilot. Everything but a catapult and a battering ram. No glorified taxicab or dump truck like Maverick was horsing around the sky, no, this machine was an honest-to-God awesomely Old Testament Engine of Destruction.

Those TAC officers at Fort Wolters had been right about Dick all along. He was glamour.

That was the day that Maverick saw the light. Standing there in the hot sun and the blowing dust of Qui Nhon, he accepted the Huey B-Model gunship as his personal savior. He might even have fallen to his knees, stricken with the absurdity of flying a virtually unarmed aircraft, even though he'd not been shot at more than once or twice, and then only by small arms, when everybody else in the country had guns. He loved that gunship at first sight, and his little wheels ground into motion. But on that particular day even the intensity of the revelation could not keep other things from taking precedence.

Beer, for example.

Maverick and the Outlaws and the 101st were living in what was still the sticks up at An Khe, and while they weren't starving or stinking too badly, rare was the man who had no craving for even a slight increase in the amenity level. At An Khe, beer was an Impossible Dream, but the guys in civilized Qui Nhon were swimming in it.

So, being a clean-living honest American GI, Maverick went to the officers' club and tried to buy some to go, but the bastards wouldn't work with him at all.

"Yeah, we'll sell you a few beers over the counter, but no cases."

Maverick pleaded. "A couple of six-packs, at least?"

"Naw, you guys from the hills take it out of here, what do we have left?" Asshole. Till then, Maverick thought they were all on the same side.

"But I have a duty to my buddies back at An Khe. You know what the Uniform Code of Military Justice says: 'Always Bring Beer.' "

"Wish I could help ya . . ." No you don't, prick.

Steaming, Maverick stalked back across the concrete to the repair hangar. Over to his right, on the other side of the runway, he noticed a big open area with tall barbed-wire fencing all around. Inside the wire were stacks of cartons and boxes and bales.

What can this be? Maverick asked himself, already knowing the answer. It was, in fact, a supply depot, but not just any supply depot. An abnormally large, well-endowed supply depot. If there's no beer in a place like that, there's no beer, period.

He ran to the chopper and grabbed his clipboard out of the cockpit. With it in hand he strode through the compound gate looking just like he knew exactly what the fuck he was doing and had every right to be there and what are you looking at, asshole? He strolled around, shoulders square, back straight, a Man with a Purpose, an Official Man, and competent. He stopped when he rounded the corner between two huge ribbed Conex containers and found himself face-to-face, like David facing Goliath, but twice as awed and twice as confident, with a hundred and four square yards of pallets, and on every pallet were one hundred and forty-four cases of beer and in every case there were twenty-four delicious cans. Like the man with seven wives and each wife had seven sacks and each sack had seven cats and so on. But with beer instead, which is better.

Then things really started looking up. The pallets were stacked right next to a generous helipad that had obviously been placed in that very spot for his convenience. One-stop shopping. Drive through, you're in, you're out.

He ran through a quick situation analysis:

1. The supply depot was on the far side of the field, away from the active runway. The controllers in the tower would be paying attention to the active, looking the other way.

2. The supply depot was right next to the maintenance hangars, where traffic would come and go constantly. Helicopters would taxi, hover, move in and out all the time. No big deal.

3. This round-faced big-eyed Spec-4 was hitching a ride back

to An Khe with the crew, so reserve troops were available if necessary, and could, in extremity, be committed to the operation.

4. They had their very own empty Huey now in perfect operating condition with a full tank of gas.

5. They were thirsty.

Seditious ideas, vague at first, bounced merrily to the surface like bubbles in champagne. Maverick forced himself to walk calmly out of the depot and back to the hangar. Szabo was there, bent underneath the chopper looking up into the hellhole where all the linkages were. Maverick squatted down, grabbed his arm, and dragged him outside into the white sun.

"Listen. That supply depot over there is loaded with beer, and we need to get ourselves some."

"I'll go along with that," Szabo agreed.

"So let's get the chopper out of the hangar and you cover up the numbers with tape. That Spec-4 who's riding with us? Don't tell him shit."

"How about if I don't even ask what you're gonna do?"

"Good man." Maverick punched him once on his expansive bicep.

Battery on, fuel on, throttle to indent, push the start button, listen to those igniters click.

"Qui Nhon tower, this is Outlaw Two Six on the maintenance ramp. Request takeoff clearance, short test flight, local area."

"Roger, Outlaw Two Six, cleared for immediate takeoff. You got an A-One-E on short final. Stay east of the field, call when reentering pattern."

"Roger. Outlaw Two Six on the go." And they went.

Flew the pattern like good boys, went out east of the field and checked out the machine, killed a little time. Szabo kept looking at his watch; the Spec-4 tried to get comfortable in the back.

Then Maverick made a broad, descending, sweeping turn toward the supply depot, checked the wind, and began The Mission.

"Qui Nhon tower, this is Outlaw Two Six. Maintenance flight complete, all systems go. Departing your AO for Nha Trang. Request frequency change."

"Frequency change approved. Have a good flight, Outlaw Two Six."

"Outlaw Two Six, roger."

Nha Trang? Well, maybe Maverick fibbed a little, telling them he was heading south when he was really going north. But they had a dirty, dirty job to do here, and extremism in the pursuit of beer is no vice.

A textbook surprise attack. It was over in seconds and the enemy never knew what hit him. Maverick came in low and fast, pulled back the cyclic, and, barely skimming the squat stacks of bales, slammed the machine toward the ground, keeping the rotor rpm up, the chopper barely in contact with the pad, so he could pull it into the air in a hurry. Szabo dived out the cargo door and hit the ground running.

Suddenly this horrified pink-and-white moon face stuck itself over Maverick's right shoulder. The Spec-4 felt he needed to demonstrate some concern.

"Sir! Is there something wrong? What's going on?"

"Listen, soldier," Maverick yelled back at him, wrestling the cyclic to keep the chopper steady, holding the collective in a delicate balance so that the machine was flying, but just barely. It swayed in the upwash and the heat. "Get the fuck out there and start throwing beer on board this aircraft right now, or I'll leave you in the middle of this compound and you can explain to the MP's what you're doing here."

"But . . . but . . . but . . ."

"Or maybe we won't leave you here. Maybe we'll take you halfway to An Khe and leave you there. Now, move your ass!"

He moved his ass. In fact, he leapt, vaulted, bounded out of the Huey at warp speed and ran smack into Szabo, all six-feet-five of him, who was just running back with his first three cases. They both fell down, did a little Laurel-and-Hardy getting back up, fell down again—being, as they were, in the right part of the world for a Chinese fire drill—then started to slam-dunk beer into the chopper so fast their arms moved in blurry motions like little windmills.

In seconds they had a Budweiser brigade figured out, two of America's fighting men in action, working in perfect unison, hand over hand, throw-catch-pass, flinging beer, hurling beer, pitching beer, tossing beer, propelling beer into that helicopter with such reckless intensity that they lost half of it out the other side, the cases sliding all the way through, dropping on the ramp, breaking open, cans rolling along the ground, exploding, white with foam. Larry, Moe, and Curly would have been proud.

"That's enough," Maverick tried to yell over the roar of the engine. "Let's get the fuck out of here!"

The crew chief and Spec-4 came diving headfirst through the big doors, did a tuck and roll into the chopper, and Maverick yanked that collective so hard he had tennis elbow for a week. The Huey lurched straight into the air with no forward motion at all, pulling G's, mashing the crew chief and Spec-4 into the cold metal floor, then rolling them forward as Maverick pushed the cyclic away from himself, nosed the chopper down to build up some much-needed airspeed, asses and elbows all tangled up, the Spec-4 screaming God knows what, grabbing at anything so he wouldn't just go *whup-whup-whup* and roll out the door on the turns.

"Helicopter departing the supply depot, this is Qui Nhon tower. Identify yourself!"

"Say again, tower. You're coming in broken," Maverick replied, yelling like he was talking to deaf people. "Say again, tower."

The tower tried to contact him half the way back to An Khe, but he didn't answer. Instead, he listened to Szabo trying to calm down the Spec-4, who lay in the back for the whole trip, giggling at the edge of audibility, and moaning.

EIGHT

The last six days had been a roil of emotions, all of them bad, but to them now was added something new. Horror.

Just as he began to feel like a human being, albeit a sick, injured, captured one who is facing certain death, he started pissing pink. He was aghast. There was something unnamed and awful happening inside his body and he couldn't even help himself. Being helpless was most emphatically not *part of the chopper-jock mystique. Military aviators are self-sufficient, they show no pain, no fear.*

Maverick was hurt down deep and frightened down deep. Internal injuries don't clear up all by themselves. Not like the pulled muscles and the bruises he got when the Cobra rolled itself up into a fetal position.

He thought furious, panicked thoughts. Maybe if he could lie very still and quiet, whatever was burst or ruptured or torn would miraculously heal or at least not get any worse. And so he did, not moving even when the little girl came in with the rice, not moving all day long, listening to the sounds of the village outside the hooch, listening to his life seep away with every beat of his heart.

The days were very long.

It had been a bad morning. The platoon was flying at fifteen hundred feet, a covey of metal grasshoppers in right-echelon formation. To fly in formation you position your chopper to either the right or left of the aircraft in front, just a bit higher, and look through his skids. When you line up the far-front-skid cross tube with the near back one, you're at a perfect forty-five-degree angle. The choppers toward the back fly slightly higher than those in the front, for better visibility. In a long diagonal line to the right, amid enormous racket, well above the kill zone, where the ground fire couldn't get to them, turbines and rotors doing just what they're supposed to do, they were making their way back from a medevac mission to Qui Nhon. They'd just dropped off a tragic pile of troops, and all Maverick could think of was: I'm glad I'm not one of them. So young. So many.

They were making time, nose down for airspeed, hitting it as hard as they could over the An Khe pass. Even with his helmet and headset on, Maverick imagined he could still hear the moans and screams of the wounded. There was a lot of loose tissue in the cargo hold. Reich, the gunner, was sitting in a puddle of drying blood, his short thick legs doubled up in front of him.

The radio came to life:

"Mayday! Mayday! Mayday! This is Outlaw Two Four . . . we're . . . aaahhh . . . going down northeast of the field." Then silence.

Well, shit, Maverick thinks, we're northeast of the field. And yes, off to his right he sees smoke starting up from the green thickness. Black, then a column of red. Somebody was smart and popped off a smoke grenade to mark the position.

Maverick looks over at Cates, his copilot, then pushes the button and speaks.

"Outlaw radio, this is Outlaw Two Six. Red smoke from Outlaw Two Four in sight, approximately three miles northeast of the airfield. We're on our way."

After Fort Wolters, Maverick had gotten better at keeping his voice pitch under control in extreme conditions. This is the first real emergency he's faced in Vietnam, and thank God he doesn't sound like Mickey Mouse anymore. Instead, he feels like giggling.

Big sweeping turn around the column of smoke, looking for a clearing. Look some more, but there isn't a naked spot of earth to be seen. Nothing but green jungle and red smoke . . . Wait! There is a small—*small!*—bare spot about fifty meters from the crash.

This isn't good. They can see the Huey on the ground buried in the foliage except where the impact has crushed the trees and it's burning and twisted and gray-brown smoke is pouring out of every orifice and little ringlets of yellow flame are starting to spread around it like ripples in a pool.

"Look, can you see those guys running around?" Reich asks

from the back. Maverick has brought the chopper just above them, swinging in the sky, looking at three men standing on the ground, panicked, legs spread, waving their arms. One tries to stamp out the fire around him. Two men lie on the ground, not running at all. More people than a normal crew. The chopper had been carrying four or six passengers.

And the whole mess is down right in the middle of triple-canopy jungle. Maybe the pilot didn't have much choice, but the son of a bitch could at least have found a clearing so he wouldn't have to chop his way in with the rotors going *whack-whackwhackwhack* and the branches and limbs and all that other green tree shit exploding around them, flying away like a flock of startled bats. Maverick brings the Huey in, swaying it from side to side in tight little circles, mowing down a small area around the aircraft. Be a bitch to bring it straight down and have solid vegetables all around so nobody can get out. Now he knows why they call them choppers.

They slam into the ground.

"Cates, you stay here," he yells to the copilot as he yanks his seat belt off and heaves himself out the door. "Reich. Szabo. Come with me!"

Maverick hits the ground, falls, gets up, and begins to run. Curiously, things start fading into the background like those stream-of-consciousness Italian art movies, overexposed, washed-out color, slightly slow-motion.

Reich, Szabo, and Maverick push through the jungle, leaving Cates to monitor the radio. Reich is in front, his short frame, about Maverick's size, crashing through the tangled green brush. Closer to the crash it gets hotter and smokier and they begin to see little flecks of flame in the air.

There are one or two men moving around, others not moving anymore, some just sitting dazed on the ground. And there is a lieutenant, who runs toward them wearing a bridal veil of blood on his face . . . skinny little rivers from his forehead down over his eyes, his nose, his cheeks.

"It's on fire," he yells. Well, no shit, is that why all these little hairs on our arms are curling up and turning black this way?

"Scott's still on board. The pilot. He's pinned in his seat."

Through the Italian movie Maverick suddenly realizes that he has no idea why this chopper crashed. There was no clue from the Mayday call on the radio. They're in the middle of the jungle, miles from the base, and they don't know. Was it engine failure? But somebody had set off a red smoke grenade, which means enemy fire. Is that the first color grenade that came into his panicked hand, or did they get shot down, maybe? Are we standing here in the middle of thousands of enemy troops? Have we run into some kind of VC religious feast day that requires the ritual sacrifice of young American boys?

Maverick grabs the lieutenant by the sleeve and pulls him along toward the chopper. The bloody rivers on the man's face have receded from flood stage. He's not badly hurt, but he looks awful.

"What happened? Were you shot at?"

"Beats the shit out of me," he says. Looks like it did, too. "The chopper kind of lurched to the left, suddenly lost altitude, then we were in the trees. I was sitting near the door, got thrown out right away."

A few more yards through the brush, and there it is. Not pretty. Scotty must have had some forward motion when he hit, because the machine is smashed in against the trees, which has collapsed the whole left front end back into the cockpit. Fuck me with a meathook, thinks Maverick, if he's pinned in there, we'll have to suck him out through a straw.

And God, it's burning like a motherfucker. A college bonfire after a squeaker homecoming victory. He leaves the lieutenant and starts to run. The crew chief and gunner start to run.

The machine is crushed into the trees tilted upward, so they have to climb up through the open cargo doors. Inside to the right, Scotty is semiconscious, rolling his head and moaning, saying things nobody can understand, and the whole goddamn instrument console is mashed over the front of his chest and stomach.

Jesus, it's getting *hot* in here. The quilted silver soundproofing material on the walls is burning and turning brown and giving off choking fumes; paint is peeling off the cargo hold. They decide to yank Scott out sideways.

Grab a handful of flight suit and pull. *Pull!* He doesn't move.

Maverick has no time to feel stupid as he reaches in to unbuckle Scott's seat belt. Tight fit for his hand, since there's an altimeter, airspeed indicator, and engine tach pushed into his stomach. Try to slide the seat back on its tracks, but they're as twisted as Scott is. Things are hot and red and hot and gray and hot and choking.

Pull again. Again! God *damn* you, Scotty, why do you have to weigh damn near two hundred pounds? And if you weren't so short you wouldn't be so hard to get a handle on. He starts to slide out from behind the console, but only halfway. He's still stuck. His legs don't do a thing. They just sit there. Nobody can bend like that. Please be unconscious, Scotty. Please.

Reich and Szabo tumble back out through the cargo doors. Maverick can see them outside through the cracked plexi of the cockpit, tugging at the shattered metal and plastic, doing a Harpo-and-Chico, trying and succeeding in pulling the front of the helicopter apart with their bare hands. The Italian movie has not stopped, and Maverick knows this is happening, but marvels at how . . . *apart* from it he feels. There are noise and fire and smoke and shit all around him, and he is *in* it, somehow, but not *of* it. Until the ammo starts cooking, bringing him back in an instant.

There's this *crack!crack!crack!* behind him because the flames have finally started doing a tongue job on the linked M-60 rounds in the ammo boxes and the loose rounds that were rolling around on the floor next to the guns, and now he starts to think that the only thing that'll keep him from getting shot to death is getting burned to death while this poor wretched motherfucker Scott holds on to his seat like it's on the fifty-yard line at the Super Bowl.

Reich yells and bangs on the ruined front of the chopper, but Maverick can't hear him. He can't hear anything but those goddamn bullets *crack!* beginning to sound like the people in Chinatown celebrating the Year of the Dog.

The gunner shouts again, bangs on the plexi with his palm, and makes vehement pointing gestures, which are not lost on Maverick. Reich is trying to demonstrate that Scotty's feet are seriously jammed under the antitorque rotor pedals. His boots are wedged in there like he did it on purpose and the pedals are crushed down over his ankles and his shredded flight suit is bright wet red and everything looks like hamburger from the knees to the floor.

Maverick climbs over the top of Scott, now mercifully unconscious, headfirst into the cockpit to get a closer look at what his feet are doing with the pedals down there, but Maverick can't pull at him with his ass up in the air like that. No leverage.

"Reich," Maverick yells. "Run back to the ship and get the machete. Move it."

"What!"

"The machete! Now! I may have to cut his feet off." Reich looks at him like he's just sprouted another head, but he turns and goes.

Ohgodohgodohgod . . . please don't make me butcher this hapless bastard to save his life but I will soon if I have to and if he lives long enough *crack!crack!* and what will he say to me when I visit him in the hospital?

"Mom, I'd like you to meet the guy that pulled me out of the burning wreckage and saved my life."

"Mom, I'd like you to meet the scumbag who cut my feet off."

Maverick pulls and pushes and wonders where that machete is, when four or five rounds all go off at once. He dives from the cockpit back into the cargo hold, out the cargo doors, right over the M-60 rounds, but by this time he's lost forty points off his IQ anyway, and runs around to try to pull Scott from the outside, through the pilot's door. He runs smack into Cates.

"What are you doing here, you bastard?" Maverick screams. "Why aren't you on the radio?"

"They sent some units out be here in a minute what do you want me to do?" Cates says in a rush.

"I can't move him from inside. Help me get this fuckin' door off."

They grab the edge of the door, which has a long crease from top to bottom and sticks out from the fuselage like a broken arm. They can hardly breathe because of the smoke and heat and adrenaline, but they both rip the door right off the body of the machine, and Jesus, Scotty's flak vest is hung up on the cyclic and his feet (what's left of them) are still cruelly jammed under the rotor pedals. Szabo is rampaging around the front of the cockpit, taking furious kicks at Scott's feet, trying to get them free. If Scott lives, he'll never do the tango again.

Cates climbs over Scott back into the cockpit between the seats and tries to lift him out, with Maverick pulling from the outside. They claw at his flak vest. Claw at his helmet. Try to bend the cyclic to get him free.

Meanwhile, it's the Fourth of July in a closet. There's all this *burning* going on and Scotty's still floating in and out but now he's saying "My back, my back" so if he's got a spinal injury or broken back Cates and Maverick are certainly going to kill him anyhow but by this time Szabo has gone completely manic and begins to tear away the whole front of the chopper by means of brute strength and fear of God alone and he's got his hands on Scotty's boots twisting and bending and banging. Scott can forget the fox-trot too. He'll be wearing special shoes the rest of his life, if he has a life.

One foot pops free. Then the other. Come *on!*

It's getting hotter by the minute. Every once in a while bits of lead flit past, and when they come close enough, they sound like nasty little bees, and the flames from the cargo area reach the cockpit and give Maverick a hesitant tap on the shoulder like an old acquaintance who's not sure he'll be recognized.

By this time Cates has pulled Scott forward a bit and the two of them grab him under the arms and heave back as hard as they can and the place is full of big-time fire and there are all these M-60 rounds whistling through the air, so fuck you, Scott, if your back *is* broken and fuck you if we leave your feet behind because we're getting out of here one way or the other.

Scott comes loose like he's been shot from a gun and all three of them tumble backward out the door, Maverick landing on the bottom with the bulk of the unconscious Scott on top of him and an extra thump added by Cates. Reich and Szabo are standing right above them and they pull Scott off him at once, flip him onto a litter and start to run. Cates starts to run. Maverick starts to run.

Boosh! What's left of the Huey explodes in one pyrotechnicolor glittering visceral blast and all of them go down in a tumbling heap.

They crawl back into Outlaw Two Six as Scotty is loaded aboard. Maverick falls into his seat. Gotta take him to the medics *right now* but the fucking rotors are all banged up and the thing will barely fly because he used it like a Weedeater and breath comes hard and fast and he's living a million miles an hour. Pull up on the collective.

Up. Then down. The flight takes three minutes. It takes forever.

The medics are upon them as soon as they land, and run Scott's litter through the swirling red dust as the rotors wind down. Maverick lies there on the floor of the cargo compartment, just now starting to shake a little, now more, on the hard metal surface with the cargo doors closed. The Italian movie slows to a stop as he hears two troops walk by outside, talking about the crash and rescue. They're talking about him.

". . . and Reich said that Maverick is inside the cockpit in the middle of all the flames trying to pull Scotty out of there with the rounds going off all over the place and he's in there like he does it every day . . . working at it like a fucking machine."

"Maybe we oughta call him the Iceman." Their voices fade.

That's him, okay. The Iceman. While it was all going on, he didn't know what he was doing, he practically wasn't even there. It was just a guy in trouble who needed help, and none of them even thought twice about giving it. He could have run up to the chopper, seen the flames spreading around it, and said: Fuck you, man, you just bit the big one, because nobody in his right mind would run into that shit for you or anybody. But he did. Not through bravery, not through heroism. Those impulses never presented themselves. There was, in fact, no actual choice made. He just did what he did and now he's trembling all over as the tension fades and the adrenaline wears off, leaving him depressed like when you take amphetamine for a long time, then stop. Fear flows in like the tide, swirling in long stroking waves, asking the question: What the fuck did you just do? He still hadn't been exposed to combat, and so far this was certainly the craziest, riskiest thing he'd ever done in his life, the most extreme situation, the most intense personal danger he'd ever experienced. He couldn't believe it of himself. He couldn't believe he'd done it and couldn't believe he'd remained so calm, so . . . inhuman. Would he be like that the next time? Is this how it feels to face danger? He didn't like it much now, as the energy left him, as he came down, as the Italian movie ended and sound and color washed back in, as time resumed its normal course, as all-too-human terror, stored under pressure during the past forty minutes, released itself, melted through him, made him weak.

NINE

His flight suit was gone. His derringer was gone. His body protested its condition with unremitting complaints of internal injury. If the NVA had left the tiger cage wide open, he couldn't even have crawled away.

His wristwatch was gone too, and he was pissed. Stupid, he knew, because considering the ass-is-grass nature of his present plight, he was lucky to have a wrist at all. But shit, it had been one of his proudest possessions from the moment Lynn had given it to him when he graduated from flight school. It must have taken her months to pay it off. Part of the uniform, part of the hot-dog-chopper-jock mystique, *an* aviator's *watch, a badge, a talisman, exactly the kind of instrument worn by almost every single helicopter pilot in Southeast Asia, and those who didn't wear them were conspicuously excluded from the customary postcombat storytelling and were consistently chosen last for jungle-rules volleyball. The watch was a massive, thick, dense black Swiss Glycine* aeronautical chronometer, *for God's sake, about six pounds' worth, with a face the size of a salad plate. Cold white numerals surrounded the outermost circumference, severely angled hands jutted from the center, sets of smaller numbers arranged in multicolored concentric circles disappeared into the infinity of the center. It had a dizzying multitude of tiny inset dials, and a red stiletto second hand that goose-stepped from number to number with an imperious precision that quashed even the slightest concern as to its accuracy.*

Without it, he had no idea how long he'd been in the cage. He had no idea where he was . . . disconnected in space and in time. All he knew was the hot yellow metal taste of fear in the back of his throat.

• • •

When the medics pulled Scotty out of his chopper at An Khe, they took Maverick aside and told him Scotty would never walk again. Then they shipped him out to Qui Nhon and then to God knows where. Probably Hawaii. About six months later the Outlaws heard that he'd taken his first step by himself. Maverick was glad he hadn't used the machete.

For pulling Scotty out, Maverick, Reich, Szabo, and Cates all received the Soldier's Medal, the highest award given for bravery in a noncombat situation. Maverick thought it was a nice thing to have, but he still hadn't gotten over the way he felt lying on the floor of the chopper. The medal made it seem like bravery is something you choose to do, but it isn't. It's something you do almost unconsciously when you're excited or mad or pissed or crazed. If you live through it, you're brave. If you don't, you're an asshole.

Months later, General William Westmoreland His Own Self pinned those medals on Maverick's crew at a ceremony back in Vinh Long. He had a hard time with it, since his right arm was in a cast to the elbow.

"Enemy action, General?" Maverick asked.

"Tennis net," the General replied.

Vietnam showed the Americans many things. All kinds of new experiences, emotions, ideas . . . diseases. No, not the usual kinds of venereal distress that soldiers historically suffer when surrounded by willing native women far from home. There was plenty of that, though, because the Americans were too tight-assed and puritanically twisted to admit that soldiers in wartime will, God bless 'em, fuck their brains out if given the chance. The Vietnamese Army, for example, ran a licensed pleasure house with clean women, as did the worldly French before them, so it was only the clean wholesome American boys who were reduced to combing the bars and whorehouses of Saigon and Qui Nhon in search of pleasure . . . and the inevitable dick rot that followed. Our rate of VD in Vietnam was the highest of any war we'd ever fought. Some strains continue to baffle researchers to this day.

So there were plenty of sore dicks, but the infirmity which concerns us here was far more debilitating, humiliating, mortifying, and humbling than any kind of genital disorder. And far less curable. This disease was commonly known as Ho Chi Minh's Revenge, and everybody got it at one time or another even if he didn't fuck. It was a vile, virulent, poisonous, pernicious form of dysentery that made Montezuma at his most vengeful seem like a kindly old uncle. If you had a choice, you'd drink water from a pig trough in Cuernavaca and joyfully suffer the consequences before you'd even think of subjecting yourself to the Tan Son Nhut Two-step.

It could have been anything. A drop of water from that disgusting ice, a microbe in the air, but at An Khe, just after Scott's rescue, Maverick was struck down in the prime of his life by some amoebas unknown to Western science even at its most advanced. There is no scientific name for this disease, no cure.

Yes, he took all the little brown pills, got the gamma-globulin shots, ate the salt tablets, did this, did that, but when Uncle Ho hit him, all his infantile potty training and twenty-four years of absolute sphincter control—"8,760 days without an accident"—were as chaff before the wind.

It was cold at night in the highlands, so Maverick slept in his flight suit, all zipped up and toasty inside the heavy one-piece garment that gripped tight around his wrists and ankles. But early one morning, with no warning whatsoever, he woke up on his narrow metal-frame cot, frigid sweat popping in little globs on his forehead, trembling in all extremities, doubled over with a horrible flushing sound in his stomach and a convulsive pain in his lower bowel, suddenly alert, every nerve vibrating with a condition-red sense of urgency. It was like waking up in the middle of a mortar attack. Cold sweat exploded from his armpits and his groin.

Then, as he hugged his knees in his heavy gray flight suit, sweaty, cold, nauseous, feverish, shaking, sick, all abdominal control deserted him and he experienced the very most loathsome form of nocturnal emission. First he was afraid he was going to die, then he was afraid he wasn't. He felt as though he was falling through his asshole, saturating himself, filling his flight suit with a foul brown semiliquid mess that smelled like a nightmare beast on the verge of agonizing death had crawled out of him to seek a final resting place.

Since the garment was zippered at the ankles, there was no place for the pollution to go, so it just filled up the legs and sloshed around in his pants. Babyhood memories of diaper days, delicious warm wet feelings, came flooding back, subtle, cerebral. But *this* was unthinkably disgraceful, inexcusably fetid, unpardonably squalid. His humiliation was infinite. Had he been Japanese, he would have committed *seppuku.*

Then he became afraid he would wake up the other pilots in the tent with his gastric discourse if not with the smell. If they caught him with his pants full of putrefaction, it would be known in all four corps in a matter of hours. Nobody but a drill instructor can dish out the shit better than a chopper jock, and he had enough to contend with right there in his pants already.

The latrines were right behind the tents, but they were a cruel joke, a mockery of basic human needs, every bit as offensive as his current situation. Besides, it was way too late for that. He'd been hit too hard and too fast. He needed a place to drain his suit, wash it out, and clean himself off.

A couple hundred meters behind the tent and down a gentle hill was a shower point on the bank of the Song Ba River. But since nobody took showers at night, the ambushes and the rest of the perimeter defenses were set up there. The only people you'd find down there after dark would be infiltrating VC or Americans with a sick desire to get thoroughly wasted by their own frightened and trigger-happy troops.

But Maverick had an *urgent need* here, he was suffering from agonizing cramps, biting his lower lip to keep from crying out, and he stank so bad and felt so awful that a few rounds from an M-16 would have seemed like comic relief. He decided that his objective must be the shower point. Okay. How to accomplish it? Walk down the path and say to the guards, "Excuse me, gentlemen, would you please allow me through this heavily defended area because I've just beshit myself?"

Not at three in the morning, and not with a bunch of kids out there in the darkness who were famous for shooting at anything that moved, including each other. He'd never even get close before they took his breath away.

"You asshole! He's one of ours! You killed him!"

"Well, what the fuck was he doing crawling around the perimeter in the dark?"

That left him one of two choices. Stay in the tent, embarrass himself, and gross out his fellow pilots, committing himself to months, perhaps an entire career, of cruel and intolerable bullshit, or take the initiative like a trained professional soldier, draw up a battle plan, and execute it, by God. Anything, almost, would be better than the present situation.

Analysis: Maverick knew where the mines were set up, he knew where the Claymores were mounted, those nasty little rectangular green boxes that explode into huge volleys of buckshot by remote control, he knew the location of all the ambush positions, so, sloshing in his suit, he crept out of the hooch in the darkness and low-crawled through the bushes, trying hard to ignore the total sensory experience of the dead smells and squishing sounds and cold lumpiness, heading for the river and hoping he could get there and back without having his malfunctioning ass shot off by some trembling troop who couldn't wait to kill his first VC.

Around the bushes, under the trees, pitch-dark highlands night, no moon, no sound but the squishing of the repulsive mess he'd made of himself, thinking to what astonishing lengths humans will go to preserve their self-respect—including *seppuku*—down the hill, inching, inching along, his flight suit weighing ten pounds too much and . . . *something* oozing out around the ankles, but he tried to ignore it, pretending he'd just been mud-wrestling maybe, slithering down the riverbank and oh so quietly easing himself into the frigid muddy water of the mighty Song Ba. Ahhhh.

The water was so cold he could hardly move, but carefully, carefully, he took his flight suit off underwater, turned it inside out, and swirled it around slowly, making no noise, grabbing it in his fists, scrubbing it together under the water as best he could, then putting it back on. He trapped so much air inside that you could have put a few ropes on him and floated him through the Macy's parade. He discreetly hugged himself all over and the air blurbled out in explosive belches. He froze.

Flashback: Because of all the red dust in the area, Maverick and Szabo would fly the helicopter out to a shallow sandbar in the middle of the Song Ba to wash it down. One day they were standing in water up to their waists, throwing it all over the chopper, sucking it through the turbine, and Maverick felt something that wasn't him moving in his crotch. He pulled down his shorts and found a two-inch leech firmly attached to his right ball. Long, dark gray, almost black, writhing and glistening. It took three burns from a cigarette to get the disgusting creature to let go. Leech spit contains an anticoagulant that made his insulted genitalia bleed for three hours.

In the frigid water, worried sick about all the leeches that might be attaching themselves to his intimate parts—you don't feel them when they latch on—he could hear the scrape of the patrols walking back and forth on the riverbank, so he forced himself to work very slowly and carefully. Agony. All he wanted to do was get out of that goddamn polluted, infested river, get out of that shitty flight suit, and into a nice warm sleeping bag. Slow and quiet, slow and quiet, because the troops on the riverbank never learned to say "Who goes there." They only learned to pull those goddamn triggers. Maverick just knew that one of them would spot him sooner or later and blow him away, flight suit, leeches, dysentery, and all.

"Dear Mrs. Marvicsin, It pains me to inform you that your husband was killed during a dysentery attack in the Song Ba River. Your souvenir American flag and a stool sample are enclosed."

The shuffling footsteps disappeared into the silence, allowing him to pull himself up out of the dark water, sopping wet but relatively clean, freezing cold and shivering, feeling all over inside his suit for leeches and other repellent life forms. Again, the low crawl back through the big bushes, the small bushes, the ambushes, where the mines were set up, where the Claymores were mounted, back past the foot patrols, back past the latrines, and, finally, into the tent. He peeled off the wet, dirty flight suit, which now contained, thank God, only polluted water and mud, with no colonic products mixed in, and just sat there on his bunk, exhausted, disheartened, weak, cramped, cold, naked, listening to the snores and night sounds of five helicopter pilots.

Then the Fear finally overtook him, just like last time. The trembling set in and he shook and shuddered and quivered in the cold dark inimical Southeast Asian night, totally alone, totally forsaken, totally sick. How much stupider could he be? Sneaking through an armed camp? Playing hide-and-seek with novice soldiers at war? Risking his life?

It took a while for him to calm down, as he quietly pulled on a blessedly clean, dry flight suit. It wasn't cold, it wasn't wet or stinking, it felt wonderful. The fright and the physical reaction made his insides seethe. He caught his breath and lay carefully back on his narrow bunk, easing himself down from one elbow. As soon as his back touched the damp sheets, he sat straight up once again, doubled over in the twisted grip of one last prodigious gastric upheaval and emitted yet another explosive torrent of putrescence.

He slept in it.

TEN

Where's Brownie? Where is *Brownie? Still in the fuckin' Navy, probably, on a carrier on the ocean white with foam, but I'm not in the Navy, shit, I may not even be in the Army anymore, after all this time lying in this goddamn bamboo cage . . . fuckers probably forgot about me already, just rolled up my mattress, took my beer mug off the wall. Rector, Arkansas, that's Lynn's hometown, just me and Lynn and little Michael Paul. No more Navy after four years because I got married and couldn't go to NAVCAD and fly . . . Lynn, stop crying, please, please maybe your father isn't* that *sick, maybe he'll get better, is there anything I can do? Well, brain tumors don't get better all by themselves and they won't let you run a Western Auto store like you're supposed to, so forget about flying and learn the parts business, and I realize that eighteen months of selling brake shoes, tires, and water pumps hasn't completely crushed my obsession with flight and maybe I* can *fly, thanks to the local congressman my father-in-law knew who gets me in to take the tests for the Army's warrant-officer flight program . . . one day I get The Letter— "We are pleased to inform you that you need to get your ass to Fort Wolters, Texas, right away"—and I'm in the Army now, I'm in the Army now, at Fort Wolters, all alone, crying into the phone to Lynn back in Arkansas, telling her: Listen, I'll never be able to fly one of these fuckin' contrary machines. And she said: Yes you can. She always said yes you can and that's why I could. Right now I wish I hadn't.*

And then, after the first tour when we went back to Fort Wolters, she stayed, and little Michael Paul too, then Scott was born a month before I came back here and she was alone again, just herself and very tiny Scott and not-so-little-anymore Michael.

• • •

Up until September 17, 1965, Maverick's role in the "police action" had been surprisingly tame and, frankly, somewhat undistinguished. He did expend about a month's worth of precious bodily fluids helping pull Scotty out of that little time bomb, but none of his flying, none of the missions, had brought him within range of serious hostility. Most times, when they inserted troops into an LZ, things hadn't warmed up yet. When they extracted them, the VC had already been allowed to slip back into the jungle. He was beginning to feel like Mr. Roberts in that movie—doomed to spend the war hauling toilet paper.

But the night of September 17, 1965, changed all that. That's the night when he found himself sitting on a hard wood plank in a hot, close, damp briefing tent under the white glare of unshielded lights, hearing all about the next day's mission.

Two buttoned-down neatly pressed intelligence officers were standing on a low riser up front, the inevitable map on a gray metal easel alongside them. They were telling the Outlaws that they'd been given the admittedly dubious privilege of carrying three companies of the 101st Airborne and a company of ARVN Rangers on a large-scale operation into the far end of Happy Valley. Maverick couldn't have been more delighted.

They pointed out that Happy Valley was shaped like a horseshoe and that the landing zones were all the way in, through a narrow pass with mountains blocking everything on three sides and rice paddies going up to the foothills. He remembered that ambushes are customarily set up in a horseshoe pattern, but dismissed the thought. After all, these men were intelligence officers. They knew what they were doing.

"It's no big thing," said the briefing officer. "A minor operation. We'll insert the three companies and let them do some ground reconnaissance. Our intelligence tells us there may be a company of VC somewhere around there. Maybe a bit more than a company."

The other officer took over, waving a long skinny pointer at nothing in particular. "We'll be calling in some heavy artillery to prep the area, and there'll be air support at all times to cover you. This will soften up the LZ so you guys can get in and out with no problem."

Nooooo problem. Artillery? Air support? This was the first time that Maverick thought he might be flying into some shit, and as every little fact was added, the event began to sound less and less like a "minor operation." Think nothing of it, just the tiniest little insertion and sweep, kind of like an exploratory, look around a bit, give the 101st some more experience on the ground, be home by lunch? Get that fruit cocktail and pound cake ready.

Just as the second officer finished talking, a major from the Special Forces stood up, the hard-edged lighting in the tent making brilliant little pops off the beads of sweat on his high black forehead.

This is what he said:

"With all due respect, gentlemen, your intelligence is fucked up."

Stunned silence. Anybody who hadn't been looking at him when he stood up was looking at him now. In fact, he commanded at that moment the rarest of things—the complete attention of all the Outlaws at the same time. He didn't seem to notice. Instead, he gestured toward the map on the easel.

"Our sources tell us that there's at least a battalion in the vicinity, possibly a regiment. If you go in there and try to play ball with only a few companies, Charles is gonna stuff it right up your ass."

The Outlaws stopped looking at the major and started looking at the intelligence officers, who just looked at each other.

The conversation between the major and the two intelligence officers proceeded in an atmosphere of courteous debate among professional soldiers, but you know how these things are, and you know the old joke about military intelligence. The commanders decided the Special Forces major was, simply stated, full of shit, and stood behind the original reports. Operation Gibraltar was on. It was a very bad idea.

Morning. September 18, the staging area. Seven days after Maverick and his crew had pulled Scotty from the burning fiery furnace. A whole week to replay the thing in his mind, and he was just beginning to understand what it had cost him. The effort, the heat, the stress, the post-horror horror at the very real danger he'd let himself in for had completely drained him. He was flat out of energy, having spent day after day going over it in his mind, spinning out sick fantasies about what could have happened. Besides, it had rained all night, the conditions were shitty and the ceilings were so low they'd had to fly through the An Khe pass instead of over it, and he'd spent several passionate minutes waiting for that VC small-arms fire to come spraying through the roof of the Huey. They'd been lucky. The fog and mist had kept the VC at home, so the covey of dark shapes clattered through the pass heard but not seen in the gray morning. So far so good.

Just east of the pass on the way to Qui Nhon the Hueys and troops formed up in single file on a usually dry riverbed that this day was ankle-deep in mud from the previous night's rain. The Outlaws, along with other slick platoons, accompanied by a sprinkling of gunships—this was a small operation, after all—would lift into the LZ from there. Why? Who knows.

Small operation or no, the staging area was black with soldiers from the 101st, and the additional aircraft that had been brought in were parked in a line that snaked itself all along the riverbed, around the bend, out of sight, all the rotor blades in perfect alignment, front to back, a very precise touch, like hospital corners on a bed. There were ships from Qui Nhon and a few Marine H-34's, the ones that look like pregnant guppies. Sitting in the cargo-hold doorway in the half-light of morning, Szabo half-turned to Maverick and spoke through a cloud of Marlboro smoke. "This begins to look less and less like a 'minor operation.' "

Maverick looked down along the line of aircraft. "You ain't kidding. Shit, these choppers stretch clear into next week."

"Where we supposed to get our fuel from so we can get back?"

"There're some tanker trucks on their way up from An Khe. They'll wait for us here."

"What if they don't get here?" Szabo asked.

That's just the kind of thing Szabo would ask. "What do you mean?"

"Well . . ." Szabo stared into the mud. "Like they could get ambushed or something, couldn't they? This is Vietnam, ain't it? Nothin' ever happens like it's supposed to. Ain't I right?"

"Asshole." Szabo was right, he was always right about the bad shit, and he was always depressed because he was always right. Reich was the optimist, but Szabo had been in-country longer. He'd seen a few things.

But he got Maverick thinking. What if they got back and the trucks weren't there? They'd be caught in the open, subject to ground attack, mortar fire, a dozen unpleasantries. No fuel trucks, and nobody would make it back to the base on the other side of the pass.

Szabo stood up, leaned against the big square cargo door, and spat in the rust-colored mud. "Home by lunch," he said, and walked away.

The LZ was only about five minutes away from the staging area, but there were so many men and the spot was so small that the lift took place in three groups. Maverick was in the second. As seven 101st troops clambered into the back, all cursing at once, Captain Weber, the platoon commander, worked his way down the line, his famous .45 hanging inevitably at his hip, talking to each pilot in turn.

"No air support," he said to Maverick as he leaned in the window of the right-hand door.

". . . Sir?" Suddenly Maverick hated him even worse than usual.

"The weather is shit, the Air Force can't get here, we can't spot the artillery in. We have to go in with gunship support only. But it's no big deal. This is gonna be a piece of cake."

Swell. Gunships are fearsome machines, but there is a good deal to be said for a few well-placed 105mm howitzer shells, or some of Dow Chemical's finest jellied gasoline. Or even a little Willie Peter liberally applied in waves of rockets, bursting into hot white smoke.

"Piece of cake. Yes, sir," said Maverick, and took a deep breath. He looked at Cates next to him and over his left shoulder at Szabo in back, who just sat there shaking his head. Slowly Maverick pulled on his chicken plate, the armored vest that helicopter pilots wore because they were so exposed up there behind their encompassing bubble of Plexiglas. They sat on armor plate too. It was all the protection they had.

Maverick looked over at the gunships lifting off, Fortenberry no doubt among them, with their guns and rocket pods and grenade turrets and flex kits sticking out on all sides like the antennae of an evil insect. Chicken plate or no, he thought about his two mingy M-60's sticking out the side doors and felt naked, like he was going into battle with his dick hanging out. He took his .38 out of its holster and tucked it down between his legs. A little extra metal couldn't hurt.

The first lift took off, about two hundred yards up the line, wheeled, and assembled itself into a diamond formation. Radios came alive as Maverick cranked up and waited his turn. Two minutes later, with a roar that upset the air, the second group throttled up, shuddered, and took to the air. In just a bit under two minutes, as the first lift approached the LZ, the headsets began to simmer with cross-talk.

Then the simmer boiled over with reports that the lead group was receiving small-arms fire. Okay, Maverick thought, I can handle that. Never expected to remain un-shot-at forever, this being a war and all. He became uncomfortably aware of his ship, how fat and heavy and big and slow it was. They were flying into a bad time and there was nothing he could do about it.

"Yankee One Niner . . . I'm hit . . . hydraulics are out . . . going down."

"There he is . . . over there . . . wait . . . say again?"

"Look! In the tree line . . . there they are . . . there's more . . ."

The grunts were taking fire and the pace of the chatter began to pick up a bit. The pitch got higher. Maverick could feel it in his ears.

Smoke grenades were used for all kinds of signaling purposes. If an aircraft went down, they'd pop a yellow or green to mark their position for the pickup aircraft, like Scotty's crew did. Or ground troops would set them off to show position, wind direction, and safe landing areas. They used any color but red, because red meant only one thing: enemy fire.

The approach. It looks like they left all the cool colors back in the States, because the first wave is (barely) on the ground and there's red smoke on the approach end, red smoke on both sides of the LZ, red smoke right in the middle of the LZ, and red smoke on the departure end of the LZ. There's red smoke all over the fucking place.

Dusty crimson, it swirls together with white smoke from the guns, flows along the ground, boils up. There's enemy fire up the ass and the whole second group is flying right into it. Up to the open end of the horseshoe, trees on both sides, wet brown rice paddies underneath, and what they can see in front of them through the smoke and dust looks like New Year's in Chinatown sans the paper dragons.

Plan is to go straight in, touch down, heel and toe, the back of the skid hits first, the aircraft rocks forward, the front of the skid touches last, and they're airborne. During that process the grunts pour out the side, jumping to the ground and charging toward the tree lines. Takes only seconds, just like stealing beer at Qui Nhon. Sure. And your check is in the mail.

Then the screaming really starts. Maverick's headset is

jammed with voices from the first lift, high and tight. "Receiving fire!" "Receiving fire!"

"Automatic fucking weapons down there, goddammit!"

"There's one!"

"Kill the motherfucker." Radio discipline is always the first thing to go.

Damn. Some of those guys never did learn to keep their voices down. It's some kind of corrupt Saturday-morning sick little horror-cartoon show, listening to them yelling into their mikes in high squeaky voices like they're all talking to babies.

Fly on. They look down at the very edge of the jungle, unrolling too slowly below them, when this minor figure scampers out of the trees with his black pajamas and pith helmet on—at once Maverick knows he's seeing something he'll never forget—and he's got this M-1 carbine, the kind with the long curved banana clip that sticks out the bottom, a garrison belt around his skinny hips, and Maverick and Cates are looking straight down at this prick from no more than fifty feet up as he puts his goddamn gun to his goddamn shoulder and calmly empties the whole clip right into the bottom of the helicopter. Must be twenty rounds, and every single one of them zings directly up through the machine.

There are seven live human soldiers back there, plus a crew chief and a door gunner, and Maverick has no way of knowing if any of them are taking this guy's bullets in the butt. The grunts have no headsets, no intercoms, so if they're wounded and screaming, he can't tell. Besides, he's in the process of flying a chopper directly into the gaping Jaws of Hell and it's taking every bit of his concentration.

"Reich, you bastard, get him! Get him!" he screams at the gunner, but he's directly below the chopper now and the gunner can't tilt his M-60 down that far. Maverick is honest-to-goddamn scareder than he was during the midnight-river-bath episode and nobody can even get a shot off at this little son of a bitch who looks like he just got out of bed.

Maverick banks left to give the gunner a better angle at this infidel on the ground. Everybody in the group is taking shots at him and the tracers fly all around in glowing neon bursts. But the air is rough and the choppers are bouncing around and banking and maneuvering to stay in formation and the gunners keep spraying all over the place. The little man stands alone, in a charmed circle.

Now he gets down on one knee. Maverick's ship is still pretty close as he assumes the classic firing-range position like there isn't really a war going on and he's a hobby target shooter out for a little practice on the old rifle range and there aren't really a dozen American Imperialist Yellow Dog Death Machines clattering by a few feet above him and those little puffs of dust around him that make exclamation points in the ground aren't really M-60 machine-gun bullets and he isn't really absolutely for certain going to die horribly within the next very few seconds. He pulls a second one of those banana clips from his back pocket—he grows in Maverick's sight, he suddenly looks bigger, like a poisonous insect under a microscope, and he's very very clear and bright—slams it into place with the heel of his hand, and gets off another twenty rounds, every one of them in the red, an absolute sweetheart shooter. He's shooting at me, Maverick thinks, astonished. He's shooting at me! The man doesn't waste a single round, as though he had to pay for each individual bullet himself.

The crew never hears the rifle go off, they just hear that nasty little *snick!* as the big lead pellets pop through the thin skin of the chopper.

They get past him but Maverick can still see him back to the right, down on one knee in the middle of his own endless hell, calmly emptying clip after clip into the aircraft behind. Nobody touches him.

Maverick discovered later that nobody could hit him. The asshole used up a few more clips, and when he was out of ammo he got up off his knee, brushed off his pajamas, and calmly walked back into the jungle.

The spot comes up, Maverick drops the chopper, collective down . . . cyclic back to flare . . . touchdown. The troops are noticeably slow in tumbling out the back and Maverick bounces in his seat from impatience, his chopper swimming in a sea of red smoke. He doesn't feature doing the sitting-duck act in the middle of this shooting gallery, but finally the grunts jump out into the molten-lead thunderstorm. Maverick looks back and everybody's gone except Reich and Szabo but he can't take off until the slicks in front get their asses out of the way, so they sit in the middle of the LZ unable to do anything but be afraid and anxious.

Jesus H. Christ on snowshoes. The tracers twinkle by all around them like headlights on a highway, and behind every single tracer that they can see are four real live bullets that they can't see and they're strapped into that Huey with a death grip on the cyclic and there's not a goddamn thing he can do to defend himself and all the while the air is filled with the sound of the rotor blades and the insidious *snick!* sound of a switchblade in a dark alley on a Saturday night as the enemy rounds explode through the fuselage and the plexi. Minor operation, my ass. Every VC in the country is in the jungle, firing into the landing zone. "They're *shooting* at me!"

He looks up through the plexi to his left. A nice fat gunship hangs in the air, unloading bullets and rockets and explosives and fiery death a mile a minute at the nearest tree line. If that's you, Dick, Maverick thinks, I hate your ass. You and all your goddamn wonderful guns.

Finally, *finally,* the lead aircraft waddles into the air. Maverick gives the collective an eager pull and throws the cyclic all the way forward and to the right and they're in the air, thank God. Szabo and Reich firing their M-60's out the sides, just holding the triggers back as they fly through the guns and bullets and glowing streaks of tracers and billowing red clouds of smoke. Outside, it is some backwoods clergyman's favorite vision of hell, with fire on the ground and fire, praise God, in the air and sulfurous cascades of smoke and the kind of Chaos that we're all supposed to go through at the end of the world, complete with damned souls wailing and gnashing their teeth. It is like a sky box at Armageddon, but it's an easy ticket.

On the way out Maverick sees two Hueys down and burning in the LZ, another floundering just above the ground without a chance of making it, a big-bellied Marine H-34 chopper over on its side and guys running and guys lying very still indeed and the VC mortars making such a mess of things that the third lift right behind them executes a precision 180 and turns back.

The first lift gets out, maybe half the second lift gets back in the air, and the third lift gives up completely. The 101st is left behind in the fire and brimstone.

"What did you think?" Cates asks over the intercom.

"Well, now I know why they say war is hell. It sure *looks* like hell."

Back to the sandbar. Regroup.

The radios bring back the news: four aircraft down and burning, first- and second-wave troops, around 250 of them, on the ground, pinned down by enemy fire, doing an incredible job against overwhelming numbers of VC that nobody except that major knew were there. They'd set those poor bastards down right in the middle of a battalion-plus-size contingent of VC, like opening a real big beehive and just sticking your face in there with eyes wide open. Not only are there a zillion guys named Charlie out there, but the operation has stumbled into some kind of monster fucking training base, like the Asian equivalent of Fort Benning, and why is everybody so surprised that there are all these enemy soldiers around?

The major had been right. The intelligence twins had told everybody they were going to the beach on Sunday, but the place was swarming, teeming, *abounding* with enemy troops. Things got hot as soon as the first lift landed. The VC had been surprised at breakfast, caught somewhere between the orange juice and the cornflakes, with weapons close at hand.

By the time they'd jumped up and manned their positions, the second lift was in prime position for the duck shoot. Before the third wave was anywhere close, the VC had the whole thing set up, popping the choppers right out of the sky. The newspapers said there were about three hundred VC, but there were more, lots more, because they had fifty-caliber machine guns, mortars, and heavy stuff that smaller contingents can't carry. All nicely laid out in dreamboat horseshoe defensive positions awaiting the lovely waves of Americans in helicopters to simply float into their sights. Trite as it may seem, imagery of shooting galleries, little pockmarked ducks, smiling past your sights in an endless parade, comes inevitably to mind.

So. Those that made it at all are back at the sandbar, low on fuel, waiting for the trucks from An Khe to show up. That had been part of the deal . . . home before lunch and a free tank of gas, but the goddamn convoy had been ambushed, just like Szabo said—Maverick whirls to look at him; he stares back through squinty cowboy eyes—in the An Khe pass and are probably sitting somewhere in the jungle burning and exploding at that very moment. The choppers are only three or four minutes away from where the 101st is proving itself beautifully under somewhat-less-than-ideal conditions, with about a dozen perfectly good aircraft on the ground, out in the open, no fuel. Maverick wonders when the VC will find out where they are and start pouring mortar rounds down the pipe to make the Yankee Imperialists think twice about running out of gas in the open. He resists the temptation to glance skyward.

Meanwhile, what they hear on the radio isn't exactly American Top Forty. Radio discipline is completely broken down and the FM is filled with anguish and terror and death from the pilots and troops pinned down in the horseshoe. They're fighting back as hard as they can.

"I'm shooting . . . I'm shooting. I got him!"

"Look at that fucker! *Look* at him! We hit him seven times and he's *still* giving signals!"

"Oh, Jesus, I'm hit!"

"Help him! Help him!"

"Help *who?*"

"Holy shit, look at 'em all . . . there's more! Shoot! Shoot!"

They're screaming and yelling and shooting and killing and dying all at the same time and there's not a damn thing anybody can do about it but sit there and listen. Maverick remembers how before they had a television set they would gather around the radio on Sunday nights and listen to Jack Benny. This is the same thing, but they don't hear classic radio comedy. They hear bravery and fear.

It is Maverick's first introduction to a certain unique sensation of cosmic helplessness that he would encounter again and again in Vietnam. There's nothing they can do to refuel those Hueys, and the ones that aren't out of gas have been so shot up that they can't fly, so everybody sits there on the ground glued to the garble, listening to the destruction that's going on almost walking distance away, and they might as well have their feet nailed to the ground. They can't fly, they can't help.

Meanwhile, even more tragic irony takes place right over their heads. Elements of the First Air Cav are off-loading from aircraft carriers in the South China Sea. Beautiful formations of helicopters, neat diagonal lines in the sky, drift right over this carnage, filled with troops on their way to An Khe.

The grounded pilots get on the radio and yell "Help" as loud as they can, but the troops in those choppers are right off the boat and have no idea what's happening, and they aren't armed or ready for battle, so they keep right on going.

Later in the afternoon, some fuel trucks rumble into the staging area with just enough gas to get the flyable choppers back through the pass to the base at An Khe. They can't go back to the LZ because they don't have enough fuel, and besides, it would be suicide. They fly the machines that can, sling-load the ones that can't with those big Chinook cargo helicopters, and everyone limps back to An Khe and Qui Nhon.

Half an hour later, Maverick is again alone on the floor, in the dark cargo hold, listening to the ice melt. The shaking comes, harder than last time.

On the second day of the battle, one of those big Chinook cargo choppers landed at An Khe on its way to pull some more of the dead aircraft out of the staging area. One of the crew was a full-blooded Indian of some sort, with that burnished ruddy skin and noble look that loyal Americans had tried so hard to exterminate.

He'd been in-country only a few days, and wanted to know all about Operation Gibraltar, so Maverick, bursting with the fear and excitement of his first time in combat, told him.

"Shit," said the Indian, "I'd sure rather be doing this than doing that." He liked his big Chinook. Didn't want to be down there on the ground where the bullets come straight at you. Didn't want to be in a gunship where you go looking for trouble. Didn't want to be in a Huey where you had to fly right into the middle of the shit on purpose and just sit there, exposed, uncovered, endangered.

They swirled that Chinook off the ground in a cloud of familiar red dust, but half an hour later they were back. Maverick got to the chopper just in time to see them unload the Indian kid. Dead. On the way to the staging area, somebody on the ground just popped one toward the chopper and caught him right behind the ear. A one-in-a-million shot.

The battles of Operation Gibraltar went on for three days, and the First Air Cav took over the resupply and extraction of the troops because everybody else was shot up so badly. It was the first chance the 101st had to prove themselves in real battle, and damned if they didn't all come out looking like Audie Murphy. Their losses were moderate in fighting that at times brought them so close to the enemy they could see their uvulas. Enemy losses totaled 226. The 101st had finally arrived. They behaved like veterans, and everybody said so.

Fuck me silly, thought Maverick. While he was sitting there recovering from having dipped his toe into the swift black current of formal armed confrontation, one thing became perfectly apparent. It was this: even with an M-60 machine gun sticking out each side door of that Huey, he wasn't exactly facing the enemy on equal terms. If the rest of the war was going to be like this, inserting a bunch of grunts into a landing zone or extracting them while the universe apocalypsed all around him, would he just have to sit there in his cockpit strangling that cyclic and letting those bastards shoot at him? Would he have to sit still, strapped into his seat, watching those little holes suddenly *snick!* appear in the Plexiglas, right in front of his face? It was scary . . . and it happened so silently!

Who needed it? With all the explosions and the noise of the rotors, he never actually heard the shots. Just a silly little *pop* as the plexi shattered. He couldn't shoot back, and for that he was very, very pissed.

After he'd stopped shaking, he crawled out of the cargo hold and found Szabo sitting on his bunk in the crew hooch, naked except for his boots, tall and skinny and pale.

"Listen, Szabo, is it like that all the time?"

"Like what?" Szabo was relaxed, and his Tucson accent flowed through, as though he'd just come back from a brisk gallop in the purifying desert.

"Like that! Like we sit there and let them shoot at us? Look, I'm a fuckin' soldier. I went to war school. I took Armed Conflict 101, and on the very first day they told me that in combat, if some son of a bitch is shooting at you, it's often a good idea to shoot back at him. Remember General Patton? He *loved* that idea."

"What's your point, Maverick?"

"What's my point? What's my fucking *point?*" Maverick was practically screaming, because the more he thought about it and the more he talked about it, the more he realized how scared he should be, and so he was, and the more scared he became, the more hysteria and anxiety took him over.

"Hasn't it occurred to you that it's goddamn stupid to go through a war with a candy-ass thirty-eight Special tucked into your crotch, for all the good that does, when everybody else is seriously armed and dangerous?"

Maverick paced the three steps up and down the hooch, which was all the room he had, and pressed on. "Anyway. I can tell you right now, as God is my witness, you see this right hand in the air? Do you? I am going to get my ass out of these goddamn bare-ass slicks with their diddlyshit M-60's and into a real live gunship just as soon as I can. Okay?"

Szabo just stared at him. "Well, there's sure as shit a lot you don't know about gunships, ain't there? Us in the slicks, we just get in and get out. You think all them gunnies do is sit in the air and protect us? They got to go out lookin' for trouble, they got to go out and *draw fire,* and between you and me, I think that's fuckin' nuts."

"I don't care!" Maverick screamed as he ripped open the screen door and stalked out into the twilight.

Please, God, he prayed as he half-walked, half-ran into the night. Please give me a gunship.

ELEVEN

He had good days and bad days. This was a bad day. He didn't move for the longest time, drifting in and out, sleeping, dozing, waking, staring. He gazed for hours—surely it was that long—at the tan thatched roof of the hut, watching little particles of dust and bamboo and palm billow and swirl in the sunlight. Odd images floated before him, like a surreal landscape: Father Wah, the Catholic priest, puffed up, pointing at the pile of corpses, equally puffed up. Downtown Nha Trang after the bomber crashed, Szabo the cowboy. Eagle and Frair, his first gunship crew.

He waited for his pain to diminish, willed *it to cease, with little success. He couldn't help thinking about the blood in his urine. Every once in a while, when he thought he could stand it, he tried to move, sweat shining on his face and arms, flimsy black blouse and pantaloons sticking to his skin. Gradually the hurting became, if not less intense, at least more tolerable. Again he pulled himself up to his elbows, slowly, with the exaggerated delicacy of a man peeling a raw egg. He worked himself into a sitting position, leaning back against one of the joints where two skeletal rods of bamboo were lashed together. The discomfort was comparatively minor. He sat with his head bowed. The cage was very low.*

He stared at the ridiculous, forbidding lock, unspeakably tired and thoroughly terrified. His pulse throbbed in his stomach. The tiger cage was a simple device for imprisonment, just a few thick bamboo rods lashed together at the corners with rope and palm frond. But they were a hated symbol, and he felt about them the way Jews feel about swastikas. Each war brings us something unique. Last time it was the concentration camp. This time it is the tiger cage. Americans had never seen them before, as they had never seen naked burning children running from a napalm attack down a jungle road. People who ended up in tiger cages usually lived lives of most unquiet desperation, lives that were, as Thoreau or somebody might have said, nasty, brutish, and short.

Well, now, Maverick said to himself one afternoon. Sitting in the tent at An Khe, holding his hand over the top of his C-rations so the ubiquitous and eternal swirls of red dust wouldn't give his lunch that delicious crunchy topping, he watched the Hueys and Chinooks come and go, huge clattering insects.

Well, now, indeed. Until just last week he had spent four months hauling Ash and Trash around a godforsaken subtropical paradise half a world away, and even though his situation hadn't been exactly the Platonic ideal of calm and tranquillity, neither had his character been thrust to its outer limits by the Supreme Test of Armed Combat. Not until now.

But *then* the whole situation seemed to get . . . denser somehow. Ghastly events tumbled over on themselves like a litter of eager puppies pouring out of a sack. Horrible happenings began coming closer to each other, closer to him.

All in one week, they had to pull Scotty out of the chopper, then this whole Gibraltar mess came down, complete with some guy he didn't even know kneeling in the dust to shoot at him, which nobody had ever really done before, and later he had to listen to that sadistic radio show, then the poor bastard Indian kid bit the Big One for no particular reason. So much air, so much space, and that bullet took up no room worth mentioning. It was mere milligrams of metal in billions of cubic kilometers of air. But it found the Indian, yes it did.

Are you coming down with the thousand-yard stare, Maverick? Isn't it a little early for that? Wanted to fly choppers, did you? Asshole. This isn't *The Sands of Iwo Jima,* you silly shit. Look at you, Mr. Army Aviator, surrounded by limitless Asian Communists, all with little children in school who carve punji stakes as a requirement for graduation. All with an ancient cultural predilection toward cruel and unusual punishment.

He felt like his skin was on too tight.

"Surrounded," by the way, is just exactly the right word. Alone in his tent, hot, dirty, tired, reaching what he thought were the limits of disgust, scared, mentally bankrupt, emotionally twisted, he could feel the VC all around him. He was on a more-or-less-secure military outpost, but concentrating the troops in the bases left the countryside to the enemy. There were so many bases with artillery emplacements that they could shell literally every square foot of the whole country, but the VC were all around them. There were bases like An Khe with its famous Golf Course, with tons of troops and hundreds of tons of hardware, but the VC were all around them. There were bases every goddamn where, with—yes—VC all around them. The only territory the Americans controlled was the thirty or so square inches under their boots, and they were none too sure about that. Most times the enemy was underneath them as well, like in the tunnels at Cu Chi. Besides, if the Americans and ARVN ever did get control of any geography, they had to give it back at night and go back to the base. One shakes one's head.

There was a Tokyo Rose–type woman named Hanoi Hanna on the radio, and everybody listened because the NVA had the only radio station that played any American music worth listening to until Adrian Cronauer came along, and he got canned in five months. The day Maverick arrived in Vietnam, Hanna welcomed him to the country by *name.* And rank and serial number and unit. Then there was Mr. Ho, the barber on the base at Vinh Long, who turned out to be a lieutenant colonel in North Vietnamese intelligence. He used to shave the pilots with a straight razor. Americans, little islands in a turbulent sea of hostility, weren't safe anywhere. Captain Weber with his .45 showed Maverick that maybe they weren't even safe from each other.

That afternoon was the first time he had started to wonder What It Was All About. He wasn't asking the other question: What Are We Americans Doing in Vietnam? No, there were already too many people coming up empty on that one. In fact, nobody was ever able to tell him why they were there. Some said they had to bring Jesus to the heathens. Best answer he ever got was: "We have people here, and we have to support them." At that time he had never taken a class in formal logic, but he recognized circular reasoning when he heard it.

He was not asking Why Are We Doing This?, but rather, Why Am *I* Doing This? He was asking Why Would I Even *Want* To Do This? This isn't fun, this is death in the dirt. He loved flying so much that he enjoyed it even when he was being shot at, so maybe if they'd had action every day and were always flying, he wouldn't have had time to let all that shit run around in his head, but it's true what they say about war being hours and hours of sheer boredom punctuated by moments of stark raving whatever. In the past week, Maverick started getting his long-delayed share of the stark-raving stuff, and it dizzied him. There was too much time to think and wonder and remember. This was a war, after all, and the happenings of the last seven days had not, given the context, been unusual, except in their density. And their proximity. All along, other kinds of crazymaking events had been occurring with a disheartening regularity.

Take dying, for example. So many people were dying! Maybe one should expect that in a war, since dying *is* kind of the whole idea, but these unfortunates weren't dying from enemy bullets and bombs, they weren't dying with a purpose, they were dying from accidents and anger and stupidity and technology run amok.

Accidents. War makes you handle lots of things that go bang, and some of them do so unexpectedly, taking you with them. The technology is always new, it is always the most complex of its time, so sometimes it's hard to stay alive around it. New equipment, new weapons, new techniques, were being tested under combat conditions for the first time, and young Americans were the testers. Bob Capitano, whom they called Captain Bob, one of Maverick's best friends from flight school, bought it in a midair collision right over the airstrip at An Khe. Somebody just wasn't paying attention. And look at Joe Worth, another classmate from Fort Wolters. Nice guy, round face, very fine sandy brown hair with one little sprig over his ear that never lay down. One day he cut it off himself and left a silly little bald spot. About nineteen when he got to flight school, twenty when he graduated, and twenty-one when he died screaming and screaming and screaming in front of everybody.

There's this device at the very top of a helicopter's rotor system called the Jesus nut. You wouldn't want to try to get by without one because it's the only piece that holds the entire rotor system together. The whole thing. Well, one day as they were flying through the An Khe pass, Jesus called Joe unto himself. The nut came off, the complete rotor system just ceased to exist in this universe as the myriad component pieces, driven by centrifugal force, asserted their individuality all at the very same instant. No rotors, no autorotation, no glide.

Straight down from fifteen hundred feet, at thirty-two feet per second, squared.

On the front of the cyclic there's a little trigger that opens the mike and lets you talk on the radio. Well, when Joe's rotors gave out and he started to fall, he grabbed the cyclic as hard as he could, giving Maverick a whole new understanding of the term "death grip," and opened his mike. He screamed all the way down. Everybody who heard him then still hears him now. Another small radio show they could have done without.

Maverick had signed up. Become an Army aviator, worn the uniform, saluted the flag, even believed in the domino theory. He had bought the whole package long before the starry-eyed Kennedy Youth, because in his family it was a heritage. But when he opened the box he found a little card that said, "All My Love, Pandora." It was an obscene mess inside. Filled with sticky red liquid, fatal fantasies, screams, bits of bodies, occasional pieces of skin, limbs, people with sickening holes in them, heads on a stick, atrocious visions, men with bullet holes for eyes, dreamers of dark dreams, delusions, dementia, and the intimidating presence of men on both sides who become truly alive only when the killing starts.

Some package. No returns. No refunds. All sales final.

Accidents. About a month earlier Maverick and two other choppers were refueling in Nha Trang on the South China Sea. It was a hot clear day with the kind of sky that looks like baby powder made of pearls. By coincidence, Dick Fortenberry and his goddamn gunship were there, lounging on the flight line. As he always did, Maverick ogled the machine and lusted. He almost wanted to fuck it.

The sky is mentioned here only because Maverick suddenly noticed that everybody around him was looking up and pointing at it.

About a thousand feet above them and getting lower all the time, an Air Force B-57 bomber made lazy circles over the city and the bay. Not an approach, actually, not really in the pattern, just . . . up there. But not for long. As they watched, the bomber's canopy blew off and two crouched forms rocketed into the sky. Up and back they went, each sprouting a parachute. They were ejecting? Here? Right over the city?

The bomber, meanwhile, relieved of human control and therefore any obligation to conform to human wishes, coursed out over the bay, a silver javelin, as the pilots floated gently down to the water. Pretty. Across the flat green expanse a chopper was already on the way to fish them out. They'd hardly have time to get wet.

The pilots were safe, but the failure of technology would cost the Vietnamese dearly yet. As the pilots splashed in the water below the rotor wash, the plane made a long slow perfect turn to the left and headed back toward the city. Nobody was driving.

Lower and lower. Floating across the city skies once, then out over the bay, then again over the city. Suddenly another B-57 appeared and ripped the air with long bursts of machine-gun fire. Staccato white puffs of smoke from the rounds. Roaring in the sky. The runaway bomber began to shed its skin as pieces came off and burst away. But still it flew. More bursts, more pieces startled into the sky. But still it flew. Overhead, and closer.

Flash forward: A story came out later that the aircraft was fully fueled and armed, heading off to a mission. The pilot had had some problem, so he aimed it out over the sea, trimmed up the controls to keep it that way till it ran out of fuel and splashed in, and then got the hell out of Dodge. But as they ejected, a knee hit a trim control or something got messed up or whatever and the bomber wound up holding a constant turn . . . but not, sad to say, a constant altitude.

Finally, on one low pass, not more than four or five hundred feet up, the machine rolled gently over onto its back like the last act of *Swan Lake* and made a long slow, slow descent directly into the middle of the city. Nightmare.

Here's what it says in *The Vietnam War: An Almanac:* "6 August 1965. SOUTH VIETNAM: A US B-57 crashes into a residential section of Nha Trang with a full load of bombs; the crew survives but twelve Vietnamese are killed."

Now, think about that for a second. A huge piece of jet-propelled hot steel, loaded to the gunwales with J-4 baby-pink highly flammable kerosene and a full load of bombs, bullets, and other destructive products of the world's foremost military-industrial complex crashes under power into a densely populated city and only twelve people are killed?

As soon as the plane disappeared behind the trees, foul gray smoke started pouring into the sky and everybody in the immediate world scrambled for transportation. As soon as Maverick and Dick stumbled out of their jeep in the middle of town, they began to wish they'd never made the trip. If what Maverick had seen of war looked like hell, there must be a much worse place, because compared to downtown Nha Trang at noon on August 6, 1965, hell would be a night on a Jell-O water bed with your favorite sex object.

This particular U.S. B-57 bomber fell headfirst, not into a residential section but into a movie theater in the center of town, right off a major marketplace at high noon, and as long as you live, you never want to see such a screaming tortured mess.

Hundreds and hundreds of people, including bargain-hunting members of the 101st Airborne Division, were blown to pieces by bombs and incinerated by flaming jet fuel and julienned by tiny shards of incandescent American metal. Or they were crushed or trampled or wounded, crippled, maimed, dismembered, mangled, folded, twisted, spindled, and mutilated. Everything disgusting and awful that can happen to a human body had happened to them. The soldiers had to be identified by their teeth, when teeth could be found. It was worse than any battle, worse than almost any kind of devastation you can think of, a scene that Dante himself, with all the descriptive richness of the Italian language at his command, would never attempt to describe.

It was like one of those television commercials for kitchen gadgets: "It slices, it dices, it makes hundreds of french fries *in seconds!*"

It looked like where the devil will go when he dies.

And all the bombs and bullets that the jet carried kept exploding at no predictable interval for hours, so that nobody could even get near the unlucky survivors or the burn victims or the people missing pieces of themselves, because after the flaming gasoline and the hot metal had done their stuff, the miscellaneous little explosions went on and on. More helplessness. More standing around feeling like one of those dreams we all have, like running in glue, running so hard, so hard, and not getting anywhere and waking up exhausted in the morning.

Lots of people died from stupid things that were tragic, funny, and sometimes both. Case in point: Thomas Tsarius, a short, stocky dark Greek from Tarpon Springs, Florida. Everybody called him Bits. A little under medium height, but taller than Maverick, with black curly hair, olive skin, and an authentic Mediterranean aspect. He was a gunner. At An Khe he lived in a Conex container, a big heavy Sealand freight box, about a third the size of a boxcar, solid steel, with corrugated sides. Vietnam was full of them, because when equipment or supplies came off the ships, they'd just leave the Conex containers wherever. After all, they cost only a few grand each. More expensive garbage, like the disposable airplanes.

Didn't take long—3.18 seconds—for GI's to figure out that, in a war zone, a solid-steel efficiency apartment was something devoutly to be wished. So big holes were scooped out of the ground everywhere, the containers buried and covered with sandbags. They were used for bunkers, storage, and light housekeeping. It was hot inside, and stuffy, but it was underground, it was steel, and it was safe.

Back to Bits. The setup in his freight box was adorable, with a cot and a chest of drawers he'd bought in An Khe, a personal electric fan, the inevitable pinups, every single one of which showed more than our GI fathers ever saw of Betty Grable and Rita Hayworth, and a full-time resident rat. A four-pounder.

Later in his tour he would become twisted enough to give the rat a coy little name and cherish him as a house pet, but in September 1965 he hated the vicious fucker. The beast was undoubtedly rabid and lived somewhere in his stuff, among the boxes and empty beer cans and litter, but Bits could never catch him. It would run across him at night, chew up official U.S. government supplies, and drive him crazy with visceral boojums that all of us have about rats.

Like the rest of the platoon, Bits had gotten good and scared and pissed off and shot at during Operation Gibraltar, and when the platoon got back that evening after waiting all afternoon in the open for the fuel trucks, he was nobody's sweetheart. He staggered down into his bunk, ripped open a drawer in one of his cute little pieces of native furniture, and came face-to-face with The Rat, who, unafraid, looked him stolidly in the eye. Later, Bits was to swear that the rat gave him the finger. Bits took one look at the diseased rodent just sitting among his intimate apparel, so nonchalant, suave, and blasé, and slapped leather, like Gary Cooper on that dusty street at lunchtime. He whipped out his official U.S. Army forty-five-caliber automatic pistol and squeezed off nine rounds in about four seconds.

If he'd gone deaf, nobody would've been surprised, and if he'd gotten himself killed six times with the same ricocheting bullet, nobody would've raised an eyebrow. He had discharged nine rounds while standing smack inside a steel box with irregular corrugated sides, and those big heavy slugs bounced around for what seemed like days, going *wheeee!* and *wizzzzzz!* and *ptchooooo!* just like in the movies and whipping back and forth between the walls before they just got tired and lost their momentum and fell down, but that crazy Greek bastard just stood there, smoking gun in hand, and never got touched. Never even felt the fucking breeze!

He had big bullet holes in all his underwear, but the rat got away.

Just when Maverick got finished thinking about the rat story and about how the whole country was full of people who wanted him dead—including a few of his own, who would kill him if he just got in the way—and about how not to take it all so personally, Ty walked in.

He'd been flying somewhere and had once again become Temporarily Disoriented with Respect to a Preplanned Position, so he stopped in to "ask directions."

As glad as Maverick was to see him, he didn't even have the energy or the will to stand up and roll around in the dirt. Ty took one curious look at him, pulled up a chair, spun it around backward, and straddled it with his arms crossed over the back.

"Okay, what?"

When Ty managed to run three or more words together, he was worth listening to. This time, though, it was Maverick's turn to talk.

"I don't know, man . . . I've been . . . look, I can't stand this. We got people out there who're getting the shit kicked out of them and nobody can do anything about it. I got my chopper all shot up yesterday and everybody aboard coulda died and that little bastard with the M-1? When he was done shooting at me he probably just strolled back into the jungle and had lunch. . . ."

"Look, Maverick . . ."

"That poor son of a bitch Scott, for Christ's sake, there's a guy just like us, wants to fly, wants to have a career in the military, he's got hopes, he knows where he wants to be in ten years, got a wife and maybe kids, and where is he now? Paralyzed in some hospital in Honofuckinglulu, his life is shot in the ass and it could just as easy happen to me. Or you."

"Yeah, but you don't . . ."

"And the Indian kid, God, the Indian kid . . . Now, that was fucking insane. This just hurts too damn much, Ty. Maybe you get it, but I sure as shit don't."

"Hey! Shut up and listen." Startled, Maverick shut up.

Ty just looked at him like he was some kind of foundling who had been brought up by wolves and couldn't talk or think or use language or walk without dragging his knuckles. He looked at him with utmost incredulity, like where the hell you been hidin' out and ain't you got no sense at all and you been here how long so why is it you haven't caught on to what everybody else in the world already knows?

"It's medals and glory. The whole thing."

"What?" Maverick poked his head forward a bit, cocking it to the side and raising his eyebrows. It's the expression you'd have if somebody said something completely alien and unexpected to you, like "Please cut my leg off."

"Don't you understand? It's just medals and glory. That's what this is all about. Really."

Maverick was stunned. Ty was attached to the First Squadron of the Ninth Cavalry, arguably the most gung-ho group in the war, if not in the world. He was intensely militaristic, believed in the country, the flag, the whole package. Even though his little present from Pandora might have contained the same bleeding unpleasantness Maverick's did, he apparently was able to see past it to his own personal understanding of some ancient creed, some inborn urges. Ty's motivation, his purposes, had nothing to do with Vietnam, nothing to do with helping the yellow man. Or killing him. It had much to do, however, with an urge that was not American, not even nationalistic or patriotic, but very fundamentally human. Ty was of the warrior caste, he understood war as an inextricable part of human behavior because he believed that if war were not some sort of genetic urge we would long ago have done away with it, the horror and the dying and the keening mothers at graveside. Given that belief, he was something of an American Samurai, a professional soldier who knew that he was doing something honorable and that if he stayed alive, his society would bestow that honor upon him, as they had bestowed it on the victorious warriors of the past.

Ty wasn't the best chopper pilot who ever clutched a collective, but he had the perfect mind to be the perfect soldier. Medals and glory was what he believed, but he never knew he felt like that because he never knew how it was to feel any other way. Besides, he and Maverick had never discussed it. Maverick had never heard him state it before. Never heard anybody state it before. Ty's words had literal sense, but they were strange to hear, like somebody saying "Today is June thirty-first."

Maverick looked at him more closely. "You mean to tell me that's why men fight?"

"No, asshole. I mean to tell you that's what *war* is about. The only reason men fight is that the women are watching."

Pause. Ty seemed so . . . positive about it all, as though there were no questions and no room for any. As positive as you are that when you drop something, it will fall down and not up.

Ty was one of the few people in Vietnam who had, at least, a perfectly clear picture of his own personal goal, his mission, his purpose. He wanted to be a good soldier, a great soldier, and medals are the way you keep score of how great a soldier you are. Great soldiers do heroic things, so Ty expected to be a hero. He had to be, because he was doing his job right. That's what war was. Soon Maverick would realize that that's what he believed too, coming as he did from a family that was proud of its participation in World War II, coming as he did from a childhood that caused him to take to heart a kind of patriotism that had been written in the sands of Iwo Jima.

The glory? Ah, now, that was another question entirely. Glory is the recognition you expect to receive if you make it home with all your medals. That part didn't turn out so well, but Ty never got the chance to find that out.

Ty never got the glory. Nobody did. Ty got the medals, though, and soon, at a different time and place, he would be a hero. At that moment, Maverick loved him.

Abruptly Ty unfolded himself from the chair, looked down at Maverick once more with those cold steel-gray fucking eyes of his, smacked him hard on the shoulder, said "Medals and glory," and walked out of Maverick's tent. And out of his life.

While Ty's Huey bore him into the sky, all Maverick could do was sit there and think. God, people must really love war. There must be something about *Homo notsosapiens,* something dark and squirmy and dank, something that rejoices in the noise and the fireworks and the stench. Something that makes men feel most alive when they're closest to death. Else, why would they spend so much time doing it and thinking about it and planning it and preparing for it? Why?

Maybe Ty understood something that Maverick never would. Or at least was better at finding words for it. To Ty, war was part of the human condition, a vestige of the hunter/predator days that never got bred out. It was a drive and a need, only slightly more manageable than hunger and excretion. This was the milieu Ty had chosen for himself, and he was going to be as good at it as he knew how. He understood that if we abhorred war as much as we say we do, we would treat it like the family's memory of Uncle Roger, who killed his wife and stashed her in the potting shed. We would hide it in the very back of the attic, where no one ever goes. We would never speak of it. Hush the children if they ever bring it up, like we do with sex. If we really hated war, Maverick thought, really hated it, there would be no monuments to it, no cannon on the courthouse lawn, no little boys' dolls complete with flamethrower and antitank gun, no movies about it, no toy guns, no *real* guns, no open house at the Air Force base on Sunday afternoon—Bring the kids! See the Machines of Destruction!—no poems, no paeans, no parades.

No medals. No glory.

TWELVE

Maverick spent the day furious. He was furious because he had gotten caught, *because they'd taken away his derringer, because they'd stolen his fucking* watch, *because they had dressed him in* black pajamas, *another symbol of everything Maverick hated and wanted to kill. Black pajamas tortured Bennie, killed Ty. The cloth felt like cold worms on his skin.*

He was furious because he didn't know what they'd done with Quinlan, because the possibility of medical care for his injuries was laughably remote. And during those long crazy days inside the skeletal beast, he heard from deep within himself the voices of dark dreams, the echoes of dead eyes, the whisperings from under the rock, the words that dripped fear, the words that told him when the enemy finally got around to paying attention to him they would proceed according to neither the Hippocratic Oath nor the Geneva Convention.

He stared at the lock and the chain. He stared at the little nicks he had made with his thumbnail on one of the bony bamboo poles, one for each day of his captivity. There were nine.

That night they moved him again.

On September 30, 1965, after sixty days in the field, after two months of living in shit and red dust and bad dreams, the Outlaws were sent back to Vinh Long, and they felt like they had fallen among the lotus-eaters. They were in a land in which it seemed always afternoon. Civilization at last.

But there was a war going on outside, and even though they enjoyed the proverbial comforts of home by the boatload, people were still dying on a depressingly regular and nearby basis.

There was a Hawaiian named Bennie, one class behind Maverick at Fort Wolters, whose unpronounceable last name was eight and one-half syllables long and contained thirty-two vowels. He flew with the First of the Ninth Air Cavalry, Ty's unit. Bennie and his crew chief were shot down in early October just at dusk in a light observation helicopter. Missing, which is the worst thing to be, and just at nightfall, too.

Nobody could do anything about it at night, but the next day the air was black with choppers out looking, and finally somebody spotted the wreckage in a tiny clearing about ten miles north of the field. The choppers went in low, the deep green gliding beneath them, because they didn't know what or who might be hiding in the bushes. They circled above. All quiet. They spotted the crew chief, a dark form sitting against a tree not far from the wreckage. Wasn't moving. Wasn't waving. Unconscious? Dead? Somebody had to go in and find out.

They called for a platoon of grunts and inserted it as close to the crash site as they could—a clearing about three hundred yards away. They were to sweep the area, plodding through a stretch of virtually impenetrable jungle, working their way to the crash site to see if the crew chief still drew breath on God's earth. And where was Bennie all this time? Besides, they had no idea if there were enemy troops around or if they might be in for any kind of surprise, or what.

As soon as the grunts hit the ground, they were fired upon by every VC in the immediate world. Small arms, automatic weapons, fifty-caliber, mortars . . . everything but slingshots and spitballs.

A trap, with an American crew chief as the bait.

The grunts got out of it with minor casualties, after one of those standard Vietnam firefights when you don't know who's shooting at whom and you're mouth-down on the jungle floor, nose in evil muck with no fucking idea what's going on. Charlie melted back into the undergrowth like always, probably down into the tunnels, and the grunts finally reached the wreck.

The crew chief under the tree was dead, pale of face, eyes rolled back under his dark eyebrows, tied up in a semirealistic position. They had nailed his arms to the trunk. When the grunts swept into the little village about a half-mile away, they found Bennie, dangling by his heels from a low tree, skinned from his ankles all the way down to his neck. On the dusty ground below him, blood and other fluids pooled and trickled and clotted.

Know what a skinned human looks like? Well, if somebody put an arm down your throat, grabbed the bottom of your stomach, and pulled you inside out, that'd be close. Nothing deprives a corpse of its last remnant of dignity or humanity more than this particular treatment. Nothing makes one look more like dead meat.

That's when Maverick first started to hate. He didn't get hardened to all the shit during Operation Gibraltar because there wasn't enough time, or even after the Indian kid got killed, or even when Ty told him what he told him. It was what happened to that smiling Hawaiian, what they did to him, what they did to his nine kids. What he looked like, raw and wet and slimy and bleeding and black with deafening flies.

That's when Maverick stopped thinking of the enemy as human beings. That's when he stopped thinking at all. He took the first step toward becoming Ty's kind of soldier.

The things he was exposed to became easier to look at. He was still flying slicks, so he wasn't pulling the trigger, but, God, he wanted to. It didn't bother him a bit to see Charlie die; in fact, he was almost happy about it. Almost. Now, he thought, now I've seen the worst, and it didn't take long. I've had horror and nausea and revulsion. They can't show me anything worse than this.

The gods of war smile at such conclusions, and nudge each other playfully in the ribs. Even standing in the heat of the village, staring at Bennie's dripping remains, he had a long way to travel before he would learn the Big Lesson: no matter how bad things are, they can and will always get worse.

Maverick had read somewhere that of all the troops in Vietnam, none were exposed to enemy fire on a more regular or consistent basis than tunnel rats and helicopter pilots. He couldn't argue with that.

The grunts had it rough, but they'd usually go out for a few days—even if they didn't get shot at, they paid the price in stress—then come back in to a base camp and have to wait around for who knew how long. The Ash-and-Trash pilots flew in and out of LZ's, some hot and some not, four or five or eight times a day. Hours and hours of dropping off whole human beings, then fighting back in later on to take out the pieces.

As the weeks went by, his exposure to combat became more frequent and more intense. He started to crash a lot. Not through incompetence, at least he didn't think so, but because flying conditions were very much inimical to safe aircraft operation. Maverick and his fellow hot-dog chopper jocks strapped themselves to the controls of a big, wide, slow green sitting duck with a propeller on top, and even with M-60's and suppressing fire from gunships and heavy artillery preceding them and napalm for dessert, they were vulnerable as hell. To shooting, to mechanical failure, to Acts of God, to anything.

He suffered an inordinate number of "unscheduled landings" for a lot of other reasons as well. His blossoming hatred for people who would skin a man alive drove him into combat situations that more self-possessed pilots stayed away from.

It amazed him that a Huey could take a zillion shots and keep on flying. And it also amazed him that just one lucky shot could knock one of those suckers out of the air in two seconds. There were times he'd just stand there after a mission and gaze awestruck at all the holes in the skin and the round shattered places in the Plexiglas that suddenly appeared before them in flight.

Nine days after they found Bennie, they pulled a resupply mission to an ARVN compound in the Ca Mau area. The troops in the compound had VC all around them, were under siege, and were running out of ammunition.

Three Hueys full of fuel and food and ammo, mostly ammo, take off that afternoon, Maverick in Number Two, forming up on the lead ship to his left, sighting through the skid supports to maintain his position. Gunships swim in the air to his right and left, floating like almost-seen objects in surrealist paintings . . . big green heavy metal absurdities, mysteriously suspended. It is almost an hour before Ca Mau comes into view, a brown smudge across the green carpet of jungle. The gunnies swim downward to lay in suppressing fire. The slicks hang back.

The gunnies glide to the west, drop in. Right away tracers come flitting up from the tree line like dragon spit. Not so bright in the daytime, but bright enough, bright enough. The gunships pull up, one, two, three, turn, make another run. The slicks circle in formation, marking time at about fifteen hundred feet, above the kill zone and not too far away, listening to the radio and waiting for their chance to make a nice calm safe approach. The Huey rattles and wallows from all the iron in the back, and all Maverick wants to do is dump that shit out the side door and haul ass. But every time the gunships roll in, those deadly little sparks dance before them. They go in three times, and three times they turn back.

"Outlaw Two Six, this is Maverick Three One." One of the gunship pilots. The gunship platoon is called, by coincidence, the Mavericks, and Maverick himself hungers to be one of them. "We gettin' shot to shit in here. They got too damn many guns."

"Roger that. Wanna fall back and figure this out?" If the gunship guys don't want to go near the place, damned if he'd fly in low and slow and stupid. And unarmed.

So they clatter off a few miles and make lazy circles in the sky, chattering on the radio to decide a plan of action. The gunny leader decides that the gunships should go in from the west, draw fire like a decoy, then the slicks can sneak in low from the east. Great plan. Can't miss.

The two gunships roll off with great authority and determination to begin the run, while Maverick circles around in the opposite direction, a slick to each side of him. He drops down, the trees blur by underneath, the overloaded choppers bump and mush through the heavy air.

There! Automatic weapons open up from the side. Then the other side. Tracers blur up at them, flitting by on the right, on the left. Maverick flashes on Ken Smith at Fort Wolters, flying him through the trees ten feet off the ground with fire in his demented eyes. *Snick!* A hole in the plexi, about a foot from Maverick's face, then they're clear. Then they're not.

The high, irritating-and-comforting whine of the huge turbine engine suddenly drops off. The Huey becomes a whale on roller skates. It dips, it spins, bodies strain against the seat-belt webbing, like flight school all over again. The motion of the ship tells them they've taken a round or two in the tail rotor, and that means no antitorque action and that means they spin around on the axis of the rotor, a sick and deadly carnival thrill ride. All Maverick can hear on the headset is "Oh, shit." Did he say that?

They lurch from one side to the other, trying to get some control.

"Maverick Three Six, this is Outlaw Two Six. We're hit. Going in. I say again, we're hit, we're going in." Shit, thinks Maverick. This is absolutely the last thing I want to do today.

He's pissed, insulted, angry, frightened. The machine absolutely does not care.

Those well-drilled emergency-landing procedures click in, his reflexes and training take over: Level out. Maintain airspeed, sixty-knot attitude, make it just as much like a normal landing as you can. Slide about three or four feet when you hit. Everything just like Ken Smith told him. He flashes again, this time to that autorotation he shot at Fort Wolters, and the crazy forty-foot slide down the icy runway.

Keep the nose up. Maintain airspeed. When they hit, they're gonna slide three feet, maybe four, and that's it. Just like it says in the book.

Silly, silly Maverick, to think he has control over this machine, to think he has control over anything. When the ground comes up and hits them, they have abundant forward motion, they are rich in momentum, rich enough to glide all the way back to San Francisco. The fat green Huey slides and slides through that muddy water across the rice paddy, wrenching him to the right as he fights to keep it straight. "Don't roll over, please don't roll over and make me into a sticky little ball." They stop—hard—when they hit the paddy dike. Forward motion goes from sixty to zero in no time at all as they shudder to a halt in the middle of the foul water.

Silence. Deep breath. A nasty little ride. Luckily, they seem to be clear of enemy fire, which is a good thing because Szabo starts screaming about his broken leg and Maverick personally feels like his asshole got moved about a foot and a half to the north. The copilot and Reich are shaken up, but at least they can walk. Harness off, Maverick unfolds from the seat and stands up very slowly, as far as he can in the cockpit. Surprise! Long lances of pain shoot up from his spine to his head. He doubles over like he's taken one to the gut.

Above, the two gunships swirl about in a cloud of noise, laying down fire, roaring all around them. Maverick staggers to the cargo bay, swearing at himself for going through all that enemy fire without being able to shoot back. Soon another Huey rises over the treetops, settles into a hurricane of paddy water, and takes them aboard.

He was in pain for days. Cramps, backache, ice picks in his spine. But the flight surgeon checked him out, said he was fine and why doesn't he just get right back into combat. Over the next two days he flew two missions, including a medevac to Saigon. But he called a halt when he started pissing blood.

The injuries were so severe they took him all the way to the

Army hospital in Hawaii, threw him on an operating table, and watched him curl up in a fetal position. While two corpsmen held him down, a third ran a stainless-steel tube with lights and mirrors and stuff on it all the way down his throat and into his stomach, looking for the internal bleeding. If he didn't die from the helicopter crash, these bastards were going to kill him with the tube. His arms showed the corpsmen's finger marks for a month, long after he had gotten out of the hospital and was taken back into the war.

After two weeks in Hawaii he was once again proclaimed "fit for duty" and was forced to spend a few days in the officers'-club bar, waiting for his flight back to never-never land. It gave him a whole different view of the war. Darker. More personal. Next to him at the bar, the doctors would sit, like a row of tombstones in the rain, reflecting upon how inadequate their medical training was, having never prepared them for the kind of meatball trauma they were seeing every day. There was, for instance, a sandy-haired, balding oral surgeon from Indiana who spent all afternoon telling him about the eight hours of reconstructive surgery he'd just performed on the jaw of a nineteen-year-old kid who'd had his face blown away in an ambush. One Scotch and soda turned into another, and then into ten, while the doctor's words ran together and the comfortable numbness set in. As he spoke, his watery blue eyes floated behind his glasses like jellyfish. For months he'd been looking at the kind of physical and mental devastation that medical school does nothing to prepare you for, that a doctor from Indiana never gets to see, even in the emergency room. Here, thought Maverick, is another victim. A bright-eye who every day was turning more and more against the steady stream of wasted youth the war was showing him. Maverick had taken a step. He began to understand that war creates casualties of every sort.

If it was hard going to Vietnam from San Francisco, it was even harder going back to Vietnam from Hawaii. But Maverick didn't mind exchanging one torture chamber for another. He flew back with a renewed resolve that he would pay any price, bear any burden, if only they'd let him fly a gunship.

Looking down on the coastline on the approach to Tan Son Nhut, Maverick became aware of yet another little tragedy. From where he sat, Vietnam looked so good. Just like Hawaii—long craggy coastlines, lush green cliffs sloping down to pure white beaches endlessly soothed by the improbably blue sea . . . sandbars, coral reefs, mountains, valleys. But Hawaii was a paradise, and Vietnam only looked like one from far off. The contrast was not merely cruel, but brutish.

The peculiar mix of people who fought the Vietnam war divided itself into all kinds of cliques. There were two very broad ones: the people who wanted to fight the war and the people who didn't. Below that distinction, groups branched off racially, ethnically, geographically. There were mission cliques too. If you were flying slicks, you stayed with the slick pilots . . . and you stuck with your platoon. If you were flying guns, you did the same thing, only more so. Even at the officers' club, the tables were divided into Us and Them. Say hello, walk on by. Any other time, he'd look at a table full of gunny pilots and think: Fuck 'em, bunch of goddamn happy hot dogs, what makes them think they're better than us?

But Maverick came back to Vinh Long from Hawaii and rejoined the Outlaws with mutinous thoughts deep in his mind. He looked at guys like Cates and Reich and Szabo and the other slick crews and started to believe that the gunny pilots *were* better than them. Gunship pilots didn't deliver bodies and food and ammo. They delivered death. They flew guns, and wasn't war all about guns, and who had more of them and who had better ones? And who could use them the best?

Then, one night it happened. Just after his return from Hawaii, Maverick sat in the officers' club with Cates, catching up on two weeks of war stories, doing what soldiers have always done after the battle, which is drinking and lying. Just as Maverick was pushing his chair back to order another drink, a gunny pilot named Logan appeared at the table. Maverick was so surprised he stopped halfway up.

"Excuse me, Mr. Marvicsin, the Mavericks would like you to join them for a drink when you're finished here." How formal of him. But then, Logan was one of the two section leaders of the Mavericks, a West Pointer, but not a ring-knocker like a lot of them. He was tall, blond, a recruiting-poster soldier, and reputedly the best rocket shot in the company.

Maverick looked at Cates. Cates looked at Maverick. They both looked at Logan. It is happening, isn't it? Maverick thought. This is wish-come-true time even though I'm a lowly W-1 in-country only a few months—invited to the gunship table? If he'd ever been to college, he would have felt like a scared freshman during rush week, getting the glad hand from the one fraternity that does all the drinking and gets all the pussy. But in a way it was inevitable. His nickname was Maverick, the gunship platoon was called the Mavericks, shit, he *belonged* there. Was this a cosmic coincidence, caused by the concatenation of improbabilities that a war always generates? Had he accomplished this through outstanding performance and reputation, or was it sheer force of wanting?

Maverick couldn't get up fast enough. "See you in a while, Cates." He was smiling so hard he could have bled from the corners of his mouth. He forgot about getting another drink, instead forcing himself to walk to the gunny table at a sedate pace, not too eager. His hand reached out of its own accord and pulled up a chair. He didn't bother trying to remember any names—after all, these guys looked just like everybody else; they were warrant officers too. They flew Hueys, dressed themselves in the normal manner. He even vaguely recognized a few faces from classes ahead of him at Fort Wolters. They looked like everybody else, but they flew *guns.*

Obviously subscribing to the ancient Roman tenet about where Truth really lies, the gunny pilots bought him a few drinks, then dinner, then a few more drinks and maybe a couple extra after that just for dessert, and talked about the war and the mission and how did he like flying slicks and what did he think of gunships. It was all Maverick could do to keep from falling on his knees from the liquor and the eagerness and debasing himself and panting like a puppy and groveling and crawling on the sticky floor. There was a chance, a chance that these guys might actually invite him to join them in the real war. Please, please let me fly a gunship. Don't let this silly drooling offend you.

They discussed a lot of things that night, and Maverick couldn't remember a one because the insistent buzzing in his head drowned out most of the conversation. But apparently his thinking was compatible with theirs—You like to shoot? Hate the VC? Wanna kill some? Hey, us too!—and as he bumbled his way back to the slick hooch, he was too buzzed and fuddled to decide whether he'd come across as a great guy or an asshole. But he was sure they knew he was a stand-up troop, the kind who would bail your ass out if you were in trouble, the kind you'd want to be in a foxhole with if you had to be in a foxhole.

The next morning, Logan knocked on the door of his hooch well before first light, told him he was In, and asked him if he felt like packing his stuff. His headache was intolerable, his teeth had little angora sweaters on, and the aftereffects of severe alcohol poisoning racked every organ of his body, but Logan's words soothed him as a miraculous cure from On High. Praising the Lord all the while, he flew around the hooch, jamming everything he owned into his bags. Cates and Dave and Walt and the rest looked on, some in admiration, some with the kind of look you give to brave fools, and others with the kind of look you give to stupid fools. He didn't care, he was in! The paperwork would follow.

The Mavericks. At last. Their symbol was the head of an angry bull snorting smoke from its nostrils. The platoon had silver pins made in the form of the bull-head logo and you got one if you received hits from enemy fire. Some guys had been in the platoon for a year and never earned one. They'd been fired at, sure, but never actually hit. Maverick collected his on his first mission. In fact, he got hit so many times that they painted "Magnet Ass" on the back of his helmet, and by the time they discovered, to their horror, just how well he deserved the nickname, he'd lost them four choppers.

To learn the techniques of operating a machine that was more weapon than aircraft, they assigned Maverick as Logan's copilot. Quite a compliment. It was like starting all over again, orientation rides, learning the systems, learning how to shoot and fly at the same time. When Maverick became an aircraft commander, Logan gave him his personal chopper, crew and all.

It was a Huey Model UH-1B gunship, just like Maverick's slick except it had been converted into a fully armed attack aircraft. He decided to call it the *Littlest Maverick,* and painted the name in big white block letters just under the window of the right-hand cockpit door. It carried four people: the aircraft commander in the right seat up front, the copilot gunner in the left seat; in the back on the left, hanging out the cargo door, sat the crew chief with an M-60, and on the right, also hanging out the cargo door, sat the gunner, similarly equipped.

For a jerry-rigged converted troop carrier, it had an awesome amount of firepower. The *Littlest Maverick* carried four 7.62mm machine guns mounted in "flex kits," two on each side, hydraulically linked to the copilot's gun sight. The flex kits were mounted on lumpy pylons that jutted out from the side of the chopper. To fire them, the copilot had only to look at a red-lighted reticle in the boxy gun sight that hung down in front of his face. When he twisted the hand grip on the side, the sight followed his vision, the guns followed the sight, and the bullets followed shortly thereafter. The gunship carried about five thousand rounds of ammunition per gun for the flex kits, about the same for each of the M-60's. There was a stop on the flex-kit mechanism so you couldn't point the guns inward at the chopper. Maverick always considered that a good idea, but tried not to think about the guys who had originally discovered the need for it.

They also had a fat cylindrical rocket pod on each side, carrying seven rockets, each with a ten-pound warhead. They were in fixed position, tilted up so they'd be level when the ship was in its forward-pitched flying attitude. The AC aimed them by pointing the whole chopper at the target like a big gun sight and pushing the button.

Another good thing. Unlike slicks, the enemy usually avoided shooting at gunships. Gunny pilots were known to be fond of overreacting, and whenever they saw a muzzle flash, they'd dump every round of ammunition they had right on top of it.

The platoon was also the proud owner of a Hog. It was a normal Huey gunship, but it had rockets up the ass. It carried twenty-four on each side, along with a few hundred 40mm grenades fired from a turret on the forward underside. It looked like an udder with one teat. They called it a Thumper. With all the other armament, the gunships still boasted the door gunner and crew chief with their M-60's poking out each side. They were true engines of destruction. Heavy artillery that could fly. Maverick loved them.

The crew that Maverick inherited from Logan consisted of the gunner, an Indian from Gallup, New Mexico, named Eagle, and Frair, a lanky six-foot-two slow-moving crew chief.

Eagle was short, broad-faced, with ruddy high cheekbones and long straight hair the color of midnight. Of his ethnic derivation there was no doubt. He loved to shoot, and somehow being shot at in return only made it more fun for him. From the side of a moving helicopter he could pick an enemy troop off a water buffalo at fifty yards and leave the animal standing traumatized but unharmed. Eagle was actually stationed in Hawaii and rotated to Vietnam on temporary assignment. He could have gone back to Honolulu after six months, but after discovering how good Maverick was at attracting enemy fire, he decided to stay on.

Frair, well, Frair was another case entirely. He was tall, sallow, thin-faced, and droopy, a man in whose eyes you could see a harsh childhood and the necessarily harsh view of the world that is its legacy. His every spoken word, and there were precious few, told of his Virginia Tidewater upbringing. Maverick at first mistook this solemnity for depth, but it was actually because Frair never had anything good to say so he just didn't say it. He was dour, cynical, pessimistic. Maverick never found out whether that was his natural disposition or whether the war had made him that way. He suspected the latter. But Frair did know every bolt, every seam, every linkage, every inch of piping on his ship, the way one knows the body of a longtime lover.

When Maverick became a gunny, he started getting shot down a lot more than before. First of all, his mission was to expose himself to enemy fire. Second, the VC moved everything at night. Slick pilots got to stay home at night, but gunnies had to go out and try to mix it up. They'd find a canal or trail or a couple of sampans out on the water where they probably shouldn't be and harass them until the little bees started whizzing by. Most times it took a lot of badgering because the VC absolutely did not want to fire on the gunnies. So the pilots kept themselves entertained by developing innovative ways to get shot at.

The gunny pilots were like those early World War I aviators, men who had brand-new, untested machines in war for the first time, having to drop bombs over the side by hand, or take their rifles up with them. The Hueys had all these hi-tech weapons, but in some situations they just weren't worth a shit, so the Mavericks would fly over a canal, flip on the landing lights, spot a few boats lying to, and throw rocks at them. The sound of the rocks crashing through the jungle canopy would sometimes spook the VC into shooting. But as soon as they did, they would suffer incandescent death from above.

Peanut-butter jars were great. One could pull the pin on a hand grenade, stick it in a Peter Pan jar so the handle stayed closed, then put the lid back on. When it was thrown out of the chopper, the glass would break and a few seconds later the grenade would go off. The VC, thinking they were under attack, would start shooting. Then *everybody* would start shooting.

They'd make Molotov-style napalm cocktails from laundry detergent and gasoline; they'd use buckets of nails. There was this one restricted canal that had been declared a free-fire zone, but the VC didn't care. They floated their people and supplies up and down the thing all night long. Logan and Frair went into downtown Vinh Long one day and bought a couple of kegs of nails, which they poured out of the chopper from about two thousand feet. The nails went right through the sampans, making dozens of little holes, sinking them.

This is about Father Wah. Maverick met Father Wah shortly after the Mavericks opened their arms and their armament to him. Father Wah was a tall, thin Chinese Catholic priest with a long face and drooping eyes, who had led a band of refugees out of China when the Japanese invaded in World War II, and walked them all the way to southern French Indochina to set up their village. It was located in a dense black forest smack in the middle of boggling square kilometers of absolutely nothing but swamp and mangroves and jungle and pestilence and undergrowth and Vietcong. Every square inch of land around Father Wah's settlement was completely and totally under control of the Communists.

How controlled was it? Well, the VC used to go there for R&R. It was said that forward air controllers could spot them water-skiing on the rivers and canals.

Father Wah was much beloved by the Americans for two reasons. He hated Communists and his village was a perfect operating base in a dense enemy zone. Even had a tidy little PSP landing strip, compliments of Uncle You-know-who.

The good father, who was known for his personal symbol of "The Dove of Peace," believed fervently in the paradigm "Praise the Lord and Pass the Ammunition." He hedged his heavenly bets by supporting his own private little army. His troops were mostly Chinese refugees, but if any Vietnamese could find their way to him through trackless VC territory, they were more than welcome to pull on a uniform. Oh, yes. Father Wah's army had dress uniforms and fatigues, weapons and fortifications. They'd built a series of concentric moats that encircled the main part of the hamlet, crossed by tiny footbridges. From the air the place looked like a huge sparkling wagon wheel. They had machine-gun emplacements, Claymore mines, concertina wire. Everything but a PX and a movie house.

Actually, the VC could have had Father Wah's ass anytime they wanted it, but they left him pretty much alone because they knew if they fucked with him every Yankee Imperialist Devil-Dog gunship in Southeast Asia would descend from the heavens and blast the whole district right into a parallel universe.

In the exact center of this mini war zone was a kind of tower over forty feet high made of that beige stone and mud, with a stairway sunk into the wall surrounding it. The brooding structure supported a weirdly modernistic cross which jutted to the low sky through a kind of open circle that centered on the point where the arms crossed. There in the middle was welded a pivoting mount for a fifty-caliber machine gun. Father Wah and God worked in mysterious ways.

The first time Maverick met Father Wah was on a mission flying a load of high-level brass into the compound. The day before, the gentle clergyman's troops had killed fifty-one VC in a furious firefight and the Americans wanted to confirm the all-important body count. No doubt about it. If anyone could Point with Pride, the good father could, and he did, showing the officers the bodies, stacked up like fire logs along the canal, already purple and puffy, a gruesome pile of meat quickly ripening in the stifling heat of the jungle.

This added another set of impressions to Maverick's image file, which was beginning to fill with a healthy dose of unpleasantness. The image of death piled high was bad enough, but for weeks, Maverick dreamt only about the smell.

THIRTEEN

The Traveling Maverick Road Show and Marching Society moved from village to village in the very small hours of every morning. After two or three of these excursions, Maverick knew what to expect. When his low tumbrel bounced into town, the citizenry would be waiting in long angry lines on both sides of the path. Again, he would carefully pull himself up on his elbows to see every infant, toddler, tot, adolescent, teenager, young mommy, grand- and great-grandmother standing together to greet him. Sprinkled among them would be a few pitifully wizened old men in various stages of ambulatory degeneration, with skin like dried apricots. No young men. None at all.

For just a moment he forgot about his urinary terror and concentrated instead on the people outside the cage, who were going to pull his guts out hand over hand. For them, this Grand Procession of the Abject Aviator was better than the circus coming to town, and everything necessary for his reception was ready to hand. Not palm fronds, plentiful though they were, not rose petals, but sticks and twigs and pieces of tree and rocks and dirt and offal, unmentionable organs of creatures long dead, chicken heads, and a small fortune in excrement. It was almost as though they'd been saving it up in anticipation. As the cart jounced into the village, the clutch of people surged forward with enormous noise, hurling foul slime of every description. He curled up on the bony bottom of the cage, jerking as the sticks jabbed into his back and shoulders, terrified, angered beyond anger, humiliated.

The soldiers finally pushed the crowd back, halfheartedly, and hauled the cage down to the riverbank. One of the NVA, the short fat one, pulled up a rusty bucket of muddy water, clambered onto the bed of the cart, spilled half of it on his leg, and poured what was left through the top of the cage over Maverick's head. A small blessing. Very small.

Again, they put him on a sawhorse kind of platform in a dim, stifling hooch. Again, some old woman, looking just like every other old Asian woman he'd ever seen, hunched in, scowled at him, spat a few foul words, and shoved a small bowl of indefinite rice through the bars.

Maverick, moving gingerly once again, tried to eat the rice with a minimum of motion. It tasted fishy, it revolted him, but he knew he had to eat. He felt a tremendous pressure at the base of his belly, and as horrified as he was, he yielded to it. The stream ran clear. He would have cried in relief if he'd known whether or not that was a good sign.

One day early in 1966 Dick Fortenberry found himself transferred to the 114th Aviation Company at Vinh Long. The 114th was a sister company and shared the compound with the Outlaws and Mavericks. Dick, experienced gunny pilot that he was, had been sent in to fly with their gunship platoon, the Cobras. When Maverick walked into the officers' club that night and saw Dick sitting there, a sudden flush of elation came over him, a feeling like he might survive the war after all. His occasional meetings with Dick and Ty and some of his other friends from flight school had been the only familiar things in a very strange situation. Now that some VC had shot at him—at *him*—he was starting to understand what a bowl of maggots he had really gotten into. It is hard to keep friends during any war, but in Vietnam friends got lost suddenly and unexpectedly, through booby traps, accidents, stupidity, and, oh, yes, enemy action. You never knew when somebody you came to care about would die in your arms, some of his pieces missing. Or just not come back from the latrine one day. But Maverick knew Ty was around somewhere, and now he had Dick right there. He was a lot less alienated than most people. It would cost him.

Out of Vinh Long the gunnies flew countermortar standby missions. After dark, when the slick pilots were snug in their beds, one fire team, two choppers, from each platoon stayed on call till sunup to react to mortar attacks, infiltration, sappers, nightmares, fevered visions, hallucinations, revelations from on high, whatever. The nine-to-five war had long since come to an end. Now they had to stay up at night, looking into the darkness and saying to themselves: Not tonight, please, don't let it be tonight.

Normally, they'd fly two missions each night, always at different times so the enemy couldn't pick out a pattern. But when the mortars started raining down, which they did on an irregular but frequent basis, the gunny crews would haul ass to the flight line, whatever the time, through the sinister whistling, the dull thumps, the whirring shrapnel, explode aloft and locate the mortar positions before things got too far out of hand.

It is a bad, bad feeling to sit in a compound and listen to the mortar explosions walk toward you as the forward spotters talk the rounds closer and closer. Everybody had his own way of dealing with it. The favorite method involved taking shelter underground at an accelerated pace. There were plenty of bunkers around, big holes in the ground squared off above with layer upon layer of inevitable tan sandbags, topped with pierced steel planking, then more sandbags, like frosting. But. It was often neither convenient nor possible to run to the bunker through a goddamn hail of mortar fire in the middle of the night, so lots of people built their own. Powell, the paranoid in the next hooch, who was just sane enough to convince people he was sane enough to fly, excavated his entire floor and put a shelter trench right down the middle so when death came from the sky he could roll out of bed into the hole and pull the steel over himself. He didn't even have to wake up. Maverick, no dummy he, had about the same arrangement, but he and Logan and some others dug the bunker outside the hooch and got into it by crawling under Maverick's bed through a hole in the wall. If the sound of incoming didn't wake him up, he could count on the six panicked happy-hot-dog chopper jocks squirming naked under his cot, dragging themselves through the wall into the shelter.

Dick got transferred in during one of the quieter periods and instantly started to make a big thing out of "how *quiet* it is down here in the south." He was from the north, where the shooting, like the fun, never stopped.

"Is this all you do is fuck around in the sky all day and drink all night?" he belched, slurring his words as he leaned back in his chair. Maverick had dragged him around the room for an hour, buying him drinks and introducing him to everybody, even people he didn't know. "Maverick, you don't really think this is the war, do you?" Maverick, who had been sitting on the other side of the table beaming at him, stopped beaming.

"In the north," he continued with a remarkable lack of tact, "we never had time to sit on our asses and drink beer all night."

As the poet wisely reminds us, words wear hard boots, and a mere twenty-four hours later Dick found out, much to his horror, that there was a war going on in the Delta too.

It was the following night. It was quiet. The Mavericks had been flying all day and had already done one night CMS mission, so everybody was hot and tired and dragging. It wasn't uncommon to fly eight or ten or twelve hours a day, and too many pilots had bought the farm because they were just too goddamn tired to control the machine anymore. Chopper pilots received one Air Medal for each twenty-five hours of combat that they flew, and Maverick wound up with over four dozen of them, plus the noncombat flight time. It's hard to describe how you feel after ten hours in the cockpit of a Huey, so never mind. It's just that helicopters don't have autopilots, so you have to fly them every second. They require constant attention from both hands and both feet. Add the excitement of having to shoot rockets and machine guns at the same time and the stiff penalty exacted by your constant rush of adrenaline, never knowing when the routine mission will turn into a legendary Rat Fuck, and you develop a chronic emotional overdraft that causes a killing fatigue. It never goes away.

The night that Dick got his initiation, the Cobras and Mavericks flew the first, uneventful mission just after dark and then hit the showers. If anything did happen, the choppers were on the flight line, preflighted, switches on, ready to go. Crews could just jump in, flick the battery switch, push that bright red start button, and roar into the air.

Due to intelligence information that was operating at its usual level of . . . well, intelligence, just about every pilot from both gunship platoons was on call that night, and almost every one of them was under the tepid running water, wet and pink and soapy and singing, swearing, laughing, shouting. The noise level was high, yells and laughter echoing off hard surfaces, but it was not high enough to keep them from hearing the *thump* as the first mortar blew into the earth on the other side of the compound.

Before the noise had even faded, fourteen naked bodies bolted, falling out of the stalls, a jumble of arms and legs writhing like so many pale pink eels, glistening and slippery, grabbing towels, groping for shoes, elbowing out the door.

In the hot open air, the resemblance to spirited high jinks in a college dorm diminishes rapidly. Explosions are raining from the sky, close and terrifying and arbitrary. Dick runs along the path about ten yards in front of Maverick, holding his skimpy towel up with one hand and trying to get his sandals on with the other. He looks like he's hopping down the bunny trail. His high white young ass flashes vertical smiles out the back.

Dick slides down a path to his left, rounding the corner in a four-wheel drift like something out of a Road Runner cartoon, and makes for his hooch. Maverick cuts the other way, stumbles up to his own hooch, and Wile E. Coyote things start to happen. The front door sticks and recoils, catching him smartly with the very edge on the bridge of his nose. Rather than stopping cold, he spins inside, crushing the third toe of his naked left foot precisely on a metal folding-chair leg. He screams and hops to his low metal bunk, catches his knee on the edge, falls forward, grabbing double handfuls of miscellaneous soldier clothes—he doesn't care what he puts on if he can only get out of this fucking hooch alive—hurls himself out the back door.

The random explosions continue, in clusters of three or four, then silence, then three or four more. Maverick, hurting, panicked, tries to run along the path and struggle into his shirt at the same time, collides with Dick as he comes around the corner from the Cobra hooch, wrestling himself into an undershirt. Dick starts to run again, maintaining the lead even as he continues the soon-to-be-legendary bunny routine, expanding on it, improvising, innovating, refining, adding subtle touches, pushing the very frontiers of comedy as he hops on one leg, then the other, struggling into his pants.

Mortars make emphatic sounds when they hit, and Maverick thinks he can feel the concussion even when they fall at a distance. They're not hitting that far away. *Thump!* Directly in Maverick's face, before his astonished eyes, so to speak, the earth throws up, expelling cruel tiny fragments of dirt and rock into his chest and stomach and legs. The last thing he remembers is flying off the ground, in the air, then pain as he drops into the mud and rocks alongside the walkway. Quick fade to black.

After a short time, or a long time, it was hard to tell, he sits up and looks around stupidly, as if seeing the place for the second time, and trying to remember it, and by the way, why won't his eyes focus up? On the ground just the other side of the crater are Dick's towel, one of his sandals, and the shirt Maverick had seen him carrying. He looks at the three objects for a long time. The rounds are still coming in, but all he can do is sit there. He is disappointed he does not see birds, like in the cartoons. Dick is gone. Blown up. Not even pieces remain. Not a shred, not a slice. Everyone who was running around like crazy is gone. How long was I *out?* Are they all in the bunkers by now, or are they blown up like Dick, who has gone and left no pieces, just a smoking hole? Not a button, not a finger, not a recognizable organ, only a towel, a shirt, and a fucking flip-flop. Between the vehement *thumps* of the incoming mortar rounds, he hears the gunships clatter up into the distant dark.

He heaves himself to his feet, runs in circles, screams for medics, the FBI, the police, the hall monitor, anybody, because he thinks Dick is blown up and the fact that he's splattered with blood has not been lost on him and he doesn't know where his clothes are and there are little bits of shrapnel or rock or whatever embedded in his skin like filthy little pimples. Suddenly two medics are next to him trying to lay him down, but he's way too stupid for that. He wants to find Dick or at least a few of his components, and besides, there's a goddamn mortar attack going on around here, or haven't you noticed, and he's supposed to be flying a helicopter because he's a helicopter pilot, and that's what he's going to do.

The medics can't hold him. They've seen crazy before so they don't even try. Fuck him, because they have enough people around who are really hurt and they don't need to bother with some sawed-off asshole square-headed chopper jock with skinny legs.

Maverick raves down the path across the compound and runs out to the flight line in a frenzy. The falling mortars continue their pointed commentary in the night. Every five steps he hears the freight-train sound and hits the dirt, trying to dig through the runway's PSP with his fingernails. The *thump* comes. He stands, runs until the next *thump* comes, hits the hard steel again.

He's nuts and he knows it, but he doesn't care. He climbs into his chopper and he's goddamn well going to fly and get up there and find those mortar positions and shoot them with his guns and rockets and kill them. Yes! Don't give me that Italian-movie shit this time, we need a whole different image here, a different image quality, a new metaphor, sharp pictures this time, not soft-focused, not diffuse, but *sharp* like little silver nails, and by the way, you can keep the audio. We don't need the sound of explosions, no *whupwhup* of the rotors, no exclamations of fire in the sky, just Mozart, perhaps, yes, and plenty of him. Utter divorce between sound and picture in this movie. The mind will cohere the music and the action, creating its own images.

No crew chief, no copilot, no gunner. Maverick guesses they waited long enough for him and crawled into the closest shelter. Fuck 'em. He jumps into the right seat, knowing vaguely that he shouldn't even think about flying at all, but flying alone exceeds mere irresponsibility and actually extends all the way to manic hebephrenia. But fuck that too. He hits the button, giggles, reaches up to pull on his helmet, and shrugs into his flak vest while the rotors spin up.

Dimly he hears a cargo door slide open behind him and turns to look over his shoulder. A helmet named "Frair" pokes through the opening, with a crew chief inside, a crew chief who may be the skinniest, most angular, most disjointed human Maverick has ever seen. And crazy, too, because as he starts to pull his long white body into the back, he looks at Maverick and begins to scream. It is a high, shrill sound, unexpected from a man as tall as he.

What? What? Maverick is in no shape for this. Is he in shock and hideously wounded and doesn't know it? Is there something those two medics didn't mention? "Hey, Fred, let's not tell this guy what his arm's hanging by." Is he missing any important pieces? Frair screams again, sinks to his knees, grabs his stomach, and collapses to the cold dark floor behind the cockpit. Maverick, confined by his harness, loses sight of him, looks down to release his belt, and sees his dick.

Except for his flight vest, he's barefoot all the way up to his neck, and Friar, lying on the floor in hysterics, took one look at him and got crippled.

Fuck it. Grab the collective, twist the throttle, push the cyclic forward, leave the ground. When he was in slicks, he felt like he was going into battle with his dick hanging out. Now he is.

They lumber into the air, wheeling toward VC Island, a crooked finger of land in the middle of the Mekong, notorious as a mortar site.

"Going hot." Maverick arms the weapons, and when the muzzle flashes begin to appear, little fireflies among the dark bushes below, he rolls in, with Friar already squeezing his M-60 like a madman.

By the time Maverick gets there, the first gunnies have already made their runs and headed back to rearm. It's just naked Maverick now, his bare ass pressed tightly against the armor-plated seat, amazed that he should feel so much more *vulnerable* just because he was lacking that one layer of cloth. And it's Frair, making pass after pass across the island, rolling in, rolling out, launching rockets, firing flex kits, swooping down, racketing across the water toward the target, breaking to the side that Frair is on so that he can cover them as they leave. Maverick gradually comes to his senses enough to call the tower.

"Vinh Long tower, this is Maverick Three Two inbound. Need to rearm and refuel. And send somebody to my hooch to bring me out a pair of goddamn pants. And a shirt and some boots too."

They settle to the PSP in the refueling area, and just as Maverick throttles down the rotors, Dick comes running toward him.

"God damn your fucking ass," Maverick yells through the window, clutching at Dick's shirtfront. "I thought you were dead."

"Yeah, and what about you? I was way in front of where that round hit, so I kept running. I thought you were right behind me."

"Right. I was on my ass," Maverick screams, wide-eyed, his hands now full of Dick's shirt, shaking him. "I was knocked completely fuckin' out, and when I came to, all I saw was your fuckin' towel and your fuckin' shirt and that goddamn shitass sandal. I thought you got blown to bits!"

Dick's gray eyes crinkle up and he just laughs. Maverick hits him weakly on the chest. Dick peers into his face to make sure he's okay, glances down at his naked lap, cold shriveled penis sticking up, weak and sorry, from between pale hairy thighs. Like Frair, he screams and falls down like his legs have disappeared, rolling on the ground, kicking, writhing, hooting, bellowing, screaming into the night.

Meanwhile, Frair jumps out of the cargo door and trots in front of the chopper to check on the refueling. As he walks away, Dick and Maverick see two white half-moons wiggling just below his flak jacket.

He's naked too.

FOURTEEN

They kept him in that same hooch for three days, which was just enough time for all his other agonies to catch up with him. After so many nights of sitting and sleeping on a thin bamboo mat on top of heavy bamboo bars, after so many days of diarrhea and trying to clean himself with pieces of his black pajamas, after so many hours of keeping his body in an eternal bend because he could not lie down or sit up, he was exhausted and light-headed from the pain and the uncertainty and the fear.

He also had enough time to start thinking like a soldier, reason things through, calculate his opportunities, plan his—dare he think it?—escape. He pondered the lock in a whole new way, not as something ridiculous yet effective, but as something to be defeated.

He was a pilot, so he made a checklist.

First, his captors. He'd seen seven soldiers, all in NVA uniforms. He allowed himself to feel a bit smug about the fact that, after dragging him around the jungle for however many days, they were looking a little the worse for wear. Good for them, the fuckers.

But where was the rest of their outfit? Maybe they were separated from their unit, trying to catch up. If so, they would have shot him and left him at the crash. Is that what they'd done to Quinlan? Or maybe they weren't even the ones who'd shot him down, but were assigned to hold on to him, take him to the north. Maybe they had to keep him alive to collect a reward.

Periodically they would come inside the hooch to look at him, five or six or seven slight dark figures, thin and brown. They would poke him with sticks to wake him up, give him a "bath" from a huge rusty pail filled with noxious water. It took two of them to carry it. They chattered at him constantly, making jokes about him, he guessed, causing each other to explode into high-

pitched trills of laughter. He may have imagined it, but the stupid-looking older one did not torment him quite as severely. Even so, Maverick wisely refrained from using his smattering of Vietnamese on them, believing that since he *was the one in the cage and* they *were the ones outside, they would be perceptibly less than amused to hear him suddenly utter "Motherfuck Uncle Ho." Similarly, Maverick correctly reasoned, they would be equally distressed if he said, with creditable accent, "Your whore sister fucks big black donkeys" or "Stick your head up your slope ass and fart your brains out." So he didn't.*

He hungered for the sound of an American voice, an English word.

Maverick soon discovered that gunship pilots enjoyed a whole new fantasy world of combat. Slick pilots tried to avoid trouble as much as possible, because it wasn't their purpose and they weren't equipped. But the gunnies went out and got themselves into the shit *on purpose,* like street gangs on the subway. Night reconnaissance, countermortar standby, lightning-bug flights where they put big lights on one of the slicks and, escorted with a dark gunship, flew around at altitude in the night hoping that some asshole would shoot at them, and when he did, the gunship would remove him from the planet, a smorgasbord of delightfully dangerous war things to do. Oh, yes . . . and the snatch missions.

With the full authority and consent of the Vietnamese government, such as it was, and accompanied by an ARVN adviser, gunnies would escort a slick to an area where the VC were active and loaf around in the sky until they found some poor bastard, or a group of poor bastards, down on the ground. They would look at the ARVN adviser for a Pronouncement. Using that mysterious Asian sixth sense that Yankees have never understood, he would divine on the spot whether the hapless citizen or citizens beneath them were "VC" or "No VC." To Maverick and the crews, it seemed like everybody in the whole goddamn country was VC. That's why they were so fond of saying, "Kill 'em all and let God sort it out." But they had to depend on these ARVN advisers and their peculiar clairvoyance.

The slick would land; grunts would arrest the guy and take him back to the base for interrogation by one or more of his less-than-sympathetic countrymen. If the snatchee was lucky, he'd fall out of the helicopter on the way.

On this bright clear day, Maverick is at about a hundred feet, letting his paisano copilot named Cicio fly the right seat, and the slick hanging improbably off to his right. A sighting: a man in black jammies is walking along the paddy dike below, trying very hard to pretend that he absolutely does not see or hear the two enormous green clattering imperialist death machines that hang in the air just above his head. He doesn't know it yet, but his ass is in for a very bad day, because one of his fellow citizens is about to determine, through occult intuition, that he's an Enemy of the People.

"VC," says the adviser, and points.

Okay, if you say so. Cicio radios the slick and they start slipping closer to the "suspect," but—what a surprise—he's known they were there all along because he starts running, jumps off the paddy dike, and disappears into the muddy brown water.

"Outlaw Two Six," Maverick radios the slick, "he's in the water just about fifty feet ahead of you."

"Roger that, Maverick." The chopper pulls in closer, hovers here, hovers there, dangles above the ground on a long imaginary string, a forbidding dark green figure above brown water. They see the crew leaning out the big doors, scanning the paddy. Cicio says, "They can't find the fucker."

Well, hell . . . Maverick had seen just where the "suspect" went into the water, but the slick flies back and forth right above the exact spot and can't flush him out.

Buzzing angrily, the slick makes a few more passes a foot above the water. Finally Maverick calls him off and cruises in closer, creeping forward, the brown muck flowing beneath the chin bubble. Between their feet and directly below them Cicio picks out the suspect, lying flat on his back in three feet of water, eyes screwed shut as tight as his asshole, breathing through a reed stuck in his mouth. Maverick had never seen anybody ever do that outside the movies.

He pushes the pedal and spins the Huey around on its rotor axis to put Frair right over the place. They hover, making a tremendous racket, the wash from the rotors making fine sprays of muddy water explode into the air all around them, and the unfortunate who lies beneath the waves pretends that nothing is happening, he believes that if he can't see them they can't see him, so he lies in the middle of this percussive blast of air and water, his whole scalp holding his eyes closed, very, very still indeed.

As they hover, the rotors blow most of the water away from him and he ends up lying in a kind of liquid hole like when Moses parted the Red Sea. His eyes stay shut.

Frair stretches out facedown on the floor of the cargo hold with Eagle holding his feet, squiggles out over the edge of the door, grabbing the skid with one hand, reaches down and plucks the reed out of the Asian's mouth. Maverick pulls up and away, the water rushes back in.

The "suspect" lies there for about thirty seconds, then a minute, then as long as a human being can possibly hold his breath. He gags, chokes, lurches to his feet. Maverick slides the Huey sideways toward him, four American hands grab him under the arms and assist him into the chopper. Then comes the part Maverick hates most—flying the prisoner back to Vinh Long to hand him over to his countrymen.

There was another thing Maverick hated: when the VC mortared them in the daytime, because the gunny pilots couldn't see where the muzzle flashes were coming from. Sometimes, if they were lucky, they'd see a dark gray puff of smoke somewhere in the endless green, but it still took them longer to locate the enemy position, and it was more dangerous. One day they suffered an especially serious downpour, so the Mavericks scrambled into the air like always, even though they were terminally exhausted from flying ten hours a day like always, and headed for VC Island like the time they flew naked. But this time they had an ARVN adviser aboard.

VC Island was misnamed. It was more like a come-hither finger of land poking into a wide point of the Mekong River. When they got there, hundreds of refugees were straggling out of the area, long ragged ribbons of humanity on the dirt roads.

They fly back and forth, just waiting for those sparkling tracers to reach up for them, but they can't find the mortar positions and nobody shoots at them, dammit, so the ARVN adviser leans forward into the cockpit, puts his hand on Maverick's left shoulder, and says, "Go there." He points down about a hundred feet to a group of villagers shuffling along in the brown powder of the road, pushing or pulling or dragging or carrying whatever worldly goods the war has decided to leave them.

They settle into a small field next to the road while the wingman circles overhead for cover. The ARVN gets out, looks around, points out a young man about twenty or twenty-five years old, and damns him with a word: "VC."

The man freezes, eyes wide, as Frair lopes toward him, pulls his .38, and brings him back to the chopper. Maverick sits in the cockpit watching the tableau through the plexi—dusty villagers, stripped of all their goods, their homes, their dignity, lined up in the road, looking on frozen-faced as one of their number is taken from them at gunpoint and lifted into the sky by the liberators of their homeland.

Hell, Maverick thinks, maybe the guy is VC, maybe he isn't. Maybe he's the very one who lobbed the mortar into camp and killed the two cooks the day before. Maybe I should hate him and kill him right now. Or maybe he's just some poor slob in the wrong place at the wrong time and flatass out of luck. The ARVN knows, maybe, but I never know. How much longer can I watch them do this?

Running vertically through the cargo-door openings, they had mounted old litter poles, because the M-60 machine guns hung from the doorframes by bungee cords, which allowed the gunners to fire them in any direction. Sometimes, when the boys got real excited, they'd swivel the guns around too far and the M-60's would get inside the aircraft with everybody. The Cobra platoon lost a pilot in just that way, shot in the back at close range by his own crew chief. They considered that kind of additional stimulation unnecessary, so they had mounted litter poles vertically in the doorways to act as a stop. But they had another purpose as well.

The detainee clambers into the back of the helicopter, chattering furiously at the ARVN adviser. Maverick speaks no Vietnamese except for the "fuck-you" stuff that everybody learns, but he understands every word. Despite frantic, and undoubtedly heartfelt, protestations of innocence, the detainee is made to sit on the edge of the doorframe alongside the pole with his feet dangling over the edge, resting on the skids. If he doesn't want to fall out, he holds on to the pole. Why does he think he'll fall out? Because Frair is on the seat behind him with his size-thirteen canal-boat combat boots square up against the base of his spine. If the prisoner misbehaves, a slight shove gives him a flying lesson without benefit of aircraft. The platoon had lost more than one chopper to grenades brought on board by suicidal VC who weren't properly searched. Another hard, expensive lesson.

To the prisoner, the significance of his posture is dismayingly clear. It is the closest they ever come to an international language.

Since VC Island is only about two minutes from the Vinh Long airfield, they stay about a hundred feet above the river, which at this point is a fat brown ribbon almost half a mile wide, streaking beneath them. The tower speaks.

"Maverick Three Four, enter right base at one hundred feet, report turning final."

Maverick flies the base leg at ninety degrees to the end of the runway just above the thick brown water. The riverbank rushes toward them, running across their route.

"Vinh Long tower, Maverick Three Four, roger."

Just as he gets the words out, the detainee in the back has a Personal Revelation: if he jumps right now, he'll land more or less safely in the river, and even a high dive into the muddy Mekong is better than what awaits him when the Americans toss him to his ARVN interrogators. They are, he knows, notorious skeptics who are unlikely to believe anything he says, and capable of causing him large and prolonged agony even if he is a solid, honest, tax-paying citizen in good standing and a registered voter on top of it all.

All in one motion, the little man lets loose of the pole, stands up on the skids, pushes himself into the air, and disappears inevitably downward.

Well, it's true that he took the fall right over the river, but it's obvious to one and all that he remembers nothing of his high-school physics, because even though he has a working knowledge of gravity, he has completely neglected considerations of imparted forward motion, trajectory, momentum, friction, and Coriolis force. He accelerates downward at the traditional thirty-two feet per second, squared, and forward at seventy miles an hour, exactly the speed of the helicopter, minus wind resistance. He lands very much facedown, not in the water but about ten feet up the riverbank, and a foot straight into the mud.

He looked like he was making angels in the snow.

Thing is, the troops who were fighting the war were confused, angry . . . Let's start again. The troops who were fighting the war were *pissed off,* and they were pissed off *all the time,* because people were sending them all these mixed signals. Somebody wanted them to fight, but couldn't tell them exactly whom. Somebody wanted them to kill, but a thing called the Rules of Engagement permitted them to kill the enemy over here, but not over there, tomorrow, but not today, or only after nine P.M. on odd-numbered Thursdays. Somebody wanted them to sacrifice themselves, but couldn't tell them exactly why. Sometimes they just went ahead and made the killing and dying decisions on their own, with appalling results. But that's the Cambodia story, and even though Maverick thinks he's seen it all, he hasn't. Cambodia will have to wait.

Then, there was the News From Home. After Operation Gibraltar, Maverick got written up on page six of the Mansfield *News-Journal:* "Local Serviceman Sees Action in Vietnam." No shit. But on the front page, where it counted, it was all hippies and hardhats.

The Democratic convention in Chicago was far in the future, but morale still wasn't very good. The troops were living in shit and dying in shit, and all Maverick could do was watch. All kinds of people were trying to kill them, and vice versa, and nobody could tell them why or when it would end or whether they were accomplishing anything. They had no idea at the time how much worse it could get in another year or two, but they were still hungry for any kind of support or appreciation. And they got it, actually, but from unexpected directions.

The officers' club at Vinh Long was a large single-story rectangular building with a flat tin roof. The wooden walls went halfway up the sides; then screening ran to the top. There was a large bar inside, with tables and chairs crammed in so tightly that you had to walk on your toes and hold your balls in one hand to get to your seat. The decor was an imaginatively eclectic mixture of VC Modern and Traditional Military American—captured enemy flags, weapons, assorted memorabilia. There was a separate dining area, attached barber shop, covered patio. Fans hung from the ceiling in neat little rows, and in the corner one of those oscillating fans stood on a tall chrome pole. It had a huge round semiglobular wire-mesh guard around the blades, crusted with damp dust, the kind of thing that nobody would ever clean, and it swayed its head from side to side like a confused Martian taking in his new surroundings, making rattling and racketing noises unendingly. It was surrounded by scrofulous greenish-yellow banana trees of all heights that had been brought in to provide a cynical accent of tropical charm. When youthful spirits were high, certain officers would shove those banana plants through the space in the back of the fan's blade guard, causing shredded frond to spew from the front. They all thought this was very funny, no matter how many times it happened. In an average week, six or eight banana plants might be sacrificed in this manner, but in Vietnam they were as cheap as life.

The club had a stereo system that was so big the lights dimmed when you turned it on. The floors were hard, the walls were hard, it was hollow, it was raucous, a place you could clean with a garden hose, and often had to. It was a place that all the bar fights in the world couldn't destroy, a peculiar kind of gentlemen's tavern, an exclusive club whose members came home from work every day pumped, and pissed, and shaken, if they came home from work at all.

The war had heated up more than somewhat, but there were still quiet days. In mid-October 1966, Maverick opened the door to the officers' club and ran into the usual brick wall of rude noise. On this day, however, there was another sound, one he had never heard in there. It was the sound of a woman's voice.

It wasn't the greatest woman's voice, kind of hoarse and throaty, but it absolutely didn't belong to a man. It belonged to Martha Raye, who had been in the neighborhood and decided to drop in.

She was sitting with her elbows on a table, surrounded by six or eight grinning pilots, dressed in loose-fitting fatigues, a Special Forces green beret on her head, topped with a light colonel's silver oak leaf, drinking straight vodka—that's when Maverick fell in love with her—listening to the stories and trying to decide whether to laugh or cry.

Maverick pulled up a chair at the back of the circle. She was absolutely the very most famous person he had ever seen up close and in color. He sat entranced. For two and a half hours, all she did was talk to them. But her impact went far beyond the simplicity of the act. First, it was a thrill for kids like Maverick, from places like Mansfield, Ohio, to suddenly come upon A Famous Person just sitting around being one of the group. He was all of twenty-five at the time, a year older than the average in Vietnam and seven years younger than the average soldier in World War II. Second, being with her and listening to *her* stories helped them take their minds off the blood and guts, if only for a little while.

Martha Raye became something of a legend during the war because she had spent so much time in Vietnam doing just what Maverick was now watching her do. It was said that during a mortar attack at Soc Trang, to the south of them, she had run out during the shelling and helped carry in the wounded. After he met her, he believed it.

Not many people back in The World knew it at the time, but there was a whole clutch of celebrities who visited the troops and helped with morale. They'd come over and go on "walk-around tours." Just fly unannounced into base camps and outposts, sometimes into the middle of an operation, or to a staging area where choppers were waiting to take troops into combat, and stroll around shmoozing the troops. Raymond Burr was one. So was Hugh O'Brian.

Just after he joined the guns, Maverick was sitting on the skids at a staging area under a low sky doing what everybody does in the Army—waiting.

"Look at this," said Frair, who was, as usual, leaning against the chopper next to the cargo door, looking around and spitting in the red dirt.

"What now?" Maverick asked.

"Catch this guy in the tiger pants walking up the line."

Maverick got up and walked a few steps away from the chopper to lean out and look down the line of machines. There was a guy in tiger pants, wearing a khaki shirt, combat boots, a Marine flop hat and gunbelt. He was strolling slowly in their direction, surrounded by pilots, gunners, everybody. He looked very familiar.

"He looks very familiar," said Maverick.

"Damn. That's Wyatt Earp, son," said Frair in his best Southwestern dry-gulch high-desert OK Corral Arizona accent. "Hugh O'Brian."

"Shit me silly," Maverick said, as Frair finally condescended to be interested. He pushed himself off the chopper and walked over to get a better view, standing next to Maverick, but about a head and a half higher.

Then there he was. Wyatt Earp, all six-feet-forever of him. O'Brian looked down at Maverick. Maverick looked up at a legend of the West. He wasn't John Wayne, but he was a cowboy.

O'Brian stuck out his hand and introduced himself. He made it sound like nobody ever knew who he was *right away,* when Wyatt Earp, brave, courageous, and bold, long may his story be told, suddenly appears from nowhere. He started asking Maverick and Frair about the Huey and what they did, and like that. He sounded actually interested.

Also impressive was the single-action Army Colt .45 slung low in a quick-draw holster on his right hip. Maverick looked at it once, twice. He couldn't help himself.

"There's something I always wanted to know," Maverick said when he had collected sufficient assurance. "Are you as fast with that gun as you make it look on television?" Surely a graceless question, but O'Brian just laughed.

"Tell you what," he said. "Let's find out. We'll have a little test." He positioned himself in front of Maverick, about three feet away.

Maverick swallowed hard. Is this cowboy going to make me draw against him? If I lose, will he shoot me?

"Put your hands in front of you, about waist-high." Maverick did. "Now, clap them."

He felt a little dumb, but he clapped them.

"Now, clap them again."

He clapped them again.

"One more time, hard and fast."

Maverick gave his hands a quick, abrupt slap together, and when they met, the cold blue steel barrel of O'Brian's revolver was right between them, pointing at his belly button. Everybody—there were at least fifteen troops standing around—was thunderstruck, but Maverick was practically catatonic. He gaped. He gulped.

"What do you think?" O'Brian asked, pulling the barrel slowly out from between Maverick's damp palms.

Maverick managed to choke something out. Nobody could understand it.

There were, of course, the bigger shows, the ones that were filmed for network specials back home. Stars like Ann-Margret and Wayne Newton, after the shows, would sometimes mingle with the troops. But actors like Hugh O'Brian and Robert Drury and Raymond Burr just *showed up.* No fanfare, no hoopla, no big shows, no oil company sponsoring an hour-long

TV special back in the States. They just talked to the troops, posed for thousands of pictures, and made them feel like somebody back in The World actually cared.

It took no time at all for the Americans to discover that, given the kind of war it was turning out to be, the helicopter gunship was more than just a handy little gadget. Even with defoliants and bombing and Rome plows that could level hundreds of yards of jungle in seconds, Maverick was flying the most effective, most lethal piece of hardware in the arsenal, always excepting the Nuclear Solution, of course. Even with all the aircraft carriers, bombers, fighters, B-52's, A-7's, and everything else doing incalculable damage on a daily basis, when you get close in and the nitty gets gritty, when you're flying along five or fifty feet above the ground, when you can hover or run or go straight up, when you wear rocket pods on your hips and flex kits in your holsters, you can walk tall. You almost have to be a genius to miss.

Back home in The World, the Americans' dinnertime news show provided a body count that was, in the main, a result of what the gunnies could do to thirty or forty people at a crack. The ground troops could manage to kill only a few at a time. A poet speaks of certain weaponry as "skilful." Gunships are that.

Surprisingly, there weren't that many helicopter platoons in Vietnam dedicated exclusively to gunships, but in the ones that were, everybody was scrambling around trying to make the Huey carry weapons and more weapons. As their realization of the chopper's potential deepened, the Mavericks and no doubt the Cobras and every other gunny platoon in that little corner of the world spent all their leisure hours devising sick schemes to carry additional armament into the air. Weapons are like potato chips. When you have one, you always want more. The pilots and crew chiefs and gunners were certifiably insane. They'd try anything.

One of the biggest problems with gunships was that their armament could deal pretty well with most types of combat situations, but not all. If they came across the enemy in a deep bunker, there was no way to get him out with the stuff they carried unless they could thread the needle with a rocket and send it right into the slot. Not much chance of that, when you're dangling in the air, swaying.

Besides, the enemy in bunkers usually fired fifty-caliber machine guns, so it was impossible to fly in close enough to get a good shot without getting your ass knocked out of the sky.

One night, not a special night, the Mavericks were sitting around in their usual condition, and Logan, with great effort, lifted his eyelids and said: "If Charlie has a fifty-caliber machine gun on the ground, why shouldn't we have one in a chopper?"

Brenner reminded him, "A fifty-cal is a major piece of armament. It's huge and it's heavy, it's got this big long barrel, and it vibrates like a son of a bitch."

"The fucker kicks like crazy," said Maverick. "You'd shake the chopper apart in midair."

Wellllllll, the longer they sat there, the later it got, and the later it got, the more beer disappeared and the better the idea sounded. Maverick, as armament officer for the platoon, was volunteered to go out the next day to that burned-out armored personnel carrier up the road. He was to take Eagle with him to help rescue the fifty-cal turret and mount from the APC.

The next day was, thankfully, quiet, leaving most of the platoon free to watch and ridicule as Maverick, Eagle, and Frair took a regular D-Model slick Huey, covered the cargo-hold floor with sandbags, put a massive piece of plywood over them, and mounted the turret on it. It was over four hundred degrees that day so they sweated and cursed and dripped shirtless in the sun as they ran heavy white nylon straps through the hold and underneath the aircraft to keep the whole misbegotten structure in place. Around them, looking on the way the Hebrews watched Noah, and making many of the very same comments, ranks of smirking doubters tolerated the heat for the sake of the spectacle.

"They don't think this is a good idea," Maverick told Eagle.

"Fuck 'em." Eagle's favorite expression, except for the Indian ones.

When all was tightened down, they whirled into the air and out over the muddy Mekong, Maverick driving, a newby copilot named Bishop, "My friends call me Buzz," who was celebrating his last twenty-four hours on earth and didn't know it, and Frair and Eagle in the back.

Up to fifteen hundred feet, circling, getting ready for the Big Test. Eagle decides to fire it single shot the first time, and if it goes well he'll put it on automatic. He sends a few single rounds into the wide brown ribbon below them.

"It works," he yells to Maverick over the intercom.

"Try it again." Even with the noise and vibration of the chopper, they can feel the kick and hear the concussion when the fifty-cal spits. So far, so good.

Eagle fires a few short bursts. *Bupbupbupbup!* Five or six rounds jolt the chopper as they leave. He fires another burst, another. No serious consequences. Everybody is still in the air and Eagle smiles over his big deadly new toy.

He points the gun back down toward the river and squeezes the triggers. The aircraft trembles as the heavy slugs rocket toward the water and all at once, *surprise!* the cockpit becomes a living tribute to the Dust Bowl of the Thirties. It's a major Lawrence of Arabia sandstorm and it's whirling around them in blinding circles, hurricanes of it, tornadoes of it, monsoons of twisting red dust in their eyes, their noses, and when they open their mouths to scream or speak, it coats their tongues like your worst nightmare of a hangover. They can't speak, they can't breathe, and worst of all, the man with the cyclic can't see shit.

"I can't see shit!" screams Maverick. "What the fuck happened?"

"The plywood came loose and tore up all the goddamn sandbags!" coughs Frair. "All the dirt's loose back here."

The copilot yells, "Turn it sideways!"

Again, through the whirling dirt, "Turn it *sideways!*"

Understanding shines through the sandstorm. Maverick brings his foot down hard on the right pedal to slip the machine so the wind will blow in one cargo door and out the other, taking the sand with it. Smart kid, Bishop, for a newby. Maverick pedals one way, then the other, blowing most of the sand out of the chopper. They struggle, shaken, back to base.

The Army runs on borrowing, and Frair happened to be especially good at it. He found a storage shed full of old mattresses, liberated a few, and installed them in the chopper in place of the sandbags. It worked. The aircraft withstood the vibration, the mattresses held up better than the sandbags, and they liked to think about how confounded the enemy must have been every time he received fifty-caliber fire from the sky.

But they still weren't satisfied.

"Why, for example," asked Maverick of himself and anybody else who was conscious at the time, "why do gunships carry two mingy little bird-fart rocket pods? And why do they hold only seven mingy little baby-dick rockets? Why?"

Shit, he thought, a few months ago all I wanted was a fucking gunship, and now that I got it, I'm still not happy because it has guns but not enough of them. Maverick was, after all, your healthy American boy whose job it is to rain death and despair and evil destruction as far as his mechanized steed would carry him, so his young man's fancy naturally turned to those Air Force rocket pods he'd seen that carried nineteen rockets each. Unbelievably, the things were disposable. The part that carried the rockets was made of heavy paper, good for one use only. He coveted anything that would get him in the air with thirty-eight rockets, so he obtained one. It is best not to wonder how.

The paper pod could be set up to fire a full salvo, or one rocket after the other in a ripple effect, or one shot at a time. The fire mode was selected with a little black three-position flip switch in the back of the pod that had to be set before you ever took off. They had a tough time figuring how that switch worked because they couldn't test it and, since they had obtained the equipment under the most dubious of circumstances and since the rocket pod was a one-use item, they had to apply keen logic and incisive reasoning to the problem, so they guessed.

Eagle and Frair mounted the pod on the right side of the Huey where the normal seven-shot pod would go, and went off to war. Maverick stayed high and behind the formation because nobody had any idea how it was all going to work out. In happy ignorance, they were experimenting with two hundred pounds of jet-propelled high explosive.

In theory, the gunships below would find the enemy, draw fire, and soften him up, then Maverick would come roaring in with all these rockets and assure victory for Democracy in the hemisphere.

It was supposed to be a quiet mission, but then the radio spoke:

"This is Maverick Three One, we're over here gettin' some small-arms fire from the tree line." As he went in with his rockets, the rest of the gunships veered toward his location all at once, a flock of deadly birds, wheeling in the sky, following the leader.

"VC in the open! VC in the open!" The cry comes as a small black figure breaks from the clearing and runs along the paddy dike, a wide-eyed rabbit, doomed, scampering alone in the clear.

"This is Maverick Three Four. I got him spotted. If you guys clear the area, we'll see what this nineteen-shot pod can do."

How many rockets does it take to kill one man? Multiply the day's body count by a million dollars, and that's how many.

The gunnies separate below, curving away to give Maverick a clear shot. He rolls over to begin his first pass. It's a big rice paddy and that lone running figure stands out gloriously atop the long straight line of the dike. Maverick can approach him slowly, fire upon him at leisure, kill him whenever. The man runs at ninety degrees to the gunship's path, like a silly duck in a carnival shooting gallery and twice as easy to hit. Maverick points the chopper at him, leads him just enough, arms the rocket pod, and hits the button.

God's balls. There is the biggest, goddamnedest explosion you ever heard, the chopper comes almost to a halt in the sky, it lurches backward, heads whiplash on top of sensitive spines, seat harnesses cut into shoulders and bellies. Rocket motors burn in all directions as the pod throws up every single one of those nineteen rockets all at the same time. They go right and left, high and low, corkscrewing off into the distance, arcing gracefully upward, diving straight down into the paddies and jungles below. The whole sky is knit with lacy lines of gray smoke from motors gone berserk and screaming into the afternoon.

Frair's voice crackles in the headset, "Ho-ly *shit!* I guess that little flip switch wasn't on single-fire after all."

The rockets go so far in so many directions that the American advisers on the ground two miles away report incoming fire. Don't you worry, Captain. It's just some of that good old American technology coming your way as your friends the chopper jocks experiment with new ways to win all those hearts and minds down there.

Maverick tries to overcome his astonishment and regain control all at the same time. Once he gets it straight and level, he looks back into the cargo hold and sees Eagle staring back at him. He looks like that cartoon coyote on a particularly bad day. His arms and legs and the front of his flight suit are covered with smoke and soot and burns. His helmet visor is down, but through the tinted plastic his agitated eyes can be seen, two iridescent cartwheels, staring in total astonishment and awe and scared-shitlessness. He is black, minstrel-show black. If he'd started singing "Mammy," they all would have listened.

Maverick turns to the front just as Eagle's voice scrapes in the headset.

"Maverick . . . the mounting shackles broke and the pod is stuck under the chopper."

Dandy. "What do you mean, stuck? Can you reach it?"

"Not a chance." He sounds breathless, tight. "It's lodged between the belly and the skid strut, and holy shit, it's burning!"

Sweet Jesus of Nazareth in a Coupe de Ville. "Burning? What the fuck's burning?"

"There's . . . there's a rocket still in the pod. They didn't all fire. One's still in there, and the motor's on. It's burning!"

There is no way to disconnect the pod, no way to cut it loose or otherwise give it some healthy distance from the aircraft. They can't land because there is enemy down there, so Maverick hits the pedal, pushes the cyclic over hard, and starts flying back to base as fast as he can make it go. They have a burning rocket on board with a motor that can go off at any time, and if it does, they can all forget about their wives, children, sweethearts, and drinking it up in the officers' club ever again. Thank God the warhead doesn't arm until it's hit by the G-force of its launch, but that rocket fuel can still kill the shit out of a chopper in flight.

Nobody breathes. They clatter through the sky, nose well down for top speed, every second an agony, trying to find a place to set it down before the beast in the belly can destroy them all. Will the warhead explode? The motor? Will the motor set the chopper on fire? Speech is silenced, breath is held. Come *on,* baby. They don't even bother to call the tower because nobody expects to make it.

Again, the gunner's voice from inside his blackened flight suit, from behind his moon-eyed fright.

"Hey! I don't see no more smoke." He leans over the edge and looks underneath the machine. "No more smoke. The motor's burned out."

In his headset, tight against his ears, Maverick hears three men issue their sighs of relief. He adds his own.

• • •

The gunship pilots were different from slick pilots in other ways. Since they were capable of doing so much damage, they became infamous to the VC and the NVA. If the enemy knew any English at all besides "Hey, GI, you fuck you motha," it was the name of their friendly neighborhood gunship platoon. Around Vinh Long, even the most illiterate remote peasant was likely to know the words "Maverick" and "Cobra."

The enemy was so woven into the fabric of society that even in downtown Vinh Long, right outside the base, "Wanted" posters covered the walls, naming people in the gunship platoons, mostly the pilots. Everybody in town knew their names. Bring in a gunny pilot dead or alive, they weren't fussy, and pick up a cool million piasters each. So going into town alone was never a good idea, and going into town at all was something to think about twice. But then, nobody was too safe in the compound either. If sappers came in, they went for the aircraft first, then the gunny pilots. That's where the money was.

In any direction the Americans looked, they could see enemy. They were surrounded by threats, by cunning little booby traps. Like Bouncing Bettys, for instance. These are little land mines that work with a trip wire. Step on it and the device hops up out of the ground to about waist-height and explodes, leaving you with a nasty raw gaping hole in your belly or legs or crotch and probably a double handful of perforated bowel, depending on how tall you are at the time. It was also possible to lift a latrine seat and catch one in the face.

When the gunships went down, they often had unfired rockets on board. Manna from heaven to the enemy, who carried them off in sheaves. It takes 1.5 volts of DC electricity to fire a 2.75 rocket. A flashlight battery would do it. The VC would lean a rocket up against a paddy dike and angle it on a trajectory toward the compound. They'd fill a can halfway with water, put a needle or nail through a cork, and float it in the can. A wire attached one end of the pin to a pole of the battery, and the other end . . . well, you get the idea. The water evaporates, at some impossible-to-determine time the cork makes contact with the bottom, completing the circuit. The rocket whizzes into the compound, sowing terror, confusion, and consternation among the liberating forces, and the perpetrators have been home with their families and children for days. The GI's could but shake their heads in grudging admiration.

FIFTEEN

Maverick just couldn't help naming the soldiers. It had been in the back of his mind for days. Since there were seven of them and they were all characteristically slight in stature, his choices were pedestrian, yet appropriate.

The one who had carried him that first night and had given him a "bath" he named Happy, for his round face and his slightly malformed mouth that wasn't a harelip exactly but sort of a permanent idiot smile. He looked like somebody had given him two handfuls of water-buffalo shit and he was glad to get it.

Dopey, the other one that he'd seen early, was an NCO, much older than the other six, tall and thin, with huge ears, very pale, wore his front teeth parted in the middle and his eyelids at half-mast. He looked like what your modern six-year-old would call a total goofer. You wouldn't be surprised to find him in a Three Stooges movie. But if anyone during those nightmarish days demonstrated the merest hint of compassion, of sympathy toward his situation, it was Dopey. Maverick often caught him looking into the cage with a "you-poor-son-of-a-bitch" expression in his eyes. He did nothing to help, nothing to ease Maverick's pain, but neither was he harsh. He'd probably seen it all already, at Dienbienphu and before.

There were two troops of medium height who were, for all practical purposes, mutually indistinguishable. At least Maverick hadn't seen them enough to be able to tell them apart. He called them Sleazy and Scummy.

Number five had a long, thin, pockmarked face that looked like someone had lit a fire on it and put it out with an ice pick. He became Scabby. And Greasy was short, round, and sweating, covered with a squalid patina of glistening body oil. He had foul dark circles under his eyes and under his arms.

The apparent leader of the platoon was as tall as Maverick, which is to say not very, barrel-chested, and dark. He carried himself so differently from the rest of the them and had such an aura *about him that Maverick figured he'd come from a relatively high-class family back north. As soon as Maverick had begun to sit up and take nourishment, he would insert his round face into the hooch to look at him and spit curses like bullets. Maverick was convinced that this man resented having to haul him around the landscape and would rather see him dead, so, in a departure from tradition, he named him Attila.*

The Mavericks had been on a mission along the Cambodian border, three bloody grueling days of flying and shooting and killing and dying. Charlie had been caught in the open, crossing a vast expanse of elephant grass. Nobody knew how many there were—hundreds, probably—but they had no place to hide, so the gunships were called in from all over the area, like fire engines to a major blaze, and they pounded the shit out of the VC as long as the sun stayed up. The trapped VC tried to sneak away at night, but the sky was lit up with flares, brilliant white pinpoints on little swaying parachutes. Like Mexican *bandidos,* the VC were making a run for the border, and the gunships flew and flew. A turkey shoot.

The third day of the mission was another shitty day in paradise. Wingman high on the right, skimming along above the impossible green, dull today in the gray light, westward out of Vinh Long, making lazy zigzags in the damp sky, working their way to the north.

By that time, most of the VC had either died horribly or escaped. But fire teams were still sent in just to pick up the stragglers.

"We're probably pretty close to the border by now." Connie, the copilot, who had drawn the short straw for the day, pointed ahead and to the left. Connie had been in the platoon about three weeks, but Maverick had never flown with him before. He was holding one of their enormous worthless maps, trying to match up the patchwork of paddies and streams and canals with the green-and-white markings on the paper. Three days without rain, and all those fucking little waterways shown on the map dry up and change shape. They could have been just outside Altoona.

"A few klicks to go yet, I figure." Maverick put it in a slow bank, carrying them even farther to the north.

Below, a huge plain of elephant grass rose into view. Long, slim tan feathers in an eternal oceanic undulation, and among the ripples, little trails and paths and beaten-down places leading off into the distance. On the horizon, at least two klicks away, a stand of trees reared up against the sky.

"Wonder what's in those trees?" he asked Connie. "Want to check it out?"

"Not especially," he said, his wide flat face puzzled as he tried to fold up a map the size of a bedsheet.

"Come on. I have a hunch." Connie was in no position to say no. And after all, they were supposed to be looking for trouble.

"Maverick Three Two," Connie called to the wingman. "We're gonna swing up ahead there to the left. Our aircraft commander is just dying to know what's in those trees."

"Roger that. Hope we don't die with him. Let's go."

They bring the choppers down on the deck, well under the overcast, a few feet above the feathery tips of the elephant grass, making for the trees at seventy knots. A mile away, half a mile, low and fast, the low line of trees runs in a ragged curve across their path. It rushes toward them.

They get as close as they can, pull a cyclic climb, burst up over the top, and right there on the other side, in the middle of a clearing surrounded by trees, are all these fucking tents laid out in neat little rows with pathways and stacks of rifles and cooking facilities and guys walking around in khaki uniforms with pith helmets on and everything but clotheslines, lawn chairs, and backyard barbecues. He couldn't believe it. Wartime Asian suburbia.

"Praise the Lord," Connie says to nobody in particular. "He has delivered up to us an abundant community of North Fucking Vietnamese Army regulars."

"God damn," says Eagle from the back. "Look at all this. They got regular housekeeping down there."

Maverick pulls up, makes a quick turn, takes all the weapons off safe, "going hot," and they throw everything that gunship carries right into the exact middle of the camp. They just can't shoot fast enough. The rockets go, two and two and two, like deadly marionettes on delicate strings of gray smoke, the flex kits chatter, the M-60's on the side start rocking the boat. Maverick fires the rockets, Connie fires the flex kits, Eagle and Frair accompany on the M-60's.

On the ground below, it's like what happens when you kick over one of those big hills of Georgia fire ants. Men burst from the tents, almost erupting out of the ground, running here, there, confused, scared, taken completely by surprise. Clearly, they'd never expected the attack.

Just before they break after the run, Maverick calls the wingman. "Pull up to about fifty feet, dump, and salvo! Break to the left and get out of here."

They do. They throw up all their rockets and bullets in one convulsive heave, then run away into the sky. By the time they land at Vinh Long it is too late to go back out, so Maverick reports on the mission and goes back to his hooch to lie down and make another attempt at coping with his perpetual state of fatigue. He is tired of being tired.

At ten o'clock in the heavy night the company commander knocked at the door of the hooch.

"Mr. Marvicsin." He stood in the doorframe, not coming in. "We, meaning you and myself, have been requested to appear before the battalion commander at zero nine hundred hours tomorrow. Will you be ready to go?"

"Uhh . . . yes, sir. But what's this—?"

"Thank you very much." He turned and left. He was pissed. Maverick could tell.

The CO arrived on the flight line about fifteen minutes after Maverick, who was waiting in the early light and the swirling dust, placed himself in the right seat, and flew them the fifteen minutes to Can Tho. A jeep was waiting on the flight line. It was a short ride to battalion HQ.

If you knew everything there was to know about U.S. military history and tradition, and if you had to close your eyes and picture in your most fervent imagination the World's Ultimate Grizzled Military Veteran, you would see Sergeant Major Novak, and you would see him clearly, indeed.

Sergeant Major Novak stood six feet, three and one-quarter inches tall and it was a good thing, because he needed the room on his uniform for all the stripes that he'd accumulated over the decades. Two hundred and ten pounds, give or take, lean, mean, square-jawed, a man of no nonsense, a man of steel, with gunmetal-gray hair and gunmetal-gray eyes and a perfect gunmetal-gray handlebar mustache like a tightly wound mainspring that coiled itself to either side of his weathered face. Mature, tried, tested, combat-hardened. The kind of man who knows where everything is and how to get it, one of the men who really run the military.

Maverick took one look at him and knew that Sergeant Major Novak must be the wisest man in the world, the King Solomon of soldiers. Maverick thought: He's taken one look and he knows me.

Sergeant Major Novak unwound himself from his chair, walked around his desk, and stepped between Maverick and the company commander as he greeted the senior officer. Then he turned his attention to Maverick. Jesus, he must have been in the Army when Patton was a private.

"How was your flight down, Mr. Marvicsin?"

Gulp.

He knew just exactly how scared Maverick was. He knew everything.

"The colonel will be with you in just a moment. Would you gentlemen care to have a seat?"

The CO hadn't said a word to Maverick all morning, and he said less than that while they sat together for what was surely a small eternity. The phone rang, the sergeant major stood up, opened the door, and stood rigidly to the side, allowing them to pass before him into The Presence. Maverick hit a brace and pulled a stiff salute. He didn't know what the CO did.

"Sir. Warrant Officer Marvicsin reporting as ordered, sir."

The colonel kept writing and Maverick kept bracing, holding the salute. He drew himself in so hard that he couldn't possibly shake as much as he wanted to. He remembered the TAC officers at Fort Wolters, and how much time he'd spent up against the wall in this exact position.

Behind him, Sergeant Major Novak put a hand on his shoulder and squeezed, twice. A thoroughly man-to-man gesture that said much in little time.

"Mr. Marvicsin." The colonel finally looked up, returned the salute, and addressed Maverick in his Officer Voice. His silver-streaked hair was perfectly manicured, as though each strand had been individually clipped with a tiny scissors. He wore a darker brown mustache, very fine, just a bit too small for his face. The desk at which he sat was very slightly smaller than an aircraft carrier, the few papers and files precisely lined up like jets on a flight deck. He sat in dim light, the curtains drawn, his head and shoulders illuminated by the aura of a track spotlight that hung from the ceiling. Other track lights to the right defined shelves full of captured enemy weapons; still others picked out the flags on the wall behind the seated figure. To Maverick he looked like God's boss.

"It has come to my attention," he said, "that at approximately eighteen hundred hours yesterday, being the date of twenty-two March 1966, you did, on your own volition, attack a detachment of soldiers of the Army of the Republic of Cambodia and render numerous casualties thereupon. Is this true?"

What! Maverick felt like he was on a fast elevator and it had just stopped way too quickly.

"What? Uhh . . . What, sir?"

"Allow me to repeat." Choke, you sarcastic bastard. "Yesterday an encampment of friendly Cambodian regulars was attacked by an American Huey gunship. An undetermined, but no doubt exceedingly large, number of friendly soldiers were killed or wounded. Was that gunship under your command?" A rhetorical question, because the colonel plunged on.

"What the hell were you doing in Cambodia to begin with? And what did you think you were attacking?"

Maverick was so stunned and so scared and so appalled that the words came out one on top of another.

"Sir . . . sir . . . we were, ah, flying around yesterday to the northwest looking for enemy movement, so when we pulled up over that tree line and saw all those assholes, excuse me, sir, enemy troops, running around in khakis and pith helmets, they just had to be NVA. So we . . . took care of them."

"What do you mean 'took care of them'?"

"We . . . wasted them."

"You killed them?"

"Yes. Sir."

"Is your combat experience such that you are an expert in identifying enemy troops?"

Maverick decided to take the plunge. Maybe the colonel liked spunk. "Sir, they had to be. And if they weren't, then they were out there supporting enemy troops. All due respect, sir, they could have been Yugoslavians, but if they're supporting the enemy, they *are* the enemy, so I salvoed and told my wingman to do the same, so if it's anybody's fault, it's mine. And besides . . ."

Maverick stopped and looked at him. "I . . . had a hunch, sir."

"I guess I can see why they call you Maverick, but the fact is, mister, that you weren't supposed to be there. However, it seems that you're right . . . the Cambodians weren't supposed to be there either. It is possible, just possible, that they were assisting the NVA. Let me remind you, in case you need reminding, that the United States considers Cambodia a friendly government . . . but I don't think they'll scream too loud about this." The colonel muttered the last part, almost under his breath.

"The fact still remains, and I cannot overlook it, that you did violate the neutral territory of the Republic of Cambodia. Many of their soldiers are dead. Many are seriously wounded. That leaves me the following choices."

Maverick couldn't wait to hear them.

"One. I can court-martial your ass, make an example of you, and exploit this incident all the way to make sure that your kind of shit never happens again."

Maverick's knees got watery. He started having trouble holding the brace. Little spasms scampered around in his stomach. He was seriously considering just giving in to the feeling and relinquishing control of his bowels on the spot. Again, he felt the hand on his shoulder. The colonel must have seen it, but seemed not to notice.

"Or, there is choice number two. Placed in the same situation, given the same opportunity, I'd probably have done the same fucking thing, God help me. So I could give you the Distinguished Flying Cross for all your 'heroic deeds' across the goddamn border, which gets you off the hook, and if I make you a hero, it gets me off the hook.

"Besides," the colonel went on before Maverick could choke or cough or faint or void himself, "due to . . . attrition, General Westmoreland has received one hundred serial numbers to promote people in the field. So I can recommend you for a direct appointment as a second lieutenant. Would you accept such a commission?"

His mouth must have come open. He stood there staring at the colonel's little mustache. His mind worked furiously, but none too clearly. First, he thought, the son of a bitch accuses me of committing a genuine wartime atrocity against supposedly friendly troops, and then he tells me that my war crime may not be a crime at all, but it all depends on how you look at it and who's on the hook and who needs to get off.

But this is the kind of thing that gets written up with ire and fury in places like the Washington *Post* and the New York *Times,* and what about all those poor bastards I killed who probably didn't deserve to die, but who does, really, and Jesus, my stomach is killing me and maybe I'm facing thirty to life in the stockade, and excuse me, sir, but would you mind if I just threw up right here on the carpet?

And now I have to think about giving up the rank of warrant officer, a pilot with officer's privileges, and actually becoming a second looie, an El Tee, a Second John, a butterbar, starting all over again at the bottom of the pecking order, this time in the commissioned ranks. Who the fuck needs it?

But, on the other hand, the alternative is thirty to life under trying circumstances. If I take the commission I'd have a chance to command, provided I can survive the war, which many people can't seem to do, and commissioned officers make more money. The tiny brown mustache is waiting for an answer.

"Yes, sir. I would accept such a commission." He croaked it, because his voice wouldn't work.

The company commander, who had been stifling small choking sounds during this interchange, began to do a sort of twisted motorboat act.

"But . . . but . . . but . . . sir, with all due respect, this man violated another country's airspace, he fired on friendly troops, he killed who knows how many—"

"Major, think about it. Which would you rather face? This man is, after all, under your command. Now, they could make an international incident out of this thing and court-martial him, so you and I get to answer a lot of hard questions. Or we can recommend him for an award, promote his ass, and probably never hear a peep out of the Cambodians. Looks to me like he pursued a contingent of enemy troops into their sanctuary, and if the Cambodians happened to be there . . . well, sometimes regrettable things happen in wartime. Now, would you care to advise me on this?"

Not a word from the major. The colonel stood up and stuck out his hand. Maverick wanted to kiss it.

He walked out of the colonel's office with a commission pending and a recommendation for a Distinguished Flying Cross. His CO never spoke to him directly again until the night before he got shot down with Shanahan.

SIXTEEN

How many days have I been *here? How many days before they decide I'm too heavy and not worth the trouble and make a little finger squeeze and throw me in the bushes? How long? They're not stupid, it'll come to them sooner or later.*

I've been wounded twice and killed at least once, remember? During the first tour? Shit, Lynn went crazy . . . a five-day mission with the Mavericks and I couldn't write and she didn't hear from me, but somebody's *wife hears that one of the Mavericks has been killed on the mission and she thinks* The *Maverick has been killed so she calls up Lynn and goes into the oh - dear - I'm - so - sorry - please - accept - my - sympathy - is - there - anything - I - can - do - for - you - now - that - you'll - never - see - your - husband - again - you're - all - alone - with - your - little - Michael - Paul and then Lynn starts getting* sympathy cards *but the military doesn't tell her squat because they wait thirty days and when they do tell you squat they send somebody around to your house, the notification officer, the Angel of Death. No more "Dear - Missus - Marvicsin - we - regret - to - inform - you" telegrams, but a real person with the world's shittiest job comes to the* door *and says to your* face *that your husband or son or sometimes daughter won't be coming home because he or she was caught in that epidemic of death in the rice fields, and suddenly, just outside Lynn's house* there he IS *getting out of an Army car just like he's supposed to, military uniform and all, and Lynn looks out the screen door at him on the street, feels all the fear and dread and trepidation and horror and panic and terror that she's been living with for so long come rushing to her heart and to her stomach. He looks like a colonel, at least, walking slowly up to the door like a man with the world's shittiest job, each step heavier than the last, somber expression, fatigued, unhealthy dark puffs under the eyes, what does he* want?

Oh, God . . . I know what he wants.

Early morning on the flight line, looking like one of those fast-paced high-action don't-you-wish-this-were-you Army recruiting commercials. Pulsing music under . . . shapes move in stark relief against the dramatic Asian sky . . . half-seen men appear and then vanish among swirls of red dust . . . glimpses of hulking machines of war . . . rotors whirl as turbine sounds start low, then scream their way up the scale, drowning out the music. Now we hear the real sounds, the vengeful roar and clatter as gunships ascend into the pearl sky, cargo doors open on both sides. The sun shines through, making them seem improbably hollow. With M-60's sticking out like antennae, they are swarms of deadly crickets that wheel and veer, departing on their errands of war.

At the staging area, ARVN troops clamber into their slicks, ten soldiers each, tiny hunchbacks under the weight of their equipment. They are borne into the sky. Gunships alongside, they are lifted to the LZ.

It looks like any other clearing, any other tree line. Suspended there in the dawning sky, Maverick can swear they'd fought for this place ten, maybe a hundred times before. But he is ready. Recent exposure to the excitement of wartime has made him a believer. His rabbit's foot hangs from its now-customary spot on the air-vent control knob, the five-leaf clover his four-year-old son Michael had sent him is in the pocket over his heart, the curved white tiger claw from the Montagnard village chief dangles from its gold chain around his neck. He is shielded in his armor of amulets, trinkets, and talismans.

They arrive above the LZ, just north of Vinh Long. The first group of gunnies breaks and heads in, firing flex kits and rockets at the tree line. Maverick's turn. He has the whole run pictured in his head. After he breaks to the left, Walt in the ship behind him will streak in under his tail to emit his 2.75 rockets that race to the ground dangling on their strings of gray smoke.

They come in low on the very first run, racing across the checkerboard rice paddies firing everything they have toward the trees about three hundred meters ahead. Maverick flies in as close as he can, and prepares to break and give Walt a shot. But a small piece of the paddy dike lifts up right in front of them, a painfully thin VC appears out of the spider hole, whips his rifle to his shoulder, forcing Maverick and Brenner, the misfortunate copilot whose turn it is to fly with Magnet Ass, to look directly down the barrel. On full automatic, at point-blank range, so close he couldn't miss if he were aged, blind, and palsied, the VC shoots the shit out of the chopper.

Bam! The chin bubble explodes. *Bam!* The windshield explodes. *Snicksnicksnick!* Little angry bullets race around Maverick, through him. His left leg flies up and hits him in the chin as he tries to pull to the left. Brenner yells that he smells smoke. Eagle and Frair yell the same thing. Maverick smells nothing.

"Everybody okay back there?" Fighting for control, he yells into the intercom. Everybody is. Everybody but him.

He's been shot. Shot! He can't believe it. He flashes to how offended he was when that bastard at Operation Gibraltar emptied his clip into their chopper. This time, he's worse than offended. He's been goddamn shot, he can't feel a thing below his knee, but he knows when the sensation comes back he'll be less than happy, and he's already starting to get furious.

Brenner takes over and heads them back to the base. Maverick finally looks down at his leg. Oh, God.

The alarm went off at five o'clock. Maverick's hand groped in the darkness and strangled it to silence as he lay still, waiting for his eyelids to come unstuck. The sound of the other pilots filled the hooch. Polish Walt coughed his guts out in the morning. Pat always farted.

Walt finished his morning coughing fit, walked past Maverick's cot, and pulled the covers off him.

"Come on, Guinea, out of bed." He bent down close to him. "And beware the ides of March." Maverick had to think for a second. In Vietnam they never much cared what day it was, only how many were left before they could go home. It was March 15, 1966. He had three months to go. Ninety-one days and a wakeup.

As he pulled on his fatigues, he realized that he'd become pretty cocky. So far, he'd come out luckier than Scott, who got his feet crushed, and Bennie, who got skinned, and Joe, who died screaming, and the Indian kid in the Chinook, who died before he knew it. He was alive, he had all his pieces, and he hadn't been hurt too badly. No holes where there shouldn't be any.

In the early orange light, Maverick and Frair preflighted the chopper. Frair had painted a pair of black-and-white eyeballs on the underside of the horizontal stabilizer because he'd heard it was some kind of bad juju for the Vietnamese. He'd mounted a bright red MP's siren on the skid, painted purple hearts on the doorframe, one for each mission on which they'd taken hits. There were dozens of them and he was running out of room. And big as life on the underbelly, a red-and-white target—a little help for the VC during the aiming process. Beneath it, they'd written a phrase in Vietnamese that meant, translated in the loosest possible fashion, "Motherfuck Uncle Ho." They were young and strong and invulnerable.

Today they'd escort a company of ARVN troops to an insertion across the Mekong into an area around Cai Lay, about twenty-five klicks away. It was an RF, a reactionary force, a rat fuck, in response to rumors of a VC supply depot. Maverick couldn't help thinking about Operation Gibraltar. Just like the last time, the briefing officer told them the mission would be a cakewalk, a boat race, a tea party. Put the troops in, do a sweep, pull them out. Nooooo problem.

Maverick's stomach is sick from shock. He can't take his eyes from his horribly violated leg. Blood seeps insidiously, bright red through his green fatigues. Eagle is lying on the floor between the seats, tying a tourniquet below his knee. Maverick can't believe they shot him.

Brenner: "Vinh Long tower, this is Maverick Three Four, fifteen kilometers northeast, inbound. The aircraft commander is wounded, we have an electrical fire on board, severely damaged aircraft. Need medics standing by. ETA thirteen minutes." Brenner has the cyclic pushed all the way forward, making top speed. There is no windshield, so they sit in a seventy-knot gale which blows away the acrid, choking smoke from the electrical fire. They have no instruments. Only the radios. Maverick can't believe they shot him.

Vinh Long is right up the street, but it might as well be in East Kishinev because the shock is wearing off too fast. The pain is becoming grating, piercing. Eagle huddles on the floor, loosening the tight strip of cloth around the leg, then tightening it. So much blood! The warmth soaks the cloth, creeps up his leg, turns frighteningly cold. Everything starts to throb like the pulsations of the rotors, like the kicking of his heart. He feels sick, scared, light-headed, angry, astonished. He can't believe they shot him.

The machine settles to the ground with a hurried thump. Hands pull off Maverick's shoulder harness, his chicken plate. He is lifted from the seat, dragged out into the sunshine. The first person he sees is Dick, who understands right away that he's not looking at a terminal case.

"Well?" Maverick asks him. "How do you like this shit?" He hurts, long throbs of pain from his leg, but he's a chopper jock, and chopper jocks don't show pain.

Dick looks at the red sopping violated leg, then back into his eyes as the medics tear the bloody cloth away.

"We were just getting ready to relieve the other fire team. I heard your copilot on the radio. Couldn't believe it was you." He looks down again at the awful wound. John Wayne screams at him from somewhere deep within his fatal fantasy: "Look what they did to your buddy! Goddamn Commie bastards shot your best friend! What are you gonna do about it? Are you a soldier? Are you gonna get one back for the Maverick? Are you a pussy?"

Dick is fired up. He is enraged, he suffers a rush of cultural testosterone. "Jesus, those motherfuckers. I won't let them do that to you, buddy. Those bastards're gonna pay for this."

He ran to his chopper, wrenched it into the sky, flew headlong into the AO and got shot down in three minutes.

Onto the stretcher, then a quick slide into the ambulance. The pain was enormous, compounded by the deepest, most intense rage he'd ever felt. He couldn't believe they shot him. All he wanted to do was go back out there and shoot some of them. His mind had turned itself off, backing away from the body's huge hurt, so Maverick decided not to accept the occurrence. This, he thought, has not happened. There is nothing wrong with me, I am not wounded, and the pain does not make me want to scream from my guts.

They carried him in to the flight surgeon. Maverick took one look at the mild-featured doctor, decided the guy was an asshole, and tried to get up from the table and walk out the door, bad leg or no. The doctor was a fucking kid, maybe about twenty-five, not much older. Round-faced, soft, tender, with a tentative, eager smile. A teenage Marcus Welby in green.

Maverick's mind worked furiously. What is this shit? Is this a doctor? I wouldn't want to be in a foxhole with this silly son of a bitch, and he's gonna fix my leg? From the looks of him he's been in-country ever since breakfast this morning. Fuck me silly with an Easter lily. Look! Look! He's staring at me like I'm the first wounded human being he's ever seen.

"Am I the first wounded human being you've ever seen, or could you just get the fuck on with this?"

The child doctor blinked twice, swallowed once, and leaned over the table. With two fingers, the way you'd handle a rotten frog, he pulled aside the gauze and looked at Maverick's leg. He couldn't avoid letting a faint sound of distress escape him. His eyebrows climbed up his forehead. Maverick looked down too. From his knee to his ankle there was pure hamburger. It looked like what you'd see in an inner-city emergency room on payday during a full moon. It was ground round.

Baby Doc, overcoming his hesitation, rubbed gauze over the calf, up, it becoming gradually apparent that the bullet had shattered coming through the floor of the chopper and Maverick's leg was perforated, ankle to knee, by dozens of pieces of metal, like a bad shotgun wound. The shrapnel had left in its wake a whole collection of angry red holes, little mouths with lips of skin that drooled blood and fluid.

"Okay, mister," said the doctor. "I'm gonna medevac you to Saigon. Let's go."

"What? Hold it. No medevac. No Saigon. Just patch this fucker up and let me get out of here."

"Can't do that. These holes go all the way from your ankle to your knee. It's nasty."

Maverick looked at the doctor's round innocent smooth face, unmarked by time or by war. He obviously had no idea what he was dealing with. Here was a happy-hot-dog gunship pilot, shot in the leg, peaking on the crest of his life's most intense adrenaline high so far, getting crazier by the minute with anger, fear, pain, blood lust, and nonspecific suicidal frenzy. "I'm not going to fucking Saigon, you dip. There's nothing wrong with me. Look here. Look!"

Manic, driven, he got up from the metal table and started stalking around the room, shaking from pain, from the deep sense of violation, beating his leg, stamping it on the floor to show the doctor how much it didn't hurt. It almost cost him a fainting spell, but Baby Doc didn't know it. The corpsmen were stunned.

Maverick started to grab the doctor's white coat in his fist, but caught himself at the last minute and simply clutched his shoulder.

"Listen. Just get some goddamn bandages on this thing so I can get back to the AO." This poor bastard doctor who had maybe never seen a war wound before this particular March morning had certainly never seen a case of the Southeast Asian War Game Crazies, and even though Maverick's symptoms were far from full-blown, they were intimidating. Welcome to Vietnam, Doctor.

"Wellll . . . I'll bandage it up, but you certainly don't think I'll let you fly in that condition?"

Maverick just looked at him for about two beats. "Swell, Doc, I won't fly," he swore fervently, trying to keep himself from crossing his fingers behind his back. "Now, please just bandage up my fucking leg and let me get the fuck out of here."

"All right. But I'm gonna give you a shot of morphine."

"No medevac, no Saigon, no morphine. Give me some pills."

Baby Doc slowly shook his head as he pulled out all the little fragments of bullet while Maverick sat on the metal table and dug his nails into the shiny silver surface. He poured alcohol on the wounds and Maverick bit his lower lip and pushed his blood pressure up forty points holding in the screams. The doctor wrapped the leg in gauze and gave him five or six assorted pills to swallow, at least one of which would soon make him feel fine, pain or no pain. Bandaged, bloody, he limped out of the dispensary to find Eagle, Brenner, and Frair waiting.

"How is it?" Frair asked.

"They wanted to cut it off at the neck but they decided to let me keep it. Go out to the flight line and find us another chopper. I'll change my pants and be there in a minute."

The three of them looked at him like he'd turned purple and grown an extra head.

"You want to fly like that?" Eagle asked. Brenner had heard about this kind of behavior, but had never actually seen it before. He kept quiet.

"Don't give me any fucking arguments. Just find us another ship!"

Maverick limped back to the empty hooch, tore off his bloody fatigue pants, and pulled on another pair. Every time he took a step, the pain sounded a deep bass note all the way up his leg, almost to his heart. He'd never hurt worse in his life, never been crazier, never been angrier or more violated or more lusting for revenge, never been more pissed off. Never felt so much pain, never wanted to cause so much pain.

On the flight line, Brenner and Eagle had gotten another gunship preflighted, armed, and fueled. Around them, Hueys landed, rearmed, refueled, took off again, engines never quitting, just down, load up, get into the air. Insanity. Frair stayed behind, because the new aircraft had its own assigned crew chief, a horse-faced guy named Gaskins with huge protruding front teeth like big pieces of Indian corn. He climbed aboard, none too happy about the way Brenner and Eagle had commandeered his ship.

When Gaskins saw them actually helping Maverick into the right seat, he started getting second thoughts, but he had no choice, so off to war they went. Maverick was in a daze. If the crew had known how spaced he was from the pain and shock and anger and pills, they would have jumped out the cargo doors with little if any regard for their altitude. He couldn't think of the course they had to fly, couldn't see the instruments. All he could see was that piece of ground opening up, that bastard pointing his automatic rifle at him. Maverick wanted to kill him with his bare hands, and his mother too, and all his brothers and cousins. But he didn't have to use his hands because he was in command of a high-tech flying arsenal, ready to use up every round and every rocket. From here on his reflexes would take over.

As they lifted off, Brenner flipped the switches to arm the weapons systems. "Going hot," he said.

It was time to rock and roll.

As expected, the "small operation" they were prepared for turned into the kind of rat fuck that hadn't been seen since General Custer strapped on his gunbelt for the very last time. At least a regiment of VC had been surprised in transit through the area outside of Cai Lay and they had all the weapons and ammunition that a unit of that size customarily has, which is lots. What the VC didn't throw at the Americans in the sky they threw at the hapless ARVN troops that had been dropped in the jungle among them.

Brenner is strapped in the left seat, astonished at the maniacal turn the day has taken, Eagle is in the back with the bucktoothed crew chief, who keeps asking "Is he okay? Can he fly? What happened to him?", and they make their way through the morning air back to the battle. Amazingly, only about an hour has passed since they got shot up.

In a dim haze of yellow pain and green tracers and death, they fly back and forth, escorting resupply missions and troop insertions into LZ's that make Operation Gibraltar seem like a fond childhood memory of spring days in the schoolyard. They fly through hailstorms of tracers, streaking like frenzied fireflies in a drag race. They fly through red smoke, gray smoke, they throw rockets and bullets and grenades by the long ton.

An endless hellish nightmare of rearming and refueling, of dangling in the air as bullets pour up from the ground like rain in reverse. Then they are hit. Again and again they are hit. "It's okay," yells Brenner, "she can fly! She can fly!" They turn away, banking crazily above the trees as the chopper gets harder and harder to control. She can't fly.

"Feels like the hydraulics got shot up," yells Brenner, then keys the mike and starts yelling Mayday. Gaskins chatters crazily in the back. Will they lose two aircraft in one day? They turn toward base, forcing the crippled machine through the air, but it does not go, it does not go. Down again, an unscheduled landing, completely unintentional, a controlled crash to the floor of the rice paddies just minutes away from base. Gaskins, damn him, is screaming scared, about how he knew they were lunatics the minute he saw the crew load this limping, drooling, lust-crazed pilot into the right seat, and now, after hours of horrifying wartime desolation, his chopper is shot down, it's crashing with this coven of madmen at the controls. He hates it, he hates them, and when the ground finally hits them, he sits as far away as he can safely get while they wait for a slick to come out and carry them back to base.

The LZ is hot all day and all night. Gunnies fly suppressing runs for hours, scrambling futilely to protect the ARVN troops, who are being decimated on the ground. There are dozens of medevac flights streaming back and forth with precious little escort, the gunnies being otherwise occupied. So it's almost dark by the time the crew gets picked up and deposited back at Vinh Long. But Frair and Eagle find yet another chopper, and another crew chief, this time a skinny kid who speaks Brooklynese through a harelip. They call him the Genius because he can fix anything. He must be a genius, because he's being stubborn in the most negative fashion. He sure as shit doesn't want to fly with Magnet Ass.

Brenner and even Eagle are giving Maverick unusual looks by this time, but they finally convince the Genius that Maverick's wound is strictly superficial and that he's totally under control. Their actual dialogue is best left to the imagination. They take to the air looking for flashlight markers on the ground that show the medevac slicks where to land. When they see them, tiny palsied points of light, they turn on all the lights they own, rotating beacon, landing lights, spotlights, everything, dancing like malicious fireflies in the dark, and they make gun runs around the marker, drawing enemy tracers toward them like millions of glowing snowflakes in a blizzard, firing while the medevac and resupply slicks get in.

Nine and a half hours in the air, nine and a half hours of drawing enemy fire, screaming on the radios, streaming smoke as machines fall, nine and a half hours of the dead, like little dolls below, twisted victims of Vesuvius, surprised by volcanic termination in mid-stride. Details are impossible to remember, Fellini has called for lights and camera and action. He is making a new movie here, stringing together surreal images, beads on an absurd necklace.

SEVENTEEN

The doorbell rings. Lynn wants to run, wants to lock the door, please, God, let it not be him, make him go away, please, God. Stop ringing my doorbell, I won't answer, I won't I won't, but of course she does. She looks at him right in the face and sees her Sunday-school teacher, just back from his National Guard drill, stopping by, the unpardonable asshole, in his uniform, in his colonel's uniform *and his goddamn* olive-drab car *to find out why she* hasn't been to church *because he doesn't have enough fucking sense to know that when a woman has a husband who's a crazed chopper jock in Vietnam and she hasn't heard from him in a week when she usually hears from him every day and everybody's saying he's dead so that she believes it because there's this stack of awful* sympathy cards *on the kitchen counter right next to the toaster, the* last *thing, the* very *last thing she wants to see on this planet is some goddamn mournful-faced Army officer getting out of a car in front of her house. She yells at him, she cries, she beats the door, she threatens him with death, she promises severe damage to his genitals and worse, she kicks in the screen and two panels of glass at the bottom.*

"Mizz Marvicsin, please, what is it?"

"You asshole! You inconsiderate asshole!"

"Mizz Marvicsin, please, *what have I* done?"

The ides of March wasn't the only memorable day during that month in 1966. The Mavericks had much else to occupy them, as the tempo of the war began to quicken yet again.

The first of the major increases in troop strength that had started six months earlier were being felt. America was not exactly jumping into Vietnam, it was plodding in, like walking through heavy mud, step by inexorable step. Not many there knew the myth of Sisyphus, but they felt the same kind of unending fatigue and futility. They pushed the boulder up the hill unendingly, flew combat missions every day and every night, hundreds of hours, until time became a blur of takeoffs, landings, tracers, deadly sparkles in the sky, people coming back shot up, people not coming back at all.

They all kept score. Every pilot, every gunner, each with his own hideously necessary tally. They kept score like the folks back home did, by the sacred body count. How many did you get today? Ten? Fifteen? How many did they get? They got Wilson, Evers, and that tall quiet crew chief, the one whose girlfriend just married another guy.

The month of March, coming in as it does like a lion, added much to the ceaseless flow of grotesque events and ghastly images. Example: They patrol fifty feet above the ground. Below them, a VC breaks from the tree line and runs along a paddy dike. Maverick sits in his elevated position, judges him, fires a round of rockets. One hits him right away, directly in the back, before it has a chance to arm. It passes through his frail body, opening him up from the waist. It travels a bit farther yet, hits the ground, explodes.

Things kept happening, spooky things, the kind of things that make you glance over into the corner to see if Rod Serling is standing there with his frozen upper lip and unforgettable voice, narrating. "Presented for your consideration . . . the Vietnam war . . . the grandest of all excursions into . . . the Twilight Zone." Example: In the middle of a paddy dike, an inventive VC has built and concealed a homemade cannon. The essence of elegant simplicity, nothing more than a length of six-inch steel pipe buried in the ground, pointing upward at an angle. It is crammed with C-4 explosive, rocks, chain, bits of metal, old Ba Muoi Ba bottles, tin cans, and assorted debris of impossible description. The poor bastard who rigged it sat there in the jungle for three years with nothing to do but wait for some poor slob gringo chopper jock to fly low-level between the tree lines over that exact spot at just the right altitude. The VC remote-detonates the cannon and blows the tail boom all to hell. Another unscheduled landing.

Example: There is a truck, an American deuce-and-a-half, traveling quietly down a trail in the delta jungle with two of the Mavericks flying low-level escort right above. The poor bastard hits a mine, the truck explodes violently directly beneath them, blowing them both out of the sky. Eagle and Frair had to fly with Maverick, because they were assigned to his chopper. But the copilots, who flew with different AC's every day . . . let's just say that their understandable reluctance to climb into the cockpit with him gradually became evident. They thought he was fucked up, crazy, jinxed, or in league with Satan. Some of them went to the company commander and begged not to fly with him at all.

Every day it became easier for Maverick to believe what Ty had told him. Maverick had received fourteen Air Medals, one for each twenty-five hours of combat flight, most of those in the previous two or three months, the Soldier's Medal, the Purple Heart, and recommendations for two Distinguished Flying Crosses. He'd been shot down way too many times, but everybody realized that from a flying-skill standpoint, he was probably the best pilot they had. What chilled Maverick during the dark of the night was the realization that up until then the war had been pretty slow. What would happen to him when things began to heat up?

Late in the month, the troop buildup gifted them with a gaggle of brand-new gunny pilots, attached to the Twenty-fifth Division. They were assigned to the Mavericks and Cobras for a few days of "practical experience" before the Army unleashed them on the enemy.

Maverick was given the companionship of Major Marion Z. Shanahan, platoon commander. Everybody else was assigned to train W-2's and second lieutenants. Maverick got the platoon commander. And that wasn't the worst of it.

Major Marion Z. Shanahan was a soldier's soldier, like Ty. About forty-one years old, about Maverick's height, a combat veteran, one of the few survivors of probably the most famous battle of the Korean War, holder of a battlefield commission and, rarest of all things, a living winner of the Congressional Medal of Honor. He was low and stocky and leathery, with a pepper-and-salt brush-cut and a pepper-and-salt mustache. His eyes were directly and emphatically blue, his words like machine-gun bullets. He talked fast, he moved fast, like a little bird, in quick jerks. Since he'd won the CMH, he could go pretty much anywhere he wanted, doing public relations for the military. So apparently he really wanted to be in Vietnam, but he sure as shit didn't act like it. He was spooked, and it was obvious. His days were one long cigarette. His nights were one long beer.

The Twenty-fifth had been gracious enough to bring their own aircraft with them. Marion Z. Shanahan's bright shiny Charlie-model Huey even smelled new, just like cars do, only different. It had just come off the showroom floor . . . had only twenty-five Vietnam hours on it. New, faster-engine, new-design, smooth 540 rotor system that already had a reputation for self-destructing at randomly selected moments.

They'd flown just one training mission together, getting the feel of the area, doing some orientation. That same night, in the whirl and clatter of the mess hall, a face swam into view over Maverick's shoulder. The company commander, who hadn't spoken three words to him since his act of stupidity in Cambodia, called him outside.

His eyes were like little tunnels through his face and he wasted no time on conversational niceties. "Listen, Magnet Ass," he said, "we have a mission tomorrow, and it could be a hot one. I want you to fly with Shanahan and show him what it's like when things get crazy. But . . . you will stay back. You will not engage in any solicited action, you will not fire your guns unless fired upon. If that motherfucker gets killed, it's like Audie Murphy gets killed. He's an honest-to-God government-certified war hero, a living legend and winner of the Congressional Fucking Medal of Honor, and if anything happens to him, if he even gets airsick, your entire ass, both cheeks and the little crack down the middle, will belong to me. Now, tell me that you understand."

"I . . . uhh . . . understand. Sir." Fuck me silly with a rubber duck.

Morning on the flight line. No sunrise, no glowing apricot splashes against the horizon. The dawn does not come up like thunder. It comes up like wet toilet paper, low dirty clouds and dampness and heavy air. But Shanahan's brand-new Charlie-model Huey, well, they just fire it up and it purrs aloft, upward into the Asian day, young, juicy, and full of energy, not tired and abused like the *Littlest Maverick.* The new chopper floats them, wafts them just under the drooping overcast well behind the flight of gunships, on the way to the area of operation. Smooth. Very smooth.

Ahead, the gunnies drop in for their first run. Maverick, flying from the left seat, holds position, loitering at the edges of the formation, calm and clearly out of danger . . . until the world blows up.

Gunfire erupts from the ground, tracers, big ones, little ones. The ship lurches, shudders, jolts, hesitates in the air. Automatic-weapons fire comes rudely through the windshield, through the console, through the radios and instruments, little sharp pieces of . . . *stuff* flying around, exploding, cracking, shattering. It happens in half an instant. Faster than that.

Hydraulics? Don't be silly. Radios? Please.

Maverick screams to find out if everybody is okay, but an inch of the intercom cord dangles from his helmet where it is shot through. He looks at the frayed end, stunned. Did I just come that close? The crew chief is hit; Eagle, who came along for the ride and should have known better, is returning fire out the side; and Marion Z. Shanahan's eyeballs swell up like a kid's on his first visit to the carnival freak house when he confronts Madame Aurora the Six-Hundred-Pound Bearded Lady. He doesn't believe his eyes.

Make no mistake. Shanahan is anything but a stranger to combat. He's been shot at before, and the ribbons on his chest say that he is without question the bravest of the brave, but that was thirteen years ago and he wasn't suspended helpless two hundred feet in the air. For him, this is a horse of a different wheelbase.

Things are turning ugly. It's not a nice ordinary little shootdown where the engine stops, you pull a standard autorotation, and you bump to the ground. No, this is bad, very bad. They are thoroughly shot to shit, they have no control, but they do have an electrical fire that fills the shattered cockpit with choking, acrid black smoke. Maverick, who learned a thing or two from the sandbag episode, tries to slip the dying machine sideways to blow the smoke out, then turns it away from the LZ to fall into the paddies about a hundred yards from the enemy tree line. The good news is that this time Maverick pulls the autorotation By the Book and the brand-new Huey with the 540 rotor system comes to rest in the rice paddy, soft as a baby blanket. The bad news is that they are less than fifty yards from the enemy position, facing directly into the line of fire.

The chopper pings and pops as the VC bullets rush in. Shanahan is in the right seat, having assumed the grapefruit position so hard you could get juice out of him. Maverick slaps him on top of the helmet. No response. He slaps again, harder.

"C'mon. We gotta unass this thing. Get out!"

Shanahan doesn't move. Maverick falls out the door on the left side, runs around the aircraft, stopping for a second on the other side to help Eagle pull the wounded crew chief out, then throws the cockpit door open and beats on Shanahan's head with both hands, crazed, furious. Enemy fire whistles around him as the chopper takes more hits.

Shanahan's seat belt comes loose, but he is now a man who has just experienced some of that old heavy life-and-death stimulation that war is famous for, and he just sits there, terrified, gasping and wheezing. Maverick grabs a double handful of his fatigues and jerks him out into the wet rice paddy. As they stumble into the water, bullets make silly little splashes around their feet.

Eagle has dragged the crew chief, bleeding from a wound high on his thigh, into the shallow water below the tail boom. By now Shanahan is back, uncurled enough to grab his Korean War-vintage M-1 carbine that he somehow brought with him from the States. Maverick goggles for just a moment, then sends him back to cover the crew chief, away from the line of fire. The air is full of noise and anger and lethal little bees. All the President's gunships make runs overhead, laying down suppressing fire. This is Marion Z. Shanahan they're talking about and he is on the ground in enemy territory and he's taking fire because some semirectal pilot that everybody calls Magnet Ass, and with good reason too, took him out on his very first mission in his brand-new Charlie-model Huey with the 540 rotor system and got his ass shot down, and God help everybody if he receives so much as an insect bite. Maverick huddles on the wet ground, returning fire, calmer than usual in such a situation, because every Caucasian in Southeast Asia, probably including some old Frenchmen left over from Dienbienphu, is coming to the rescue.

Behind the paddy dike they lie in the muck and slime and fire their M-14's as fast as they can. Then Eagle dashes for the cargo door, pulls one of the M-60's off its mount, stands in the ankle-deep water with his pelvis thrust forward, legs braced, gun jutting high and proud from his hip, the imagery so obvious that even Maverick sees it right away, and starts firing like a madman, and God help them if they ever stop, because if they do, even for a second, those motherfuckers are going to pour out of the trees and carry them off like Gypsies do with little babies.

But the VC bullets keep pouring in like donations to those TV evangelists, making *chunk* sounds when they hit the ruined body of Marion Z. Shanahan's brand-new Charlie-Model Huey with the fancy 540 rotor system, only now it's fancy garbage and it's on fire like a motherfucker but they don't dare step away from it because, garbage or not, it's an umbrella that keeps the storm of enemy fire off their heads.

The noise, the shooting, go on. Air strikes are called in and A-7's shatter the sky, appearing from nowhere with an awesome roar fifty feet off the deck, sowing seeds of napalm that blossom into incandescent fire in the trees not a hundred yards away. Hot wind and concussion rush around them. The medevac chopper lowers itself from the sky, hands reach out to lift the screaming crew chief, and he's gone.

The noise, the shooting, go on. The look on Shanahan's face at the butt end of his rifle demonstrates that the whole combat thing has come back to him in a rush. He's home again. Eagle still fires the M-60. It's only been half an hour. It's only been half a lifetime. Then a slick, the Blessed Angel of Mercy in a fevered vision, descends, taking hits like crazy, God from the machine, enfolds them into itself in a blinding swirl of muddy water, and lifts them into the sky.

Marion Z. Shanahan probably knew more about war firsthand than anybody Maverick had ever met. But he rode into Vietnam on the American illusion of the times. Nobody back in The World knew what was really going on. Somehow, to them, it wasn't a "real war." That night Shanahan stood at the bar smiling, with his arm around Maverick's shoulders, telling him of Korea and of what one must do to receive the Medal of Honor. Across the room, the company commander stared at the two of them in silent disbelief.

EIGHTEEN

Another sleepless night rambling through the jungle like a doomed French noble in 1789, rolling around inside the skeleton, another desperate day, another mass of hostile villagers, another shower of shit. Where the fuck were they going? *When would they get there? And what would they do to him when they did?*

Actually, the first several days had gone quickly because he'd been unconscious most of the time, but how many days had there actually been since then? Maverick had slept through most of them, and kept right on sleeping, since for some reason he never had the knack of resting quietly while being hauled in pitch blackness through triple-canopy jungle so thick that he couldn't even see the stars to get his bearings, in a tiger cage on a square-wheeled bamboo cart pulled by a water buffalo. He was exhausted, drifting in and out, having delirious dreams—he dreamt that Dopey was staring at him from the door of the hooch—about Lynn and his children and all the people and places he was certain never to see again.

But now, as his hurts slowly faded and his dark unending distress burrowed down into his bones to set up housekeeping for the long term, and as he began to have faith that the daily ration of rice, sometimes with a few pieces of fish or chicken or other enigmatic substances, wouldn't kill him, at least not right away, and because of the incredibly human facility to adjust to anything, *even standing on your head in shit, certain inimical speculations began to bubble up to the surface of his mind like evil-smelling sulfurous eruptions in a primeval lake of gray mud.*

The very first thought was the least thinkable. It was this: There is no fucking way I can get out of this alive.

• • •

March didn't exactly go out like a lamb. As April began, the filthy weather and the unceasing horror continued. During the first week, the weather was barely marginal in the mornings, but missions were canceled in the afternoon. By the time Maverick's crew landed on that Wednesday, April 6, they were cold and damp and ready for the officers' club. All the choppers on the ground told them that the rest of the crews had already come home.

It had been another heavy operation in Muc Hoa, near the Cambodian border. In the middle of vast miles of elephant grass, in a place called, not surprisingly, the Plain of Reeds, a complete Vietcong hospital had been uncovered. There were over one hundred and fifty beds in the place, medicine, equipment, operating rooms. The troops who first found it bumped their noses on the outside walls before they ever knew it was there, so perfectly was it concealed. From ten feet above, the only way the chopper pilots could find it was when the Special Forces sergeant stuck his head through the roof. Brilliant.

The Vinh Long officers' club was always noisy, but on this particular Wednesday it was noisier than usual. At least until Maverick walked in. The magnitude of the operation had brought pilots in from all over. Cobras and Mavericks based at Vinh Long, Tigers from Soc Trang, Razorbacks from Saigon, a regular family reunion. Everybody in the place had been flying insane hours for days and was unwinding as hard as he could.

But when Maverick opened the door, the conversation died the way it does when the orchestra conductor raises his baton. In the center of this, Dick Fortenberry, dressed in fatigues, sat hunched over a table, staring down at the damp rings on the brown tabletop. He stood out; he and his copilot were the only stationary people in the room.

Neither one of them would look at Maverick. All he could see was the top of Dick's brush-cut, a bit of pink scalp showing through.

"Dick. What's going on?"

"Sit down." His copilot took the hint. The opposite chair was suddenly empty, and warm. Around them, the tide of conversation began to flow once more.

"Davey Moore is here, from Soc Trang." Dick still hadn't looked up. "I gotta tell you what he told me." The tabletop still held a hypnotic fascination for him. He wouldn't meet Maverick's eyes.

"Dick, what?"

"Ty is dead."

Maverick just looked at him. "Say that again."

He said it again. "Ty's been killed."

Down at the bottom of his feet, Maverick felt a curious numbness, not a tingle like when things fall asleep, but a deadening that quickly chilled its way upward.

"Moore!" Maverick yelled as he stood up. The place got quiet again.

Davey stood up from the table behind him. He was thinner than when Maverick had seen him a few months back. Dark circles under his eyes matched the color of his brush-cut. He wisely stayed on the far side of his table.

"Where'd you hear this shit?" Maverick demanded.

"Everybody's heard, Maverick."

"Everybody's heard *what?*" They faced each other like gunfighters on the dusty street of an old western town.

"Well . . . the story."

"What story? What story?" Maverick leaned forward, knuckles down on Moore's table. "Tell *me* the goddamn story."

Troops scattered from the table as though Black Bart had just pushed open the saloon's swinging doors and swaggered in, looking for some sucker to take him on.

Davey waited till Maverick sat down across from him. They looked at each other through sunken eyes, faces gaunt, more weary than anybody should be at twenty-five. The numbness in Maverick's legs worked its way just a bit higher. He felt like he was dying by degrees.

"Well, you know how much shit the Cav has been taking up around Bong Son." Everybody knew. Up there, nobody said anything about "advising" the ARVN or about "police actions." Up there, they were all fighting an honest-to-God war almost twenty-four hours a day.

And then Moore proceeded, in a flat voice, to tell Maverick about the death of his best friend.

"It was about a week ago," he said. "Ty's unit inserted two platoons into a landing zone up in the highlands. It was a typical operation."

Everything was easy as Sunday morning, all the troops were on the ground, all the choppers were away, and the NVA were mouselike in their quietness . . . at least until they opened up with practically every weapon in the eastern hemisphere. Machine-gun fire sputtered across the clearing, cutting men in half. Mortars rained down. There was no time to dig, no place to go. They were surrounded, ambushed.

Most were killed where they stood. The rest screamed for medevac, they screamed for air support, they screamed for gunships, they screamed to be pulled out. They just screamed.

"None of the slick pilots could go back in but Ty. He was the only one. In the middle of all the fire and all that smoke he flew his chopper right through all that shit, slammed it to the ground, and started taking guys aboard."

Davey stopped, licked his lips, took one more gulp from his long-neck beer bottle, went on.

"Maverick, those guys just about ate that chopper alive. When Ty took off there must have been twenty of them aboard, hanging on the skids, falling out the doors. Ty pulled it into the air somehow, but there was no way he could carry all that weight. The ship took dozens of hits, and when some of the guys got shot and fell off, he managed to get a little more altitude.

"When he was about fifteen feet off the ground, the chopper rolled over in the air and exploded."

Davey stopped talking again. He took another nervous sip. Maverick just sat there feeling the freeze as things began to sink in. Davey smiled, a halfhearted movement of the lips, and went on.

"When Ty was trying to pull the chopper up, he was taking hits big-time. Somebody said he was hit himself. But just before the explosion they heard him screaming on the radio, 'Fly, you motherfucker, fly!' "

Maverick smiled, though he had no reason to. It was just like Ty.

"Ty's dead?" He had to ask one more time. Had to.

"Yes. He is. It's the truth. I'm sorry."

When Davey said that, the freeze spread upward in a rush, engulfing him, kicking him in the stomach. He felt like he weighed eight hundred pounds. He felt like there was a metal band tightening itself around his forehead. He screamed, "No! No! No!" over and over. He heaved himself to his feet, jumped over the table, and tried, like ancient kings, to kill the messenger. Hands were on him at once, lifting him outside into the afternoon dampness. Somebody gave him a water glass full of bourbon, and he drank the whole thing. They put him to bed when he passed out.

He was so crazed and depressed and outraged and hurt that they grounded him and he spent four days stalking the compound, all his crazies boiling on the surface. Nobody could go near him. He was so manic that he bribed a grunt platoon sergeant to take him out on a foot patrol, just to see what it was really like in the jungle. Somewhere inside, he hoped they would walk into some shit and he'd be killed. Those days and weeks became a blur. Inside, he had turned to wet cement from the waste of it all. That whole country and all the people in it weren't worth one Ty Hisey.

Ty's death was a turning point for him. Ty had personified the grand tradition of the warrior class, something every kid understands when he grows up dreaming of becoming the Duke. Ty made Maverick feel, back then at least, that they were heir to a long and cherished history, a part of human culture since the most ancient of men marked himself with the blood of his prey and returned to the campfire to receive his just glory and adulation. It was the same code Maverick unconsciously lived by, but he hadn't realized it or verbalized it until Ty gave him the "medals-and-glory" speech.

In 1966 there were tens of thousands of troops in Vietnam who most emphatically didn't want to be there, but there were others who most emphatically did. Most of them had bought into the Pay Any Price, Bear Any Burden idealism of the New Frontier. They asked what they could do for their country, and the country said, "Step right this way." Then Vietnam showed them a kind of New Frontier they never expected to see and sent them home with shattered ideals, shattered bodies.

But Maverick had come along too early for the Kennedy years. He was a child of Eisenhower, a child who remembered waiting up for his father and uncles to come home from the Big One, Doubleya Doubleya Two, who remembered all the family being there when they arrived, who remembered the homecoming, the uniforms, the sands of Iwo Jima, the medals, the glory.

Maverick's patriotism, ideals, standards, concepts of service, or whatever you call it dated from before 1960. They dated, now that he thought about how nicely Ty had laid it bare, from practically the dawn of time. It was not a fad, not the sudden flush of a generation's sentiment, but something more deeply rooted, more interior, more ancient, more fundamental than whatever drove the others, no matter how old they were.

Ty couldn't be gone. Not him, of all people. He, and what he stood for, had been around far too long. If you're a professional soldier and you do everything right, you don't die.

But even as Ty was killed, he taught Maverick one last paradoxical lesson. Dying is one of the things a soldier knows best how to do.

Tyrone Hisey got his medals. The Distinguished Flying Cross for piloting resupply missions to a unit trapped by enemy fire. The Bronze Star, all the Air Medals.

Ty got his medals. The Vietnamese Cross of Gallantry with Palm and the only medal nobody wants, the Purple Heart for the wound that killed him.

Ty got his medals. But his glory, the recognition he felt he deserved, knew he deserved, did not exist then and exists now only dimly. It can be found, if at all, in very few places.

On Panel 6E, Line 64 of that long, low black shiny wall.

And here.

Before he heard about Ty's death, Maverick had been friendly with almost everybody in the platoon. He felt close to Eagle and Frair, had been with them long enough to know he could depend on their experience and reactions. Besides, Eagle was the best goddamn shot with an M-60 he'd ever seen. He saw Dick often. He felt like part of a team, a group of Americans banded together for a common purpose. He dimly realized that in war it doesn't pay to care too much. You'd hang your ass out for a guy because you needed to know that he'd do it for you. But as soon as you'd seen all the pictures in his wallet and knew the names of his wife and kids, you closed the door. Maverick had never been able to do that. He tried to stay open.

But after Ty was killed, well, rage and anger and blood lust took over. During the last three months of his tour he became stupidly fearless. And isolated. The more VC he killed, the more he wanted to kill. He took bigger chances, he hung his ass out ever further, he pushed the edges of the envelope in every direction. He could have destroyed the entire population of Southeast Asia with his rockets and flex kits and grenades, then gotten down on his hands and knees to pull up every bush, every tree, every blade of grass with his teeth, and still have felt unvindicated.

They let him be. He was a veteran pilot, sensational with the rockets, and he somehow kept from getting shot down anymore. When he got into the short time, though, with only a few weeks to go before his return to the States, they started to hold him down. Less combat, more Ash and Trash. Good policy, considering everybody's fear of the Supreme Irony. Get your ass killed with two days left on your tour, which is the scariest thing of all. They all knew somebody who had just five days and a wakeup to go and made the trip home lying down instead of sitting up.

They kept him out of combat, which made him furious, but not out of the air, which made him less furious. So his limited-combat status made him the perfect choice to fly Frank Harvey when he showed up. Harvey was a writer, working on a book about aerial combat in Vietnam, fresh off a few weeks on an aircraft carrier. He came to Vinh Long to go in for the close-ups.

Frank was a combat expert, having already written aviation books and articles for major publications. He was also a hundred and fifty percent behind the war, believing mightily in the rightness of the American presence and the superiority of the American cause and the capability of the American hardware. On this trip he was gathering material for a book entitled *Air War: Vietnam* and had gotten permission to fly night reconnaissance with the gunnies. The men who looked after such things figured he wouldn't be in much danger, and with the precious naiveté usually reserved for children and others of undeveloped insight, they assigned him to fly with Magnet Ass. They had surely forgotten the little episode with Shanahan.

It is cool the night that Frank loads his six-foot-two, white-haired frame into the back of the chopper. The three gunships aren't supposed to be looking for any action, so they fly him to a free-fire zone to show him how to do gun runs. The first two ships pick an area for target practice and Maverick stays in close so Frank can have a good look. And he's looking as hard as he can, jammed up in the cockpit, between the front seats, grinning. Ahead, the fire team breaks for the run. Rockets go down, motors glowing orange in the night. Tracers pour downward like water from a garden hose. And look, tracers pour back up the same way and the next thing they know they're in the middle of the goddamnedest firefight. Frank's grin disappears as he scrabbles out of the cockpit back into the cargo area, holding on to whatever sticks out from the walls.

Eagle's voice on the intercom: "Maverick, you should see this old guy."

He doesn't have time to look, but then Harvey's face appears forward once again, eyes glowing like headlights on a dark country road, skeletal knuckles white as his hands grip the backs of the seats for support. He looks all around, his head a constant swivel as tracers fly back and forth, as the ship sprays rockets and flex-kit fire into the night. Combat! Action! Holy goddamn, we're getting *shot at* and isn't it *great?* What a story! He never got to see this back on the aircraft carrier.

He's scared, excited, thrilled, and crazed all at the same time. Just like the rest of them.

Maverick's tour ended in mid-July 1966. When he got on that Caribou to fly to Saigon and take the Big Freedom Bird home, he could only marvel at the changes he'd seen in just twelve months. The buildup that had started in mid-1965 was now at full flood. Troops were pouring in, and guns and money and huge rust-red steel containers of matériel. By comparison, that first shipment of troops was a small fraternity party. It was obvious that the level of the war was rocketing skyward like never before. There were more NVA troops, more firepower. Areas that had been safe were suddenly dangerous, complete with radar-guided antiaircraft guns. The VC couldn't make those in their hooches. He felt like he was deserting, getting out just when the war was becoming real.

The morning light through the transport's window made a bright pool in front of him, picking out the small square white box he held on his lap. On the top, a scribbled message in black marker bore the traditional admonition against peeking before Christmas. Frair and Eagle had run onto the plane and tossed it to him just before takeoff. He tore open the box. Inside, he found a small piece of unauthorized military booty. It was the handgrip from the cyclic of the *Littlest Maverick,* ripped from its mountings and presented to him gift-wrapped, a fond remembrance of what he was leaving behind. He couldn't decide whether to mourn or rejoice.

The Caribou started to taxi. From the window he could see Eagle and Frair standing on the flight line next to the chopper.

The *Littlest Maverick* had a big red X hanging in the windshield—grounded for repair. A key component was being smuggled out of the country.

The aircraft shook and made the kind of noise you never hear if all you fly is commercial. It was time to go, but Maverick could easily have stayed. When he'd arrived he was sure that he would see the end of the war. After all, everybody said that all they had to do was clean up the situation and go home. Fix up those politicians in Saigon, win some hearts and minds, use a little superior machinery and firepower to wipe out all those little bastards in the jungle, and besides, what harm could they do with their black pajamas and antique weapons? Shit, they didn't even have shoes. Well, Maverick thought, it wasn't that simple. It might take the rest of the month.

But like the man who plays the slot machines, certain that just one more quarter will give him the jackpot, he thought that if he could fly just a few more missions, stay one more month, one more week, everything would be wrapped up nicely. But so far, nothing had been resolved. So far, Ty had died for no particular reason. The war had taken a lot out of him, taken a lot away. It had stolen his compassion, stifled his emotions, drawn him apart from his fellows. It had shown him some of its faces, not all, but some. It had told him things he didn't really want to know, things we'd all be better off not knowing, since nobody ever seems to learn the horrible lessons gained at such a horrible price. He was afraid that if the war lasted much longer, they'd make him come back. He was even more afraid that he'd want to.

NINETEEN

Just outside Mansfield, Ohio, in the middle of another kind of rolling green land, two straight roads cross each other precisely. On one corner there is a plain square clapboard country church. It is perfectly white and it stands out sharply, clearly defined edges of country rectitude against a crisp deep blue sky. The colors are deep and meaningful, the image has a shine to it, like the glossy polished back of a postcard. Behind the church, low rows of aged gravestones sit like broken teeth in the grass. Ty's marker stands out. It is the newest.

It is July, it is hot, and Ty's mother stands in the small graveyard, holding Maverick's arm. He remembers her from his childhood when Ty lived around the corner. She was pretty back then, average height, with light brown hair worn short. Fair skin, good cheekbones. Now her hair is longer, and grayer, now the laugh lines have turned to wrinkles, the sparkle in her eyes is caused by her tears, and her joy has been leached away, replaced by a cruel dull dead grief.

Mostly this day they stand together in silence. She says little, but does ask Maverick one question. She wants to know what Ty gave his life for. After all the demonstrations, the riots and the controversy, she wants to know whether or not Ty's life was wasted. She wants to know if she lost her son for nothing.

Maverick truly doesn't know. After seeing all that poverty and suffering and death and horror, he can't honestly tell her whether anybody would ever be able to help those people, and he certainly couldn't tell her with a straight face that they had advanced the ideals of democracy among the Asian peoples. He was just . . . doing his job, for all sorts of reasons that he can't find words for. But now, for the first time, it bothers him that he doesn't know, that he doesn't have an answer for this woman who stands next to him, a mother looking down at the grave of her young son, the most tragic of sights.

She needs to know. Maverick needs to know. He needs to know whether all those lives and all that equipment and all that money and all that agony were for anything. He needs to know whether Ty Hisey has died for nothing, whether he himself has wasted a year of pain and being wounded and being shot down.

He almost hopes they send him back. It is the only way to give Ty's mother an answer to her question. She deserves it.

For now, he doesn't answer her. He can't tell her he doesn't know and he can't tell her he does. He can't tell her that Vietnam is a fucked-up place and they fight for the same hill, the same clearing, over and over again. He can't tell her *the* truth, but he does tell her *a* truth.

He tells her the one thing he knows for certain. He tells her that if Ty had to do it all over again, he would.

TWENTY

All through the first tour, all through the second tour, I've written to her every day, every *day, but now how long has it been since the letters stopped coming? Days, maybe* weeks *now, she hasn't heard from me after I've been writing her like a good boy. One summer when I was at camp they wouldn't let you into the dining room unless you showed them the postcard to your mother that you'd written that day. I tell her not to worry but she knows me well enough, she knows what I really mean, especially this tour, which, frankly, looks to be ending, and very badly, too, and* then *what will she do with the kids, little Michael and little Scott and Lynn alone in some small Texas town?*

Where's Daddy, Mommy, when is he coming home?

As Yogi Berra might say, it was déjà vu all over again. When Maverick arrived back in The World, the first place they sent him was Fort Wolters, Texas. As a TAC officer.

The base was teeming with khaki. Sixteen months before, he'd left behind a nice quiet little military installation in a nice quiet little town with about a hundred training helicopters and two companies of nice quiet little warrant-officer candidates who flew and did push-ups all day. But in late summer 1966 the air was black with choppers, as though the dreaded thousand-year locust had made its way up from South America and was preparing to devastate the central plains of Texas. And below, ten companies of helicopter-pilot hopefuls, with two or three hundred candidates per company, hit their braces and did their push-ups, just dying to get into that Southeast Asian action they'd heard so much about.

The people, the landscape, the whole panorama had . . . intensified. Vietnam was chewing up chopper jocks at a horrifying rate, and spitting them out in shreds. If you were a male of any species, had warm blood, breathed air, and walked upright, you could probably have gotten through the course at Fort Wolters in 1966, because so many of the pilots that Maverick went through with no longer had warm blood and no longer breathed air.

The fresh-faced TAC officers with zero hours of flight time were gone. The ones Maverick met were, like him, veteran pilots with hundreds of hours under conditions far removed from the amicable flat countryside, and country folk, of central Texas. The people of Mineral Wells had never shot at them. Never.

By late 1966 the Warrant Officer Hall of Fame had been long established at Fort Wolters, and boasted a dispiriting number of memorial plaques and pictures. There was an honor scroll with Ty's name on it, and Jim's and Bennie's and far too many others. Only sixteen months ago they were all just a bunch of little boys learning how to fly. Maybe they'd be sent to that Vietnam thing or maybe they'd wind up in Europe or somewhere. Not anymore. By this time, they all knew just where Vietnam was and knew the names of all the cities and rivers and hills and provinces and they had heard enough war stories to last them till they went out and created their own and they left central Texas knowing more about that remote place than they knew about their hometowns.

They knew just what it would be like in Vietnam. They had no idea what it would be like in Vietnam.

When he began his assignment as a TAC officer, Maverick was the junior man in the training company. About three weeks after he reported, he'd had enough time in grade to be promoted to WO-2 and three days later his direct commission came through. Suddenly, thanks to his Cambodian misadventure, he was a lieutenant, second in command of the company, outranking men who had outranked him the day before. It is the severest type of discomfort the military can inflict outside of battle.

Fort Wolters was full of second lieutenants, most of whom had come from OCS or ROTC programs. Brand-new officers, brand-new aviator candidates, still shiny. Unblooded.

So Maverick was in an unusual, uncomfortable position. Since he didn't go to Vietnam as a lieutenant, since he'd received a battlefield commission, he'd never been to OCS or

ROTC. Or even college, for that matter. He didn't have much to say to his fellow officers.

The day after his commission came through, he pinned his brand-new butter bars on his flight jacket and went to lunch in the officers' club. As a warrant officer, he'd always had officers' privileges, but it felt different, somehow, to sit at the table by himself.

Just as he finished the macaroni and cheese and started on the chocolate cake in the little green plastic dish, he sensed a buzz of discomfort behind him. His chair scraped back as he looked at the cafeteria line. A gaggle of brand-new aviator-candidate second lieutenants shuffled along in clumps, back-to-belly, whispering to each other. He glanced at them once, then again when a tallish sandy-haired figure degaggled himself and took one, then two hesitant steps forward.

"Lieutenant," he stammered, looking down at Maverick, "please don't misunderstand me . . . I don't mean to be a smart-ass or anything, but that leather patch with your wings on it there? Well, you're not supposed to put that on until . . . umm . . . *after* you graduate from flight school."

Having gotten it all out, he shifted from one foot to the other, glanced right and left, tugged at his shirtfront.

Maverick looked up at him, a forkful of crumbly brown cake halfway to his mouth.

"Really?" He began to tingle, sensing the onset of a classic *faux pas,* the kind of blunder that would follow Second Lieutenant—Maverick glanced at the man's twitching nameplate—Tully for the rest of flight school, if not for the rest of his life. The kind of "did-you-hear-what-Tully-did" story that his classmates would tell again and again with ever-increasing relish. The kind of personal fuckup that, if it happened in Vietnam at midnight, they'd know about from the delta to the DMZ by morning. He summoned deep reserves of strength to keep himself from smiling. The poor bastard was on the hook. Maverick couldn't wait to reel him in.

"No shit?" he continued, putting down his fork and looking around the room, trying his damnedest to appear fearful, to keep the giggles from sputtering out from between his lips. "Jesus, what would happen to me?"

There were no second-lieutenant pilots at Fort Wolters. A lot of firsts, but all the seconds were just like this uncomfortable, courageous wretch. They were all just candidates. Aspiring chopper jocks with an itch for the action. Whale shit.

"I don't know," replied Tully. He put his hands on the back of the chair across from Maverick and leaned forward, bringing his sandy hair and broad forehead closer. "But they won't let you off easy. Especially those asshole TAC officers."

He must have thought Maverick was some sort of overzealous, dewy, virginal candidate who'd gone to the bookstore, bought his flight computer, pencils, legal pads, and pilot's wings and brought them all proudly back to the barracks to spread them out on his bunk.

"I'd take 'em off before somebody sees them and gives you a hard time. We don't need to be doing any more push-ups than we already are, know what I mean?"

"Roger that," said Maverick. "I don't need no shit from those assholes. I guess I'd better get rid of the goddamn thing right now, huh?" He put down his fork, pushed his chair back, and stood up, glancing around once more, looking back at Tully with what he hoped was a grateful "we-Army-aviator-candidates-have-to-look-out-for-each-other" expression.

He peeled off his jacket. On his shirtfront, of course, were five—count 'em—five rows of the most colorful campaign ribbons and citations the Army and the Republic of Vietnam could bestow upon their soldiers, red ones and green ones, a purple one, some with stars, some with V devices for valor, a stunning display, the size of a polo field, topped off by honest-to-God silver Army aviator wings with lots of mileage on them.

The English language, rich in so many thrilling ways, pregnant with so many possibilities, has no word, no phrase, no idiom for Second Lieutenant Tully's inward emotion or outward expression when this spectacle was presented to him. If you had a long, heavy plank of some incredibly dense wood like teak or mahogany and swung it into the center of his forehead, using a healthy windup, getting your shoulders and torso behind it, putting plenty of wrist into it just at the second of impact . . . No, too gentle. Forget it.

Some pundits use the word "klong." A klong is a sudden rush of shit to the heart, like the way you feel when you're sitting in the movies about seven-thirty P.M. and suddenly remember you invited the boss and his wife over for dinner at seven that night. Tully had one of those: an obvious, prolonged, fervent klong. Waves of shit rushed to his heart. Silverware hit the floor behind him. His fellow Army aviator candidates hooted and shrieked. His color became as a summer sunset. His mouth made onomatopoeic motorboat noises. His appetite disappeared. Slowly Maverick put his jacket back on.

When Maverick came face-to-face with his first Cobra, there was the smell of fog, the heavy wetness of a cool, moist Georgia morning. The sight quickened everything in him that was a pilot.

Here, at last, was the AH1-G, the gunny's great American dream machine. Anybody who had ever flown in Vietnam wanted a chopper just exactly like this. It was perfect. It was a vicious beast made of metal, crouching on the misty ground, floating almost, fog rolling around its belly, stroked by smoky fingers. It was the most menacing, most appallingly wicked contrivance he'd ever seen. If form follows function, this creature's every line and curve proclaimed its predatory purpose.

As the war had expanded past the first thousand days, then the second, the shortcomings of the Huey as a gunship continued to become fatally obvious. It was fat and it was slow. Perfect for cargo and troop transport, but never intended for cruel use as a gunship. Every chopper jock in the Army knew that a new machine was in the works, and now Maverick, after almost a year at Fort Wolters, had been chosen to attend one of the first Cobra flight schools in Georgia.

He felt like he had been ushered into The Presence. He was looking not only at the machine he thought would save him from certain death in the jungle sky, he was seeing something of a modern miracle. The powers that be, having realized almost at once that the Hueys could go only so far in fighting an Asian jungle war, began designing a new kind of airborne weapons system almost from the start. But the American military-industrial system being what it is, you just don't get on the blower to Bell Helicopter and tell them you'd like to pick up a totally new kind of chopper by the end of the day, or could they have it ready by lunch?

It takes ten years to put a new war machine in the field, what with all the initial concept work, preliminary drawings, design, specifications, bidding, congressional wrangling, committee debate, nay-saying, horse-trading, politicking, lobbying, dinner-buying, budgeting, budget cutting, boondoggling, funding approval, prototyping, designing, crashing, cost overruns, debugging, tooling, manufacturing, testing . . . and then if the thing didn't do what it was supposed to, well, it wouldn't be the first time.

But they put the Cobra into Vietnam in just under three years, start to finish, and they did it by cramming a bunch of Huey parts into a new package, kind of like the relationship between a Volkswagen Beetle and a Porsche.

The Cobra was essentially a skinny Huey, using many of the Huey's basic components, including the 540 rotor system from the Charlie model and a new turbine engine that could have lifted a sizable residence off its foundations. It was longer, but with a higher profile. From the side it had, despite all its menacing slope-nosed sleekness, much of the grace and all the subtlety of an earth mover. But from the front . . . oh, baby. It was *this* particular perspective that thrilled Maverick to his toenails, a man who had been shot down so many times in one tour that he was amazed every time they gave him a new helicopter.

Seen head-on, the Cobra practically disappeared. It was only three feet wide, except for the stubby stabilizer wings on either side. Two men did the work of four, the pilot seated high in the back, looking over the head of the copilot/gunner in front of him. In the Huey the pilot and copilot sat side by side right up front, directly behind a Plexiglas picture window that extended midway to the floor and even curved under their feet so they could look almost straight down. Here, two men sat in an honest-to-God cockpit, like in a jet, sleek and skinny, no gunner, no crew chief, no more low-and-slow.

The Cobra was as close to a fighter plane as a helicopter could get, faster than the Huey, more maneuverable, more powerful, with a kind of performance that Maverick would not accept until he pulled one up to fourteen thousand feet one day and watched the 707's fly by below him. You could dive it, you could put it into highly unusual attitudes, you could damn near barrel-roll it. In a steep dive, you could glance up through the fighter-style canopy and actually look at the ground through the disk of the rotor blades. In the history of rotary-wing aircraft, the only pilots who had ever seen that sight were the ones in the process of crashing upside down.

It had miniguns and a 40mm grenade launcher on a rotating turret up front, fired by the copilot. It had fixed miniguns on the wings, it had twice as many rocket pods as the Huey, and they would fire high explosive, white phosphorus, fléchettes, chocolate pudding, whatever.

Maverick had a delicious fleeting thought of the Vietcong on the ground, hiding in the jungle, firing frantically, futilely, at his narrow silhouette as he sped directly toward them at two hundred knots, spitting assorted death. He was absolutely dead certain, there on the flight line at Hunter Army Airfield in Savannah, Georgia, that short of a few well-placed tactical thermonuclear devices, this machine would win the war, and he hoped he could get back there before it was all over.

When he saw the Cobra that first day at Hunter, his second tour was a certainty, not because he was overwhelmingly patriotic—though he believed he was doing a job for his country—not because he was consumingly committed to American Asian policy as handed down by the Kissingers and Johnsons and Nixons, not because the Army doesn't teach you to fly a Cobra unless you can fly it someplace that will do them some good. Not even because he was among the first to join a highly select fraternity of Army helicopter pilots.

It was because when he looked at the Cobra he saw an aeronautical miracle, which he admired, and a personal Sword of Retribution, which he lusted for. As a pilot, he was awed by the design, the thinking, the genius that had conceived it. As a human being, he was awed by the possibility of getting one back for Ty, for Bennie, for the Indian kid, for Scott, for Joe, who died screaming, for all those grunts who lay bleeding and oozing, holding their bowels in the back of his chopper. He felt, just for a moment, a twinge of pity for the enemy.

He never thought that he'd be going back to a very different war, and that the enemy had surprises for him, and that he would, ultimately, need all of his pity for himself.

He left for his second tour on May 1, 1968. He flew from San Francisco, like last time. Drunk, like last time.

TWENTY-ONE

Once Maverick allowed himself to think the unthinkable, still more fetid bubbles of ugly thought worked their way up from the depths: If I could escape right now *and get out of the village unseen . . . then what? I don't know where I am—in Cambodia, a mile outside of Hanoi, or halfway to Rumania. I have no flipping idea where an American base is, but I'd bet it isn't right down the block. I haven't heard a chopper in ten or fifteen days. And even if I* did *know where the base was, how far, in which direction, how long would I last in the fucking* jungle *with no food and no shoes and no matches and nothing but a pair of black pajamas? And* then, *if I* did *get to a base, some trigger-happy nineteen-year-old grunt would waste my ass because they waste the asses of* everybody *who comes running toward the base in black pajamas.*

Shit, there's always somebody outside the hooch. They never let me out of the cage and I can't tear out with my bare hands. Even my coveted black belt in tae kwon do, bestowed upon me by Lieutenant Yoon Hee Nam, the chief master instructor of the whole goddamn South Korean Army, mocks me, like the huge rusty lock.

I'm fucked. I'm going to die. I wonder what it will be like.

When Maverick returned to Vietnam in 1968, it was just after the famous Tet offensive and most of the troops fervently wanted to be someplace else. But if they couldn't be someplace else, then the place they wanted to be was Tay Ninh. An ancient city, about sixty-five klicks northwest of Saigon, Tay Ninh had been sacred land since the sun came up for the very first time. Neither side wanted to offend the gods and the Buddhists by smearing it off the face of the earth, like they'd been doing with the rest of the country. Tay Ninh, bless it, was an island, a refuge, not too dissimilar to being home in bed.

And that's where they sent Maverick. But before he even got near the place, he began to see omens, portents that whispered and gibbered in his darker places. Gradually his conviction would grow, gradually he would become more and more certain. He would never, but never, live through his second tour.

The 707 from San Francisco was a bit late taking off, due to a silly little bomb scare, the consequent evacuation and search occupying no more than three and a half breezy, congenial hours. The next day, when the aircraft broke through the clouds over Tan Son Nhut, it was obvious right away that a whole different war was going on down there. First time through, the place made Maverick feel like a college kid on his way to Lauderdale for spring break. Second time through, even before landing, even from above, he felt like he was entering a war zone. Not at all the same sensation.

The base had expanded, grown, burgeoned into a vast military city. Once the small airport of a small Asian capital, it had become without doubt one of the busiest airports in the world. Around the clock, men and matériel poured from the sky in raucous waves of piercing uproar. On the ground itself, Maverick could see nothing but a boundless spreading stain of aircraft, vehicles, machinery, supplies, bales, boxes, pallets, crates, and people.

But there was one familiar touch: the buses still had steel mesh on the windows.

Maverick reported, waited in line here, waited in line there, found that his orders had been changed en route and he was now assigned as section leader to the Third Squadron of the Seventeenth Air Cavalry. Charlie Troop, in Tay Ninh. He didn't care.

Somebody gave him convoluted directions to the officers' quarters, and it took him the rest of the morning to find it. He wandered through the streets and alleys of the military metropolis that Tan Son Nhut had become until he stumbled upon the BOQ about twenty yards behind the sprawling main mess hall, on the far side of a low, light brown sandbag wall. For most of the day, in solemn amazement, he strayed through the complex. He was sure that it grew and multiplied even as he watched, like flowers in time-lapse photography.

That night, Maverick lay awake on a strange cot in a strange land for the second time, the relentless scream of the machines in the air already becoming mere background noise. He was astonished to be so astonished, like the man who returns home after twenty years and wonders how everybody got so old.

If there hadn't been a lull in the air traffic, he never would have heard it: an odd, high-pitched whistling sound at the remotest edge of perception. The pitch changed, it got lower. The volume increased. The sound began to take on ominous overtones, like a freight train, like a tornado, the kind of sound he would hear far away during twister season in central Ohio. A fatally familiar sound that he hadn't heard for a year and a half. It was far away, then closer. Then closer. Too loud for a mortar.

Artillery. Incoming.

The night turned into day around him, the ground lurched beneath, betraying him, like the planet itself had been kicked in the belly. To the right, just beyond the sandbag bunker, a major fraction of the mess hall spasmed skyward in a grand eruption of gorgeously glowing fragments that ejected themselves into the night, flaming and spinning.

Just above his head, the gray tin roof of the hooch peeled up from front to back, lifted off, flew away, leaving him lying on his back, tingling from concussion, eyes wide, dust swirling down onto his face. Through his dead ears, he barely heard the yelling from outside: "Incoming! Incoming!" Well, no shit.

He rolled onto the floor under the one-eighth-inch protection of his government-issue cot and counted the explosions till he couldn't anymore. Back in the first tour, somebody yelled "incoming" and everybody got pissed because their showers were interrupted. But this is the second tour and now the explosions are big and close and loud and real. It was not the welcome he expected.

Up from Saigon, through the window of the Caribou, in the middle of a raw blue sky, Maverick looked down on Tay Ninh and the startling heap of ragged black rock that rose abruptly from the rice paddies three miles to the north.

"Nui ba Den," said the sergeant in the next seat, who saw the question before Maverick could ask it. "The Black Virgin. Never seen it? Well, the situation is this. We own everything around the bottom of the mountain. Own it, no question. On top, there's a Special Forces camp with a radio relay station, so we own that too. But everything in between, well, *they* own it."

"Say again?"

The sergeant leaned forward to stare past Maverick out the window. "The whole middle of the mountain is full of tunnels. We hear that some are so wide you can drive trucks through 'em. In fact, there's a suspicion that a tunnel runs right out of the heart of that thing into Cambodia." He leaned back. "Wouldn't surprise me a bit."

The approach to Tay Ninh took them all around the mountain. Maverick could see cave openings up and down the sides. On top, the isolated Special Forces camp, not much bigger than a suburban residential "homesite," squatted uneasily, a dusty brown smear against the deep green, surrounded by barbed wire and sandbags, bristling with antennas. In the center, on a tall thin pole, a lonely, defiant American flag.

He reported to C Troop, Third Squadron of the Seventeenth Air Cavalry, another precise, anonymous grid of long low buildings, got assigned to a hooch, and started to circulate, getting the feel of the place, meeting some of the troops. It didn't take him long to evaluate the situation. The troop commander was Major Norman Norskin, who seemed mild enough. He looked like the type who stayed behind his desk, buried himself in paperwork, and kept out of everybody's way, but Maverick was ultimately to see him in a different, less flattering light. The exec officer was a little better, a round-faced short guy named Kaskey, with oyster eyes and a damp forehead. There were a few pilots that Maverick had put through Fort Wolters, first-tour pilots, by this time almost ready to return to The World. Familiar faces. He began to feel that things, at first glance, were not too bad. But then he met Garcia.

There were two sections of gunships at Tay Ninh. They called themselves the Assassins. Maverick, by this time a first lieutenant, was to be the leader of one, and First Lieutenant Raul Osberto Garcia de la Vega was already the leader of the other. He was a short, lean, olive-skinned East L.A. Chicano and everything about him was dark, from thick black brush-cut hair to eyes of cold ebony fire. Maverick bought him a few drinks that afternoon, to find out who was who and where the assholes were, and discovered that all the assholes in the squadron, perhaps all the assholes in the Far East, were sitting right in front of him, all rolled into Raul Osberto Garcia de la Vega.

Dark eyes catching every pinpoint of light, hands trembling as he leaned intensely forward, Garcia delivered an intense, rambling speech, a discourse, an oration, an address, a harangue, like the kind you can get out of religious fanatics if you know how to stir them up. It made no sense, but it was brilliantly performed. All about how he'd gotten out of the barrio under his own power, received a commission through ROTC, and was happy as shit that the war was being held in his honor, practically, for the sole purpose of giving him the chance to show what "his people" could do. The more he talked and the more stories he told about his combat experiences, the more Maverick realized that the man was a dangerous maniac, certifiable in any society but this. It was evident that he believed his bravery could best be demonstrated by leading his men into the kind of lunatic kamikaze situations where even the Light Brigade would ask for a time out and a glass of shandy. He was also, however, the unit instructor pilot and outranked Maverick by about a week. Another omen. He should have been wearing a sign with hundreds of tiny blinking bulbs around the border, like a theater marquee, powered by a backpack battery, saying, "Hello, I'm thoroughly demented and dangerously suicidal."

In no time, Maverick discovered that Garcia, understandably, had no friends. None. In fact, an insidious undercurrent of talk had it that if any man on the base believed he could get away with it, one of those fragmentation grenades would somehow find its way under Garcia's bunk and when it went off everybody would just roll over and sleep through it. He was a marvel, a classic, like Erich von Stroheim, who used to play sadistic Prussian generals in the silent movies: the Man You Love To Hate.

Maverick needed only a few days to get up to speed. Military procedure dictated that he take a checkout ride with Garcia in the Charlie-model Huey they were still flying. The new Cobras hadn't arrived yet. It seemed odd to Maverick that, with all the flying he'd done, he'd flown this model only once before—the time he demonstrated to Shanahan what helicopter aviation is like from the ground up.

He also had to take a series of check rides with Garcia to get familiar with the area. Garcia was crazy, but he wasn't insensitive, and he picked up right away during the discussion in the bar that Maverick had the same reaction to him that everybody else had, and since Maverick was the other section leader, Garcia would have viewed him as competition even if he weren't a manic suicidal psychopath. It was hate at first sight, so naturally he tried to bust Maverick's nuts on the check rides, but it took only three or four seconds for Maverick to demonstrate what a year of combat flight experience could do for your flying skills. Garcia pushed as hard as he dared, but could find no fault.

And so, off to war. It had been a year and a half, but some things never change. People still wondered what they were supposed to be accomplishing, only now there were more people doing the wondering. They still flew Hueys, they still ran fire teams of two and usually three ships. The tactics, the procedures, the land, the dying—all the same.

But Tay Ninh wasn't like the south. It was hills and jungle and elephant grass and rice paddies and rubber plantations. And one huge, menacing mountain.

They weren't escorting major troop insertions into LZ's anymore. The mission was different. This time it was "target of opportunity," which means hunter-killer-search-and-destroy-fly-around-all-day-and-if-it-moves-shoot-it.

Procedure: the Light Observation Helicopter would go out, circle a target area at very low altitude, which was the only way you could see anything on the ground anyhow, and try to draw fire. It was the kind of exciting, challenging, pulse-quickening job that is available only in wartime. Hueys fluttered above, waiting for the enemy to be so unconscionably stupid as to fire on the LOH. When he or she did—and they had to sooner or later—the Hueys swooped like falcons, not with talons but with rockets, miniguns, grenades, M-60's. Some of this was very much like before, when they'd scoot around the paddies hoping for a few bullets to reach up at them.

This time, though, with their platoon of blues on standby for immediate reaction, they were *looking.*

And finding diddly. The first few days Maverick flew out of Tay Ninh as an aircraft commander, all he saw were empty bunker positions, abandoned camps, all the places the enemy had been, but no place the enemy was.

Was it always going to be like this? At least back at Vinh

Long there was something going on. Call it an anti-omen, the serenity before the inevitable tempest. Before too long, in fact very soon, Maverick would be up to his ass and well past it in enemy, fervently wishing he weren't.

TWENTY-TWO

To pass the time, he talked to himself incessantly. That's how he knew that things were getting very bad: he started to refer to himself in the past tense. He had pretty much given himself up for dead, convinced that the Americans couldn't possibly be looking for him. Where would they look? He'd been shot down close to the border, so he could be anywhere inside Cambodia or North Vietnam by now. No, what he hated was the impersonality *of it all. The first new Cobras had arrived in July '68, and the machines, like the men, were interchangeable. That meant you flew a different Cobra every day, with a new copilot. No crew chief aboard, no gunner, no tight little teams. No flying with the same troops, coming to depend on them, knowing what they would do when you were all in the shit. The people were like all the other parts of the machine. Indistinguishable. Expendable.*

Maverick had become Assassin Three Six. The Six meant he was platoon commander, another promotion he got instead of a court-martial when the sniper got squashed. Garcia had been sent home, after they took him off flying status and put him in operations. He had become so manic and deluded that nobody would go near him. Kaskey had been promoted from executive officer, but he took a direct hit while sitting on the john during a mortar attack, so Maverick had moved up the line through a combination of talent, luck, and attrition. The pinnacle of his military career and the finale had come sooner than he expected, in a tiger cage in the jungle.

Charlie Troop, Third Squadron of the Seventeenth Air Cavalry, numbered 209 souls. On bad days, there were fewer. The Army divided them into four platoons: aeroscouts, the hunters; aeroweapons, the killers; aerorifles, the grunts; and service—maintenance, supply, and so on.

They were a proud bunch. They boasted the highest body count, they found more weapons caches, staged more ambushes, and kicked more ass than anybody. So they believed, and so they boldly said to anyone who would listen. Each platoon had its own particular kind of *esprit de corps.* The blues, for example, all fifty-seven of them, were dirty, bearded, and combat-crazed, with bandannas around their heads and dark holes where their eyes should have been. They knew who they were, why they were there, and what they had to do. No existential angst in any of these young lads, no "what are we doing in this war," no *weltschmerz,* no hell-no-we-won't-go. Just a bunch of playful lads living in the wonderful world of weapons and liking it there just fine, who held little contests to see which of them could go into battle wearing the most ordnance. They garbed themselves, festooned themselves, with every lethal amulet they could find: M-16's, M-60's, M-79 grenade launchers, shotguns, .45's, grenades, .38's, Claymores, LAW's, antitank weapons, an alphanumeric arsenal.

The blues *loved* the jungle and pursued their missions with an almost priapic passion. When they were turned loose in the underbrush, they killed people, captured weapons, found rockets, seized antiaircraft guns, killed people, confiscated propaganda leaflets and mortar rounds, along with jillions of rounds of American and VC ammo. Once they brought back a ton and a half of American rice in fifty-pound burlap bags, the kind with that cute little hands-across-the-sea drawing on the side and an unintentionally mocking line of copy: "A gift of the people of the United States of America." They crawled into tunnels, something that only a very small group of Americans with slight physical stature and peculiar emotional orientation would even dare attempt. Theirs was the kind of attitude that prompted them to have playing cards printed, the famous cards with the ace of spades on one side and the unit logo—on a blue background a white horse gallops, ridden by an indigo cobra with wings—on the other. These they left pinned to the shirts, the foreheads, or the eyeballs of the enemy dead.

The aeroscout platoon, the "we-find-'em" pilots, were Army aviators too. They flew crews of two men in light observation helicopters, LOH's, except everybody called them loaches. These were sort of half-armed with a pilot-controlled minigun mounted on a pylon that allowed it to shoot straight down. Other than that, they were virtually defenseless except when the observer leaned out the side with his M-16. The pilots flew these machines only *this far* above the treetops and were highly vulnerable to enemy fire. They were hot dogs, and fancied themselves possessed of titanic testicles. Likewise the slick pilots who carried the grunts into battle. They were all brave, all dedicated, all had, more or less, a clear sense of purpose. If they didn't believe in the war, at least they believed in the Army. But the gunny pilots reserved unto themselves an oddly idiosyncratic mystique, one that was strictly the purview of the aviator who is also a combat soldier. They were more like fighter pilots, and would have been perfectly at home in an aircraft-carrier wardroom, shooting the shit with the A-7 jocks.

They all wore the traditional crossed sabers from the caisson days. The more gregarious affected handlebar mustaches and sported flat-brimmed black Stetson honest-to-goddamn cowboy hats with gold braid or silver braid, depending on grade of rank. Very nonregulation, but nobody would dare think of asking that they be removed. Their platoon patch, the badge of the Assassins, the one Maverick wore, boasted a dark-cloaked figure, like something out of a Bergman film, wearing one of those yahoo hats, with burning red eyes revealed beneath the brim. Skeletal hands brandished a saber.

They drank screamin' mimis in the officers' club, a shot of brandy flambé that would, if you didn't knock it back fast enough, set your handlebar mustache afire. They flew by the seat of their pants, they told outrageous lies, and even more outrageous truths.

Poppoppoppop! Poppoppop!

Now, what the fuck was this? It was two o'clock in the muggy morning and these absurd little sounds were coming from somewhere outside the hooch. *Poppop! Pop!* Faintly, then louder. From off to the right at first, then moving across, and closer. *Poppop! Poppoppoppop!* Comical exclamations. Maverick lifted himself up on his elbows in his bunk, puzzled.

He could barely see over the sandbag lower walls of the hooch. Above the wall, he looked through the screening that ran up to the tin roof. Outside, the blackness was suffocating. He couldn't see shit, but he could still hear: *Pop! Poppoppop!*

The screen door stuck a bit as he pushed it to go outside, so he gave it an irritated little shove. The rough wooden step bit into his bare feet. Was this some kind of local Tay Ninh thing that they did here all the time and he just didn't know about it? He was a newby, right? He barely knew where the mess hall was, he didn't know that the screen door would stick, and he for goddamn sure didn't know about these curious sounds in the night. Like a little gun that shoots Ping-Pong balls: *Poppop!*

He strained his eyes toward the ditch that ran diagonally from far to the left around the back of the huge bunker about forty meters from the hooch door. Second tour, you learn to wangle a hooch as close to a bunker as you can get. Let the newbys run through that goddamn mortar mist. Since Tay Ninh was about three times larger than the base at Vinh Long, the bunker was a massive underground affair made from those huge metal Conex containers, sandbagged ten feet down. Full of radios, manned around the clock, it served as the troop command post and was the safest place in the area.

"Hey, what *was* that?" yelled Maverick, turning back over his shoulder. Inside, there were only strangers. He'd been there three days, didn't know anybody, and didn't much want to. First tour, you make friends and they get blown up or shot down or simply never come back. Second tour, you make no friends.

Far off to the left he saw . . . muzzle flashes? Then the funny Ping-Pong noise again. Next, the deadly little bees—*bees!*— flit through the air around him. Ah. Finally, a sound he could understand. Finally, a situation he could recognize. Of course. He was being shot at.

He dropped facedown on the rough wood porch like he'd been poleaxed. Then he started yelling.

"Hey! *Hey!* Some asshole's out here shooting up the fucking place!"

"Don't worry about it," answered a voice from the inside. "It's probably one of those civilian construction workers. They get juiced up and do that all the time."

"They got *weapons?*" Maverick was appalled.

"They buy AK-47 'souvenirs' from the grunts."

Dandy. Maverick had been on the business end of those legendary Russian rifles more than enough times, but he was always in a chopper and never actually heard the sound they made. He heard it this time, though. Getting closer, too.

"Fine," said Maverick. "But these motherfuckers are firing through the hooch!"

Poppoppoppop! Pop!

Flash! The night becomes a blue-white specter as aerial flares incandesce, dangling their harsh radiance on little parachutes, crazily swinging back and forth like bare bulbs in cheap hotels. The shadows lurch and sway. More muzzle flashes appear from farther along the ditch, then come closer. Maverick watches, amazed. Some little bastard is running along down in there, jumping up to empty a magazine, ducking down long enough to slam in a new one, then jumping back up again. Nobody is doing a goddamn thing about it and now he's almost to the hooch and it will be Maverick's turn at the wrong end of the barrel.

The figure sprouts from the ground once more, showing Maverick a small round head with a pith helmet on it. No civilian. A North Vietnamese Army regular, sworn loyal to Ho Chi Minh, high on death.

Maverick's words, had they been uttered, would have been these: "That ain't no fuckin' construction worker!" The words had, in fact, actually been formed. They were there, in process, little electric sparks on their way from the brain to the lips and teeth and throat, just now ready to make the sounds begin. Never had any words been more on the tip of any tongue.

But just then the entire firmament lights up with an infernal eructation of towering orange fire, apricot magnificence shot through with greasy black smoke, ground-shattering rumble, visceral concussion, the Big Bang itself. On the other side of the road, the base's entire ammunition bunker, a chaotic roiling ascendant blaze of glory, utterly ceases to exist.

The impact of exploding atmosphere launches Maverick backward through the screen door, which will never stick again, just as the roof peels back. Torrents of hot metal fragments pour from the air.

It begins to sink in. Even though Maverick has already spent one action-packed year in Vietnam, he's never had this particular experience before, but he suddenly understands the situation. This fucking camp is under attack. There's an NVA shooting at him from a ditch right over here, and no doubt that ammo dump went up because some sapper, fired up on loyalty to the cause, had clothed himself in satchel charges, run in, and pulled himself off for the greater glory of Uncle Ho. Works almost every time.

Now Maverick hears the worst sound he's ever heard in Vietnam. Worse than explosions. Worse than the deadly little bees. Worse, even, than the screams and moans of the wounded strewn on the sickening slick floor of a Huey cargo hold. This sound is simply voices.

Voices that yell: "They're in the wire! They're in the fucking wire!"

The enemy himself, up close and personal. Not hundreds of feet beneath Maverick now, not seen from the relative safety of altitude and distance. Now he's on his way into the camp, trying to overrun the base. The next meeting will be face-to-face.

Everything happens at once. The machine guns start chattering, the Claymores scatter hot little pellets, sounds are dull and cottony, heard through eardrums still sizzling from the impact of the ammo-dump disaster.

World records for the forty-yard low crawl are shattered as Maverick propels himself along the ground from the hooch to the main bunker, knees, toes, and elbows, with every other GI on the base right behind him. People run over his head, up his back, because those motherfuckers are *in the wire,* probably halfway through the camp by now, gaining yardage and racking up first downs like mad.

Down through the crush, Maverick crawls into the bunker, and into another one of those unforgettable radio horror shows, just like before, horrified voices pouring out of the night sky, tinny voices, shrill with fear and pain and damage.

Every radio in the place is turned on, and each tells the same story. Confusion. Pandemonium in the most original sense of the word. The demons are there. Nobody can find the company commander. Nobody can find the troop commander. The TAC frequencies are loaded with screams from the artillery batteries.

"Oh, man! There's a hundred of 'em on the north side. Put the mortars over there!"

"Get some one-five-fives!"

"Shoot direct! Fuck it, shoot direct!"

"Get the beehives!" The barrels of the big guns come down, parallel to the ground, hurling exploding canisters of little nails full in the face of the invasion.

"Oh, shit, man . . . they're comin' in the west side too!"

"Charlie Horse Five, this is Charlie Horse Six, over."

It's Maverick's troop ID. Norskin, the troop commander, God only knows where he is, is calling Kaskey, the exec officer, whose round face, even more moist than usual, reflects the orange underground light in tiny wet sparkles. His eyes swim in their own little puddles.

"Six, this is Five. Go."

"How many gun crews you got sitting there?"

Kaskey scans the room, his face a pale damp full moon, squinting into the eerie orange light.

"I see four pilots."

"Good! Scramble the guns."

Kaskey's damp eyes widen, moons within a moon. Maverick sees stunned disbelief.

"Uhhh . . . say again, Six." And Six is just about to say again when, from another speaker, a shrill scream erupts: "They're on the pads! They're on the goddamn pads!"

Then Six does indeed say again. "Scramble the guns! Get 'em in the air. Now!"

Kaskey looks around again, directly into the face of ranking-pilot-section-leader First Lieutenant Maverick. "What are you gonna do, Lieutenant?"

Fanfuckingtastic. So *this* is what the goddamn bars on his shoulder are for. Garcia and his boys are nowhere to be found, probably in a bunker on the other side of the base, the fucking place is being overrun, the ammo bunker has been blown into an alternate space-time continuum, the radio says that three sappers crawled up the barrels of the eight-inch guns with satchel charges and pulled themselves off, and nobody needs to worry anymore about the enemy being in the wire because they're not anymore. Now they're on the fucking pads!

"Scramble the guns?" says Maverick. "Scramble the *guns?* Do you hear what's going on out there? The gooks are on the goddamn *pads.*"

Kaskey, almost apologetic, would have lowered his chin if he'd had a chin. "Maverick, we gotta get something in the air. We need support up there. The fuckers are all over the place, man, we gotta do it." His voice falls off. "Now."

"Sir," says Maverick, taking a deep breath. Even here, at the beginning of his second tour, even after years in the Army, he vainly believes the situation can be handled with reason, cool heads, and good sense. He already misses the old days back in Vinh Long, where shit like this never happened.

"Sir," he begins again. "The choppers are over half a mile away. We're in our underwear. Do you honestly believe that me and all these people can walk from here to the airfield, cross the fucking runway to the pads on the other side, stroll to our aircraft, fire them up, and get off the ground when there's nothing between us and the airfield but combat and killing and looting and raping and dying and North Fucking Vietnamese? What time next year do you think we'd get there?"

Kaskey just looks at him and delivers his line like it's the end of the act and the curtain is already coming down: "Maverick, it's a direct order. Get the goddamn guns up, and do it now."

Maverick turns, looks around. He sees three other pilots, two crew chiefs, and two gunners. Seven people, still strangers, but now bound to him by a common threat. Ty flashes through his mind. Seven faces look at him. Fourteen eyes say "No fucking way." He takes a deep breath, pulls himself up to all of his five feet, seven and one-half inches, puts his slightly oversize square chin in the air. He has no choice.

"Okay. I'm gonna go. Either you guys'll come along and die like idiots or maybe be heroes, or you'll stay here and get your asses burned because you knew I was going and you didn't come with me." Then, like a good salesman going for the close, he just shuts up and waits.

There is a lot of glancing back and forth. At a boardroom table they would have shuffled papers and poured glasses of water with trembling hands. At the prom they would have clustered and elbowed, trying to decide who would ask the Dream Girl for the next dance. One stands up. Then another; then they all do.

Maverick starts breathing again, calls the troop commander and asks for a deuce-and-a-half truck. He pities the poor bastard who'll have to drive it over. Then he turns to the crews.

"Back to your hooches, get your gear, and be back here in five minutes." They go outside into the maelstrom.

Minutes later the crews straggle back through the fire and explosions, running hunchbacked with all the weapons they can carry. A big green truck is rumbling in front of the bunker. Inside, Maverick discovers a trembling driver with short blond hair, nineteen, wide-eyed, white-knuckled.

"What's going on, Lieutenant?" he shrieks.

Maverick pulls himself up to the window. "We're going to the airfield."

The kid's eyes get wider, his hands strangle the steering

wheel. "Hey, I'm not going to the airfield. You may be going to the airfield, but—"

"Forget it," yells Maverick. "Get out of the fucking truck." He jumps down and wrenches the door open. "No sense in you getting your ass blown away too. C'mon. Out." The kid comes down. Around them, flashes, noises, screaming in the night, cold swaying light of flares in the sky, dust, whirlwinds of confusion, anger, fear.

Maverick turns to the crews. "Give me an M-60 on the hood and one out the back and one on either side of the son of a bitch and everybody else lying down flat in the bed." More asses and elbows, then Maverick pulls himself up and spreads his arms across the big black steering wheel. With a shudder the truck lurches forward, creeping through the chaos toward the airfield, toward the enemy.

That old Italian-movie feeling starts coming back, like sitting in a time capsule, like being at one of those marine parks where you can stand and watch the big fish swim behind the glass, they in their world, you in yours. Here, too, it is happening behind glass. All the fire, all the noise, all the fury of the night is out there. But in here, Maverick hunkers down inside his flak vest, inching the truck along. Stray bullets hit, one creasing the hood a foot in front of him. The M-60's in the back jabber in response.

Through all the roar, he hears, from the back of the truck, the ancient soldiers' litany, a low sound, a chant that was traditional at the time of the Trojan Horse: "I don't believe this shit. I don't believe this fucking shit."

But the real trouble doesn't start until they get to the runway. When Maverick pulls up, he looks out toward the strip like Moses looking at the Red Sea before he found out what kind of show God was going to put on.

The runway is a highway of PSP running north and south. They pull up to the west side, but the helicopter pads and the enemy, they think, are on the east. Can't drive across the runway because there's a big ditch on either side. Could drive all the way south on the perimeter road, which comes dangerously close to the enemy-laden wire, then back north again. Not a chance.

"Everybody out!" Maverick yells. "Let's unass this thing." The group assembles in the lee of the truck.

"We're gonna walk across the runway, all abreast, all at the same time. You know which aircraft you're taking, I know which one I'm taking. Bowers, you fly with me. We get in those motherfuckers and we fire 'em up. No lights. No instrument lights, no navigation lights, no beacons, nothing. Only radios. Ready?"

They look this way and that way. Eight of them line up abreast, four carrying the M-60's, others with .38's or .45's or M-16's, and they march across the steel in the middle of the night with all these flares and all this noise and all these tracers and rounds going off, across the naked runway to the revetments where the choppers are parked, not knowing who will greet them when they arrive.

The revetments are low walls of PSP welded on edge and stuffed with sandbags. They surround each helicopter in a U-shape, with the choppers parked head-in and the blades dangling over the top. They protect the machines from a close mortar round, but little else. Under normal conditions, which these are not, you: (1) fire up the aircraft; (2) pull it into a slight hover; (3) back it up; (4) and (5) make a pedal turn and begin to taxi; (6) turn left; and (7) go out to the runway for takeoff. Normally, but not tonight.

"As soon as I get that sumbitch cranked," says Maverick, "as soon as you hear me hit the igniter, you do the same. The next thing you'll hear is when I'm at five hundred feet. You stay here cranked up till I tell you I'm gone."

Maverick, Bowers, and the other pants-pissing maniacs frantically make ready and fire up. The riot of their engines is lost in the sound of the battle. Preflight? Forget it. No time for the niceties of safe military aviation they learned at Forts Rucker and Wolters. Now it's set the indent on the throttle end of the collective, push the ignition button, listen for operating rpm, and pull that unfortunate machine straight up out of the revetment, vertically into the sky, fully loaded with rockets and minigun ammo and four scared soft creatures who have already come close enough to death just getting to this point, straining, groaning, creaking, and shuddering. If the Huey were alive, it would hemorrhage internally.

Above the revetment now, hanging in the air in a furious whirl of dust, kick the right pedal, put the nose down to get some airspeed, any airspeed, and then a hard steep cyclic climb all the way up to five hundred feet, a runaway elevator, stomachs left behind.

"Assassin Three Two, this is Three Four. Over!"

"Where the fuck are you?" screams the wingman from the ground below.

"I'm at five hundred feet heading south. Get up here."

The night is dark, cloudy. No moon, no stars. Just the tipsy light from the flares swaying in the air around them, the tracers, and the explosions. There is light, too, from the furious battle taking place atop Nui ba Den.

The top of the mountain is ringed by an unappetizing black doughnut of gunsmoke. Within, tracers flash through the clouds like chain lightning. Queasy terror erupts from the radio. The base is also under attack by hundreds, at least, or thousands, it seems, of VC who have erupted from the tunnels below, bats at dusk from a Texas cave. They're attempting to overrun the camp and succeeding brilliantly. On top of the mountain, men scream at the base below, begging for help. A gunship, just one gunship. But only two gunships have made it off the ground, and they're a little busy right now. So the screaming goes on.

Meanwhile, inside the camp, a certain cook, Spec-4 Ronald P. Landers of Opelika, Alabama, unable to make it to a bunker, huddles weaponless in his tent, watching the Man in the Ditch, untouched to this point, continue his assault, spidering along, jumping up to shoot, ducking down to reload, and realizes that he, Ronald, will be seriously dead soon because he, the Man in the Ditch, is getting closer every second, and he, Ronald, can completely kiss good-bye his dream of having some culinary creation named after him; beef would be nice, like "Filet au Landers" or "Tournedos en Sauce Landers," but he'd settle for "Chicken à la Landers," so he summons every ounce of courage he has, which, he discovers, is more than he previously supposed, grabs a meat cleaver, jumps out of his tent, hunkers down in the depression, and, as the Man in the Ditch scuttles by, rises up, driven by fear, desperation, excitement, and adrenaline, and looses a long, sweeping upward roundhouse blow which deprives the Man in the Ditch of his head, or at least the part from the bridge of the nose northward.

Only two gunships will make it off the ground this night, Garcia's troops being stuck in their respective bunkers with Charlie crawling around on top. Maverick and his wingman desperately pour their ammunition down from the sky, flying around the camp directly above the wire, firing straight down, strafing the perimeter and sometimes firing directly on the bunkers. Below, the NVA, in waves, swarm and scatter, regroup, swarm again.

The Hueys fire incessantly, dodging the little parachutes that hold the flares aloft, through a sky that has taken on the kind of cold electric blue-white color you expect to see in morgues. All fingers aboard strain at the shuddering triggers and firing switches and little red buttons. Four minds *will* the bullets from the barrels. Four minds *will* the rockets from the pods, and in long, convulsive, rippling pulses, they go.

The Huey lands, reloads, takes to the sky again and again. They fly for seven hours.

The next morning a detail is sent out along the wire. They count three hundred and sixty-seven NVA corpses. They do not count the trails of blood that lead back into the jungle. They do count the American corpses, but they tell no one the number.

TWENTY-THREE

Humans are wonderful. They can bear almost anything as long as they know it's only for a certain period of time. Even if you're sentenced to twenty years, after the first day you can say to yourself, "Well, it's only nineteen years, three hundred and sixty-four days," and begin counting. That way, time moves for you. Otherwise, it doesn't.

Once Maverick began to think the dark thoughts, he realized just how little hope he had and started to give it up. How long will this go on, this moving every night through anonymous locations, spending days in little islands of nowhere, surrounded by strangers whose kindness he could not depend upon, whose utterances he could not understand?

And on top of these rank eruptions of fatalistic thinking, he was afraid that he was going crazy. Two things made him think this. One was that some of the villages he was taken to began to look familiar to him, though he knew in his mind they had to be different. The second was that the Vietnamese he heard all day started making sense.

He dwelled on the darker thoughts, like the tongue dwells on a missing tooth: I'm never getting out of this cage and they're never taking me out. If I'm in Cambodia or somewhere in the north, no American Devil Dog gunships are ever going to drop out of the sky suddenly, wipe out Happy and Dopey and Attila and the rest of these motherfuckers, and lift me into the sky, a free man. I am beyond reach. Alone.

Let's just take a minute to recap here. So far Maverick has been in-country six days. One hundred and forty-four busy hours. In that time we've had a major mortar attack on Tan Son Nhut, the strongest of all American strongholds, that cost them who knows how many young lives, the mess hall, and an undetermined amount of taxpayers' property. The enemy has attempted, with near-success, to overrun more than a few bases, thereby causing frenetic all-night battles and death by the long ton.

Things are very much out of hand, and it's still early. If it gets worse, nobody will be surprised.

The Tay Ninh area nestled along the Cambodian border, which surrounded it in a rough horseshoe shape to the north, west, and south. The land was scrub, swamp, rolling hills, rice paddies, and rubber plantations. God, mindful of every detail, had created a Garden of Eden for the delight of guerrillas and infiltrators, who were going forth, being fruitful, and multiplying.

To the east of Tay Ninh the aspect was even less attractive. First, there was the area called the Iron Triangle, north of the enormous base at Cu Chi, where American guns sent the flaming death of artillery fire miles and miles into the countryside. What they didn't know at Cu Chi was that directly underneath their boots the earth was riddled, permeated, infested with an elaborate complex of enemy tunnels, astonishingly elegant in design and construction, one of the marvels of modern warfare.

Meanwhile, the troops inside the base at Cu Chi never stopped wondering: "Where do all these snipers come from? Seems like they just pop up out of the ground." And so they did.

Then, ah, then . . . there was the Michelin rubber plantation, a vast, sweeping flat expanse of land planted with thousands of trees laid out in perfectly neat columns and rows. The rubber trees were much like the enemy, in that they were a permanent part of the scenery, covering the ground as far as human vision could encompass in every direction. Incredibly enough, the Michelin people still pulled rubber out of the place. At one corner of the property squatted the little village of Dao Tieng, where most of the workers lived. And in the exact center of the vast estate was the headquarters. It was a three-story "mansion," a beige structure of concrete and stucco, with gracious steps leading up to the front entrance, wide veranda all around; in back, a sweeping patio surrounded a generous swimming pool. A fine example of French Colonial architecture.

At least it had been. But its best days were now over the horizon and out of sight, the mansion having fallen into the hands of a battalion of the Twenty-fifth Division of the Army of the

United States, who had a job to do. With a lack of sensitivity bordering on downright wartime callousness, they ripped up the grass airstrip that looked like it had been manicured daily by hundreds of indefatigable gardeners with tiny scissors and threw down hundreds of square yards of PSP. Then they filled the place with radios, weapons, and young soldiers who made war.

Familiar image: The mansion, like all bases in Vietnam, was a tiny boat full of Americans bobbing in a bottomless, endless sea of enemies. The VC and NVA loved the plantation because it was practically inviolate. The Americans had agreed to pay 150 U.S. dollars for every tree they destroyed, though it was unclear whether the Communists were similarly charged, so, with American pilots reluctant to send their favorite fiery projectiles into the place, it became an encampment not unlike the Annual Boy Scout Jamboree at Valley Forge, except this one attracted all sorts of Communist infiltrators, sappers, snipers, fellow travelers, regulars, irregulars, semiregulars, sunshine soldiers, guerrillas, sympathizers, supporters, toadies, yes-men, hangers-on, groupies, innocents, unfortunates, and others of that ilk. When Maverick stood on the front porch of the mansion and ran his gaze around the horizon, there was nothing in any direction but rubber trees and people who wanted to kill him.

Nothing much ever happened at the plantation, but late every afternoon a fire team from Tay Ninh flew in to spend the night on countermortar standby, just in case. It was precious duty because the crews got to stay in a real house, with semidecent food, bathrooms, comparatively luxurious sleeping arrangements, a swimming pool, and besides, the place felt so . . . so French, somehow. The boys fought for the duty. Over the weeks, Maverick's turn came around once, twice, and then a third time.

He arrived late in the afternoon of June 3, 1968, in a Huey—the Cobras still hadn't arrived—with two newbys: a confused, slack-jawed Mississippi farmboy named White, who until very recently had never been more than fifty miles from East Jesus, and a street-smart Philadelphia hustler called Bradley. He chewed gum with his mouth open, slouched when he walked. You'd expect him to carry a pair of dice in his pocket. In the right seat there was a short, skinny first-tour copilot that everybody called Rat Man, but only because he looked like a rat:

long, protruding face, tiny little teeth, the merest wisp of a mustache growing like algae that bridged an inconsiderable gap between a verminous nose and feral mouth. If they ever held a contest for Ugliest Man in Vietnam, Rat Man would enjoy perhaps his only moment of glory.

Unlike the first tour, pilots were not assigned their own ships. The choppers, crews, and pilots were interchangeable, which might have been efficient but did nothing to foster team spirit and the sense of cohesiveness soldiers need in wartime.

In the other ship were four new troops, the pilot and gunner just up from Saigon. The pilot's name was Wallace, but Maverick forgot the other three as soon as he met them. He was burned that the fuckers had pulled choice duty after only three days with the platoon. He never had that kind of luck.

Just inside the mansion's front door was a long hallway. The first room on the right was filled with massive black and gray boxes of radio equipment. The pilots' dormitory was the second room, just past it. On this particular night, even though it was close to two o'clock, there were operations going on all over the area and the radio room was filled with snapping, crackling, and squawking, the same sounds you'd hear from your front-row seat at the parrot show. Maverick lay awake on his cot, blanketed by the heavy wet air and the noise from the radios next door. On the other side of the room White and Bradley breathed and spluttered and snored and mumbled. Next to him, the Rat Man did the same, only louder.

"Rat Man! Are you awake?" No answer.

"Shit." Maverick heaved himself up from the cot, tucked it under his arm, grabbed his blanket, and padded down the hall toward the back of the building. When the radio noise receded to the limit of audibility, he found a small dark alcove just under the stairway about half as tall as he was, tossed the cot inside, and crawled into the space. He turned over and stretched out mere fragments of a second before the arrival of the first mortar.

The tornado sound, vengeance from on high. It draws closer with alarming speed, then *whomp!* The rocket, irresistibly attracted to the mansion, falls out of the night, and with stunning, deafening concussion blows through the roof and explodes on the second floor, which instantly collapses.

Outside the alcove, gray dust and dirt and beams and stucco and huge chunks of concrete rain down as the floor above suddenly becomes the floor below. The staircase cracks, it sags, it suffers, but it does not give way. Maverick is safe. Stunned, amazed, astonished, scared . . . until it occurs to him that he might be the only one left alive in the whole place. Outside the building, all around, other rockets fall to earth, emitting dull thuds as they explode.

Gasping, coughing, breathing concrete dust, he grapples his way over the rubble in stocking feet, trying to run and step carefully at the same time, doing a kind of two-step duck-walk toe-dance toward the radio room and Rat Man's bunk. The radio room has partially survived. Two young operators grope their way out through the dust and smoke, leaning against the wall. One bleeds from the scalp; the other, arms straining, coughing, drags him along. They are the last to come out.

The dormitory has all but disappeared. There is instead a shattered doorframe—peeling plaster, rough edges of wood—and beyond it, the aftermath of instantaneous demolition: piles of rock and roofing and beams and rust-colored iron reinforcing bars and concrete dust and dirt. Through the dusty haze Rat Man staggers out, an apparition. He collapses against the wall, looks at Maverick through tiny frightened eyes, like a snail who has just discovered what the word "escargot" means.

There is no sign of White or Bradley. The rocket explosions continue in sporadic thumps, mercifully farther away.

Maverick grabs Rat Man by the shoulders. "Where's Bradley?" he yells, trying to hold Rat Man on his feet and look past him through the dust. "Where's White?" Rat Man looks like . . . well, like a man who's just had a building collapse on him.

"We gotta get in the air," Rat Man gasps. "We're under attack."

"No shit," yells Maverick. "I know that! But where's the crew? And where's what's-his-name Wallace and the rest?" The new crew had been sleeping along the far wall of the room, now hidden by a solid mound of ex-building. Maverick wipes his face on his sleeve, peers again through the clouds of concrete dust, and begins to feel that he may have to admit something unpleasant to himself. Could anybody live through that? Are they under there somewhere? "Shit. We'll have to go without them. I hope somebody can dig in there."

As the two of them stumble down the hall, a few troops make their way along it from where they'd been sleeping in the back of the building. Rat Man leans against the wall and points. "In there . . . at least six guys." The troops look at him once, then twice, since the explosion has done little if anything to improve his appearance. They climb into the ruined dormitory and throw themselves at the pile, searching, digging, pulling down the largest pieces first.

Rat Man and Maverick make it to the Huey that sits just at the base of the wide front steps, throwing a brief glance at Wallace's chopper about fifty feet away. A mortar has fallen next to it, shattering all the plexi in front and bending the machine heavily to the left, a ruined skid buckled underneath. They get in, fire up, lurch into the air as the dust swirls around them. New explosions puncture the night.

Just above the ground the dark shape skims toward Dao Tieng, then climbs a bit to look for muzzle flashes. They don't start taking hits until they reach three hundred feet, but then, right over the village, the popping sounds begin as the skin of the chopper is violated, time and again. The hydraulics stiffen up, the oil pressure drops, the shriek of the turbine winds down, the chopper starts to fall. Maverick is familiar with the feeling. Autorotation is his least-favorite maneuver, but also one he's practiced a lot. Excited, scared, resigned, he pulls the cyclic back to a sixty-knot attitude and tightens his grip on the collective, ready to yank it up just before the chopper hits the ground.

"Son of a bitch," Maverick yells. "Let's try to make it to the ARVN camp by the river." In autorotation now, rotors windmilling, trying to make the most of the forward airspeed, aiming for the small ARVN outpost just past the village. If they land long, they wind up in the river. If they fall short, there are only two things to worry about. Either they settle in directly among the VC or they put down in the mine field that surrounds the camp, at which point their asses will certainly be blown to the smallest of bits.

The Yankee Devil Dog gunship executes its unscheduled landing in a broad expanse of liberally mined terrain between the ARVN outpost and the enemy position. When the ARVN laid down the field they had accidentally received twice as many mines as they needed for the area, so they just went ahead and buried them all. But nothing explodes when the chopper hits and slides three feet forward, just as Ken Smith dictated, except the air around them as the VC or the NVA or whoever the fuck they are begin potshotting merrily away at the huge enemy devil death machine, with its soft warm operators, that has fallen among them like manna from heaven at this ungodly hour of the morning. They're destroying the machine as fast as they can squeeze their triggers, with the same boyish brio that you might find among a gang of inner-city youths who come upon an untended Rolls-Royce on a deserted back street at midnight.

Maverick and Rat Man have serious reservations about unassing the chopper and setting foot on the ground, but they like the alternative, sitting in the crippled machine and taking fire, even less, so they get out and huddle underneath, trying to lie lightly upon the earth. They are closer to the VC line than to the "friendly" camp, and even though they have sidearms, they are, for all practical purposes, defenseless. They cower on the south side of the chopper, and in spite of the bullets and the whizzing sounds around them and the continual *pop* and *snick* that the chopper makes every time it takes a hit, they feel relatively safe. And they *are* safe, right up to the minute that the friendly troops start shooting at them too.

The ARVN's at the base begin to return enemy fire in dead earnest, shooting above the chopper, around the chopper, through the chopper. The Americans are sitting in a textbook cross fire. They are not happy.

A lull. Maverick screams into the night toward the ARVN camp: "Hey! Goddammit, hold your fire! Come out here and get us!"

A voice from the enemy side: "We get you, okay, fucking American pig! You die tonight!"

Not you, asshole. Maverick yells toward the ARVN outpost again: "Jesus Christ! You ARVN bastards! Come pick us up!"

Rat Man and Maverick are trapped. They can't get through the mine field unless a few brave ARVN troops come out and guide them to safety.

The camp responds: "No can! Dangerous! Sit now. Get you first light!"

Anybody who thinks a soldier of the Army of the Republic of Vietnam is going to leave the safety of his camp at three in the morning, walk through a dark mine field in the face of enemy fire, rescue two Americans, then walk back the same way, understands nothing of the Asian philosophy of war. So Maverick and Rat Man lie under their ruined machine in the middle of a punishing cross fire punctuated by heavily accented insults, most of which are entirely ungrammatical but perfectly understandable nonetheless, having as their subject a wide assortment of commands for the commission of physiological impossibilities, descriptions of unpardonable acts involving various life forms, accusations of homosexuality, sodomy, incest, pedophilia, coprophilia, necrophilia, and a dozen other polysyllabic crimes against nature, most of which also employ the "philia" suffix.

For three hours both sides throw thousands of rounds into the shadows and thousands of insults into the air. Maverick even considers squeezing off a couple toward the ARVN camp, just to keep things interesting, but finally, at first light, the firing stops. The enemy's night shift is over; they punch their time cards and, as usual, dissolve into the jungle. After it becomes a bit brighter and the orange morning has ripened to yellow, three ARVN soldiers appear, irregular apparitions in the opalescent light of dawn, reluctant saviors who thread the Americans through the mine field back to the camp. Maverick's conviction of nonsurvival gets stronger. He prays again to the gods of war: Please, send me a Cobra. Please. Just one.

War, like life, goes on. Rubber being a chief export of Vietnam, there were plantations all around Tay Ninh and every one was an enemy refuge, if not an actual vacation spa. As before, every living soul Maverick saw on the ground below him was suspect. There were no friendlies.

The sun was low in the sky to his left as he led his fire team northeast across the low columns of rubber trees just outside Tay Ninh. There were reports of stepped-up enemy activity at this plantation, and the Assassins were running visual reconnaissance and prisoner-snatch missions. Fly around and look, grab one if you can.

Ahead, the familiar row of workers' houses filled the clearing among the trees, low, squat concrete-block affairs with no glass in the windows, no paint on the walls. A small man in black pajamas emerged from one of them, wheeling a bicycle. He hesitated in the still-bright orange afternoon sun, then threw his leg over the seat and pedaled away.

Decision time. Was this simply an innocent trying to get out of the area because the sky was racketing with American death machines? Or was this tiny black figure, legs pumping frantically on the pedals, possessed of a more inimical purpose? Maverick faced a profound yet commonplace ethical, moral, and philosophical decision: Do I waste this fucker's ass, or what?

"Let's snatch him," said Rat Man, flying again with Maverick this day. And so they did.

Maverick and the wingman both circle for another pass. One chopper will land in front of the cyclist, one behind. By this time, the tiny figure is well down the road, a solitary black smudge against the red dust, kicking up a little plume of it behind him. He is totally exposed since the American Rome plows have cleared back the trees about forty feet on either side. In the lead, Maverick drops down, practically to ground level, and eases the chopper up behind him. They dangle in the air, swaying, getting closer, closer, supported by a column of swirling dust.

The little man stops and puts his bare brown feet down. He turns around on his bicycle, pulls his hand out from the folds of his black pajamas, points at Maverick's chopper, and squeezes off at least a million rounds from a machine pistol. The chin bubble explodes in a bursting cascade of glittering plastic and Maverick feels a dull *smack* somewhere along his right leg. He's felt it before, once.

The chopper sways wildly in the air, somebody yells, "Kill him! Kill him!" Somebody else yells, "Maverick's hit!" The minigun linkages have been hit too, so they don't swivel, the chopper is right in back of the motherfucker so the door gunners don't have a shot, the pilot's been wounded, for Christ's sake, and nobody knows how badly, the cockpit is filled with dust and nobody up there has a whole lot of control, they're too close to fire the rockets, if they pull up and go over him they'll be out of danger but then nobody will get a shot and everybody wants one. Maverick is hit and bleeding and hurt and pissed and taking it personally, so he drops the evil machine down to about three feet off the deck, shoves the cyclic forward, the wind and dust and debris filling the cockpit, gets an eighty-knot attitude and, with a surge of adrenaline-powered vengeful blood lust, flies directly toward the tiny man on the tiny bicycle, who, incidentally, is still spraying rounds as fast as his pistol can shove them out the barrel.

Closer. Closer. The little man, fearless, stands his ground, becomes larger. So do his bullets. Suddenly, with the racketing machine nearly on top of him, larger than life and twice as nasty, he spins away, his hunched shoulders pulling him forward, just as the front of the right skid plunges into his back, tossing him into the air.

A black rag doll, he seems to float in front of the chopper for a brief eternal second, just long enough to burn his ghastly image into the minds of all the crew except Maverick, whose rage is now rapidly drowning in a torrent of pain. Then, suddenly deflated, the figure tumbles in the wind and red dust and rotor wash, his limp body spurting blood. Maverick banks the chopper to the right, in time to see the man logrolling down the lonely dirt road, his limbs askew, his head ninety degrees to his neck, unmistakably dead.

Maverick makes a pass over him, just to be sure. The door gunners, enraged, put a few hundred rounds from their M-60's into the body, out of anger, out of fear.

Fortunately, or unfortunately, Maverick's leg wound was not serious enough to deserve a trip to Saigon or Hawaii. It was serious enough for him to spend three weeks limping and screaming about the perceptible lack of modern armament in This Man's Army, specifically the Model AH1-G Cobra helicopter gunship. After his weeks in Cobra school, coming back to the Huey, coming back even to the highly advanced Charlie model with its 540 rotor system, was like having your father suddenly take away the Ferrari and make you drive a Volkswagen. Punishment of the ego. The enemy didn't melt into the jungle anymore; now they stood and fought. The goddamn Hueys had always been obesely tempting targets—wide, slow, never intended for this kind of use—but now the bastards could shoot and now they had bigger guns to shoot with. If I don't get a Cobra soon, reflected Maverick, my ass doesn't have a chance.

What else did this do to Maverick? It gave him another Purple Heart and a dubious reputation. The troops already knew where his balls were. They found that out the night the base was being overrun and he led the crews to the flight line smack in the middle of Opening Night in Hell and actually got off the ground while Garcia, with so much to prove, was trapped in the bunker along with his whole section. But when he unbicycled that VC with his skid in the face of point-blank fire, well, even though his stock went up, his crews could not perhaps be faulted for their misgivings as to the *compos* of his *mentis,* not to mention his sense of the macabre. Let's be blunt. They thought he was fucking nuts.

But that was not necessarily a bad thing, because in Vietnam, like in prison, people left you alone if they thought you were crazy. And there were plenty of people being left alone. Besides, first-tour chopper jocks had the traditional soldiers' respect for combat veterans, especially ones who had won the Soldier's Medal, Bronze Star, Distinguished Flying Cross, umpteen Air Medals, a Purple Heart, as of that last mission, two Purple Hearts, and all the rest. They thought, the simpletons, that returning pilots were men of steel, with uncanny insight and maturity that only exposure to combat can give. They thought that as long as they flew with veteran pilots like Maverick, they were safe. Maverick kept the Magnet Ass thing to himself.

So that's how he got away with it. Everybody figured: Look, he's a second-tour pilot, a veteran, a soldier who has Learned the Lesson, a soldier who has tasted combat, indeed, who has very nearly drained the cup. Everybody figured that flying your chopper directly toward an enemy who was firing at you point-blank as fast as he could and had already scored one palpable hit upon your all-too-vulnerable meat was not an act of bravery, not an act of lunacy, not what you do when you're thoroughly twisted, but simply a course of action to be expected of a veteran combat pilot in Vietnam. Life-and-death decisions were made every minute of every day, affected by training, habit, reflex, fear, anger, outrage, injustice, indignation, hatred, abomination, wrath, resentment, shock, pain, fatigue, alarm, horror, panic. You make those decisions instantly, and hope you're right.

TWENTY-FOUR

He tried to summon up that American-fighting-man resolve, the will to live that even then was keeping hundreds of POW's alive all over Southeast Asia in even worse conditions. Maverick felt none of it, no indomitable courage, no esprit, no defiance, and sure as shit no belief in God. He took no refuge in religion, organized or otherwise. He was absolutely certain that if there were a God, he would have gotten him out of the cage long ago. If there were *a God, Ty wouldn't be dead; in fact, if there* were *a God, none of this shit would even be happening and everybody'd be home in the U.S. of A. with his wife and babies. He felt only pity and grief for himself and for his wife, who by now, if it's been thirty days and it sure as hell feels like it, may well have been told that he is missing, presumed dead, insurance check is in the mail, and what is she going to do all alone in the world, young and blond and pretty and broad-hipped with two little boys? He also felt something* else. *A feeling that you get in the night when your mind sickens itself by spinning endless ghastly cadaverous possibilities, when your heart knows there is no way out, when your three-in-the-morning thoughts take their first faltering yet positive baby steps toward despair.*

It was August, hot, depressingly moist, the beginning of the monsoon season, and the new Cobras had finally arrived, amid great rejoicing. The chopper jocks were like kids in a new-car showroom, making appreciative noises, examining them inside and out, touching, feeling, smelling, running their hands along the plates and rivets, their dreams fulfilled. The Assassins had been flying them for barely a month, and Maverick, like a new husband, had already begun to notice tiny flaws, troublesome little imperfections in the machine he loved so much. First of all, the fuckers didn't have any air conditioning. While it might seem frivolous, even decadent, to ride into battle in an air-conditioned war machine that isn't a tank, the Cobra had been built with a perfectly clear Plexiglas overhead canopy. In the balmy Southeast Asian sun, these generated a greenhouse effect that could make orchids bloom in a week but contributed nothing at all to the physical ease of the pilots, who were already under somewhat of a strain without having to lose six pounds of water on every mission. There were supposed to be air conditioners in the Cobras. The a/c units had been shipped with the Cobras, there was even a group of holes where the fittings should have been attached. But they'd all apparently been confiscated, appropriated, commandeered, usurped and/or pre-empted upon arrival and had no doubt found their way to the trailers of the colonels at Tan Son Nhut. The situation did nothing to build morale.

Second of all, the Cobra carried two, and only two, people. There was absolutely no room for anybody else. Unlike the Huey, the Cobra was strictly a fighter aircraft. No cargo hold, no benches, no big doors on the side. To Maverick that meant if the weapons systems jammed, there was no crew chief or gunner to hang his ass out the door and give it some percussive maintenance. It also meant that if some troops were in trouble on the ground, wounded, under attack, he couldn't pick them up. He'd gotten into gunships in the first place because he hated that feeling of crippled impotence, so his thoughts began to run in more abnormal directions than usual. This is saying quite a bit.

Being platoon commander, he was the only pilot with a permanently assigned chopper, at which he looked closely and critically. He peered at the two nineteen-shot rocket pods, huge cylinders on the sides, at the two wing-store fifteen-hundred-round miniguns, long needle shapes, at the five-thousand-round minigun in the turret, at the three hundred rounds of those sassy little 40mm grenades. He'd painted a bull's-eye on the underside anyway, and mounted a bright red siren on the skid just like the old days and painted the name *Maverick's Mayhem* in big white round letters just below the canopy. The old Maverick longhorn bull's head, rendered in white paint, adorned the front.

But *Maverick's Mayhem,* Cobra Five Seven Three, just like the rest of them, siren and bull's-eye notwithstanding, still had only two seats.

"Sergeant Hobbs, will you step over here a moment?" Maverick called from across the flight line to the passing squad of grunts.

"Sir?" Hobbs was tall and thin and looked easy to break. But underneath he was made of fine steel wires, each strung just a half-turn too tightly. He wore the traditional bandanna around his head and his voice had a slight quaver to it, as though he could barely keep it under control.

"I'd like your men to see one of our new ass-saving techniques."

The grunts, having particularly vulnerable asses, were always interested in getting them saved, so Maverick and his copilot found themselves the center of an attentive, if somewhat unwholesomely aromatic, assemblage.

"Now, you'll notice," began Maverick, plunging into the lesson, "that the Cobra carries just two men. If you guys get in trouble on the ground, which you do, and if I want to pull your asses out, which I do, how would I go about it?"

Hobbs and the grunts just looked at him. They hadn't expected a quiz.

"Behold." With a flourish, he pushed the flush-mounted buttons and swung down the ammo bay door on the right side just forward of the wing stores. Then he walked around and revealed the one on the left. The doors opened to a ninety-degree angle with the fuselage and made a kind of shelf about three feet long and eighteen inches deep.

They were supported on each end by steel cables that connected them to the body of the chopper. When they were down, they were strong enough to stand on.

"You open the doors by pushing these two flush-mounted buttons. Each door will hold about three hundred and fifty pounds if you're lucky. So if this aircraft could land when you guys are in trouble, you could open the doors and sit on them . . . and I could carry you back to base."

It didn't sound too crazy to the grunts, but then, very little did, and if you had to make the choice between planting your ass on that little shelf to be taken into the air dangling off the side with no protection whatsoever, and staying on the ground in the middle of an ambush or an overrun base camp, you'd hop on in a heartbeat. So when he asked if they'd like to try it, they muttered and shuffled a little, but it wasn't any more dangerous than what they did every day, so they didn't exactly say no.

After appointing four volunteers, Maverick got the doors on both sides situated and spent a few minutes working out a way for them to sit on the door securely. They finally decided to link their inside arms and put the outside ones through the steel cable. When the grunts were installed, their buttocks packed onto the narrow shelves on each side, arms linked like two men getting ready to dance at a Greek wedding, Maverick climbed into the open canopy with his copilot in the front and cranked up the turbine. He radioed the tower for clearance, taxied, and lifted into the sky, two souls actually on board and four others hanging their asses out over the edge.

It was a flawless day, cloudless and clear, so the dark shapes against the nose of the Cobra and the four little legs hanging down made an obvious picture from the ground as Maverick flew the pattern. He went around once, getting the feel of how the chopper responded with four troops hanging on, and by the second pass he'd proudly convinced himself that here was obviously a valuable new air-rescue technique that would revolutionize the role of the Cobra in combat if not Army aviation itself. He would be celebrated, his name would be legend. When he settled the machine back onto the ramp, in exactly the same spot he'd left, his four passengers were windblown, deafened, but still in place. Major Norskin, the troop commander, was on the flight line to welcome them, hopping up and down, first on one foot, then on the other.

The grunts jumped off and Maverick threw the canopy open while the troop commander came running up alongside the chopper to demonstrate why everyone had begun to call him Norskin the Foreskin. Major Norman Norskin the Foreskin was so enraged, so irate, so provoked, so pissed off, that his roundish face was a dull cranberry color from his high forehead right down to where his chin should have been. The wattles of flesh on his neck shook from side to side as he choked and stamped his feet. He was furious. Maverick discovered where the phrase "beside himself" came from. The man was trembling so hard he looked like he was standing in two places at once.

"Lieutenant Marvicsin," he yelled, pointing at him with a wicked finger at the end of a long arm, "I saw that, I saw that." Well, shit, thought Maverick, it was hard not to, you dickhead, I was right over the base at eight hundred feet.

"What the fu . . . what do you think . . . what are you doing? These men . . . You . . ." This was the same man who had so confidently ordered the guns into the air when the base at Tay Ninh was being overrun, but this brilliant display of airmanship had apparently overwhelmed him and it was taking him some time to put the words together with any semblance of congruity.

"How dare you . . . endanger the lives of troops under your command? You . . . That was . . ." He was yelling so loud that Maverick couldn't hear him. Finally he started stringing words together.

"Don't you think these men face danger enough every day without your careless and irresponsible disregard for their safety? Don't you think they have enough trouble with the VC without having one of their own officers trying to kill them too?"

"Sir, I was trying to—"

The major was not to be deterred. "I saw what you were trying to do. I saw you play a goddamn schoolboy prank with the lives of these men."

"Actually, sir, I was looking for a way to save them from—"

"You want to save them? Well, you can save them by doing your job, mister." The grunts had gathered around the little scene, staring at Norskin the Foreskin in goggle-eyed unbelieving astonishment while he shit all over an officer who had just shown them a short way home. Maverick had proved, in front of God and everybody, that the Cobra could, in fact, be used for evacuating troops. A limited number of troops, to be sure, not like the Hueys, but still it represented to them a saving of asses where one might not otherwise exist. One of the troops who'd taken the ride muttered to another, "This guy ain't got no fuckin' sensitivity."

And he had no fuckin' imagination either. No inventiveness, no desire for the old higher-faster-stronger, no urge to make his machines or his men do their lethal work more effectively. He ran his world by the book and by the clock, and as far as he was concerned, Maverick had just violated every tenet of morale, safety, principle, an officer's responsibility to his men, and quite possibly the Code of Hammurabi as well. As Maverick stood flatfooted and agape, as Hobbs and his squad, embarrassed, shuffled their booted feet in the dirt, the obloquy continued unabated. For long minutes Norskin the Foreskin hollered at Maverick, yelled and roared and bellowed, reviewing his shortcomings, his irresponsibility, his immaturity, emphasizing the more salient points with stampings of the feet, wavings of the arms, and wigglings of the fingers. Maverick was torn between dumbfounded surprise, a visceral urge to kick him in the balls, and a puckish desire to shoot a grin over his shoulder at the grunts. Then, after running out of ways to say the same thing over and over again, Major Norman Norskin the Foreskin stopped, breathless, whirled, and stalked off into the blinding afternoon.

Even though the Assassins had moved to Di Anh, their area of operations was still the same: the impenetrable region along the Cambodian border west of Tay Ninh, in the shadow of Nui ba Den, which impended above the landscape, sullen, enigmatic, eternal.

Over this area, Maverick wheeled at fifteen hundred feet on a low gray afternoon, covering the LOH that buzzed slightly above the ground completing a BDA mission. Bomb-damage assessment required them to overfly certain sectors where jungle that had stood undisturbed for thousands of years had been reduced to fine powdered ash in a blinding instant by the B-52's that flew miles above. They would report back how completely the earth had been scorched, searching for open bunkers and exposed tunnels in a wasted landscape, where areas of once-impenetrable jungle lay peeled back, replaced by fantastic craters hundreds of feet across and deep enough for a diving competition. The earth was, to put it biblically, rent and torn asunder for hundreds of yards in every direction.

But on the edge, just a few yards from what remained of the trees, the scout reports an orange panel on the ground—a signal for the choppers to land. Then he reports that he's receiving fire.

Maverick drops down for a closer look as the LOH flits away to safety. There, next to the orange panel behind a pitifully small mound of dirt, five or six or seven Special Forces troops, probably on a long-range patrol, are taking wicked fire from the tree line. They are lying at the bottom of the crater with their asses hanging out.

Maverick's copilot, Taylor, knew what all Assassin copilots learned right away: when you fly with Maverick, you're strictly along for the ride. The chopper banks to the left, drops almost straight down, and rolls in for a pass at the enemy position. As the ground whizzes by, they can feel the sharp impact of machine-gun rounds hitting the chopper. True, the Cobra was skinnier than the Huey and presented less of a target, but when you fly one of them twenty feet away from enemy guns, you become virtually unmissable.

Taylor clenches his fist and squeezes out a barrage of grenades and minigun fire. Maverick does the same with a salvo of rockets. Red flame erupts from the ground. They do it again, then a third time. As they come about for the fourth pass, the scout pilot sounds in their headsets.

"Assassin Three Six, this is Charlie Horse One Three. You keep Charlie's head down and I'll try to take some of these guys aboard."

"Roger that, One Three. Get your ass in here."

The Cobra makes two more passes. At the end of each run, Maverick pulls the machine cruelly over to the side and around so that he can get back into position sooner and not give the enemy a chance to pop some rounds at the exposed scout, now dangling in the air below ground level, in the middle of the crater. Slight forms scamper toward the suspended machine, crouching low.

"I'm out of here, Three Six," says the scout. "Got three passengers, returning to base."

There are four men left in the crater. Taylor understands the situation instantly.

"Maverick," he stammers into the intercom, "you're not gonna . . . ?"

Oh, but yes. His question is answered by a sinking stomach as Maverick pulls the Cobra up and around, banking along the crater rim, and coming up on the stranded troops from the far side. In a whirling, blinding cloud of dust and debris, the huge clattering machine settles to earth. Maverick throws open the canopy and is about to bark orders when he discovers, in the most disturbing possible fashion, that he has not been completely successful in suppressing the threat of enemy fire.

On a Cobra, the canopy opens from the pilot's right and swings up to the left. The copilot sits under a separate canopy that opens to the opposite side, so that if the aircraft rolls over, both men will not be stuck inside. Like aircraft of old, the machine could even be flown with the canopy open, as long as the speed stayed under sixty knots. As Maverick swings open the clear bubble and holds it against the force of the rotor wash with his left arm, one whole section of the plastic blows away in blinding shards of glittering silver. A ragged hole appears in the canopy not an inch from his elbow. He stares at it for a second and thinks: Fuck me to tears. He pulls his head into his shoulders and starts screaming hoarsely at the men who hunch down on the far side of the chopper. They're safe for the moment, but Maverick and Taylor, who has his canopy open too, and is yelling at the troops on the other side, are under serious fire. Heavy leaden rounds ping pregnantly into the side of the ship.

"Listen up, we gotta get the fuck out of here. See that door right down here on the side?" he yells over the rotor noise. He can't point, because one arm, at present still unshot, holds the canopy and the other holds the cyclic. "Push the two flush-mounted buttons and pull the door open. Two guys can sit on it. Link your inside arms and put your elbows through those support cables."

One of the troops, a sergeant, yells up at him. But between the rotor noise and his helmet, Maverick can't hear him. The sergeant waves his arms and yells again. Just as he does, another section of the canopy blows away next to his outstretched arm. Big spinning, whirling glittering pieces. Fuck this, he thinks, these assholes don't climb aboard in the next three seconds, I'm taking my ass home.

The sergeant yells one more time, then gives up. He orders two of his men toward the chopper, then disappears around the front. The troops open the door, spin around, and sit. Maverick drops the canopy, asks Taylor for clearance, and swivels the machine around on its rotor axis. He sees little puffs in the dust where enemy bullets hit, and continue to hit.

On the other side, Taylor has told the other two exhausted troops how to jam their bodies onto the precarious shelf. Maverick gently pushes the cyclic forward. The nose drops, the dangling troops feel a momentary panic. Lowering its pointed nose, the chopper moves up and forward, the men clinging to the steel cables and to each other.

Maverick points the Cobra away from the line of fire, trying to keep the machine between the enemy and the four soft beings who adhere to the outside of the machine. He makes his way back to base just above the ground, low and slow, barely clearing the trees.

Is this unsafe aircraft operation? Is this playing fast and loose with the lives of the men under his command, his trust, his responsibility? Well, yes, in a way, but it's better than being stuck somewhere outside of Bhum Fuk Vietnam in the middle of a bomb crater the size of the Superdome under fire by determinedly hostile forces. The men do, in fact, dangle in space, but frankly, they couldn't be happier.

Maverick looks up at the canopy, sees the ragged, shattered places, shakes his head, and pushes the Plexiglas back. "Hey!" he yells to the two men on the right side. "How you guys doing?" The one closest to him is bent over to the right, elbow hooked through the door-support cable, sandy hair standing almost straight out from his head because of the rotor wash and the headwind. His face is red from the effort. He yells back to Maverick, who can't hear shit. He yells again. Maverick points to the side of his helmet in the classic I-can't-hear-shit gesture and yells back, "Never mind. We'll be back at the base in about three minutes. Just hold on." The man yells again and points downward. Maverick looks at the ground, sees nothing but the inevitable customary green jungle canopy, shrugs, and lets the canopy fall shut.

"Taylor," he says over the intercom, "how is it on your side?"

"So far, so good," Taylor replies, craning his head to look down and out the left side at two men who are trying to cram eight square feet of buttock into six square feet of space.

Up to this point, Maverick had done what he'd always done: turned off his mind, let the obscure Italian art movie take over, with its seeming slow-motion soft-focus imagery, removed himself from the situation, and rushed in on full automatic. Don't think, just do it. He didn't consider the enemy fire, he didn't worry about the insidious holes that appeared in the upraised canopy just this far from his arm, he just saw a responsibility, and he took action. He was no braver than anyone else, but he was brave for five minutes longer. He'd seen people hesitate in situations like that, the way Cooper did when he flipped out in the air. But if you hesitate, you never regain that special kind of degenerate lunacy that permits you to act, to hang your ass out without any interference from that silly little nagging sense of survival.

But now, loafing back to base, flying gingerly to protect his precious cargo, he allowed himself to savor the almost ambrosial irony of the circumstance. He looked up and out of the cockpit one more time at the two men on the shelf, live men who would certainly by now have been converted to numbers on the sacred Body Count, and smiled with a profound, almost visceral satisfaction, with an intimate, exquisite sense of impending gratification, like waking up in the morning with the smell of fresh coffee right under your nose. He relished the feeling, savored it, cherished it. He almost rolled it around on his tongue. To Taylor, who, like every single other human soul in South Vietnam, knew of the previous week's confrontation with Norskin the Foreskin, he said, "I just can't wait to call this in." And then he did.

"Di Anh control, this is Assassin Three Six, two miles west of the field, inbound for landing with six souls aboard."

Silence. Then: "Maverick Three Six, Di Anh control. Say again."

Maverick said again, emphasizing ever so slightly the "six souls aboard."

"Six, are you in a Cobra?"

"That is affirmative."

Silence. "Uhh . . . you're cleared for a straight-in approach."

Maverick made a gentle turn to the right and made for runway eighteen, bringing the Cobra in just past the control tower, preparing to land as close to the dispensary as possible.

"Assassin Three Six, this is Di Anh control. You have seven souls aboard."

Now it was Maverick's turn. "Say again?"

"I say again. You have seven souls aboard. There is a man hanging from your left skid just below the wing store. Be careful on your landing."

Shit, thought Maverick, so that's what everybody was yelling about. "Taylor, did you know that sumbitch was there?"

"Negative, sir, but he must be pretty tired by now."

Maverick settled the chopper gently to the ground, hovering a few feet in the air for a moment to allow the unexpected passenger to drop off, then eased down on the collective and settled in. Apparently word had spread as soon as they'd called in, because the ramp was full of people, some helping the five Special Forces troops to an ambulance, some curious, some just smiling. Hobbs was there, demonstrating his own personal understanding of the event's irony by doubling over in spasm after spasm of yocks, guffaws, and belly laughs. As Maverick watched, Hobbs crippled himself, laughing to tears, laughing as hard as a human being can without rupturing something vital; then he fell to the ground and was assisted to his feet, moist, incapable, flaccid.

Major Norman Norskin the Foreskin never spoke to Maverick directly again.

The astonishments of the war came at them in cycles. Even though the Assassins flew every day, sometimes they ran into shit and sometimes they didn't. When weird things happened, they came in clusters. August was the month of the man who walked on water. And the famous Sniper Squash.

In the first case, Maverick is escorting a scout, which flutters along the canal banks between the trees like a summer butterfly. Below them, on a dike between rice paddies, two men squat on their spare black-pajamaed haunches alongside a herd of five or six water buffalo.

"One Three, what's the story on those guys?" Maverick asks.

"Moving in now to check them out," says the scout as he drops the chopper down to dangle barely off the surface of the water. The water buffalo shift uneasily and start to move about, but the two men, as do so many Vietnamese in similar situations, pretend to be oblivious. They squat, their bottoms barely off the ground, folding themselves in half the way only Asian peasants and Alabama sharecroppers can do. The rotor wash causes one man's tunic to fly up, exposing the dark brown grip of a pistol stuck in his waistband and causing the scout pilot to yell in surprise, dump a red smoke grenade over the side, and get the hell out.

"We got one here! We got one here! This guy's got a gun!"

"Roger that," says Maverick from a thousand feet as he begins to drop his machine out of the sky. One of the Vietnamese breaks and runs along the paddy dike to the right, one to the left. The left-hand runner is closer to the tree line, so Maverick decides to go after him before he makes it to safety. He pulls a hard left-hand descending spiral, the ground whirling beneath, to come up behind the frightened, scampering man, lets go with two rockets, then two more, then again. Great gouts of water explode upward from either side of the paddy dike. Maverick is so close that he flies right through the explosions, covering his canopy with water and mud and little rice plants.

When the spray settles down, he can see the man, crazed, legs pumping, still running.

As the scout floats off after the other suspect, Maverick rolls in again, but the runner suddenly changes direction, now racing off across the flooded rice paddy itself. His little brown feet make small splashes in the mud. Maverick whips the cyclic to the right, sending the Cobra into a diving turn. His stomach sinks.

"Marco, you bastard," he calls to the copilot. "Go ahead and wax that fucker's ass before he makes it to the tree line and we lose him."

"Roger that," says Marco as he belches up a few 40mm grenades, which explode all over the paddy, making huge fountains of water and mud and filth. But that little man, he just keeps on running, now looking like one of those Canadian wood loons or wigeons or whatever they are that run across the water beating their wings madly for about fifty feet before they get airborne. As Maverick breaks to the left, Marco goes to the miniguns, buzzing them all around the poor bastard, causing tiny eructations of water to the right of him and the left of him and in front and behind, but he is untouched, he is charmed, and he just keeps on pumping it out.

"Well, shit me silly," says Maverick as he rolls over for his third pass, which is two too many. Marco hits the miniguns again, getting off about a hundred rounds, which hit nowhere near the running target before they jam completely and give up and die. Below, their hapless victim is still running his black-clad ass off, down one paddy dike, up another, across the water so fast that when the grenades start falling again, giving off their deafening explosions of mud and water and shrapnel, the rest of his adrenaline kicks in and he runs on top of the water. If he had been on the Sea of Galilee instead of a rice paddy, he could have started a new religion.

The next five grenades from the thumper create aquatic havoc in the paddy, but they miss him too; then the thumper jams and will not fire. Marco lets loose with a string of expletives in Italian that Maverick understands all too well, even the ones in the pluperfect subjunctive.

"Jesus Christ!" says Marco, finally, in English, and Maverick, leaning over to his right to look at the little man run along on top of the water, says, "Shit, that's just who he reminds me of. The fucker's walking on water down there."

Now Maverick loses the rest of his minuscule supply of patience. The thumper won't throw grenades anymore and the miniguns are constipated, but he's still got fourteen rockets left, by God, and when the day comes that he can't kill one asshole VC with fourteen rockets, he'll give back all the medals, take off the big black smart-ass hat, and hang up his spurs. Time to stop fucking with this guy and get it right.

One more pass, down and around behind the VC, who has made it to the junction of two paddy dikes and is running into the setting sun, on fumes by now, because he certainly can't have any energy left. Maverick hangs his deadly machine in the air just far enough back so the rockets will have time to arm before they wipe the exhausted VC off the planet; then he squeezes the button and ripple-fires. Ten rockets blast out of the Cobra's pods in quick succession, their motors filling the air with ribbons of gray smoke and halos of orange flame leading downward toward the scurrying figure. Again Maverick has to fly through the rocket explosions, through the fountains of water and mud and vegetation that surge skyward, coating the Cobra with more stalks of rice. Maverick looks back over his right shoulder. "God *damn,*" he says to Marco, "that motherfucker can *run!*"

There are four rockets left, so Maverick pulls a wicked pedal turn, hangs in the air like an insane apparition right in front of the frightened, exhausted target, who reverses his field like the finest NFL running back and starts to haul what little ass he has in the opposite direction. Maverick squeezes the button again.

Whoosh! The last of the rockets leap out of the pods, practically parallel to the ground, trailing heaps of gray smoke and orange fire, streaming past the man at a million miles an hour, leaving him untouched, scared, and, by God, still running.

Now the Cobra has nothing left. If they want to, they can lift the canopy and throw a few rocks, or land the chopper, get out, and Maverick can hold him while Marco beats him up a little, but basically their two-million-dollar war machine is just a few tons of hot flying metal. The thumper crapped out, the miniguns won't say a word, and the rockets have exploded all over the goddamn Vietnamese countryside except in the one place where they were aimed. And Jesus is turning in an aquatic running performance that would make the International Olympic Committee hold up those big white "10" cards.

Maverick grits his teeth, lifts the machine, spins it, and drops down right in front of the VC. He hangs there, not more than a foot off the ground, directly across the paddy dike, a shimmering hellish vision in the splash and spray of the water around him. Jesus finally stops running and stands there, facing the machine, mouth open, shoulders slumped, skinny legs trembling, tongue hanging out. He is a David before a nightmarish green-metal Goliath. He has nothing left. He stares at Maverick and waits for the machine to cut him down.

But Maverick has had a revelation. This man is obviously meant to live. Maverick wouldn't have shot him then—*couldn't* have shot him—even if he'd had the ammunition left. Not knowing that his action will, like many things in war, come back to him, he throws open the canopy, gives Jesus the smartest salute he can muster in the narrow cockpit, and leaves him, exhausted, alone but alive on the paddy dike, and lifts his narrow machine into the blue afternoon.

August 28, 1968, was a Wednesday, though not too many people in the Assassins knew it, and even fewer cared. At Di Anh, like everywhere else in Vietnam, there were no traditional chronological markers. No morning newspaper, no jazzy drive-time deejays supplying good-humored time and temperature every five minutes. If you had a calendar watch, you knew the date. Otherwise, you knew how many days till the end of your tour, and that was about it.

August 28, 1968, was a Wednesday, and Maverick knew it because it was the day the sniper got squashed.

It is two-thirty in the hazy hot afternoon, and from an anonymous tree line the VC are passing the time shooting the shit out of an armored company of ARVN's in a clearing about twenty klicks from camp. It is one of those routine clearing missions that has gone bad, or, more to the point, another one of those routine clearing missions that has gone bad. The ARVN's are taking it deeply and painfully in the ear. Two armored personnel carriers are burning, three retreating, and several just standing still. The Assassins, on station above the melee, make pass after pass at the ragged clump of trees, firing rockets and miniguns with monumental commotion but little consequence. Whoever is in there is not only unfavorably disposed toward the basic principles of democracy, but deeply dug in and heavily defended too. It is not long before Maverick is out of ammo, and tries to call for relief so he can head back to base and rearm.

But the ARVN troops below are being bloodied right and left, and the ones that can still talk are on the radio screaming for somebody to come pull them out. When they hold down their microphone keys, the circuit closes and nobody else can transmit, so Maverick can't get through to them. He decides to stay above the situation even without ammo, and watches the rest of the fire team retreat into the distance.

So there he is, at a thousand feet, circling, with Stevenson along for the ride, hoping they look mean even though the ship is totally defenseless and thoroughly without recourse. Another bad thing about the Cobras, he thinks. When they're out of ammo, they're not worth a shit. In a Huey, there was plenty of room in the cargo hold for boxes and boxes of M-60 belts, grenades, and the like. You could even pitch the grenades out by hand, and those three other guys aboard could tend the weapons, reload, fix a jammed system. In the Cobra, you just sit there in your solarium with your fingers up your nose, hoping nothing goes wrong, because if it does, you're fucked. And Stevenson, a very green, very scared outdoor-faced first-tour copilot fresh out of Cobra school, is more frightened than he's ever been in his life, but not as frightened as he's going to be, because at two-thirty in the afternoon of August 28, 1968, the enemy is before him and he's about to see the proverbial whites of their eyes.

As Maverick and Stevenson hover above the action, things gradually die down. The shooting stops. The other Cobras have not returned. Except for the inevitable clatter of the chopper, the paddy becomes quiet. ARVN troops hesitantly lift their heads, peering above the paddy dike that they'd been using for shelter. Maverick flies raucous circles, patrolling the scene, helpless. Please, God, don't let it start up again, and me sitting here with no ammo. Jesus, he thinks. What a thing to pray for. He would pray for stranger things, and to stranger deities, before the war was over.

The ARVN unit has an American sergeant along, who is the first to come out of hiding. Even from the air the pilots can see that he is a big man, well over six-five, rangy, with long arms. He carries his M-16 across his chest, climbs over the paddy dike, and begins slowly walking toward the tree line, a lone figure outlined in fuzzy sunlight against the dark brown water. He looks over his shoulder to see if any of the ARVN troops are following. They aren't.

He turns back over his shoulder, motions them forward, and continues his careful pace along the inside edge of the paddy dike. Stevenson cranes his head, peering down the left side of the chopper.

"Hey, Maverick. Take a look at this shit."

As they complete their circle, they see a lone black figure, muscling along the ground on the far side of the paddy dike that intersects the one the sergeant is following.

"What the fuck's he doing out there?" Maverick asks, a bit rhetorically. "Doesn't he see our goddamn American death machine?"

"Maybe he figures that since we stopped making passes, we're out of ammo. He ain't so dumb."

Maverick drops the Cobra down lower, skimming along the dike.

"Shit, I wish the ARVN's would get off the radio," Maverick says, keying his mike uselessly. But the ground troops, only two of whom are now following the sergeant, are still on the air, fervently expressing their keen, heartfelt desire for expeditious extraction.

Maverick flies alongside the sergeant, hovering inches off the water, kicking up a teriffic spray. He and Stevenson both motion toward the sniper's location up ahead, pointing, pantomiming, gesticulating to the extent allowed by their jammed-in situation. You don't sit in a Cobra, you wear it.

The sergeant just waves back, looking again over his shoulder to see if his troops are staying with him. They aren't.

Normally, of course, Maverick and Stevenson would have used the combined resources of the weaponry at their fingertips to incinerate the crawling form on the ground, but that was not possible. The sergeant kept walking.

"Is it us, or is this grunt dumber than he looks?" Maverick puts the cyclic forward and skims the chopper to a position directly over the sniper, who by now is at the junction of the two paddy dikes. In twenty paces, the sergeant will leave footprints on his face unless he decides to jump to his feet and empty that AK-47.

Maverick turns the chopper head-on to the sergeant, hovering just above the sniper, muddy spray rippling out from the rotor wash amid monumental clatter, tilted slightly toward him, a sinister apparition, swaying. Stevenson knows what to do. He opens his canopy, yelling, waving his arms, gesturing what he hopes can be translated as: "Look, you asshole, there's a goddamn VC right here and he's gonna blow your balls off, so watch out," when the sniper rolls over onto his back, lifts his AK straight up, and empties the entire clip on full automatic directly into the belly of the chopper from no more than three feet away.

Heavy point-blank slugs rip through the ammo bay, through the doors, through the floor, up into the cockpit, Stevenson's canopy shattering as Maverick has a brief hideous impression of his copilot's body wrenching upward with the impact of thousands of tiny bullet fragments, pulverized by the bottom of his armor-plated seat. A thousand shards of metal rip into the backs of Stevenson's legs.

At the very same time, Maverick's canopy shatters outward too, the first time he's ever seen that happen. Startled, he lurches forward. The collective jams downward, the rotors lose their lift just like that. The Cobra falls out of the sky, slamming into the mud so hard that the skids buckle outward like a cheerleader doing a split, the tail boom buckles with a tortured shriek, and the whirling tail rotor digs into the mud and water, making the ship shudder and buck and spasm. Maverick hits bottom with a shattering jolt and barely has the presence of mind to chop power to the engine. The rotors slowly spin down. Maverick opens what's left of his canopy. It is quiet.

The ARVN troops hurry toward them and gingerly extract the bloodied Stevenson from his seat. He lies facedown on the dike. By the time Maverick is helped out of his cockpit by the sergeant, the rest of the ARVN troops are standing around chattering, pointing, discussing. Everyone stares at the red mess on the backs of Stevenson's legs, but it looks worse than it is.

Maverick kneels down next to him.

"You're gonna get a Purple Heart for this, you know?"

"Great. It hurts like a sumbitch."

"And the Army's got special procedures when you get shot in the ass. You know that?"

"Listen, can we just—"

"When you get shot in the ass like this, they put it right on the citation."

"Give me a break. Sir."

"And at the awards ceremony they make you bend over and pin that medal right onto your butt."

"Is there much blood back there?" Stevenson asks, manfully ignoring the bullshit and craning to look over his shoulder. From the bottom of his ass to his knees he feels like he's been shot with rock salt.

Maverick has no mercy. "And we got a tradition in the Assassins, too. You get shot in the ass, everybody gets to paddle you."

A low moan from Stevenson. Maverick stands up, then bends to look at the chopper.

Underneath the flattened Cobra, half-covered by greenish-brown water, two skinny arms and two skinny legs protrude from the surface at ninety-degree angles. The sniper has been driven exactly downward a good two feet into the mud, easy. His extremities are arranged in a comic approximation of death, the kind of rigorous supine posture you see in cartoons and slapstick farces. The ARVN's think it's hysterical.

Norskin the Foreskin wanted to court-martial him, or better yet, have him taken outside and shot. This time, his rage surpassed even the impressive heights he'd previously attained. In no time at all he had Maverick, in an eerie replay of the Sergeant Major Novak episode, standing in a brace before the squadron commander and, barely containing himself, denounced him in a quivering voice, yet with an eloquence and a vocabulary that could only have been painfully rehearsed. The Foreskin saw his opening, and was determined not to squander the opportunity. He sounded like a revivalist preacher.

". . . did purposely destroy government property, and showed a willful and wanton disregard for his equipment and for the life of his copilot and had no respect for . . ."

The squadron commander was Lieutenant Colonel Dickerson, a thin-faced type with a caricature of a hooked nose, violet bags under his eyes, and pale skin. He had the look of a man who never sleeps. The day after the sniper got squashed and Stevenson got his ass perforated, Dickerson listened to Norskin's address with a wearily distracted benevolence. It was all he could do to keep from putting his head down on his desk. For this was not the first of Norskin's fulminations he'd had to sit through. The Foreskin had been before him on a discouragingly regular basis, at least two or three times a month, dragging in one pilot or another, wanting to hang them for an appalling multiplicity of infractions, misdemeanors and malfeasances, both real and imagined.

"Major," he interrupted, speaking as calmly as he could when he had Norskin in his office, "like you, I regret the fact that Warrant Officer Stevenson was wounded. But from all reports I've heard, Lieutenant Marvicsin certainly saved the life of the sergeant and may well have saved the lives of the fine ARVN soldiers who were with him. In fact, the sergeant has already recommended him for a Distinguished Flying Cross. Would you like me to summon him here and solicit his opinion?" Dickerson loved to talk like that to Norskin.

Again Norskin transformed himself into the classic image of barely contained rage. He reddened. He quaked. He blew air out his nose. His mouth moved, but only little croaking noises came out. Huge ropy purple veins stood out in his neck, pulsing. His blood pressure shot up forty points, and you could tell. He looked like Moe just before he hauls off at the other two Stooges.

"That will be all, Major. Dismissed."

Norskin stood there like he'd put down roots, unable to stop making tiny noises in his throat. Then, after a few beats, he brought forth a weak salute and about-faced himself out of the room.

Dickerson looked up at Maverick. "Sorry about your copilot. Y'know, you and the major don't make a very attractive couple. I was sure you wouldn't care to walk out of here with him. Give him about a ten-minute lead. You can wait in the outer office. Dismissed."

TWENTY-FIVE

Given the fact that he had nothing to do all day but sit and think, and given the fact that passage of time was virtually meaningless, Maverick drifted back and forth between grim reality and even grimmer fantasies.

What was happening made him crazy, but what wasn't *happening made him even crazier. During two tours he had recovered the bodies of men who had been decapitated, skinned, buried alive, and just plain executed. One body had every single bone broken. He knew of an Air Force pilot shot down over the North whose captors had covered his head with a burlap bag, then soaked it with water, almost drowning him on dry land. He would never breathe properly again. Of course, many of the dead Americans and ARVN's he'd seen had been deprived of their ears or their fingers, or even more intimate appendages.*

Where were the bag and the water? Where was the knife? As he sat, day after day, somewhere between waking and sleeping, he floated in alternate pools of terror, trepidation, paranoia, boredom, and dread. Every time someone came in the hooch, he had one of those rushes of shit to the heart. He found himself thinking: If you're gonna do me, you bastards, do me now. *It was all he had to look forward to.*

Maverick was nervous. Things had been too quiet for too many days, and intense experience said it couldn't stay that way much longer. Ironically, one of the hardest things to do in a war is the thing you do the most of: sit around and wait. When things are too calm, you lose the edge, you lose the stage fright or whatever you call it in combat. The delicious tinge of fear. Then, when you find yourself in the shit again, it's that much harder to deal with.

It was so quiet that there was only one crew out on patrol.

Just a gunship and a scout, flying north of Cu Chi to see what they could find to shoot at. Maverick listened on the radios in the dark, cool operations room as Fuller, the scout pilot, kept reporting that he saw nothing, nothing, nothing. Then he started screaming.

"Takin' hits here, receivin' fire," Fuller's Southwest drawl was suddenly higher-pitched. "Small arms and automatic weapons, oh, shit . . . Mayday! We're goin' in! Mayday! Mayday!"

Just then the gunny pilot broke in on the VHF guard channel, cutting off all other transmissions.

"Maydaymaydaymayday! Assassin Three One. I got a LOH down in the AO."

Maverick recognized the voice of the copilot. It was Borowski, who'd been with the troop about six months. He was almost ready to become an aircraft commander. Eastland was the pilot, a second-tour man with almost as much flying time as Maverick, but less misadventure. Things didn't seem too serious, because Borowski's voice sounded like his balls were still attached.

Maverick leaned forward and grabbed the mike away from the teenage radio operator, a gawky kid, all bones and Adam's apple. "Report the situation, Three One. Are you sure he's down?"

"Affirmative. I saw the muzzle flashes from the tree line, he took some hits and started to spin out of control. He went in. I can see the smoke."

"Report condition of the crew."

"We don't know. We're at altitude. We . . . uh . . . we can't go back in."

Wait a second. They have a crew down and they can't go back in? And why is Borowski doing the talking? What happened to Eastland?

"Borowski, what's happened to your AC?"

Silence.

"I say again, Three One. Where is your aircraft commander?"

"Here, sir," said Eastland. "We're circling the LOH at one thousand feet."

Maverick felt a chill. There is no such thing as a gunny pilot who won't drop in and check on a downed crew. There was a peculiar hollowness in Eastland's voice. . . .

"Three One, roll in and make a few passes. Report the condition of the LOH crew."

"Jesus, sir, there's some big stuff in there. I mean, we went through it one time and damn near got our asses shot off. It's *bad.*"

"Eastland, do you have ammunition remaining?"

"Uhh . . . that's affirmative, sir. About half the rockets, the same on grenades and miniguns."

"Then roll in! Flatten the tree line around them and find out about the crew!"

". . . can't do that, sir." Even through the crackle of the radio, Maverick could hear the dead tone in Eastland's voice, the quaver. He'd spent his first tour with the Cav and had hooked up with the Assassins about thirty days earlier, transferred from a unit in the delta. From the day he arrived he'd been drinking like a motherfucker, his close-cropped head bent nightly over straight Scotches. After a week of watching him pour them down in the officers' club, Maverick made a few discreet inquiries. All the WO's said he was a right guy, so Maverick had to believe them. Sometimes you could tell when a pilot was getting crazed if the crews refused to fly with him, but even that wasn't a reliable indication. Back in the first tour, plenty of crews had refused to fly with Magnet Ass.

"Say again?" Maverick couldn't believe his ears. "Can't do that" was a phrase you never heard much from gunny pilots, and even though it was perfect English, it sounded peculiar, as though Eastland had said, "September thirty-first."

"I can't go back in there, sir. I won't. There's goddamn bullets and tracers and shit all over the place . . ." His voice trailed off. Damn. The son of a bitch was completely around the bend.

"Warrant Officer Eastland, I order you to make a pass over the crash site, lay down suppressing fire, and report on the crew. That is a direct order. Do you understand?"

Silence.

"Assassin Three One, do you read?" Silence. "Borowski, do *you* read me?"

". . . Affirmative, sir."

"You are now in command of the aircraft. Warrant Officer Eastland is relieved of duty. Stay on station at altitude till I get there."

Maverick was pissed. He had a crew on the ground, and if they were lucky enough not to be dead, they'd be virtually unarmed, under heavy fire in a hot area. Meanwhile, there was a fully armed Cobra just above them that wouldn't help out. He started to get that old running-through-glue feeling again. And then he started thinking about the kind of damage Eastland could do with a U.S. Army Cobra gunship if he decided to assert himself in the wrong direction.

"Scramble the blues," he yelled back over his shoulder as he slammed through the door of the ops room out into the blinding sunlight. It was a heartbreakingly perfect September afternoon, not at all the kind of day for alarms and excursions.

If anyone in the whole Vietnam war had ever been in the wrong place at the wrong time, it was Warrant Officer Henry Alonso. He was a half-Cuban from Miami, but he was dark and *indio,* with black black hair, thick and straight, hanging over a low forehead. Everybody called him Chico. At the very second that Maverick burst through the door, Alonso walked around the corner on the way to the latrine. But his bodily functions would have to wait.

"Alonso," Maverick yelled as he grabbed him by the shirt-front, "come with me!"

"Where are we going, Lieutenant?"

"Come with me!" Alonso, half his shirt in Maverick's fist, felt himself being dragged toward the flight line. His feet scuffled along the ground, his arms waved at his sides.

"*Coño,* Lieutenant, I was just going to take a piss. Can't you find somebody else?" Alonso's favorite word was "*coño.*" He used it all the time, and said that it was a staple of the conversational vocabulary, especially among Cubans, but he could never quite tell anybody what it meant. Apparently it was some sort of pseudo-Castilian all-purpose Latino Caribbean expletive with an elastic definition and could be used to mean "damn," "gee whiz," "ass," "pussy," "fuck," and much more. Alonso did say, however, that it had better or worse meanings depending on where in the Hispanic world you said it. According to him, Cubans said it all day long, though seldom in mixed company, but a Madrid cabdriver would kill you for it.

Maverick pulled him harder. All he could think about was two guys down and maybe hurt and certainly getting their asses shot up, and some fucking maniac at the controls of a gunship in the sky who's gone clearly over the edge. "Come with me," Maverick repeated. "It's an emergency."

"Can it at least wait till I take my leak?"

"No. We gotta get in the air." Maverick realized later that if he'd just told Alonso that there was a crew down and under fire, he'd have jumped into the Cobra without hesitation, urinary distress or no.

Maverick drags him to the nearest Cobra and stuffs him into the front cockpit. He begins throwing switches and pushing buttons even before his ass hits the seat. There are clicking sounds, then the turbine spins up, canopies close, seat belts click, one, two, three, come *on,* you bastard, Maverick waits a lifetime for all the needles to shudder into the green, then drags up on the collective and pushes the cyclic forward, trembling the machine into the air. Frantically, Alonso radios for clearance.

The muddy ribbon of the Saigon River writhes beneath them as Maverick pushes the fully loaded chopper toward the crash site. He calls Borowski.

"Assassin Three One, this is Assassin Three Six. Do you read?"

"Three One, roger." The past few minutes have done nothing for Borowski's composure.

"We're on our way. Report the situation."

"Uhh . . . we are still at altitude. The LOH is burning on the ground. They're still under fire."

Maverick hates to hear that.

"Eastland!" Maverick calls. "Eastland, do you read?"

Silence, then Borowski's voice: "He says he won't talk to you, sir. He . . . doesn't sound too good."

Neither do you, Borowski. "Eastland! Answer me! That's an order!"

Silence, then Borowski again. His voice sounds like it's been tied up with wires. "Uh . . . sir . . . Eastland says he'd like to go home now."

"Remain on station! I say again, remain on station!" Maverick can't believe what he's hearing. Barely above the treetops at 140 nautical miles per hour, flying into who knows what kind of awful shit, a nut case above him in a fully armed Cobra, and he has to play military commander, diplomat, and psychologist all at the same time. He can't stop thinking about the fact that even though Borowski is controlling the chopper from the front seat, Eastland, as aircraft commander, has the override and can take control of the gunship whenever his little voices tell him to.

"Stay where you are, Borowski, you are in command of that aircraft!" As long as Eastland doesn't whack out entirely.

"Should I drop in and make a run at the tree line, sir?"

"Negative! Stay above the crash site so we know where it is. I'll come in low and fast and see what's going on before they know I'm there."

In the front cockpit, Alonso listens to the radio chatter, and the pieces of the whole ugly picture begin to fall together for him. He deduces that they're flying directly into shit, with a crew down and enemy in the area. But worse is his entirely correct conclusion that there's a berserk Cobra pilot in the area. He swallows hard, whispers *"Coño,"* and tries to forget the pressure on his bladder.

By the time they reach the crash site the blues are scrambling and other aircraft, having picked up the chatter on the guard channel, are heading toward the area. Maverick can see Eastland's chopper, ahead of him and discouragingly high above. The trees fly by as they burst up overhead and bend a steep turn around the column of smoke. Instantly, tracers spit up from the trees.

They catch a glimpse of the LOH crew on the ground. One lies still, facedown, a broken doll smeared with red. The other huddles next to him, obviously hurt, waving weakly. As they speed by, the tree line to their left opens up with seven, maybe eight kinds of gunfire. The muzzle flashes look like little twinkling Christmas-tree lights, but the bullets feel heavy as the ship takes hits all along the side. Maverick pulls up to altitude, out of range. Eastland and Borowski circle lazily just above them. Borowski is beside himself, yelling at Eastland, not on the intercom, but over the air.

"You chickenshit bastard! You asshole! What the fuck is wrong with you?" And like that.

"Pretty hot down there, huh?" Maverick grins to Alonso through the intercom.

"Coño tu madre! What are we going to do?" Maverick can tell Alonso is upset. Any time a Latin uses *"madre"* in an expletive, you can count on him for a high level of stress.

"Eastland!" Maverick yells. "You got one more chance!" You asshole son of a bitch. "Roll in on that tree line to the north and put some rockets in there! When you break, I'll be right on your tail. Do it! Now!"

Suddenly Eastland's Cobra banks to the right and begins to

roll in. Maverick drops the nose and lets down on the collective. The Cobra starts to fall, setting up on Eastland's tail. The ground rushes up.

"Okay, Alonso, we gotta wax those fuckers so the blues can get in," Maverick says. "We'll follow Eastland right down the pipe."

"Roger that, sir," Alonso says. *"Que Dios nos cuide."*

But Eastland's *mentis,* remember, is far from *compos.* He *doesn't* go right down the pipe. No, he starts firing his rockets at about eight hundred feet, much too far away to be accurate, then pulls up and breaks right, climbing into the safe sky, leaving Maverick, who is *directly* on his ass, totally committed to flying all the way in, right down into the obscenely festive twinkling lights.

Now they're on top of the trees. Alonso unleashes his grenades and miniguns. Maverick fires the rockets and they *whoosh* toward the trees, disappear, then announce their presence with puffs of orange fire and black smoke. But suddenly Maverick and Alonso find themselves about thirty meters off the ground, directly in front of the tree line, stark naked, with no covering fire. The forest creatures burst forth with everything at once, small arms, automatic weapons, fifty-cals, slingshots, spitballs, paper clips and rubber bands, the works. Then the same thing happens from the left, and the right. Cobras are only three feet wide and terribly hard to hit from the front, but the VC do it. Alonso's canopy shatters. Pieces whirl around his head. He finally goes to the bathroom.

The controls stiffen up in Maverick's hands, a familiar feeling. "Listen, Alonso, I don't know how long this thing is gonna fly, but if we gotta put her down, it's gonna be right next to that LOH." The crash site is, comparatively speaking, the safest place on the ground, and Maverick would rather be there than three or four hundred yards into the jungle in the middle of all those VC or NVA or Algerian Zouave warriors or whoever they are.

"Let's just fly it as long as we can, sir," Alonso responds. He's already soaked from the waist down; he can't be much more scared.

Maverick wrestles the Cobra to a position directly beside the column of dirty gray smoke that pours up from the LOH. They hang ten meters up, blasting the men on the ground with downrushing air. As soon as he gets into a hover, Maverick kicks the right pedal viciously and the crippled Cobra spins madly on its rotor axis, whirling like it's suspended from a skyhook, spitting minigun fire and rockets to all points of the compass. Maverick and Alonso are on a ghastly carnival thrill ride, dizzied as the horizon swirls around them.

Alonso is the safer of the two. Perched as he is on the front of the Cobra's long snout, he spins the fastest and is hardest to hit. Maverick, on the other hand, sits almost directly on the axis of rotation, making him just about stationary, the proverbial sedentary waterfowl. Now that the hungry NVA have a nonmoving target, they take cruel advantage. As the ship spins and spits, it is peppered with hostile fire from every direction. It shakes and judders in the air, it sways and swirls as the two men within spray the dizzy horizon with bullets, firing, firing.

"Assassin Three Six, this is Monsoon Five. We're approaching your location. Will extract that crew in about two minutes."

Great. Upstairs, Eastland has apparently given up completely and is not coming to the rescue. Maverick, right pedal to the floor, spinning crazily in his wounded Cobra, is too busy to deal with him and too busy to do any more than acknowledge the inbound Huey.

"Roger that." Whoever the fuck you are. "But you better get your ass in here pretty goddamn quick or you'll have two crews to pull out instead of one. Look, the heaviest fire is from the west"—*SMACK!* a hole in the canopy—"so make your approach from the south."

On the next spin past, the Huey banks gently and circles to come in from the south.

"Alonso! We've about had it with this motherfucker. The hydraulics are gone. And I got smoke back here."

Low moan from Alonso, possibly another eloquent epithet in the language of Cervantes and Lope de Vega.

The Cobra spins once more, and comes to a hover facing the south, looking for the incoming Huey. As it gets closer, Maverick can just pick out the Twenty-fifth Division insignia on the front. It sets up on a short final, turns sideways, and the first thing Maverick sees is the red square on the door with a single white star in the center.

"Jesus Christ, Maverick," stutters Alonso, "it's a fucking general."

"Assassin Three Six, back off some so we can set down," says the Huey.

Maverick backs the Cobra away from the downed LOH, still burning on the ground, and continues firing to the west, now swinging the chopper back and forth on the rotor axis, sweeping fire in a broad arc across the tree lines. The VC don't care. Automatic-weapons fire pours into the air, into the clearing, into the Cobra until they take that one hit too many and fall roughly to the ground from ten feet.

As they throw the canopies back, they are in the middle of choking gray smoke from the cockpit fires, choking black smoke now whirling around them from the LOH fire, and choking red smoke from all the grenades that the LOH crew set off. Troops from the Huey appear, drag the two broken men away from the wreckage, Maverick and Alonso scurry in the same direction and dive facefirst through the wide cargo doors, ending up facedown on the cold metal floor.

"Maverick, is that you?" Maverick rolls over onto his back and looks into the cockpit. In the left seat, staring back over his shoulder, is the wide gray face of Brigadier General Rawlings C. Persons, the assistant division commander, the same general that Maverick had checked out on the Cobra's gun systems.

A typical Magnet Ass story. Maverick had put the general into the front seat and flown to a free-fire zone for some target practice. Picking out a clump of trees, they dropped from altitude and rolled in. Persons, aiming for a big obvious tree in the center of the tree line, squeezed off a few hundred rounds from the miniguns with exquisite accuracy. On the second pass, they went in closer. When they were about fifty meters away from the target, Persons did it again, sending his streams of tracers dead center. Just when he was feeling the most satisfied, a stream of tracers came right back at them, dead center. Maverick knew better than to be responsible for getting shot down with a general, so he pulled a wicked cyclic climb, rolled over to the right, mashing them both down in their seats, and got the hell out.

"Thanks for the lift, sir. And Warrant Officer Alonso thanks you too. Don't you, Alonso?"

Alonso wasn't about to thank anybody, except maybe sweet Jesu Cristo for keeping him alive. He was petrified, he was scared, he was *wet.* The only generals he'd ever seen had been in the distance at parades, or in history books, or on pedestals in the park. But here was one bailing his ass out, just like a real person. He stuttered.

Brigadier General Persons took both of them back to base. When they landed, Eastland was standing on the ramp looking full of explanations. Maverick looked away, walked past him.

To make a long story short, there was some talk about a court-martial, but Maverick just couldn't do it. He figured that everybody had a breaking point, that people could be in mortal danger for only so many days in a row before they started acting bizarre. They took Eastland off flying status, but worse, nobody in the troop would talk to him. He might as well have been an old Eskimo woman sitting out on the ice, abandoned, waiting to die. He had failed each of them in a fundamental way that had nothing to do with courage, heroism, medals, or glory. But it had everything to do with responsibility. He didn't hang his ass out for his buddies, and therefore he was cursed. Tomorrow, Eastland, it'll be you on the ground, burning. Then what will you do?

TWENTY-SIX

Almost a month in the cage, twenty-five days in the skeletal belly of the beast, but Maverick still didn't know how long it had been. Like prisoners throughout history, like the misbegotten hero of a Dumas novel, he had started making scratches with his thumbnail on one of the bamboo rods. There were twenty-one of them, pitiful little horizontal ticks along the pole in the corner, but he had no idea of how long he'd been in the cage before he'd started doing it. There was nobody he could ask.

Meanwhile, the seven dwarfs were still struggling through the jungle with him every night. Attila always walked in front. The other six took turns guiding the cart, watching him. He searched the faces of the seven for a look, an acknowledgment, anything. *Sleazy and Scummy, the twins, looked at him as through solid glass marbles. He was a piece of meat, and a loathsome one at that, soon to be slaughtered. Scabby, with the pitted face, never came into his hooch, but stared at him ceaselessly during their jaunts, as though he were some kind of exhibit in the zoo, as though he were from another planet, as well he might have been. He couldn't decide about Dopey. The man's expression of involuntary stupidity was, in its own way, neutral and unreadable. Was Dopey looking at him through softer eyes, or couldn't he help it?*

He thought he was finished being angry, but he wasn't. He hated helplessness worse than irresponsibility, and his forced paralysis galled him to the marrow, as it had when he watched the NVA capture the downed crew in Cambodia, unable to fire a shot. He also came to hate being stared at and jabbed at and yelled at and scorned. He had virtually let his hopelessness devour him. He lay in the cage dispirited, doomed to his very soul. His mind was backing off again; he felt like none of this was really happening to him. Things inside were shutting down. He'd opened Pandora's present during the first tour, and was appalled at the obscene things that flew out. Unlike her, however, he still hadn't heard the tiny voice of the last thing in the box. Maybe he never would. Maybe he'd just lie here and die.

Brigadier General Persons was impressed. During the whole approach he'd watched Maverick swirling like a madman above that downed chopper, spraying bullets and rockets and grenades in every direction, single-handedly, it seemed, saving the lives of all those men, fearlessly, it appeared, exposing himself to enemy fire in his crippled ship, taking hits like he didn't even care. Actually, of course, Maverick had simply seen another of those *responsibilities* that drove him so hard, turned off his mind, and started shooting. There was no prior interior debate concerning risk versus benefit or how the present circumstance fitted in with his sense of right and wrong, no intellectual process whatsoever. He just did it.

But to General Persons these were the fearless acts of a hero—Maverick would have laughed—so as soon as he'd given all the boys a ride home, he wrote out a recommendation for a Distinguished Service Cross—just one notch below the Medal of Honor.

But sometimes those things go through and sometimes they don't. Chopper jocks don't generally get DSC's, and the citation was downgraded to the Silver Star. Maverick never expected any kind of recognition at all, so he liked the Silver Star. It was better than nothing.

Route One ran northwest out of Saigon about twenty-five klicks through Cu Chi and another fifteen klicks beyond that, still to the northwest, through a town called Trang Bang, and you know what the GI's called it. The road continued through Go Dau Ha, which everyone, of course, referred to as "Go to Hell." At that point the highway split, one branch becoming Route Twenty-two and continuing due west through the rice paddies and elephant grass of northwest Vietnam toward the Cambodian border. The other road wandered northwest until it reached Tay Ninh.

The pilots loved that road, because it was secure, relatively, and easy to follow. It was a main highway on the ground and in the sky.

On this day, Maverick was flying an unusual Cobra from Tay

Ninh back to Di Anh. Unusual because (1) the front seat was occupied by the Cobra's beefy, red-faced, moderately rotund crew chief, a man named MacDonald with a bulbous red-veined nose that looked like it could guide Santa's sleigh. Unusual because (2) the ship was completely unarmed. Stripped naked. The grenade magazine was empty and the maintenance crews at Tay Ninh had removed the flex kits and rocket pods so they could work on electrical systems. Maverick and MacDonald had hitched a ride in a Huey up to Tay Ninh and were bringing the Cobra back to Di Anh.

A perfectly routine flight, as are they all. Calm, clear, visibility forever, a flawless day for flying, and MacDonald was enjoying the hell out of it because even though he broke his ass on the machines every day, he seldom got to fly in one. Maverick had the urge to put the top down and tune in some rock and roll. They were relaxed, the war forgotten, actually savoring the ride. Route Twenty-two was off the left side about half a mile below them, and they just flew right down it, headed for the intersection at Go to Hell, where they would pick up Route One to the southeast. Everything was lovely until people started screaming Mayday.

"Maydaymaydaymayday! This is Army Otter Two Six Niner, going down, going down, maydaymaydaymayday, engine out, receiving fire, going down." End of transmission.

"This is Saigon control." Instantly the controller's voice cut through on the guard channel, blanking out all other calls. "Aircraft in the vicinity of Go Dau Ha, report. Any aircraft in the vicinity?"

Maverick did it again. He piped right up without a moment of hesitation, causing MacDonald to cringe. "Roger, Saigon control. This is Assassin Three Six, over Go Dau Ha. I caught that Mayday. Can you give me a vector to the area?" He should have kept quiet.

"Roger that, Assassin Three Six. Turn two two zero degrees, approximately fifteen kilometers. That was the last known position."

In the front seat, MacDonald swallowed hard and wished he had a drink. Two seconds ago he was enjoying the ride in his very own three-million-dollar flying machine, and now he was being taken along on a rescue mission bare-ass naked. There was one other thing, too.

"Excuse me, Lieutenant," he said over the intercom, "but

if we go fifteen klicks to the southwest from here, won't that put us into . . . Cambodia?" He said the C-word.

Maverick, already pulling the aircraft into a sweeping right turn to take up the new heading, looked at his map and wished he hadn't.

"Fuck me silly. I guess you're right." And not just a little bit over the border, but a good five or six miles, which surpassed infringement and went all the way to trespass. Maverick, however, was no stranger to border violations.

"All due respect, sir, but do you think that's a good idea?"

"I dunno, Mac, but we got some boys down in there and we're the closest to them. Could be us just as easy, couldn't it?"

Mac couldn't answer; he just looked out the front of the bubble and imagined that he saw the Cambodian border, a big black line like on the map, coming closer. If they got into any trouble, they'd be double fucked. They had no weapons and Mac wasn't worth a shit on a mission. He couldn't handle the radios and hadn't the slightest inkling how to fly a Cobra. The ground rushed by below.

Meanwhile, Maverick pushed the chopper forward as he called for other aircraft in the area to come back him up. One responded, then another, then another, all far away but en route. The last call he got was from an Air Force F-4 Phantom, probably six or seven miles above, returning from a mission. The border got closer.

They barreled toward the location, trying to spot the wreckage, smoke, burning brush, anything. No sign. Just an ocean of tall, waving beige elephant grass and the predictable regularity of rice paddies. They began to circle.

"Assassin Three Six, this is Silver Six." The voice crackled in Maverick's headset. "I say again, this is Silver Six. Make an immediate one-eighty and clear the area."

"Shit," said MacDonald. "He sounds important."

"Probably is," said Maverick. "Silver Six, this is Assassin Three Six, we are inbound on a rescue mission. We have an Otter down in the area."

"This is Silver Six. You are headed into number-ten country. Clear out. Make a one-eighty *now!*"

"I say again. We are on a rescue mission. A downed Otter with four souls aboard, at least. Do you copy?" You fucking asshole.

"We copy five square, Three Six. You are in violation of the Cambodian border. Take a heading of zero nine zero and get out of there."

Fuck me silly. Time for radio problems. "Ahhh . . . Silver Six, you're breaking up. Please say again." Maverick dropped the Cobra lower, continued to circle, looking, looking, seeing nothing but green and brown. He tuned out the general, who repeated his orders twice more, then began to call all the aircraft who were on their way to help. At once, he got a response.

"Assassin Three Six, this is Bronco One Eight. Meet me on Victor 125.5." It was the F-4. Maverick switched to the new VHF frequency.

"I'm in your area, Three Six, altitude twenty-four thousand feet. Let me know if there's anything I can do to help."

"Hang in there, Bronco. My ship was under repair and I don't have a single solitary fucking gun."

"My, my, Assassin. You *are* fucked, ain'tcha?"

"Roger that. And all alone, too. Stand by while I find these guys."

Meanwhile, Silver Six was still on the other radio, too loud and too clear, trying to get a response from the Cobra, talking to all the other inbound pilots, warning them off, leaving Maverick and MacDonald completely alone.

"Sorry, Silver Six, you're breaking up real bad. I do not read. I say again, I do not read." Where *are* those guys?

Ahead in the distance, a cloud of orange dust appeared above the road, obviously a truck, and a big one. It seemed logical that it would be headed toward the downed aircraft, and as they came closer, Maverick pulled his ship up higher for a better look. As he gained altitude, he spotted the Otter in a dry rice paddy halfway between his position and the truck. An olive-drab cross in the leaf-brown dried mud, surrounded by brilliant green.

The aircraft had landed in one piece. The gear was crushed beneath, but the plane had held together. It lay on the ground by itself. There was nobody around it.

"Shit, what happened to the crew?"

"Well," MacDonald said, "if they was goin' anywhere, it'd be east."

"Good for you," Maverick said as he began to turn in that direction. Below him, from the tree line alongside the Otter, the Christmas-tree lights began to twinkle. It is a most unwelcome sight, since you see it only when the barrel of the gun is pointed directly at you. Automatic weapons, possibly a fifty-caliber. They began to receive little presents, feeling them as they delicately punctured the side of the Cobra.

"Receiving fire!" choked MacDonald, who had until this point never heard the song. He knew the words, though.

"No shit." But he still can't see anybody, just that goddamn truck, now easily visible, getting closer and closer. Time to call in the F-4.

"Bronco One Eight, this is Assassin Three Six. Look, I got this truck coming along the road and I think they're on the way to the Otter crew. Can you slow the fuckers down a little?"

Of course, the F-4 could have sent the truck and everyone in it to sit in glory at the right hand of their ancestors, but they were in Cambodia illegally in the first place and didn't want to make it worse by killing anybody. Maverick just hoped to keep the truck away from the area long enough to find the crew and get them out.

"Can't wait," the F-4 jock responded, and in a matter of seconds the fighter plane's curiously assertive silhouette burst into sight above them like a steel-gray javelin against the low sky, made one pass toward the horizon, hooked a hard left, and came in low along the road, impossibly fast. In front of the truck a great gout of flame and smoke and dirt shot into the sky as the jet thundered past, leaving behind a 250-pound bomb, making an entire section of the road disappear. *Nice* shooting.

But that didn't bother the deuce-and-a-half, which was undoubtedly packed to the gunwales with enemy troops, because it just made its own road, veering to the left to avoid the bomb crater, jouncing crazily across the dried-up rice paddies, over the dikes, careening into the fields. Maverick followed, and was rewarded with the sight of four unfortunate figures lying down behind a paddy dike a hundred yards ahead, waving up at him like he was Grandpa come to stay for Christmas. One of them had his flight jacket off and turned inside out, flashing the bright orange lining up to the sky. In the foreground, the truck continued across the paddies, getting closer, not stopping.

God, if I had one rocket, just one, thought Maverick, I could take that truck out, pull those four guys up onto the ammo-bay doors, and get their asses out of here. And where is my fucking backup?

"Any helicopters in the area, this is Assassin Three Six. Need some help here, fellas, get in here and lay down some fire so we can pull these guys out." He called on the guard channel, so everybody with a radio in the Republic of South Vietnam could hear him screaming for help.

But Silver Six heard him too, and he had already done his authoritative job, forbidding any inbound aircraft, no matter how good, charitable, brave, or heroic its intentions, to cross the border. Meanwhile, bullets were still coming at them from the tree line just beyond the Otter crew. Maverick was grinding his teeth because he couldn't shoot back; it was like he never got into gunships, flying those pregnant Huey slicks—it was like that old helpless tied-down running-through-glue feeling again. He couldn't shoot back, he couldn't land, and his buddy in the F-4, even with the awesomeness of all his firepower, was useless in this kind of situation. He couldn't hover and protect the crew; they'd take him right out of the sky. The truck, now slowing down, climbing over the last paddy dike right below him, sped toward the four huddled figures.

Maverick tried once, twice, to drop in on the paddy, but every time he did, those Christmas-tree lights would twinkle merrily again, the ship would *ping* from the hits, MacDonald would start screaming, and he knew if they shot him down, six people would be in shit instead of four.

Meanwhile the F-4 made two more passes, strafing, laying down long strings of bullets around the truck, which is a very small target when your aircraft cannot go slower than a zillion miles an hour. He made much noise, but had little effect. If he used the cannon, he'd incinerate them. The truck was determined, like the little engine that could. It kept coming, bombs or no bombs.

Maverick looked down and to his left as he circled. There they were, not a hundred feet away, four young guys his age, just like him, in the shit up to their armpits, two EM's, probably a warrant officer and a major. They looked up and waved, they looked toward the truck, no doubt wondering why that big fat Cobra didn't lay down some of those juicy 40mm grenades or rockets or something. As they stared the enemy in the face, Maverick dangled impotently, watching the sad scene play itself out inevitably on the ground.

In less than a minute the truck trundled across the last paddy and skidded to a halt. Ten or twelve khaki-clad figures bundled out of the back, pith helmets on their heads, AK-47's in their arms, ran around the truck, and grouped themselves in front of the four Americans. Maverick and MacDonald watched, sickened, as they climbed to avoid the fire from the ground. The boys took their guns out of their holsters and limply handed them over. Maverick and MacDonald watched with huge empty holes in their bellies as the NVA troops herded the men together, marched them toward the truck, and shoved them in the back under the canvas top. Maverick saw the truck turn in the dry mud, raising new clouds of dust, and bear its hapless human cargo westward down the road, deeper into Cambodia.

Heavily, he swept the Cobra around to the left, steadied the compass on a due-east heading, and flew back to the border. He wanted to throw up.

Maverick thought he'd finally figured it out the night the supply officer shot Hilton.

It was this: the thing that made being in Vietnam so disconcerting was that every time you thought you could not possibly be more horrified, the place would present you with something totally appalling. Just when you thought you could withstand the pressure of events, the pressure kicked up a bit.

Some could take it and some could not. Eastland couldn't, so he went to the Macadamia Ranch one afternoon and let the LOH burn on the ground. But maybe he had an excuse. After all, he'd seen those Christmas lights twinkle many a time. He deserved to whack out. But some of them cracked up with no excuse, for no apparent reason. Like the supply officer.

Maverick had been sick to his stomach for two days after watching those poor bastards being driven off into Cambodia, thinking about how they must have felt, not knowing that soon he would find out. The last thing he needed was to wake up to the sound of gunshots. It was Harland, the supply officer, shooting Hilton with his nine-pound forty-five automatic. But he would have shot anybody else, just as well.

Late night, at least one-thirty or two in the morning, stifling, the air making everything sweat. Maverick, very much asleep, barely heard the first shot, certainly heard the second, and was off his cot and out the door in his baggy white boxer shorts by the time the third one came.

Outside, at the end of the precise row of hooches, little silvered men ran about in full moonlight. Some were scurrying along in a crouch, but others were lying on the ground in the classic hit-the-dirt attitude. Maverick ran down the path, pebbles digging into his feet. The first person he saw was MacDonald.

"What the fuck's going on?"

"Shit, Lieutenant, it's Harland, Hilton's roommate. Asshole just went nuts, pulled out his forty-five and started shooting. Got some poor fucker in the leg, and maybe Hilton's hit bad, but he's still inside the hooch."

It was dark, with only the liquid light of the moon showing anything. Through the hooch windows, a dusty yellow glow wavered, as though a bulb were swinging back and forth. Maverick pushed past MacDonald, crouched down, and scurried toward the hooch. Outside on the steps, a group of men, white skivvies glowing in the night, huddled over a figure lying at their feet.

"Alonso!" He lay on the steps, twisted, faceup, bare-chested, his naked right leg horribly bloodied just below his groin, raw flesh turned inside out, hanging. His breath came in great sickening gulps. Two men held him.

"*Coño,* Lieutenant, I was just walking up to the door to see what the yelling was about because there was this big *jaleo* inside, and when I opened the door, the motherfucker shot me. He shot Bill too. He shot Bill. I think he's dead."

Sweet Son of God on a Honda. It's not bad enough that everybody in the fucking country is trying to wax our asses for us. Now we gotta go shooting our own. Maverick backed off as two medics ran up, bent over Alonso, and began to lift him gently down the steps.

"Anybody else in there?"

"Just Harland with the gun and Hilton on the floor," someone told him.

"Nobody tried to get in and talk to him?"

"Sir?" One of the copilots blinked at him. "He just shot two people. Probably killed one of them. He's sitting right inside the door with a forty-five in his hand. No, sir, nobody's tried to get in and talk to him."

Indeed. But Hilton was a warrant officer, one of Maverick's pilots. Harland, his roommate, was a warrant officer too, but in the supply-and-service section. Not a rated pilot. Here, then, was another one of those . . . situations. Maverick's mind turned off and his curious sense of responsibility kicked in, making him, as it often did, perform acts that were not in his own best interest.

"Get going. Tell everybody to clear the area. Notify the MP's. When they get here, tell them not to come in. Got it?"

The EM looked at him the same way Reich did when he was about to cut Scotty's feet off, the same way Eagle looked at him when he wanted to fly with that bloody great wound in his leg. Maverick was getting used to it. But somebody had to be in command, and this night it was him, and one of his men was inside. He couldn't think about it past that point.

He took a deep breath, crawled up onto the rough wood porch, and huddled down next to the door. On the gravel in front of the building, medics were tending to Alonso, troops were crouched on the ground, torn between their desire to back off to where it was safe and to stay close to see if Maverick would get shot too. Like at an accident scene, the number of dark, morbid figures around the hooch gradually increased. Maverick's hand fell onto a piece of wood lying along the wall. He pushed the door open with it. Gently, gently. He slowly put his head around the corner, then jerked it quickly back. He did it once more, jerked back again.

From what he could see, Harland, the supply officer, sat at the far end of the hooch on a cot that ran along the back wall. Maverick could barely see the feet of Hilton, who lay on the floor with his head toward the threshold. Every time he pushed the door open, he gave Hilton a little crack on the head. Hilton, he presumed, was beyond caring. Son of a bitch.

Harland, his curly black hair wet and tousled from the heat, sat, head bowed, with his bare elbows on his bare knees, shoulders hunched forward, left hand supporting his right forearm. His right hand clutched the impossibly menacing black forty-five, pointing it directly at the door. As heavy as it was, it shook in his grip. He was looking up through his eyebrows, sunken eyes wide and pale, burning, glittering. A lamp had been knocked to the floor and was still lit, rolling back and forth, a little less each time, casting an eerie wavery glow from underneath. The light washed across Harland's features. His teeth were clenched; he sat, naked, in a kind of sick satanic majesty.

Maverick's eyes traveled around the scene and returned inevitably to the forty-five. It looked like Harland was sitting there holding the haunch of a Great Dane. On the floor, from under

Hilton's chest, a widening rivulet of blood seeped out along the floor.

Harland spotted him peering around the door.

"It was that goddamn tape recorder, y'know? Is what it was. Fuckin' thing. I told him to turn it off, playing the goddamn thing at two in the morning, I'm tryna sleep. I'm under a lot of pressure here, y'know, a lot of pressure. Goddamn this fuckin' place."

At least he was talking. "You're right, Harland," Maverick said as he started to slide inside the door, crabbing along on his heels and hands, dragging his ass along the floor. He pulled himself just inside, sitting on the floor, back against the wall, knees drawn up.

"That's right, man," he said again. He slowly pushed the door shut, noticing as he looked back all the frightened white faces that had crawled up on the porch behind him. He tried not to look at Hilton, motionless on the floor, bleeding.

"Why don't you tell me what happened?" You asshole, if Hilton's dead, so are you.

"I told him to turn it down. 'Turn it down,' I said, 'or I'll blow the thing off the wall.' And he said, 'Blow away, you asshole,' so I took out this . . ." He swung the deadly metal toward Maverick, who tried to make himself smaller and sink into the floor all at the same time. The huge hole at its tip was a tunnel into infinity. The hammer was cocked. Harland pointed it back at the door. ". . . and I blew the shit out of the tape recorder, and then . . . and then . . ." He giggled just a bit. The sound chilled Maverick to his soul. "And then I blew the shit out of him and some other asshole who came in the door. Boy, was he ever in the wrong place at the wrong time." He giggled again.

Maverick eased himself to his right along the wall, farther into the room, stopping next to the small brown refrigerator.

The door to the hooch opened half an inch.

"Stay out of here," Maverick called, then turned his attention back to Harland, his naked body seeming yellowed and sick and sulfurous in the light that came up from the floor. Long shadows played on the wall in back of him.

"If he listened to me, I wouldn'ta shot him."

"I know, Harland. It's okay." You silly son of a bitch, talking about the pressure. What the fuck do you know about pressure, about taking hits, about seeing guys get blown up? Spend your days counting bedsheets, mortar attack comes, you're in the bunker. Everybody else is running around in the jungle, you're back here with your inventories and manifests and receipts. I got no pity for you at all. Just give me the fucking gun . . .

From outside came the sounds of jeeps pulling up, shouting, noises, ambulance doors opening and closing; it was getting thick. A *situation* was developing. Maverick began to talk, saying whatever came into his mind, because he was giddy from fear. The forty-five had grown in Harland's hand, becoming even larger when he started to giggle. Maverick continued sliding to his right. Hilton continued to bleed.

"Listen, Harland, everything's cool." Brilliant wording. If he could just calm this silly son of a bitch down, get close enough . . . "It's not your fault. Nobody wants to be here, but we're just trying to do a job, that's all. It gets to everybody sooner or later. Shit, I feel it too. Everybody understands. Besides, you're shooting at the wrong people. You want to shoot, I'll aim you in the right direction. There's a whole bunch of people trying to kill us, without us killing each other, and now you've gone and wasted a perfectly good pilot—*Hilton, you poor bleeding bastard, I hurt for you*—and we need all the pilots we can get. We need you, we need everybody."

Harland just looked at him, and Maverick stumbled and stuttered, seeing the obscene infinity in his eyes. He tried to keep the fear and pain out of his voice, still moving, an inch at a time, along the wall, now at the corner, now along the back wall, coming closer to Harland's cot.

It took forever, but Maverick edged closer, talking, talking about the war and the pressure and how he understood and wasn't it heavy, didn't know how anybody could stand it at all, but look at all the money the government had invested in Hilton and he's just lying there doing nobody any good at all, and look at the mess. He inched to the end of the cot, just barely within reach of Harland, who was staring intently into the universe just next door. Now-or-never time.

Maverick's left hand shot out and slapped down on the forty-five from the top, grabbing it high on the barrel, just above the grip. Startled, Harland pulled the trigger, and the sharp point of the hammer lanced into Maverick's hand, tearing the skin between his thumb and forefinger. At the same time, his right fist, propelled by anger, fear, and frustration, came down on

Harland's wrist. The gun came away and Maverick threw it across the room, tearing his hand, as Harland fell apart, screaming and yelling and laughing, toppling over onto his bunk.

The door burst open and MP's filled the room, jumping over Maverick, piling onto Harland. The cot collapsed like a brand-new colt and five or six bodies writhed on the floor, legs kicking. Maverick crawled through the boots over to Hilton, who lay with his face crushed against the floor. He was breathing slowly and with gravity.

"Bill! Bill! Are you okay? Can you hear me?"

An eyelid fluttered, then opened.

"Am . . . am I dead?"

Maverick's laugh had a tinge of hysteria. "No. No, you silly son of a bitch, you ain't dead. Can I roll you over?"

"Okay, but real easy."

Two medics appeared, a black and a white, knelt down across from Maverick, and put their arms under the body to slowly roll him onto his back. Maverick just couldn't wait to see the front of Hilton's shirt.

It was a classic combat mess, torn and shredded, soaking red. As the medics delicately picked the fabric away with their fingertips, Maverick expected to see the kind of gaping hole that forty-fives are famous for creating, expected to hear that awful hollow gasp. Instead, he discovered a terrible ragged slice, not a bullet wound at all, just to the right of the breastbone. The heavy gold chain around Hilton's neck disappeared grotesquely into the cut, running in a smooth glittering line from under his throat right into his chest.

What the fuck is *this?* "Jesus! Can you talk? What happened?"

Hilton gritted his teeth. His entire upper body was in agony from the concussion. His head throbbed from the fall.

"He started bitching about some goddamn thing, we weren't listening to him, we never do. Then, before I knew it, he had that fuckin' gun in his hand. I remember standing up when he shot the tape recorder, Jesus, it went all *over* the place, and then I turned to the side and he got me. Shit, this hurts like a bitch."

One of the medics, a tall skinny blond, looked up.

"You wear some kind of a medal?"

"Yeah," Hilton grunted, "a Saint Christopher. Why?"

"Because it's inside your chest." Maverick took another look at the sickening gap on the front of Hilton's pale body with the surreal gold chain burrowing into the red flesh, becoming part of it. "You didn't get hit straight-on?"

"No. I think I turned away."

"Well, the slug must have hit the medal sideways, driven it into your chest, and bounced off. We gotta be careful moving you. It could be next to your heart."

"Ain't you one lucky asshole," Maverick said, wanting to kiss him with relief. "That's the goddamnedest thing. You're gonna be black and blue from the waist up for a month, but tell you what, I'll buy you a new medal."

"Hell you say. You hold on to that thing when they pull it out of me. I'm gonna wear it for the rest of my life."

TWENTY-SEVEN

Denial begets disbelief, which in turn begets anger, then hopelessness and despair. Then religion.

The fractured marital circumstances of his parents caused Maverick to be brought up Catholic, then Lutheran, then nothing. He had gone to church only because his family did. Now, in the most dire extremity, he started thinking seriously, as many do, about the Order of the Universe.

And he came, as many do, to mixed conclusions. If there's a God, why am I in this cage in the first place? Why doesn't he get me out? Why is all this happening in the first place? *And if there* isn't *a God, then I'm even more fucked than I thought.*

By the twenty-seventh day of his suspended animation, Maverick had begun to notice the increase in his strength, if not in his spirits, a fact he was careful to conceal from Dopey, Sleazy, and the rest. During his long hours alone he had been exercising secretly as best he could inside the cage, doing little chin-ups on the bars. But nothing could relieve the constant hot needles in his back. He'd been bent over for fifteen or twenty or twenty-six days, had not straightened out once. If he ever got out, he would need a week to unbend.

But even as his strength came back, his mind was very much in the process of going south for the winter. Or perhaps farther. He was crazed from the constant incomprehensible sound of Vietnamese, he was emptied by the loss of his wife and children, he was more than slightly whacked from having thought about nothing but slow death for the past three weeks. Plus he was having nightmarish déjà vu perceptions every time he was carried into a new village. He was convinced that he'd been in every one of them before. He was becoming increasingly twisted, and he knew it.

That's when he started to pray. Wild, feverish, manic, ram-

bling, labyrinthine discourses during which he took unto himself Jesus, Jehovah, Buddha, Mohammed, Moses, Saint Cecelia, the Blessed Virgin, in exactly that order. He would have prayed to Elvis on velvet, or to Hanuman, the Indian monkey god, if he'd known about him.

Maverick had arrived for his second tour in May 1968, and the word "Tet" was on everybody's lips. He was told time and again how the VC were everywhere and how they were eating in the American mess halls with the South Vietnamese employees. The horror, snock, and surprise of Tet had triggered an escalation of forces that made the Big Buildup of 1965 look like a Boy Scout camping trip. Now, after six months in-country, Maverick was even more amazed at the sheer size of the war. And typically, just when he thought the astonishment was over, it made another quantum leap.

The unit was losing men like crazy, and everybody hated it. Every day somebody else didn't come back, and the Assassins would look at each other, then look away. The hits just kept on coming. And just when the action began to soar to unprecedented heights, Maverick had to stop flying.

In Vietnam, the military tried their damnedest to make sure every one of its officers got rotated through a range of command positions. They might not have another war for forty years, and everybody needed the experience. Maverick's time as platoon commander was up. He was promoted to captain and made troop operations officer. His duty was not in the AO, not in combat. No flying, no missions, no shooting. The dramatic irony is too obvious even to mention. But at least Major Norman Norskin the Foreskin had been transferred to squadron. He left without saying good-bye.

The new troop commander was Major Robert P. Edge, a tall, stooped, lean individual with alarmingly straight dark brown hair in full retreat. He had earned the nickname "Razor" because he was sharp enough to admit certain things that most officers don't much like to admit, such as he didn't know jack shit about what was going on and Maverick obviously did. So they'd fly the command and control missions together, sometimes in a Huey and sometimes in a Cobra. Maverick, who was afraid he'd never fly again, wound up with two choppers sitting on the pad outside the operations building. His pad. His choppers.

• • •

The operations officer coordinates all missions and scheduling with the squadron, and sometimes even with division. He briefs the platoon leaders and pilots about the next day's events; all of his duties pertain to combat, but none of his duties involve him in it.

Maverick hated the shit out of it. It was the worst kind of hell, sitting in the operations room all day, surrounded by radios, listening to the horror show that Vietnam radio did so well, hearing the cries for help, hearing the terror, hearing the action. That helpless feeling, that impotence again, the feeling he knew thoroughly and despised deeply.

He would have pleaded, cajoled, whined, begged and groveled, and debased himself before Major Edge for a chance to fly, but he didn't have to. The major could not help but run his hands through his hair and say to himself: He's good . . . he's crazy as a wounded wombat, but he's good. It's getting so we need all the shooters we can find, so if he really wants to shoot that badly . . .

But in war, as often in life, there are people who believe that anything worth doing is worth overdoing. If Cobra missions are good, then flying with the scouts, down there close in, face-to-face, should be even better.

Ralph Barstow was the commander of the scout platoon, and Maverick decided if he was going to fly with anybody, he should fly with the best. Besides, Barstow had a reputation as a prime loony when it came to helicopters, and that suited Maverick just fine. That is how, one day very early in May, Maverick found himself slung from the left-hand door of a LOH cradling an abbreviated M-16 in his lap, four feet above the trees just west of Nui ba Den. They'd been down there for hours, giving Maverick a perspective he'd seen many times before, but only briefly, when he was in the process of crashing. They'd found nothing but twelve-foot-high anthills, huge pale cones that stuck straight up from the ground like towering dunce caps. Excellent for target practice, except now they didn't need much practice, since real targets presented themselves at more frequent intervals.

The longer they hovered five and six feet off the ground in the swirling noise, the more nervous Maverick got. They were blowing the bushes apart with the rotor wash, and if some motherfucker popped up, he'd be right in Maverick's face. Every other occasion that had placed him close to the enemy had ended in disaster, both mechanical and physical, and he knew that if the next bush revealed the enemy, they'd be looking each other in the tonsils.

And then they were.

The branches bent to the ground and away from the chopper when a small figure appeared, suddenly standing straight up and looking exactly like your worst nightmare of the enemy. A pith helmet, khaki shirt, web belt, and a huge AK-47, the size of which Maverick could only infer because all he could see was the hole at the very front. It was dark, deep, and less than ten feet away. He saw it clearly and without mistake.

They pulled their triggers at the same time, but no vicious burst of gunfire erupted. Jammed. They looked at their guns, they looked at each other, two classic Saturday-morning-cartoon double-takes. They panicked.

In less than three seconds Maverick had thrown the useless weapon into the back of the chopper and reached for the thirty-eight on his hip. He *knew* he was a dead man because that AK was one of the world's great weapons and it would start functioning brilliantly again very soon and those deadly little bees would come whistling toward him from right over there and he'd be bleeding before he ever got that thirty-eight out, but then it leaps into his hand and points itself in approximately the right direction. During the same three seconds, the VC had dropped the AK and started to run, looking back over his shoulder, wide-eyed, at the Yankee Death Machine swaying crazily just above the ground behind him. He runs jerkily through the tangling underbrush, stumbling, falling, then finally gaining speed, looking back at Maverick, who is trying desperately to steady himself for a shot with the puny pistol. And just as the VC breaks clear, just as he starts really picking up some good motion, just as he is about to burst forth into the clear, he makes the same fatal mistake Lot's wife did and looks back over his shoulder one more time and *whap* runs headlong, full tilt, into a tree, which catches him solidly dead center, flattening the side of his face against the trunk, stopping him cold. He staggers for a second, *oing-oing-oing,* the way that coyote who chases the bird in the desert does, and just as he rebounds outward from the punishing trunk, is driven back into it by the force of Maverick's single bullet, which violates him just below the shoulder blades and slightly to the left. He hangs on to the tree, holding himself up as he drains away, slithers to the ground.

Still, only a few seconds have passed. Barstow looks around at the sound of the gunshot, sees the thirty-eight in Maverick's hand, looks beyond him out the door to see the VC with the ugly red smear on his back melt to the ground, and yanks the cyclic to the right, flinging the LOH up into the air, throwing Maverick out the door, straining against his harness. Maverick fumbles for a smoke grenade, but by the time his shaking hands find one, pull the ring, and pitch it out the door, they are already half a klick away from the site.

As they circled at a distance, Barstow called in the gunnies and Maverick looked at his hands. Like the proverbial break of dawn, the whole concept of war and death and killing took on a new meaning. It was the first time he'd ever killed someone he'd made eye contact with.

The bomber pilots never saw the results of their deadly labors, but the gunny pilots did, sort of. They were in close, they saw the faces of the enemy. But their work required this great clattering airborne weapons system which interposed itself between them and their actual human targets.

But here was something more direct, more personal. This was not throwing explosives at faceless figures on the ground from five hundred feet away, this was not the splattering overkill of a grenade or rocket. This was just two men, one gun and one bullet, eye to eye, like in the parking lot in back of the bar on a Saturday night. It was awful.

Like most disasters, the mission in March 1969 started off innocently enough. Maverick really shouldn't have been there at all, was inviting trouble, but couldn't resist flying and couldn't resist trying to teach Cummings everything he knew. He liked Cummings.

Cummings was the kid next door, he was textbook, he was the charming young man that every mother wanted her daughter to marry. In Cummings' case, daughter would have jumped at the chance, even if her mother approved. He was well over six feet tall, blond, smooth-cheeked, eager, open-eyed. Fresh out of high school, fresh into the Army, and the ink on his Cobra-school diploma could yet scarcely be touched without smudging. You liked him at once because he listened to you.

A nice kid, with nothing but a military career on his mind.

His father was a rear admiral in the reserve, he could have gone to Annapolis, done anything, but what he really wanted to do was fly Cobras in Vietnam. He jittered for six months before arriving in-country, so afraid was he that it would all be over before he got there.

In spite of all the promises to himself, Maverick started to like him, his eagerness, his respect, his spirit. Yes, Maverick remembered everything he'd told himself about closeness, friends, like that. He'd seen so many go down, so many not come back, and Ty's death . . . well, that had just about crippled him.

But here was a kid who glittered! If he lived through the war, he could be a great soldier, one with all the right instincts and attitudes. He seemed to understand warfare and the seemingly irresistible human impulses toward it. He was, unconsciously, the Warrior's Creed made manifest. He was Ty, seven years earlier. Cummings was twenty years old, and Maverick, in spite of himself, treated him like a son.

It was March 19, 1969. A Wednesday. Maverick was filling in for a sick pilot, a thousand feet over the elephant grass, flying in aimless circles, a menacing presence, the Cobra's long sinister shadow tracing their path on the ground. Cummings, as was becoming more usual, occupied the front seat.

Things, for a change, were quiet. Some of the gunships on the morning mission had reported small-arms fire, but there was none here, not in this beautiful afternoon, not with the sky so blue above and the waves of grass so amber below. There was a lull in the action, almost a calm. Standing out clearly against the pale grass below them, the LOH they were escorting butterflied back and forth, darting beneath the white blurry circle of his rotor blades, until the situation became less pleasant.

"Charlie Horse One Four," the LOH pilot calls, "receiving fire here, taking a couple of hits." And he changes direction suddenly, dropping red smoke, sliding aside in the kind of turn that tears your rotors off and getting away with it, vulnerable, running for his life.

"Okay, Cummings, we got a little action here. Get a grip on your balls." Maverick pulls the chopper to the left, looking almost straight down at the red smoke that boils in the air, lining it up.

"You hire, we fire," Cummings responds. Cocky little fucker. A real chopper jock.

Dropping, the Cobra points Cummings toward the smoke, rushes him toward it, like the very first car on a roller coaster, coming up fast. His hands are ready on the grenade launcher and flex kits. First, the two of them will let go with the buzz of the miniguns and the rockets with their gray plumes, then Cummings will cough up a few grenades from the turret, peppering the area around the twisting red smoke with all their explosive might. Then, when the column of smoke blurs past them, a hard turn to the left, sliding in the sky, gaining weight, lining up again, afire with rockets, guns, and those hefty little pointed green grenades.

But none of this happens. None of it. Before they can execute the sequence, before a finger can make the merest quiver on a trigger, the entire front cockpit explodes in an astonishing hail of metal, glass, and plastic. It sounds like thunder with a razor's edge; it looks like a ghastly cascade of mirrors, a startling blossom of deadly crystal flowers.

Then come the smoke and the wind from the knocked-out canopy in front. They hunch down under the weight of rushing air. Other than the sudden roar of the rotors, there is no sound. Maverick is so surprised and startled that his throat tightens up and words don't come out.

Then: "Maydaymaydaymayday, this is Charlie Horse Three, we're hit, I say again, we're hit, fire on board. Cummings, are you okay? Maydaymayday!"

Maverick suddenly feels like he's had a basket of live snakes dumped in his lap. He's trying to fly the chopper, which is losing its will to be flown but manages somehow to stay in the air, he's flipping switches on the radio, he's trying to take up a heading to Tay Ninh, which would be easy except the compass is hidden by blowing smoke, he's chattering to Cummings, and he's just living for the moment when the next unexpected burst of fifty-caliber fire will erupt beneath him and shoot his ass out of the sky. God knows, it wouldn't be the first time.

"Maverick, are you okay?" Cummings' voice was weak, but it was there.

"Thank God, you motherfucker, why didn't you answer me? Are you hit?"

"I think I am, I think I'm hit." Oh, shit, he's got that hollow, shocked sound, the way you'd talk if you saw your arm lying next to you on the ground but the pain hadn't gotten to you yet.

"How bad?"

"I think it's pretty bad." He knows it, but he doesn't *know* it.

"Where is it?"

"In my legs."

"Hang on, man. We'll get back as fast as we can. I'll call in for medics, they'll have an ambulance right there. I know, it's happened to me." Please don't let this kid be hurt, please.

"It's in my legs," he says again, all the life gone from his voice, no presence, no timbre, like the way the dead talk, when they do.

"You'd better have a look at this, sir," Cummings says, and with that, he picks up his leg, and the sight makes Maverick's stomach lurch.

Cummings laces both hands beneath his left knee and leans back, hoisting his leg up. Maverick unbuckles his harness and half-stands up in the cockpit so he can see over the instrument panel. He stares, appalled. At the bottom, above the ankle, there is torn flesh, reddened fabric, nothing else. No foot. The foot is there, however, hanging off the leg at an impossible angle, dangling on the shreds of cloth and meat.

"Fuck me dead," Maverick blurts in spite of himself. He would have said "*coño,*" had he remembered it. He swallows hard to forestall his stomach's all-but-inevitable journey northward. He can't help but stare at the dangling foot. He leans into the cyclic, trying to push the chopper harder, faster.

"It doesn't hurt that bad."

Oh, you poor bastard. "It's okay, it won't hurt. Put it down, okay? We're almost there."

Cummings doesn't answer. The Cobra continues, nose down, rotors tilted forward, hydraulics stiffening from loss of fluid, enormous wind rushing about them.

"Cummings!" Maverick is afraid that if Cummings stops talking he will stop living. He hears a moan, a few mumbled words, like sleep-talking.

Maverick is on the radio all the way to Tay Ninh. He flies the chopper all the way into the ground; medics swarm up the side and pull Cummings out of the ruined cockpit. One carries the severed boot.

The ambulance speeds off into the red-dust afternoon, as Maverick slouches high in the cockpit, stunned, sickened, empty.

TWENTY-EIGHT

By the twenty-seventh day Maverick was as healthy as he was likely to get. His mind was clear. Twisted, but clear. Thoughts galloped through it with the miraculous lucidity granted only to the dying and the insane. The dark thoughts, once horrifying, had become commonplace—almost, awful as it is to admit, comfortable. He had given up all hope of escape, he had done what he could in his heart to say good-bye to his wife and the two young boys he barely knew. Mandarinlike, he had, willingly or not, begun to Make Peace with himself, acquiesce to the inevitable, come to terms with the hopelessness of his situation, captive of the seven hideous dwarfs.

His thoughts had clarity but no direction. Acuteness, but no order. The lessons of captivity were, surprisingly, a recapitulation of the lessons of combat: just when you think you've hit bottom, there's a new bottom to hit.

Maverick was sure he'd hit it on the twenty-eighth day, though he was pretty sure it was only day twenty-four. They were still moving him late every night and he had long since stopped paying attention to the individual villages. He just stared at them, frightened that they looked so familiar.

This is it, he decided just after the most ancient of women had tossed his evening meal into the cage. Her hands had been curled into claws, one of her fingernails was black. Digging through the gray tin cup, he decided: This is the lowest I can possibly go. The best part of my day is finding half a fish head in a bowl of slimy rice.

Day twenty-eight would bring him lower still.

His call sign was Cobra Six. Not many people knew his name, or cared to. He wasn't an aviator, he had nothing to do with aircraft. He was an LRRP.

A peculiar kind of personality emerged in Vietnam. Actually, several peculiar kinds of personalities emerged in Vietnam, but one of the most startling was the kind that enjoyed going out on long-range reconnaissance patrols. Cobra Six was one. A man who traveled alone, surrounded by enemy, a man who lived in the jungle for thirty or forty days at a time, a man who could effect more physical devastation with three inches of wet rope than Maverick could with his entire AH1-G Cobra gunship. And much more quietly.

He looked the part, he acted the part, he was the perfect foreshadowing of the ultraviolent and infracoherent he-men that would inhabit the movie screens of the generation to come.

Cobra Six did have a name. It was Lieutenant Short, and he was anything but. He was over six-three, weighed maybe 230 pounds, and every single ounce of it was writhing muscular blood lust. He was broad-chested, narrow-waisted, heavy-shouldered, flat-stomached, *basic.* The fundamental human form brought to a kind of perfection that Praxiteles would have swooned over, a war-torn, lunatic Adonis.

When Maverick met him in 1965, he was a sergeant at the Special Forces camp in Muc Hoa. Then he'd received a commission as a reward for a bit of battle madness similar to that which earned Maverick his. He'd been in-country for four years straight, had never gone home, had never even taken an R&R leave to the moist enticements of Bangkok or Taiwan. He was one of those people who, once having discovered the war, lived and breathed for it, but his involvement was an insidious animal thing, as far from the warrior's creed as a toad from the Talmud. Cummings, for example, would have been disappointed if the war ended, being deprived of the opportunity to play a part in his country's efforts, carry on the family tradition, count coup. But Cobra Six would have been devastated. He, at twenty-nine, had found his element, had become part of it. If ever a man's true nature had been spectacularly and definitively revealed, it was his, the moment he saw the jungle for the first time. The attitudes and responses of civilized humanity fell from him as scales from the eyes of the unbeliever. His transformation was virtually immediate. Nobody knew where he was from in the States, but his return to paved streets and traffic lights was out of the question.

Inevitably, he became an LRRP. His job, though he hardly considered it work, was to go on long-range reconnaissance patrols alone and unsupervised, answerable, for all practical purposes, to no one save the ravaging beast he carried around inside himself. He could range wherever he wanted, whenever he wanted, commit any heinous aggressive acts against the enemy that he could get away with, come back when he pleased, if he managed to stay alive. He was not commanded, he was unleashed.

The most frightening and dangerous thing about him was that he was brilliant. Realizing his destiny practically the second his feet had hit the tarmac at Tan Son Nhut, he set about learning the language with a fervor that bordered, like everything else he did, on the maniacal. In doing this he discovered a completely unrealized linguistic talent, becoming more than reasonably fluent, with a Saigon slum accent, faster than anyone has a right to. If any American in Vietnam tried to learn more of the language than was absolutely necessary to order a beer and get laid, he came in for incredible peer-group abuse and accusations of gook-loving. When Short did it, nobody said a word. His language ability, along with some unimaginable physical coercion, enabled him to interrogate his captives with an efficacy that the SS would have envied.

From almost the beginning of the war he was a legend. His manic lust had revealed itself early, and not long after he began his patrols, he'd been summoned back to Saigon, stripped of his weapons, and confined to the base. He was so crazy and had done so much weird shit out in the bush that if even half the stories were true, he'd have to be terminated with extreme prejudice. But the next day they came looking for him in his quarters and he was gone, disappeared, evaporated, wearing just his fatigues, no equipment, no gun, no nothing. Nobody had seen him leave. Three days later, when they heard from him on his pocket FM radio, he was nesting in the jungle, fully equipped, on patrol, fighting for his country in his own little way.

Normally, Cobra Six would locate concentrations of enemy, commit a miscellaneous atrocity on a few, report them, scramble the blues, or call in air strikes. Then he'd disappear and turn up a few days later dozens of miles away. The few times he did come into base, he'd sit in the officers' club and try to tell stories, but nobody had the stomach for them.

Late in March, in characteristic fashion, he materialized on the airstrip at Tay Ninh, sitting on the ground next to the green bulk of a Huey, leaning against his backpack. His CAR-15 was cradled in his lap and he looked as though he'd slithered into the base from a hundred miles away. If he had become part of the jungle, then the jungle had indeed become part of him. His lean face had absorbed all possible dust and mud, the rotting vegetation of the jungle floor had worked its way into every line and crease. There was a foul green cloth wrapped around his head, his lids were heavy over washed-out no-color eyes. The reluctant remainder of his jungle fatigues carried no insignia. They were caked, almost bonded, to his body. All this was overlaid with fearsome cascades of ammunition punctuated by dark blobs of grenades. He had, as closely as could be determined, two weeks' worth of hair on his face and three months' worth on his head. He was beyond dirty, beyond nasty, he was a human horror and, true to his character and his myth, had never even considered bathing.

He was hitching a ride to the top of Nui ba Den. There was fabled to be an entrance to a main VC tunnel somewhere up there, and nobody had ever been able to find it. Or if anyone did, he never lived to tell. Cobra Six said he knew where it was. He was going to fix it up.

Maverick got the call well after midnight. An Air Force chopper in the area had been contacted on the FM from Cobra Six, calling for support on top of Nui ba Den. This, for some reason, was another one that Maverick decided to handle himself. Perhaps he just went because it was Cobra Six and he wanted to help. Mostly he went because it was Cobra Six and the rest of the gunnies were so afraid of him that they wanted to leave him there.

Maverick pulled on his fatigues, walked across the compound, roused Marco, put him in the Cobra, and wafted him into the quiet night air.

Blacked out, they flew to four thousand feet, the top of the Black Virgin. They listened as hard as they could to the radio, but nothing was there. They swung back and forth in the night, pass after pass, then Cobra Six came up, talking in a whisper.

"This is Cobra Six. This is Cobra Six. Do you read?"

"Cobra Six, this is Charlie Horse Three, what's your position?"

Whispered: "I'm on top of Nui ba Den."

"I know that." You dangerous asshole. "But where?"

Whispered: "On the north side, about a quarter of the way down on the trail."

"What is your status, Cobra Six?"

"They're here."

"Who's where?"

"The VC. They're here."

"Where?" Maverick, understanding that Cobra Six walked an emotional tightrope, tried not to rush him.

"Right in front of me."

"How *far?*"

"About thirty feet." Shit, the guy is sitting right on top of the enemy, gabbling on the radio.

"How many?"

"I can see three, but I know there are lots more."

Around Maverick, mortar flares whitened the sky at regular intervals. Cobra Six had called for them so he could see the enemy. Every time one went off and the sky flooded with steel-edged light, he reported a few more.

"Can they hear you?" Stupid question.

"I don't think so."

"What are you gonna do?"

"Wait."

"For what?"

"For them to pass."

Maverick had one of those bite-on-the-ass bad feelings. He was afraid the VC would be able to hear the transmissions from the chopper, the crackling of the radio, as well as the sound of Short talking back.

"What do you want me to do?"

"Stay on the north side, stay blacked out, and wait till I need you."

So Marco and Maverick swept back and forth at a distance, trying to sound innocent, invisible from the ground. The VC, even if they were exposed, would have no suspicions.

Five minutes went by, then ten, then fifteen. A long time to make aimless circles in the night.

"Cobra Six, this is Charlie Horse Three, do you read?"

A hoarse, urgent, intense whisper: "Shut the fuck up!"

But stupidly, Maverick did not. "Are they close?"

"About ten feet. Now shut the fuck *up!*"

Just then another mortar flare went off, the parachute swaying in the night, making the shadows of trees perform an eerie *danse macabre* on the mountainside.

They waited another five, ten minutes as mortar flares burst and floated around them. Maverick couldn't wait anymore.

"Cobra Six? Cobra Six?"

"Maverick! Listen! We got a situation developing here. They . . . Oh, shit!"

The first part was whispered, but the "Oh, shit" came in the kind of voice and with the kind of volume that most people use when there's something to say "Oh, shit" about, like the airline pilot's last words on the cockpit tape before the jet goes into the mountain. And there was. At one spot on the side of Nui ba Den, about a quarter of the way down, the Christmas lights, all at once, began to twinkle. Muzzle flashes broke out everywhere. Dozens of people were shooting. A moment later, the explosions came.

Furious tongues of orange fire licked up from the ground, jagged flames, bright knives cutting the darkness. The balls of orange fire described a jagged path down the mountain.

"Cobra Six! This is Charlie Horse Three, do you read?" And again and again. When Maverick's voice became hoarse from screaming into the mike, Marco took over, and they tried until their fuel ran out. Twenty minutes later they'd flown back to Tay Ninh, refueled, and were back on station, circling, weaving across the area, waiting, listening. Gradually the sky began to lighten and blue itself for the day.

"Let's make one more pass," Maverick said to Marco on the intercom, "and then we'll have to give this up."

In their headsets, a voice, the quietest voice, just barely audible: "Charlie Horse Three, this is Cobra Six. You still there?"

Jesus, he's alive. "Cobra Six, where are you?"

Still very quiet: "I'm at the bottom of the mountain, on the north side."

"What's your status."

"I need to be extracted. Somebody's gotta get my ass out of here, *now.*"

"You know where the ammo-bay doors are on a Cobra?"

"I know where they are." His whispers became more intense, a lot of tight muscle in his voice.

"Okay. I don't know where you are, so I'm gonna fly around the mountain low-level as fast as I can go. When I start to come up on your position, you get me some sort of signal, understand."

"*Wilco!* Now, just hurry the fuck *up.*"

Maverick rolled the Cobra over and dropped it low, just to the base of the mountain on the northeast side, where the jungle turned into elephant grass. He began to sweep toward the west. Behind him, the sun was coming up just as Kipling described it, over his shoulder, pouring thunderous shafts of glorious illumination across the forbidding flanks of the Black Virgin.

"Now," said Marco, "is not a good time to be doing this."

As they streaked above the ground they could see muzzle flashes twinkling to their left, some miscellaneous VC taking potshots down at them from the middle of the mountain. They would be flying into shit.

"Slow down!" came the command from Cobra Six. "Slow down! More! More!"

Maverick pulled the cyclic back. The Cobra's snout came up, the machine began to flare, slow down. They spotted an orange panel, brought the machine to a hover, and Cobra Six came running out of the woods at the bottom of the mountain, an apparition from hell itself, covered with blood, dripping with it, frightful.

Short stumbled over the rocky earth, fell once, dropping flat onto his chest, arms outstretched like a cartoon character. Up again, running, bullets making sinister little puffs all around him, others pinging into the chopper. Finally he reached the machine and ran around to the side away from the firing, ducking unconsciously under the rotors. Marco opened the canopy and Short tossed up his CAR-15 and backpack, then immediately jammed his two thumbs into the door-release buttons, yanked the door down, jumped and spun around at the same time, planted his ass on the tiny shelf and wrapped his arms through the support cables, sagging to his left, hanging on with what little energy remained to him. Maverick jammed the cyclic away from himself, heaved up on the collective, and urged the machine forward, inches off the ground.

When they fluttered into Tay Ninh, the ambulance was already on the ramp. As soon as the skids touched the PSP, medics untangled Short from the steel cables, stretched him out, and plugged him with at least a hundred needles and tubes and clear plastic bags of fluid.

Maverick yanked his harness off and vaulted out of the cockpit, leaving Marco holding Short's pack, of which little more than basic fiber remained, and ran to the stretcher.

"Remember," gasped Short, "when I said they were ten feet away from me? Well, just as I said it, one son of a bitch turned around and looked right at me, so I shot him."

"But . . ."

"That scared the rest of them, so I had to take off running. Then the fuckers started chasing me and shooting at me and we was running all over the place down this little skinny path . . . and I couldn't stop and shoot at them so I was pulling grenades off my belt and throwing them back over my shoulder, but they'd roll down the mountain with me, so every time one went off, I got hit. Maverick, I got shrapnel all the way from my ankles to my ass." He tried to laugh, was not successful.

Maverick stood watching in the golden morning light as two skinny medics slid the litter into the ambulance and drove off into the sun.

They took him to the dispensary, then to the hospital at Cu Chi. When Maverick called there the next day to see how he was doing, his bed was empty and nobody could find him.

TWENTY-NINE

They moved him again, late at night, in fact just before daybreak. Not far, an hour perhaps. Dopey, Happy, and Scabby hauled his cage down an impossibly narrow trail into another déjà vu *village, through another storm of garbage, rocks, and excrement. Once they had set him up in the hooch, above the ground on his risers, and Dopey had given him one last pitying look over his shoulder on the way out, he had nothing to do but sit in his bamboo surround all day and think, just as he had done on the day before and the day before that, about death. His own, and everyone else's.*

Everybody had died, and now he would too. But his death wouldn't be clean. Not even a shoot-down. No crash, no purification of flame, no heroic sacrifice in battle, no medals, no glory.

He dwelled on the fact that he would die at the hands of some hateful Asian, and probably over an unthinkable period of time. He wouldn't die like Jim did, or Ty, or even Woodrow. More like Bennie. To escape whatever the NVA might have in store for him, he would even have settled for a really horrible death, like the guys on the lightning-bug mission and their dog.

Four weeks, more or less, four weeks of lying bent on the bamboo bones, eating whatever foul rice he could choke down, living in his fetid black pajamas. The garment reminded him of his flight suit after his bowels crashed that night, but the flight suit had been miles cleaner.

Maverick had been in Vietnam, altogether, almost twenty-three months. He'd seen men die in almost every conceivable way, and in some ways that were not the least bit conceivable. Many had been killed around him, but with the awesome power of his helicopter gunship he'd gotten back his share.

On one routine mission the previous week he'd made two

passes at an enemy position outside a fire base that was under attack, and after the battle the blues confirmed a body count of thirty-eight people. Thirty-eight people. From just two passes on just one mission. How many deaths does that make me responsible for, he thinks, after twenty-three months? Hundreds? Certainly.

Inconceivable. He had spent days trying to puzzle out the perversion of values with his twenty-seven-year-old mind: in the States, you kill a measly five or six people, they jump all over your ass. You can pick up the paper one morning and read of the man who went berserk in the supermarket, pulled a gun, and killed nine people in one insane, frenzied act. Think of the public horror: *nine people,* for God's sake, how terrible. In the Nam, we do four times that before breakfast, with one simple flick of the thumb.

When you get short, the prospect of the life ahead makes you think of the horror of the death behind. How close did you come? How many times? How much of it did you see? How many of those mournful, hollow last gasps did you hear, and how many boys cried in the jungle?

Maverick felt like he'd seen it all in tight close-up. Death on both sides, humiliating and honorable, bodies blown apart, severed limbs, heads on sticks, men holding their bowels in place with both hands, children grotesquely burned. He had absorbed much of the knowledge that we are best not knowing, and then, thankfully, the whole process stopped. He'd finally gotten to the point where he could honestly say to himself that this time he had seen it all. He was sure he had learned the lesson. But he hadn't. There was at least one more thing to see. Maybe two.

The room seemed much smaller at five-forty-five in the morning. Big table, buff walls, olive-drab elbows resting on dark gray metal. Around the table were Barstow, the scout platoon commander; Myers, the gunny platoon commander who had replaced Maverick; and two officers from division, a captain who would be bald in three years and a major of moist forehead and unhealthy proportion. After introductions, nods, and handshakes, the major heaved himself out of his chair and squeezed sideways along the wall to the green-and-white chart on the easel next to the door.

"We have a chopper down between Saigon and Ben Hoa."

He pointed. Their present position at Di Anh was right in the middle. "It was a lightning-bug mission and it went down late last night. If we don't find it first thing, Charlie will."

"Any survivors?" asked Barstow.

"We're not sure. The pilot's mayday call said something about a fire on board, but nobody could make him out too well."

"Think the flares went up?" Myers asked. A lightning-bug mission involves loading up a Huey with a ridiculous number of aerial flares, whose job it is to be highly flammable. They wear little parachutes, and are stacked like fire logs on the floor of the cargo bay. The Huey flies up to about three thousand feet and the crew throws them out a few at a time. The flares are hooked to a cord which opens the parachute and ignites the magnesium. They float to the ground slowly, spewing a kind of intense light that assaults the eyes like broken glass. The swaying of the parachute imparts an unwholesome sharp-edged relief to the ground and shadows below.

"It's possible. A fire on board could set them off." Great. Even ten or twenty magnesium flares going off close together would create a tiny supernova. They would incandesce with an awful magnificence, creating inhuman heat, causing air molecules to part company. Maverick had a brief unbidden thought of the chopper and its passengers becoming liquid in midair, pouring from the sky in glowing molten streams. Flesh and metal, the ultimate union of man and machine.

"How many people?" Maverick asked. "Four?"

The captain chimed in. "More than that. Aircraft commander, copilot, door gunner, crew chief. They took along some staff officer who had no business up there, and a division sergeant major who wanted to go along for the ride. They picked the wrong night."

The major put in, "Tell them about the dog."

The dog?

"Right," said the balding captain, shuffling through a stack of yellow paper. "On the flight was their division mascot, a German shepherd named . . . ?" He found it. "Romeo."

Maverick put his head down—hard—on the table and groaned.

Three choppers took to the air so early that they called it "Oh-dark-thirty." Barstow and an observer in a LOH, Maverick in the Huey, and two of Myers' men high and to the right in a Cobra. Three unlikely shapes in the opaque air.

The LOH stayed low, flitting among the trees, hurtling across the rice paddies. Maverick and a kid named Warfel—"Everybody calls me Waffles"—flew the Huey. The division captain and major were strapped to the bulkhead in back, along with the crew chief and gunner. The Cobra stayed high, a predatory fowl of impossible design.

"We got 'em," Barstow's voice broke in the headsets. He wasn't far in front, and they caught up to him in just a few seconds, circling a flooded rice paddy. As they came over the trees, the burned hulk of the downed Huey was painfully obvious against the wet mud floor. It had practically buried itself in a huge gash in the ground, was surrounded by irregular black chunks of debris.

Nose dug into the moist black landscape, tail boom pitched up, rotor in the air, tiny green sprigs of rice plants all around, the Huey was not merely charred, it was melted and softened and flowing, like an Oldenburg nightmare. A blackened form with unexpectedly elegant curves. If anything was left of the fuselage, it was underground.

Maverick followed the LOH, setting up an approach, keeping the mud square to his left, flaring, landing. The Cobra racketed the air above them.

They settled in right behind the LOH, cut the engines, and slowly approached the wreck. A single line of men, eight of them abreast, like little boys walking into a dark room on a dare, afraid of what they would find.

And rightly so. The chunks of debris surrounding the burnt-out Huey were flesh, not metal.

Maverick swallowed hard, but swallowing didn't help Waffles, because he bent his knees and gave back his breakfast on the spot. The captain stood with his eyes closed. The major stared and breathed through his mouth.

"What the fuck happened here?" Maverick directed the question at no one in particular.

The major's voice was small and quiet. "I've seen this once before."

Maverick pitied anyone who had seen this before. The pilot and copilot were invisible, pushed cruelly into the earth by the force of impact. But in a hundred-foot circle around the aircraft was a cold-sweat nightmare worse than Bennie, worse than heads on sticks, worse than anything.

The four men who had been in the back of the chopper lay on the ground in dozens of separate pieces, each, except one, no larger than half a leg or a quarter-torso. There was a complete course in human anatomy spread before them, a buffet from hell. Red, black, and olive drab, pieces of people were everywhere, arms, legs, reddened flesh and bone and cloth.

It was worse than downtown Nha Trang when the bomber crashed. There were fewer dead, but look at them! Maverick, still swallowing hard, couldn't even think about what might have happened. The eight men unconsciously huddled together, staring into the face of unspeakable carnage.

"Oh, God . . . oh, God, look at that," Barstow said. He pointed off to his left, sank to his knees, surrendered his stomach.

They followed his finger to where a man appeared to be standing in a hole, looking at them through a spontaneous cloud of flies. Barstow had seen it right away, but the rest had to get closer before it hit them. The man was not, of course, standing in a hole. The top half of him was sitting upright on the ground. He had been cleanly severed just below the waist and, with the kind of puckish improbability that Vietnam was famous for, had fallen from the sky and landed straight up. He was surrounded by black and tan dog bits, tiny German-shepherd slivers. The sheer almost-normality of the sight made it harder to take than all the open chests and stomachs and faces that they had seen before. Maverick's stomach kicked hard, but did not move.

"You said you seen this before?" someone asked the major.

"Near the border one time," the major said, looking slowly around. They could barely hear him. "A lightning-bug mission caught fire with a full load. Could have been an accident, or maybe they took a hit or something. There were five guys aboard when the flares went off. They were too high to land before they burned up, so all the guys in back unassed the thing at about two thousand feet."

"Shit," said Barstow.

"Well, what would you do? Die on impact or get burned up in the air? But they jumped just as the chopper started to fall and they all went through the rotor blades."

Jesus. Jesus. Arms here, legs there, little pieces of dog all over the fucking place. Maverick was dumbfounded. He stared at the ghastly red and pink fragments against the dark brown dirt and felt the softness of his own body and remembered the forty brief days left on his tour. That's it, he resolved. That's it. I'm not gonna put myself in the way of this anymore. I've been here two years, almost, and I've seen lots of shit. Today I can honestly say I've seen it all. They can't show me anything worse than this.

And then they did.

Just after the ghastly mission of recovery, a young, moon-faced, eager reporter about twenty-three years old showed up from *Overseas Weekly,* a newspaper published for troops in the Pacific. Wars are story machines. In this war, highly mobile chopper jocks told tales all across the country. Little histories became tales, tales became legends, then myths.

It was no surprise, therefore, that someone, somewhere, had told the tale of Magnet Ass, the pilot who couldn't help getting shot down. This kid wanted to meet that man, and he did.

When the article about him appeared, the most interesting thing to Maverick, considerations of ego aside, was the piece on the page with it. The story concerned one Bob Woodrow, a Cobra pilot with the 334th Aerial Weapons Company in the delta. This particular individual had been flying copilot, in-country only sixteen days, when his wingman was shot down during a mission. This was Aircraft Number One Thousand to be lost in the war, and why that was a cause for special recognition is anybody's guess, but a story was written on the occasion. What interested Maverick, however, was the fact that Woodrow and the aircraft commander spontaneously got the inspiration to extract the downed crew by having them sit on the ammo-bay doors. This action saved their lives. Maverick read the article almost as many times as he read his own, warming to this Woodrow character in spite of himself. A week later Woodrow himself showed up in Di Anh, transferred to the Assassins.

When Maverick saw his name on the "Newly Assigned" roster, he bolted from the operations shed, giving the screen door a nasty crack, and headed for the officer billets. Woodrow had been assigned the hooch next to his, and Maverick found him just headed out the door, recognized him at once even though he'd never seen him before. He was twenty-six years old, a lowly WO-1, stocky, with sandy hair. His face was angular, his jaw square. He looked like Maverick's twin cousin, and their rapport was as profound as it was immediate.

"You Woodrow?"

"Sir," Woodrow said, glancing first at the insignia, then at the name on the shirt. "You're . . . Magnet Ass?"

Maverick laughed and stuck out his hand. "Come on, I'll buy you a drink and you can tell me the ammo-bay-door story." God help me, I like this kid.

Over the next few days Maverick told Woodrow the Norskin story, the Scott story, and anything else he'd sit still for. Woodrow was a warrant officer and Maverick a captain, but considerations of rank, as sometimes happens, had no effect on their friendship or respect for each other. Maverick was in charge of operations, no longer the Assassin platoon leader. He didn't command Woodrow, it was not his job to critique him, all he did was assign him to fly missions with different pilots. So the long talks and the chess games and the screaming-mimi lessons came naturally. It seemed that they had never not known each other.

Woodrow caused Maverick to abandon his resolve against friendship once again. He'd lost Ty, had seen Cummings lose a body part, but he just wasn't made to be a loner. There was a month left to his tour and nothing could happen to Woody in a month.

Besides, most of the troops he met when he first got there had been killed or rotated. He was living among strangers, out of phase. He spent his Cobra time doing aerial-gunnery instruction and giving copilots their AC check rides. He was lonely. Woody was, he sensed, a good soldier, and he couldn't resist a good soldier. Ty would have loved him.

Maverick gave Woodrow his AC check ride on Tuesday, April Fools' Day, and watched him climb into the sky on his first mission the very next morning. The sky was low and damp, oily clouds suspended only five or six hundred feet up. He watched the LOH and two Cobras circle the base and disappear to the northwest. Inside the operations shack, the air was hot with the crackle of radios and the garble of abbreviated voices. All talk and no action for half an hour, then the guard channel cut everything off.

"Cobra down," reported an LOH pilot. "I got a Cobra down at X-Ray Tango seven seven four, two two four."

"That's our AO," said Maverick to nobody in particular, "but there's no action there."

"He's burning, in pieces . . . must be a midair. Must be a midair," the radio screamed. "There's pieces of the Cobra . . . and pieces of another aircraft, a fixed wing . . . stand by one. . . ."

Maverick looked at the two barely-twenty radio operators, who, like members of the television generation, were staring at the black speakers as though they expected to see pictures in them. "Who is it?" Maverick asks, and the radio answers him.

"Charlie Horse Three, this is Assassin Three Two. Assassin Three Five is down. I say again, Assassin Three Five is down."

North. And Woodrow. Maverick felt the most peculiar sensation. It was a chill, but it was hot. A numb tingling, a dizziness. It felt like somebody had stuffed cotton in his ears, because the sound of the radios became dull and heavy. When one of the radio operators said, "Captain? Are you okay?" Maverick heard it as a voice from the end of a distant tunnel, indistinct and gloomy. He turned around and walked out the door. He never felt it push against his hand, he never felt the wind on his face as he walked toward the ops pad.

All his actions were automatic as he climbed into the operations Huey and set the throttle indent. He never heard the clicking, but knew it would be there. He fired up the turbine. He couldn't see the gauges, didn't know, in fact, that there were even instruments in front of him, but when the vibration felt right, he made well-practiced automatic movements and the Huey lifted into the air.

He was solo. He had no copilot, no crew chief or gunner. He felt nothing, heard nothing, saw only what was directly in front of him as he pushed the machine, low-level because of the clouds, northeast toward the crash site.

He had no trouble finding it. Smoke poured up from the ground and the LOH and Cobra circled above. He couldn't even think to call them on the radio, but made one low pass over the crash site and then settled in.

The ground below had been desolated by a recent B-52 strike. It was waste and burned trees and craters. Down and to his right he saw pieces of the Cobra, its broken canopies lying off to one side. Farther on, he saw pieces of an Air Force OV-10, a two-passenger forward air control craft. It was practically intact, but burning, black streaks along the brown wings, rivets standing out, sharply defined.

Maverick was enough in contact with himself to set the Huey's engine at flight idle, but when he opened his door and set his feet on the devastated ground, he simply went away. Ahead of him, three pieces of the Cobra burned on the ground. On his right, shattered pieces of the Cobra lay, against a splintered tree, upside down in a small crater. He forced himself to look to his left, where North and Woodrow, or two forms he assumed to be North and Woodrow, lay one on top of the other, limbs at odd angles, blackened and thin and stinking. Their charred helmets, still in place, made them look barely human, stick figures with bowling balls for heads.

The OV-10 had come down through the clouds right on top of Woody and North. The Air Force plane had enough wing left to keep flying for a little time, but the Cobra was suddenly and ultimately without rotors. These had come apart on impact, resolving themselves into lethal shards of whirling metal that had separated the tail boom, sliced the fuselage, then ceased to exist in this universe. There was little on the ground to find.

Maverick had no idea what happened after that. He vaguely heard the whine of the Huey idling behind him. He didn't remember the log he sat on, hunched over, shaking, with his elbows on his knees, looking down at the little mounds of red dirt around his boots. He couldn't recall the rotor wash and dust and dirt that flew around him as the other choppers landed. He remembered only the cloying indelible smell of burning human flesh, his face in his hands. And he remembered crying, for the first time since he was a kid. As soon as it began, it crippled him, making him helpless, given over to the act, so forbidden in the world Maverick had chosen for himself, this release, this torrent of loss and sadness and despair. He cried in huge straining spasms, cried for Woodrow, his last friend, and for Ty, his best, and for everyone else the war had taken from him. Everything he should have cried about for years, he cried about then, hurtful wrenching sobs, his father, his mother, how he missed his wife and children, choking, shuddering, out of breath. When he felt the arm around his shoulders, he began to scream.

It was the squadron commander, a lieutenant colonel, sitting next to him on the log. The man was talking to him, but Maverick barely knew it. He heard things about letting go, about fighting too long, about understanding how he felt. It was all so . . . *sorrowful.* Maverick had just given Woodrow his check ride, had just celebrated the birth of Woodrow's new son to ridiculous alcoholic excess, winding up facedown in suspicious mud behind the latrine. Now he did indeed let go, lamed by grief and loss and disappointment held inside too long.

Once again, Pandora gifted him with poison and pain that burst into the air.

He was crazy from all the destruction, furious at himself for letting Woodrow in, allowing the war to betray him again. Saddest of all was that Woodrow, who was Maverick's idea of a great soldier, had died for nothing. He was dead, wasted, burned, and stinking on the ground right over there because two fucking Air Force zoomies came down through the clouds at the wrong place at the wrong time. And the two of them had lived.

Somehow, he got back to the base. Somehow, he found himself in the operations shack, looking at the mission board. He was numb, dumb and closed off, he knew he should have grounded himself, but he also knew that the Assassins had taken heavy losses, had indeed now lost two more, and there were no replacements. Woodrow's name was down for a mission two days later. Maverick took the stained cloth off the hook to the right of the board. With tears running down his cheeks, down his neck and into his shirt, he rubbed Woodrow's name out and replaced it with his own. He was making a final gesture, with no idea of how final it would be.

THIRTY

Maverick dozed all day, suspended, outside of time, one moment exactly like the next. Even the small interruptions, like Attila's head appearing in the doorway three or four times, had long since ceased to attract his attention. He was like one of those big helpless gorillas you see in the zoo, so far away from his native element and with such little hope of ever returning to it that he squats the interminable hours away, staring into the distance at whatever it is he's lost.

The seven dwarfs usually moved him hours before daybreak in order to arrive in the next village before first light, just in time for the now-traditional excremental procession. So Maverick had become accustomed to waking up at what he judged was about five in the morning, expecting to see Dopey, who always led the parade, bend himself into the hooch. Inevitably, he would be followed by Scabby, then one or two of the others. This night, they didn't come.

The entryway of the hut gradually changed from black to gray, then to blue and yellow. The heat closed in, sounds of the village began to swell. It was a sizable hamlet, people walked past the door incessantly, dogs barked, there were high-pitched conversation, yells, and laughter.

Perhaps an hour or so after dawn, Attila came in, dark patches under the arms of his khaki shirt, as though he'd spilled coffee in there, pie face beaming with sweat. He waddled up closer to the tan bamboo cage than he ever had before, bent down with his hands on his knees, pushed his round head forward, and gave Maverick a long stare.

"Go now," he said. Maverick was stunned. Attila had barely said a word to him since he'd been captured, and now the fat little shit comes up and speaks to him in English.

"You speak English?*" Maverick choked out.*

"Go now," Attila repeated as he straightened up and walked out of the hut. Dopey and the others, who were waiting respectfully outside the door, crouched in and surrounded the cage. They grabbed it around the top bars, heaved it up, carried it out into the dirt street, and let it drop. Maverick looked up into the sun for the first time in a month. It was warm and golden, it soaked him.

During the war, he'd become used to the spontaneous gushes of adrenaline that would kick into his bloodstream. It was an occupational sensation in combat. He'd felt it every day, every time he'd pushed the throttle to indent and lifted his sinister machine into the sky to hang his ass out over the edge. His life, until thirty or so days ago, had been a continual series of klongs, the sinking in the stomach, shortness of breath, trembling limbs, cardiac acceleration. He'd lived with all the furious rushes of shit to the heart when the green tracers licked around him in the night, and his mind told him that for every brilliant emerald flash he saw, there were four huge bullets right behind it that he couldn't see.

But he'd been totally dormant for a month, deprived of sensation, twenty pounds lighter, torpid, atrophied. So when the adrenaline rush hit him this time, it sat him up with a vicious jolt, opened his eyes, and closed his throat.

It happened when Attila began to open the cage.

He had this big rusty key, like the kind you'd see in an old castle, which fit the big rusty lock that held together the big rusty chain on the flip-up door of the cage. The door was hinged with frayed hemp at the top and secured with the chain and the impossible lock at the bottom.

The six other dwarfs had surrounded the cage, shuffling their feet in the red dust, holding their AK's across their chests. A gaggle of villagers stood beyond them, well back, craning to see.

Maverick sat panting, in the midst of a textbook panic attack, thoroughly buzzed by the shock, hands shaking, heart frantically seeking escape from his rib cage. He stared at Attila as the ponderous lock came open and he rattled the tangled chain through the bamboo bars to open the door.

"Go now," Attila said, looking at Maverick through the top of the cage.

"Where?"

"Go now," he said again, and prodded him with his foot.

Maverick crawled out of the cage into the open. He tried to stand, but his body, crumpled for so long, had forgotten how, and he collapsed to the ground, straight down, like his strings had been cut. Dopey tucked his rifle under one arm, yelled at Scabby, and they grabbed him by the armpits to wrestle him up. His back set him afire.

He managed to get his feet under him and force himself to stand, quaking, stooped. Dopey held on, just to be sure he didn't go south again. Attila yelled at the twins.

Dopey led him away from the cage as the twins put down their rifles and pulled his elbows back so they stuck out behind him, with his hands in at his waist. They stuck a long bamboo rod through the crook, horizontally across his back. He felt the ropy roughness as they busily tied his elbows to the bar. Expertly, they had another rope around his waist with his pulled-back wrists secured to it. More shabby rope tied his ankles together about two feet apart. He was beside himself with adrenaline intoxication, terror, and the agony from his back, thinking surrealistic thoughts, like how some men actually would pay for a bondage job like this.

They finished him off with a rope that looped around his neck, knotted at the Adam's apple and ran down his back, tied off to the rope that connected his ankles. If he tried to take a big step, the rope would pull back and he'd choke himself on the knot.

He looked around, the rope rubbing harshly against his bare neck. All he saw were the villagers and the seven dwarfs. This was it. Wherever they were taking him, it was the last place he would ever go.

"Go now," Attila said again. Was that all the English he knew? He pointed down the road to the west, toward the paddies that lay around the village. The early sun attacked Maverick's eyes, splashing hotly off the brown water amid the deep green rice plants. Beyond was the wall of the jungle.

Attila set off with a long determined stride, and so did Maverick the second that one of the twins shoved him hard in the back with his rifle butt. Dopey and Scabby followed as Maverick hobbled down the road, his stinking black pajamas clinging to his skin, feet tied together, arms pulled painfully back around the bamboo rod. He looked back to see the other soldiers standing on the dirt street, a tiny group of four around the now-empty tiger cage, dark forms against the early yellow sun.

It took the four of them over fifteen minutes to walk across the paddy dike, because Maverick couldn't step more than a foot at a time and had to hop and skip along. Scabby prodded him with his rifle butt more than once, enjoying it, bringing it down on the small of his back. Finally Dopey barked something at him and he stopped.

Fuck me, fuck me to tears, Maverick thought. I've spent however long it's been doubled up in a fucking tiger cage and now these motherfuckers are taking me for a walk? He could scarcely stand. With every step, long cramping waves flowed up his legs and across his back. With every step he experienced the kind of pain you have when you take your arm off the back of your date's seat after two hours in the movies. It was worse than getting your dick caught in your zipper, it was worse than anything Maverick had experienced since the medics shoved the tubes down his throat in Hawaii, and it would not stop, could not stop, because the two incredibly stupid-looking and repulsive North Vietnamese Army regulars walking behind him with their assault rifles at port arms said it could not stop. He hadn't used his legs in a month. They didn't want to work, but they had to.

And he was having such wild, feverish thoughts, of what would happen when they got him wherever it was they were going. To a POW camp? Were they taking him out in the jungle to waste him? Days ago he was challenging them in his mind, but now he felt that peculiar looseness in his bowels, exactly what he'd felt the time he'd flown into the inferno of Operation Gibraltar.

Last stop, just ahead.

At the end of the paddy dike the jungle swallowed them up in green, cool air and gloomy damp. They felt their way along a path that could be picked out only if you knew it was there in the first place. Attila had strutted ahead of them, perhaps not by much, but he was invisible around a curve in the trail. Behind Maverick, Dopey and Scabby chattered, giving him a poke with a gun barrel now and then, as if he needed reminding.

Terror has its compensations. When those prehistoric flight-or-fight impulses fire up, when all those hard-wired chemical reactions make their merry survival soup in the bloodstream, it ignites the senses. Skin tingles, ears extend their range, the heart pumps capaciously, fueled by the oxygen the lungs devour in hungry gulps. The body surrenders to its true electric potential, responds to its very most primordial drives. That's why Maverick heard it and his escorts didn't.

It was nothing, nothing, the slightest hum high in the air, inaudible, really, among the rustles and cackles of the jungle. But Maverick heard it. He knew what it was and he was ready when it happened.

There was a *click* in the air, followed by a furious roar and an explosion of infernal fire. Napalm.

Air Force jets streaked through the sky, expelling their long ovoid silver canisters of jellied gasoline. When napalm goes off, it creates flames in excess of two thousand degrees. Huge volumes of air rush instantly upward with the heat. Living creatures are stunned when the air is actually sucked out of their lungs. All of Maverick's training and instinct kicked in, forced him to take a frantic gulp of air and hold his breath as the entire world lit up orange around them. No more than two hundred meters ahead of them the jungle transformed itself into a greasy brilliant apricot-orange furnace shot through with snaky coils of gray smoke. Behind him, Dopey hit the dirt, Scabby started to run back down the trail in the other direction, and Attila, who had been well in the lead, was instantly done to a turn. Maverick, eyes wide, heart pounding, realized on some basic, almost genetic level that this was it, that he had plenty of ways to die and maybe only one way to live. He threw his head back to give himself some slack, and bolted to his right, scurrying into the jungle.

He was shaking, choking, gulping air, taking silly little steps, stumbling through the undergrowth. Every bush had fingers that grabbed him, every inch of trail had a hole or a vine that tripped him up. Intense heat from the flaming jungle washed around him as he staggered. If he fell, he had no hands to protect himself, no way to push himself up again.

And right there in the middle of his back a piece of his flesh burned with the certain knowledge that Dopey was just behind him, shaken but alive, pulling himself to his feet, fitting the butt of his thoroughly dependable Russian assault rifle to his skinny shoulder, getting ready to close an eye, squeeze a finger, and give him a final one-gun salute. Maverick twisted to the side, dared a look backward, and saw Dopey doing exactly that.

The jungle burned with an infernal vengeance. Fuck it, Maverick thought, if his reaction could be called thought. This is the last stop, the last chance. I can die now or I can die later, and if this motherfucker wants to waste me right here, it's better than whatever else they could do to me. He turned, managed a few more tiny steps, then took one more look, even if it meant certain destruction. Dopey, silhouetted in the orange light of burning jungle, lowered his rifle to his side, saluted him, and bolted off down the trail away from the flames, was swallowed up by the forbidding green, was gone.

Maverick didn't have time to think about the fact that what Dopey had done was perhaps a sort of karmic repayment from the man who walked on water. Maverick didn't know shit about karma, knew even less about the wheel of life. He continued to stumble forward, realizing that the napalm attack meant he was still in the south, when he heard the loveliest, sweetest, most welcome sound in the air above him.

The ancients believed that the heavenly bodies were set in crystalline spheres that rotated about the earth. They believed that these spheres made music as they moved, and that if we could but sense the sound, it would be the most celestial experience of all. But the sound Maverick heard was sweeter still, more moving than the songs David sang for Solomon, more deeply affecting than all the galaxies singing in concert.

Rotor blades! The sound of choppers, dozens of them, shaking the air, roaring in the fiery sky.

Maverick started to run, the rope around his throat rubbing his neck bloody and raw, choking him. He didn't care. The pole behind his back caught on the vines and trees, spinning him around. He didn't care. He pitched forward once, directly onto his face in the mud, dragged his feet underneath himself, and forced his way up. He ran forward, sideways, stumbling, careening, his bare feet in agony. He didn't care.

Abruptly he broke out of the undergrowth into a huge flat expanse of scrub and elephant grass. He stood for a moment at the edge of the clearing, tears streaming down his bearded cheeks, and looked up into a sky boiling with United States Army helicopters. He'd stumbled into the middle of a huge insertion. Hueys circled above the far tree line, sweeping onto final approach, black locust shapes, light streaming through the open cargo doors, outlining the helmeted troops within. Just above and to the sides, black Cobras outlined themselves against the morning sky. It was a fearsome spectacle, apocalyptic, all those machines of destruction hanging in the air. It was the most beautiful, most moving, most poignant sight that Maverick had ever witnessed. And then they all began to shoot at him.

Terrified, he broke from the edge of the clearing and hobbled out toward the choppers. Little puffs of dust exploded in the ground at his feet. Two Cobras veered toward him from above.

"Don't shoot!" he yelled, as though they could hear him. "Don't shoot, you motherfuckers, it's me! It's *me!*" In his relief and exhilaration, the fact that he was wearing black pajamas had completely escaped him. Above, radios crackled with the familiar shout, "VC in the open! VC in the open!" And all the Cobra jocks wanted the kill.

More chattering in the sky. More bullets. Maverick hobbled and hopped and skipped in little circles, arms pinned behind him, yelling, crying with relief and frustration. He'd escaped from a month of imprisonment and the prospect of certain death at the hands of the North Vietnamese Fucking Army, had had the incredible luck to run into a swarm of Americans who, in the best tradition of the cavalry, had come galloping over the hill in the nick of time—it was almost too perfect!—and now the assholes were going to kill him! As he darted about, dancing with little baby steps among the rattle of the bullets, his lunatic thoughts screamed about how ironic this all was and how sorry those fucking chopper jocks would be when they found out they'd wasted one of their own and how wouldn't this be the ultimate bite on the ass. His head swiveled wildly, searching for escape, frantically judging the distance back to the cover of the jungle. Puffs of dust burst up from his hobbling feet, bullets poured from the sky, danced around him. Then it all stopped. Maverick stood still, collapsed to the ground. His adrenaline had run out. He had nothing left.

With tremendous clatter and swirl, three Hueys settled to the ground not twenty meters from him. Blues poured out the doors, hands turned him over, pulled frantically at his ropes. He heard all the voices, speaking English, but made no sense out of them. He saw the faces, American faces, but recognized not a one. He felt cold steel at the back of his neck when one of the troops knifed through the choker, he heard the word "Maverick." The pole came out from behind his back, his feet were freed. Hands were on him, lifting, carrying him. Above him, swarming black choppers circled the sky.

They slid him into the closest Huey, the metal floor cold against his thin rancid garment. Familiar smells assaulted him, oil and hot metal, kerosene, gunpowder, and men. A green helmet looked down into his face.

"Are you Maverick?"

"Yeah. Am I dead?"

"No, you ain't dead. You been snatched."

"Why'd they stop shooting?"

"Somebody spotted your beard."

"Where am I?"

"About a klick from where you got shot down."

Son of a bitch, he thought. I wasn't crazy after all. Those fuckers had been moving me in a goddamn circle for all that time. No wonder some of those villages started to look so familiar.

The face smiled at him. "Let's get you back to the medics."

He lay gasping and sobbing in relief, staring at the dark gray roof of the Huey. It blurred with his tears. The cold floor pressed into his back, buoying him on the air. He was free of the green violence of the jungle, free of the oily dwarfs, free of the slimy rice, the abject boredom and appalling terror of the cage. His tour was over; they would send him home at once. Exhaustion weighed him down; the rotors thrashed the air, washing him with the wind that roared through the cargo-bay doors. The sky accepted him.

The war had one more thing to show him, one last lesson, the hardest one of all. But it would have to wait awhile. Now there was too much else. There was Bennie to cry for, and Jim and Cummings and Woodrow. And Ty.

The last lesson had, in fact, already been learned. But it would take years, perhaps, to understand. It would have to wait until he could rid himself of the most lethal part of the Manhood Myth.

Until he could open himself up to the terrible, terrible cost of his particular education, until he could gather into himself the devastating loss of what he had always thought himself to be. It would have to wait, perhaps for years, until he could find the courage to suffer.

THIRTY-ONE

Lynn stayed in the taxicab so that Maverick could have a few last minutes alone with Ty. Dick, who had driven all the way in from Connecticut just to be with him, had left earlier in the day. It was his time to let go, and his wife knew that he needed the solitude.

He stepped out of the cab into the cold, misty November air. It was the middle of the night. The Lincoln Memorial loomed to his right, a solid yellow-white cube. He stared down the long expanse of the reflecting pool toward the gleaming needle of the Washington Monument.

As he walked down the dark asphalt path, three bronze figures slowly emerged from the yellow haze, loomed above him, larger than life. Their bodies, running with the moisture of the night air, seemed to be soaked with the sweat of the jungles, the highlands, the rice paddies, and the coastal plains of Vietnam.

For some, Vietnam had meant death. For some it had meant survival. But for many it became a symbol of courage and fear and pride. The three bronze faces above him displayed two other emotions as well. One was horror, and one was the thousand-yard stare.

The detail was perfect, right down to the flak vest and the double canteens suspended from the web belt, even to the mosquito-repellent bottle stuck in the elastic band that held the camouflage cover on the helmets. The soldier with the M-60 was wearing a flop hat, like the one Maverick wore during his last tour.

They were young. They were Hispanic, Anglo, and black. He'd seen those faces a thousand times. He'd always see those faces.

The black soldier had a towel around his neck. Maverick

wanted to reach up, take that towel, and wipe their faces. He wanted to carry the M-60 for them, or the bandoliers of ammunition slung heavily across their shoulders. Or the M-16.

Across the grassy slope, the Wall was a long black ribbon of granite embedded in the hillside, wandering forever away from him. One section angled toward the Washington Monument and the other toward the Lincoln Memorial. He was amazed at the number of people walking along the path in both directions at two-thirty on this cold, damp, drizzly November morning.

Some walked slowly. Some stood quietly, as if in church. Others reached out to gently stroke the name of a loved one. Still others wept openly at the memory of a lost husband, father, brother, son, friend.

They were all separate people, with their own separate griefs, but they were sharing just then, and not one of them walked away unmoved.

He walked past the towering ghostly figures that glowed from the small footlights at the bottom of the wall, down the gentle slope to the deepest point on the path, looking for the three roses that Lynn, Dick, and he had placed there earlier in the day. The wall was inscribed with the names of the 58,132 Americans who had given their lives in Vietnam. Ty's name had been hard to find, but now Maverick knew exactly where it was. The searching had already been done. Three roses would show him the way.

He stood before the spot. Panel 6E, Line 64. It had been twenty years, eight months, and fourteen days since Ty was killed, his chopper dragged to the ground by the men he was trying to save, and Maverick prayed Ty would understand and forgive him for not coming sooner. The roses were still there, but one had fallen over. He knelt to put it back in its proper place.

Then he heard the sounds. Two panels to his left, about ten feet away, a man in a fatigue jacket stood sobbing quietly in the dim light, one hand to his face, the other clenching a white handkerchief at his side.

Maverick could just barely make him out in the darkness and the mist and the drizzle, but the two of them seemed to be about the same age, though the other man was a bit heavier, a bit taller, with longer hair and a beard. Like many there that night, he was reaching out to caress a cold name on the wall before him.

The man's sobs deepened, making the tears rise in Maverick's eyes.

He reached out toward the wall and let his fingers feel the incisions in the cold black stone. Tyrone W. Hisey. Panel 6E, Line 64. He said good-bye to Ty once again, and knew he understood. Then he stood up, walked to his left, and approached the sobbing man. When he put his hand on the man's shoulder, the stranger turned toward him. Without thought, they embraced. They wept together, shuddering in each other's arms, arms straining to hold on. They patted each other on the back.

At that moment they each knew that they weren't alone in the feeling, they weren't alone in the grief and the helplessness and the horror and the guilt and the sorrow.

When they separated, the man held out his hand and they shook. He never gave his name. They'd never seen each other before, and they would never see each other again.

Maverick looked after him as he walked away, disappearing into the mist.